A COURT OF SEAS AND STORMS
A LITTLE MERMAID RETELLING

LEGENDS OF LOVE

DANIELA A. MERA

ELAYNA R. GALLEA

This is a work of fiction. Names, characters, places, and incidents either are the product of the author's imagination or are used fictitiously. Any resemblance to actual persons, living or dead, events, or locales is entirely coincidental.

Copyright © 2023 by Daniela A. Mera and Elayna R. Gallea

All rights reserved. No part of this book may be reproduced or used in any manner without written permission of the copyright owner except for the use of quotations in a book review. For more information, address:

authordanielaamera@gmail.com

elayna.gallea@gmail.com

First edition April 2022

Second edition October 2023

Paperback ISBN 978-1-7781920-0-5

Ebook ISBN 978-1-7781920-1-2

Book Cover Design by GetCovers

Interior/Case Laminate by Shane Nel

Map by Daniela A. Mera

ASIN (ebook): B09V1XQDBD

ISBN (paperback): 978-1-960343-14-7

ISBN (hardback): 978-1-960343-13-0

❦ Created with Vellum

SUGGESTED READING ORDER

Legends of Love novels are a part of an interconnected stand-alone series. You can read in whatever order you'd like. However, we'd suggest:

A COURT OF FIRE AND FROST

A COURT OF SEAS AND STORMS

A COURT OF WIND AND WINGS

WELCOME TO ARANTHIUM

We are delighted to share Helena and Erik's story with you!

Before beginning this story, we want to take a moment and acknowledge that this book is New Adult and open-door sex scenes are present.

Reading is wonderful—it's what brings us together today. However, no book is worth your personal peace. So please note that cursing, violence, substance abuse, mentions of parental abuse, and an attempted on-page sexual assault are in this book. Take care of yourself, dear reader.

*To the people who wanted Captain Hook to have a happily ever after.
Villains can be redeemed.
Loving after heartbreak takes courage.*

PART ONE

I
CALLED TO THE KING
ERIK

"You have five seconds to tell me where to find the gold, or your blood will be coating the floor." I snarl, gripping the back of the wooden chair with one hand while I tighten my grip on my dagger. Gesturing towards the trembling woman seated nearby, I clench my teeth. "You wouldn't want to leave your poor wife a widow, would you?"

The ashen-faced man beneath my blade trembles, his face somehow paling even further. I swear, he is as white as the linen of the pompous shirt he is wearing. His blue eyes widen as they slide toward the woman sitting on the other side of the room.

She, too, is bound to her seat. Thick brown ropes are wrapped around her arms and legs, binding her in place. A large golden ring encircles the third finger on her left hand, clearly marking her as belonging to the man whose neck is on the edge of my blade.

The woman is shaking. The gag I placed between her teeth is dark with moisture from the tears running down her pale cheeks. Her eyes are pleading as she stares at her husband, trying to speak through the gag. She is struggling against the bonds, her voice muffled by the cloth.

"Please," the woman sobs through the damp fabric, "don't."

I don't blame her for being scared. I'd probably act the same way if the Pirate of Death boarded my ship and killed the entire crew in front of me.

Unlike my own ship, *The Black Rose*, this one is far less modern. Wooden planks are everywhere and there isn't a touch of metal or technology in sight. It's precisely what I would have imagined ships looked like three hundred years ago. Old. Decrepit. It even has old-fashioned cannons sticking out the side. Definitely not my choice of vessel.

Blowing out a long breath, I warn, "Shut up." Turning back to the man on the edge of my knife, I tighten my grip on his shoulder. "You should know, this is really your fault. You should never have brought your gods-damned wife on a boat. Every sailor worth their salt knows women are bad luck on boats."

The man tries to respond, but I keep going. My jaw is tense as I continue my tirade. "Even if you don't buy into the superstition, you really shouldn't have been a piece of shit. You should have known a bunch of asshattery would attract *my* attention."

"I'm begging you, don't hurt her," the weak man whimpers as a tear runs down his cheek.

I watch the tear with disgust as it lands on his shirt, dampening the already-sodden material. Gods. I hate it when they do this. The whiners are the worst of the entire bunch. Little does he know, I would never hurt an innocent woman. I have morals, even if he doesn't. Besides, it's not the woman's fault her husband brought her onto the ship.

"Time's up," I growl.

Turning my back on the sobbing female, I press my knife deeper into the man's throat. A glimmer of satisfaction rolls through me as a pearl of crimson blood wells above the blade of my favorite dagger before running down the sailor's neck in a jagged line.

Behind me, his wife begins to wail through the gag. I grit my teeth and tighten my grip on the hilt. That cursed woman is going to make me regret my decision not to kill her before this is done. I just know it.

"Wait," the man says through clenched teeth. He tries to pull his neck back from my knife, his eyes widening impossibly further as he meets my gaze. "I'll tell you."

Slowly, I pull my blade away from his throat. He gasps, the cut still leaking blood. "There are three thousand pieces of gold in the hull of the ship and another ten thousand buried off the coast of the Northern Court. We can be there in three days if we sail through the night."

"Good man," I clasp his arm. Turning on my feet, I take the bloody blade and slash it through the woman's bindings. She pulls off the gag and stumbles towards her husband.

"Oh, Marcel, I thought you were dead." She falls into his lap, weeping as she presses a handkerchief she pulled from her dress against his wound. Her clothing is as old-fashioned as this ship.

"If the treasure isn't there, you'll both wish you were," I promise darkly. My eyes narrow as I glare at them, spinning my knife between my hands. "You'd better pray to whatever gods you believe in that the gold is where you said."

Slamming the door behind me, I allow myself a moment to smile.

Another day, another treasure acquired by the Pirate of Death.

The gold is there.

All ten thousand shimmering pieces of treasure. I'm standing on the deck of *The Black Rose* and watching as crate after crate is hauled aboard by my crew.

Unlike most wooden ships that sail the waters in Aranthium, mine is only five years old and equipped with all the latest Summer Fae tech. The shipwrights who built it for me described it as "modern-pirate", whatever that means. I don't give a fishshit what those land legs call it as long as it is the best ship to have ever sailed the seas in Aranthium.

Only the best for The Pirate of Death.

Once all the gold is safely aboard my ship, I turn to Marcel and his wife. They are huddled together by the mainmast, their arms wrapped around each other as the woman weeps once more. She has barely stopped the incessant blubbering since the moment I spared her husband's life. It's gods-damned annoying. If I didn't believe in not killing women, I would have already thrown her overboard.

Rubbing my left forearm, I glare at them from my position on the deck. I'm so focused on the couple, I don't hear the footsteps coming from behind me.

A throat clears, "Arm bothering you, Captain?"

I curse, turning around.

Jean Luc, the ship's cook, is holding up his hands in supplication. He continues, gesturing to my arm. "I can bring you some cream."

"There's nothing for it," I reply gruffly. "Just the old wound acting up again. If I hadn't already killed the bastards who did this to me, I'd take pleasure in killing them all over again."

He nods, eyeing the limb as though he can see through the fabric of my shirt. "Can't even tell it's a fake."

"That's why they call it a lifelike prosthetic, man," I say, my voice dropping into a lower register. "When you pay as much as I did, it had better look and work *exactly* like a regular limb."

The Fae scientist who had engineered my prosthetic had assured me my left hand would be identical in every way to the limb I had lost. No one would ever know it was a fake unless they saw me without it. It blends in seamlessly with my skin. The prosthetic has artificial muscles and bones, and moving it requires nothing more than a thought.

Jean Luc raises his hands in the air, backing up. "Gotcha," he says. "I'll just go below deck then, Captain. Leave you to your... guests."

I nod. A sense of satisfaction fills me as I turn and place my hands on the metal railing. I watch grimly as my "guests" finally get ready to depart my ship.

My lips tilt up as the sailor—I won't call him a captain, for he barely deserves the title after his piss-poor performance a few days ago—and his wife climb into an awaiting wooden rowboat we brought from their ship. It looks out of place against the metal of *The Black Rose*, but no matter. It will be gone in moments.

We've given the couple enough supplies to make it back to shore, where they can find a FaePhone and call for assistance.

Or whatever.

It's not my problem.

Humming as I find myself in a rare good mood, I walk down to my office. All the sailors step out of the way, dipping their heads in reverence.

As they should.

I'm the captain.

My good mood lasts until my FaePhone rings the moment I step into my private space. Can't a man have some gods-damned peace and quiet for once? Groaning, I yank the phone off the solar charger and put it to my ear.

"Yes," I say as I slump down into my leather seat.

A tinny, female voice is on the other end. *"Your presence is required in Aqualis. Come immediately."*

I run my hand through my hair. "By whose orders?"

"The King's."

The call abruptly ends before I can answer and I'm left spewing curses. I slam the FaePhone down, and wince. This is top-of-the-line Fae technology. There are far too many that can't afford such nice shit. I pour myself a finger of the most expensive alcohol in my possession and throw it back. It burns as it goes down.

Then, and only then, do I leave my office to give my crew the new directions. We have to change course. The Ice Mer King has summoned me.

Maybe it won't be awful?

"I want you to kill my daughter."

I blink once, then twice, wondering if somehow my ears have gotten clogged during my journey into the underwater city. The enchantment the Ice Mer put over me is supposed to protect my "frail" human body and give me the ability to go about their city, but something must have gone wrong. There's no way he said what I think he said.

Is there?

"Sir?" I'm swimming in place with my back straight. The water chills me to the bone and this gods-damned tail is a complete nuisance. I hate the way the Mer magic makes me feel, as though my body isn't my own. The tail and gills they gave me feel so *wrong*.

The sooner I get out of this city, the better. The windows look out over Aqualis, and I see Mer people swimming far below, going about their daily business. My hands are clasped behind my rod-straight spine, trying to portray ease before the King.

I don't think it's working.

Gods. The sooner I can get back to my ship, the better.

"You heard me," the Ice Mer King says gruffly.

He is sitting at a large mahogany desk that is more than double the size of my body. His bare upper body highlights powerful, gold-clad arms that are resting atop the desk. His fingers are steepled as he looks at me. The bands glint in the spell light, and his muscles tense as he leans forward with a penetrating stare. I suppress a shudder and swallow hard.

The King's long gray hair is streaked with the deepest blues and greens. It swirls in the surrounding water like seaweed after a storm. A diadem made of pearlescent seashells rests on his head. It is imposing and reminds me of his importance.

I can't peel my eyes from the diadem, imagining for one moment what it would be like to add something like that to my own pile of treasure.

I ask, "Isn't your daughter—"

"Enough!" he roars, rising from the desk. His deep gray, almost black tail flicks back and forth. It takes everything in me to hold my ground.

A beat passes and the most powerful Mer goes preternaturally still. His eyes pin me in place as he looms over me. When he speaks, power laces every word. "It is not your place to ask questions. You have no rights here, *human*. Need I remind you of the reason you stand before me at all?"

I clamp my jaw shut, shaking my head. There is no need for that. As if I could ever forget the reason my life is no longer my own.

It hasn't escaped my notice that the one time I played hero, my public chivalry landed me a life debt to the royal Ice Mer family. That was definitely *not* my intention. All I had wanted to do was spare an Angel from the disgusting advances of the Ice Mer Crown Prince, Henrick Proteus.

Everyone in Aranthium knew Crown Prince Henrick had a penchant for taking the lives of his conquests. He had left more than a few bodies in his disastrous wake.

Had, because he finally met his match in the Winter Fae Queen's Consort two years ago. Prince Nathaniel of the Winter Court had killed Henrick in an arena filled with Ice Mer. Ballsy. They say the wimpy Fae did it to demonstrate his passion for the stone-cold badass, Queen Elvira, or something. But I'm sure he didn't know that he was saving untold numbers of women from a horrid fate at the Ice Mer's hands.

My arrangement with Henrick had been pretty standard after I had saved the Angel. I gave him a percentage of everything I earned from my raids. Enough to make him happy, but not enough to bankrupt me. At least, that's how it had worked until he had gone up and gotten himself killed. Instead of finding freedom after the bastard's death, things had become much worse for me. Henrick's cruelty had nothing on his father.

Within a month of his son's death, King Phelix had tightened my reins, took a larger cut of my raids, and invoked an archaic law.

A life for a life.

Because I had saved the Angel's life that night on the docks, I was duty-bound to take a life. Any life of the King's choosing. I had thought for sure it was a joke.

But no.

The Northern Court values brutality and strength. Such a place leaves little room for my morals. I had consulted multiple experts on the Northern laws, but each of them had come to the same conclusion: I am bound to King Phelix and stripped of my agency.

It shouldn't matter, right? Smuggling goods and stealing wealth is a deadly endeavor. I have taken more lives than I could count, for the gods' sakes. My soul has always been as black as a starless night. My soul was stained long before Phelix took over my debt.

But right now, here in Aqualis. King Phelix is asking me to kill his own daughter. The female is—at least presumably—innocent.

Just like that, I realize just how much it matters.

I don't kill innocent people.

Not for the first time, I find myself wishing I had ignored that modicum of conscience that still resides deep within me, even after two decades of pirating and pillaging and death. I try my best to atone for my sins and weaknesses, but I know the truth. Even when I saved the Angel from being raped, I had known. The black marks on my soul were already so dark, there was no saving me.

The small acts of kindness I do are for others, not myself.

If I had just ignored the nudge of morality, I could have hopped back on my ship. I would have sailed away from Angel's Landing, none the wiser. It's not as though saving one Angel from a night of harm would reach back through the threads of time and save *her*.

But instead, I am receiving orders to kill the new heir to the Ice Mer throne. This underwater land is going to run out of eligible heirs pretty soon at this rate.

As the Ice Mer King explains the mission, my mind hangs on one word: Helena.

I have never met the Ice Mer Crown Princess, but I've heard rumors about her.

They say she is as beautiful as she is cunning. She has never married, apparently scaring off every suitor with a sharp intellect and even sharper teeth.

She has always been the proverbial black sheep of her family. I know she's here somewhere in the city, but no one has seen her except for select diplomatic visits. According to *Aranthium Celebrity News*, Helena was paraded before the Queen of the Winter Court eighteen months ago, closely watched and even more closely guarded. It was all people could talk about for weeks after the fact.

"... doing so will release you from your debt to me."

With a start, I realize that the Ice Mer King has continued speaking. I barely hear him over the pull of my memories.

Shit. Shit.

I don't want to let the King know I didn't hear him, so I nod and paste a grim look on my face as I try to figure out what's going on.

Did I just agree to murder the Crown Princess?

Before I can delve deeper into the absolute insanity of... *all that*, a knock comes on the door.

"Excuse me, King Phelix?" A timid voice comes from beyond the doorway and I turn around to see a very thin Mer swimming in the hallway. She has dark, almost black skin with violet hair that sits in a tight bun on the top of her head. There is a silver band wrapped around her chest, matching her tail.

"What?" the powerful male snaps, pounding a fist on the desk. The entire piece of furniture shakes from the impact.

The Mer shrinks backward and somehow seems even smaller than before. "I was sent to tell you that the um..." she looks at me and then pales, "delivery is here for you. From your... friends."

"Is that so?" Phelix asks, swimming over to her.

She nods, her tail quivering as she mumbles an affirmative response.

"Fine," he huffs.

King Phelix turns to me, and I flinch, *gods-damned flinch*, at the barely contained violence in his expression. A green glow hides behind his pupil-less eyes, and it takes everything in me not to cower against the threat of pain I see there. "Can I assume you will do what you were told? Or do we need to have a *different* kind of conversation? One that ends up in you losing yet another limb?" He looks pointedly at my right hand.

Clenching my prosthetic fist at my side, I take a deep breath before unfurling my fingers slowly. I shake my head. "I understand, Your Majesty."

"Good," he says. "She'll be brought to you tomorrow. Remember, don't link this to me. Get her out of Ice Mer territory before you do it."

I nod. What else can I do?

The Ice Mer King barks at the servant, "Let's go."

The Mer in the doorway swims off so quickly that she leaves the water swirling in her wake.

When the King and his guards are out of sight, I slump against the desk.

What in the name of the gods am I going to do now? Stealing is one thing. Cold-blooded murder is another.

Shaking my head, I try to think of a way out.

The problem is, there isn't one.

I'm just a human.

A scary one, to be sure. But mostly that's because I'm known around the sea as the Pirate of Death. It's a title I... inherited more than earned, but I have gone to great lengths to make sure I am well-feared through all of Aranthium.

But being the Pirate of Death won't help me where the Ice Mer King is concerned.

Dammit. I'm going to have to kill her.

With a sigh, I run my hand through my hair.

At least I'll be free after this.

Free to roam the seas once more, without the shackles of the life-debt binding me. With that thought buoying my spirits, I take my leave.

A transport shark is waiting for me outside the King's office and I wearily hold on to its dorsal fin as it barrels through the water. The first time I traveled by shark had been a less-than-pleasant experience. Now, though, it has become just another mode of travel. The magic wears off slowly, allowing me to ascend without getting sick, but my body still feels off. I will never get used to this. Though, the view isn't bad. I let my eyes roam around the sizeable underwater city.

The Ice Mer King might be a cruel overlord who apparently has a fetish for filicide, but his domain is breathtaking. The coral buildings reflect all the colors of the sea. The soft pinks and blues accentuate the incredible rainbow of hues as thousands of Merpeople and schools of fish swim through the city.

Few humans ever see Aqualis, and here I am. I wish I could enjoy it and play the tourist, but everything is just so damn heavy. I wish I had never met Henrick.

Murder an innocent. Not just any innocent. The Crown Princess herself. Is it too much to hope that she's a horrible person? It would make this so much easier.

Actually, considering she is the progeny of the cruelest being I've ever known to roam the seas, I'd bet my chances are pretty high. If she's cruel, then it makes my job easier to stomach.

The beautiful city loses some of its luster because of its cold brutality. It would be idiotic to look at the artistic value of such a place and ignore the soldiers with deadly seashell swords strapped on their backs.

We're drawing closer to the surface, and I see rays of sunlight shooting forth through the water. I cannot wait to get my legs back.

The shark brings me to a dock where my rowboat is securely tied off. My ship is floating in the distance.

My whole body heaves as I let out a relieved exhale.

I'll spend the day on land. My mind is swirling with things to do. Lists are good. They provide order. And right now, that's what I need.

Nodding to myself, I pull on the spare sweatpants I had left in the rowboat for this purpose. I'll stock up on supplies and get my crew back on the ship before our unwanted guest arrives. I know they'll want to leave as much as I do. The sea calls to our very souls.

As I go about my business, one thought remains in my mind. *Let her be cruel.*

2

BEHAVE
HELENA

Two years ago, the Consort of the Winter Court killed my older brother, Henrick, in front of a large audience.

My pompous older brother had been idiotic and brash, as usual. When he underestimated Elva's lover, Nathaniel, he'd lost. If we're being honest, I was almost happy when Henrick died.

All of that almost-joy had been short-lived when my father had returned to Aqualis from the Spring Mer Lands. When the Ice Mer King had burst into the small estate he had given me, I had been floating in my softest bed of kelp. I can still remember the way his emerald eyes burned with fiery rage.

In that instant, I had known his mind. He had wanted to invoke his birthright power. The magic imparted to the beings of our land from the gods.

I had poked my head out, waving my fingers as I flashed him my best smile and said, "Hello, Daddy."

That had been approximately six seconds before he had exploded in a swirl of thick, green ink. My father had grabbed me by the wrists and dragged me into the courtyard. After some overly dramatic shouting, he had told me he was going to throw me in prison with the most wanted and dangerous Mer in the sea.

I had sweetly reminded him I was now the heir to the throne. Even for a mighty Mer, throwing his heir in prison might look a teeny, tiny bit bad.

He struck me once across the cheek, called me a bitch, and then told me the next worst thing: I would have to go live with Hallie and James in their private estate in the coral reef.

It was secluded, and Hallie had refused to so much as look at me since they found out Henrick was dead. She hated me and blamed me for his death. She made it very clear that since Elva was *my* friend, I was at fault for everything that had happened. To make things worse, my father had gleefully informed me I would not be allowed any technology. He laughed as he told me I could kiss my contact with the outside world goodbye.

Within minutes of his proclamation, he had a servant pack my bags. Mirthless laughter had escaped my father's lips as he sent me off with a team of shark escorts to live with my sister and her husband for the indefinite future.

I had known what he was doing, even then. I understood King Phelix well. He was biding time until he figured out what to do with me.

My father is a terrible person in general, but he is still the male who contributed to my conception. Growing up, he had forced us all to respect him and prepared for the possibility that any of us could take his place.

When I first arrived at Hallie's house, I had been exhausted from the journey. The house had been cloaked in darkness, and not a soul had spoken to me while I was shown to my room upstairs.

Day after day, things remained the same. They all dragged on, morphing and bleeding into each other until I no longer felt the passing of days. Like the slow growth of a coral reef, each day creeped along. It was only because of the sweet notes from my nieces and nephews that I knew nearly two years had passed while I rotted away in that damned room. I tear the little letters the Merlings bring me to shreds until the enchantment on them disappears, and they disintegrate in the water.

Hallie doesn't know about the notes, though. In fact, it was only a month ago that she let me glimpse Giselle and Ian through the slot on the door. She was convinced I was "dangerous" and had plotted with Elva to kill our brother. I was glad for the Merlings' safety that their mother didn't know about our clandestine notes. She didn't want her babies to be anything less than perfect.

Everyone had always loved pretty little Hallie. No one had cornered her as a child and made her watch while they tortured little animals. No one had hit her when they were drunk. They never had to. Hallie always ensured I was there to take the brunt of the brutality. She had always put me in the path of danger. I just didn't recognize her orchestrations until it was too late.

Two years later, I have reached a clear conclusion: Hallie is worse than prison. At least in prison, I could've made friends. Instead, I am given three meals a day, and no one speaks to me for more than ten minutes at a time.

My sentence is generous for the Northern Court. I probably should've been killed immediately. I've had a lot of time to think about why I'm still alive. Perhaps Daddy has just a bit of a soft spot for me, his embarrassment of a daughter.

My mind wanders everywhere and nowhere at once. I'm lying on my bed, counting the glittery flecks of pearl embedded in the ceiling, when a soft knock sounds on my door.

I pause, straining my ears to see if I had imagined it.

It isn't mealtime... which usually means it's time for a lecture from my Devastatingly Perfect Sister.

The knock sounds again, accompanied by, "Helena?"

I bolt up and swim to the door, my tail swishing from side to side. I look down at the doorknob and just barely glimpse my naked breasts.

Wait, I think. *Shirt.*

I pull a loose, short-sleeve shirt over my head and open the door.

Hallie's annoyingly large eyes meet mine. She's pretty—prettier than me, many say—evil, and yet still manages to be absolutely, annoyingly elegant.

"What do you want, Princess?" I snap.

Something glimmers behind her eyes, and I smile. I want her to get mad, to show me the kind of person she really is. These lectures are much more fun when I get to try to smack her. She's a better fighter than I am, though. Daddy's little girl in every single way.

"Dad's here for you," she says.

I frown because she doesn't take my bait.

"What the hell does that son of a bitch want?" I snarl, attempting to accelerate the situation.

The door opens so fast, slamming against the wall. A bang echoes through the room as I'm thrown back into the wall. Hallie's eyes are glowing green, just like the king's. I smile at her even as the back of my head aches like hell. Pain is good, though. Pain reminds me that I'm alive. It breaks up the monotony of the days.

Bingo. Now the show begins.

She swims over, grabs my neck, and pins me to the wall. "*Behave*, Helena. If you want to keep living in my hospitality, if you want to see your niece and nephew, then you will be nice. Act *really* sorry, got it?" Hallie's teeth make a clicking sound as she clenches them, her peach-colored hair floating around her.

"Got it, little sister," I choke out, still grinning.

I follow her down the stairs and find the Oh So Glorious Ice Mer King at the entrance.

I feign shock, "Daddy? Is that you? After all this time!" I put a hand to my forehead and somersault backward.

"Helena," he commands, "you will stop that this instant."

His voice is enough of a warning that I return to a normal swimming position. The back of my head is still throbbing from Hallie's outburst—a reminder of the life pulsing through me.

My father hasn't changed at all. He watches me through wary, dangerous eyes. "We're leaving. Your house arrest is over."

I stiffen like petrified wood. "Wait, really?"

He doesn't repeat himself, just turns around and swims out of the house. The water is swirling in his wake. Hallie is clinging to James, looking like the ever-needy damsel in distress. Of course, James can't see what a monster she is. I snort at my joke.

"Behave, Helena," James says, straightening his pitiful crown. "You're upsetting my wife."

I *really* want to tell him what he can do with that second-rate crown, but two of Daddy's personal guards flank me on either side and grab my arms.

"Hey! At least take me to dinner first," I say when their silky hands dig into my flesh. When we pass Hallie, still curled up in James's arms, she looks up at me and flashes a triumphant smile. I blow her a kiss, and her eyes narrow.

I'm glad my Giselle and Ian aren't here to see this. They deserve so much better than this dolphin shit.

When we enter the open sea, the guards hurl through the water at an inconceivable speed. My tail isn't used to the rapid pace, and I go limp in their arms. The sensation of being dragged through the sea sucks.

When we arrive in Aqualis, the guards hand me to my father. Continuing with the theme of the day, he then drags me behind him. The familiar, breathtaking views surround me on every side as he takes me to the throne room.

We pass through enchanted tunnels so no one will see how poorly the Crown Princess is treated.

I push water through my gills as fast as possible, grasping at the oxygen that will keep me from passing out. Once I'm in the throne room, the male who fathered me violently releases me.

I rub the purple spots on either arm. My ice-gray skin bruises so easily.

For a moment, Phelix, the Ice Mer King, just floats above me. He is enormous; god-offspring always are. His well-kept beard is a blend of a dozen shades of green and blue. It appears as if there are dozens of eels writhing around his pale gray skin and unnervingly green eyes. Eyes that are currently promising pain in epic proportions.

I stare back at him. I am his daughter and won't let myself be afraid of him, even if he hates me.

He breaks the silence first, and I smile, reveling in the small win. "You are a disappointment," he says cooly.

The slight sense of pride evaporates. "Yes, Daddy. I know," I say. This time, instead of flashing him a cocky smile, I drop my head. It's pitiful how short of a time I stood tall before him. I let the monsters inside me that I keep locked up run around as they wish. My shame makes me sink a bit lower in the water.

"You cannot be queen," he continues as though I hadn't spoken.

"What?" I don't understand.

"Silence!" he demands. The sound waves travel through the water at such a rate that they cause my head to pound even harder. "If you were to take the throne tomorrow, it would be a disaster. You know *nothing*."

He pauses, swimming back and forth across the room for a few moments. He reminds me of a caged tigerfish I once saw when I was younger. They're dangerous wild, but in captivity, they have been known to kill entire populations of Merlings.

At last, he says, "You will go to your uncle in the Gates of Hell. He is a smart ruler. He will teach you what you must know if you ever hope to become queen."

"So, you're saying there's a chance I will be queen," I flash a half-hearted smile that he doesn't return.

"This is serious, Helena."

"Okay, okay, when do we leave?" I begin fiddling with the baggy gray shirt still billowing in the water.

"*You* will leave today. I will not be coming, and you will take a boat."

My jaw falls open, and I blink. "Boat? But Daddy, why would I take a boat when I have this bad boy?" I gesture to my tail.

He doesn't like my joke. The room around us grows dark, and my heart speeds up. His voice thunders, "Helena, you talk too much. You will learn to be a queen or pay the price. I think it's time you learn another fundamental lesson."

I open my mouth to respond, but he's too fast.

"If you are going to be above water, you will need legs. But, as you know, there has to be a balance. I've thought long and hard about this... and I'm almost sad I won't be coming with you. Because, you see, my darling daughter, the price for legs will be your voice."

When the last word comes out of his mouth, my eyes fly wide open. No! I need my voice.

I open my mouth to protest just as emerald green magic shoots across the room. It snakes past my lips and down my throat like a slippery eel. I choke, the water that has been my home for my entire life suddenly making breathing impossible. I look down to see my tail fading away. Desperately, I grab at the bottom of my shirt, trying to cover the human parts that are now exposed for the world to see.

I want to say something, to scream, to yell my frustration, but nothing more than air bubbles come out. A new sensation fills me, one I've never felt before. My lungs burn, and my oxygen supply is suddenly non-existent.

The King smiles and snaps his fingers. He summons a shark that speeds through the room. It slides under me and then shoots me up to the surface. The shark swims faster than the guards. The underwater city disappears as the light gets stronger, illuminating golden-white particles floating in the green-blue water.

Black spots edge my vision as a rainbow of colored fish burst from their formation around us. The water is brighter the further we go, but the black keeps interceding in my sight. My lungs burn, and my chest seizes as we travel.

We slice through the levels of the sea. It changes from midnight to twilight to daylight, but the burning in my brain and chest makes me worry I might die just as we break the surface. I gasp for air, spitting out as much water as possible. It burns.

My eyes focus, and I realize there is a small boat. The man who is sitting there quickly reaches over. He grabs me under the shoulders and lifts me carefully into the skiff. The shark is gone, quick as lightning. I make a futile attempt to cover myself, suddenly quite aware again of the lack of clothes on my bare legs and the bitter cold. The chill doesn't feel the same anymore; it hurts me.

I've always dreamed of leaving Aqualis. I just didn't know how painful it would be.

The man sees my struggle, but I am too busy languishing in the sensation of breathing to care. He shrugs off his coat, cursing profusely, and wraps me up as best as possible. He paddles us away, and I watch his muscles tug at his shirt as he rows the oars toward a much larger ship. I'm so tired, so I close my eyes.

My breathing is returning to normal, and I start to speak as if to say, "Don't look at my legs. They're very unimpressive."

No sound comes out. Nothing. Not even a croak or a whisper or a breath of air.

No no no no no no no.

I sit up abruptly. The man, startled, turns around to look at me. His dark hair is swept to the side. He keeps it short. Dark lashes fringe his eyes, and I like how his short beard frames his lips and jaw. I want to tell him this. Something. Anything.

Again, I open my mouth, straining my voice, and... no sound comes out. I scrunch up my face. Every muscle in my neck strains as I try to scream. I thrash out with my arms and unsteady legs.

No sound. Nothing.

"Hey, it's okay. Shh, it's okay. Calm down," the man repeats the platitudes, grabbing me by the shoulders and pulling me in tight to his body.

I shake as silent sobs wrack my body, gripping his arm tightly.

When the tears leak into my mouth, they taste like the sea.

I have no voice.

3
GET HER SOME CLOTHES
ERIK

"Captain, you're bringing a female aboard?" Disbelief rings through the air as my first mate hangs over the metal railing of *The Black Rose* and stares down at us.

The Crown Princess has finally stopped crying. Now she's curled up in a ball across from me. They sent her here in a T-shirt and nothing else.

Gods. Couldn't they have at least given her some real clothes?

Her eyes are full of fire, flame, and anger, but she hasn't said anything. I can't tell if I'm happy about that or not.

"Captain?" Conrad's voice is full of questions he won't dare ask in front of the crew. For the past twenty years, we've sailed the seas together. He is the closest thing I have to family, and he knows it. He's also kind of a bag of shit. I can see a glimmer of interest in his sharp blue eyes, but his face is schooled to perfection.

Conrad's blond hair is long and tied in a bun at the nape of his neck. His face is weathered, but women still find him attractive. I found him last night in a brothel with not one, but three women hanging off him.

When Conrad saw my expression, he sent the ladies away with kisses and empty promises to return another time. They had pouted as they walked in their skimpy nightgowns past me, heading down the stairs to their madame.

For as long as I've known him, Conrad's always been able to charm the ladies. He's had to avoid multiple ports because a female wants to cut off his favorite appendage.

I've never had that problem.

It might be sentimental of me, but I'm more careful with women. In our line of work, there aren't many opportunities to meet someone.

One of my most valued rules is that I don't get involved with females.

They're bad luck on the sea and have no place aboard my ship. I have no doubt women are no problem on some ships—like a cruise ship, yacht, or even on a fishing trip—but they are definitely out of place on vessels like mine. *The Black Rose* is a pirating vessel, not a leisure craft.

Conrad has repeatedly tried to push me towards the women who cater to men like us at the docks, but I refuse to use that option more than I need to.

His eyes are narrow as he studies me. I can practically see the wheels turning in his head. It's not a surprise. I've never brought a woman on board my ship. Women are dangerous. They make men weak. I learned early on that we *never* show weakness with a crew watching. Never give them a reason to doubt your abilities.

"Erik?" he asks again. I realize that I've been sitting in the rowboat like an idiot, just staring at him.

I nod. "She is coming aboard. This is..." my words dry up as I realize I can't share her name. The last thing I need is for my men to know who this is. I cough, covering up my blunder. "Madeline," I blurt out.

My face pales as I realize what I've just said.

Madeline? Did you just give her the name of your dead mother?

She jolts at the name, her eyes narrowing as she stares at me. Her nostrils flare, but even though she opens her mouth as though to speak, no sounds come out.

"Her name is Madeline," I repeat, my voice more firm this time as I regain control of the situation. "And she is coming aboard. Have one of the men prepare a room for her below deck. Conrad, take her to the bathroom and have the cabin boy bring her a set of his clothes. She can't stay in this." I gestured to the baggy t-shirt that is *not* adequately covering her up.

Conrad glares at me, but he doesn't push back. "You've got it, Captain."

A COUPLE OF HOURS LATER, I showered and changed, and I'm standing on the deck of my ship watching Helena. She's wearing different clothes but still manages to look out of place.

My FaePhone is tucked in my pocket, and I've spent the past hour below deck. I was responding to various calls and emails that came through while I was in Aqualis. Summer Fae can be a nuisance with their tricks and glamours, but no one can dispute that they make the best technology in Aranthium.

Even if I'm in the middle of the sea, my phone gets a signal. I bought a state-of-the-art solar charger the last time we docked in the Summer Court. Why not? Money is no issue, and having expensive things is a good look for me. People have certain expectations for the Pirate of Death. Obnoxious shows of wealth are practically part of the job description. I have a reputation to maintain, after all.

When I returned above deck, my gaze immediately went to the female standing at the metal railing. It's been twenty minutes, and Helena hasn't moved since I came out. She is looking out over the swirling blue and green waters surrounding us. The ship is large, but not so big that I can't see everywhere on the deck at once.

"Has she said anything?" I ask Conrad, who is standing next to me.

"Not a word. I gave her the clothes you requested, and she dressed in the crew's bathroom. She has been standing there ever since. It's eerie, and the crew is already asking questions—"

I snarl at him. "They are not to touch her. At all. She is under my protection."

He puts up his hands in supplication. "Man. I figured as much, but do you want to tell me why she's even here?"

Shaking my head, I fix my mouth in a straight line. "It's none of your concern."

He sighs but doesn't push the point any further. A long moment passes and neither of us speaks. The atmosphere is tense on the deck, and I can feel my control over my emotions slipping.

"Don't you have somewhere to be?" I snap. As far as I'm concerned, this conversation is over. Conrad raises a brow, turning to look at me, but he takes the hint and finds something to do.

Good.

Now I'm stuck on board with a female, already something I don't enjoy. If that wasn't enough, she's here because I have to kill her.

Running my prosthetic through my hair, I start to walk towards her.

Committing murder isn't enough for her father. He insisted that I have to make it look like someone else killed her, which means we must get far away from Ice Mer territory.

Gods. I need a stiff drink.

My life is such a mess, and this woman is making things worse.

As I stroll up next to Helena, I try not to notice how the cabin boy's clothes fit her frame so well. She is wearing a long, cream-colored tunic that falls below her hips. She has on black leggings that hug her every curve and show off her lean thighs, but I suppose we didn't have any footwear for her because her feet are bare.

Despite belonging to our smallest crew member, the tunic is clearly too large for her frame. She has a large black leather belt cinched under her breasts, making it more obvious than ever that she is a woman on board an all-male ship. Her purple and cerulean hair has dried off since her ascent to the surface, and it is flowing in billowing waves all around her.

Out of the corner of my eye, I catch Philips ogling her instead of doing his job. I growl at him, baring my teeth in his direction, and he quickly turns back to manning the ship.

No matter what King Phelix has asked of me, the Princess is still a guest and will be treated appropriately. Until the time comes to get rid of her. I have morals. I won't allow for disrespect towards her.

I turn my attention back to Helena. She is holding onto the railing and wobbling. Her icy gray skin stands out against the gleaming metal of the railing, and even without her tail, it is undeniable that she is different from the rest of us. She looks so out of place, it's laughable.

She must hear me coming because she turns and looks at me. As she shifts, a wave comes over the side of the railing. The ship rocks, and she slips, her bare feet sliding on the deck.

Sighing, I grab onto the railing with one hand and her elbow with the other. The moment we touch, a shock rushes through me. She feels like she's made of pure ice. I drop her elbow the second she is no longer in danger of falling, but it isn't fast enough. Helena turns and glares at me, pure venom filling her pink eyes.

This makes things so much more difficult. We will have to coddle her every step of the way.

I sneer, stepping back from this female who has upended my entire life. She's a princess. She's probably used to having everything handed to her on a silver platter. She'll just have to get used to a different life on my ship. I can't spare any crew members to cater to her every need.

She still hasn't said a word. That whole situation is becoming increasingly irritating by the second. On one hand, it makes my job easier. On the other hand, a mute woman is very high on my "thou shall not kill" list, right under children and right before puppies and kittens.

At the top of the list is "thou shall not get thyself killed by the Ice Mer King."

Dammit.

A conundrum if I ever encountered one.

"Madeline," I bark, extending a hand toward her. "Come with me."

She stares at me, and I cringe. Her eyes are unnervingly pink, and they convey her thinly veiled contempt for me. For all humans, no doubt. Finfolk are notorious for their hatred of humans.

Clenching her jaw, Helena pushes off the railing. She ignores my hand and begins to walk away. I watch, brows raised, as she makes it three steps before her bare feet lose purchase, and she careens toward me.

I curse, putting out my hands to grab her. The moment I

touch her skin, I grind my teeth. She's so cold, it feels like being pelted with ice water.

"Can't even walk by yourself," I mutter, shaking my head as I lead her below deck. "What in the gods' name did I do to deserve this kind of hellish torture?"

She doesn't answer, just rolls her eyes.

I lead her down the hull, past my crew's inquisitive gazes. They remain silent. They know better than to ask questions.

Ten minutes and two more near-falls later, we stand before a small private room below deck. I won't let her sleep in the same room as the men. The small space has a built-in bunk against one wall and a wooden desk with a chair beside it. I shove her inside.

"Here," I say gruffly. "Make yourself comfortable. I'll have someone bring you some food shortly. Don't go wandering around the ship without me. It's a dangerous place for a female."

She glares at me but doesn't say a word. She just... watches me. It's unsettling, to say the least.

"Goodbye, Princess," I snap before slamming the door in her face.

This is going to be the longest journey of my life.

4
WOBBLE LIKE A JELLYFISH
HELENA

The door slams shut, and the loud sound reverberates through my clenched jaw. I take several deep breaths as I look around, trying to calm myself. There isn't much to see. This ship is boring.

The inside of this room is painted white with one navy-blue stripe running through the middle of it. It doesn't look like I imagined ships of old to be, but considering I spent my life underwater, I don't have much experience in the matter.

I hug my arms around myself as the same debilitating fear closes all around me. It isn't claustrophobia. That I could handle. This is different. It's the fear of being alone again. I've been alone for so long.

In those early days, I tried to talk to my best friend, Elva. Unfortunately, all my efforts had proven fruitless. Loneliness is one thing, but having friends only to have them taken away is another level of pain. Being alone after knowing the joy of friendship is like having something dangled before you, only to have it pulled away at the last moment.

The horrors of life are exponentially worse if you *know* things aren't meant to be this way. If you *know,* there's a better world out there.

When I get to my Uncle Aidoneus, things will get better. I have to believe that. My uncle is every bit as fierce as my father but has much more capacity to be reasonable. Well, at least, that is what I have heard. It's a bit hard to believe, to be honest.

Daddy Assface never invited either of my uncles over for dinner or Solstice parties.

A small desk with a drawer is on my left. I wobble over, very unsteady on my new legs, and plop down. When I open the drawer, I find a small writing pad and a pen. My face lights up.

This is perfect!

Do they know I can't speak?

I tap the pen against the pad, thinking of all the horrible, nasty things I can write to the King. My face drops when I realize there is no real way to get my letter to him. I have no FaePhone, of course.

I could write something terrible to the captain of the ship. He was so rude to me earlier. I think about him, wondering what kind of man he is. I would like to know if I can conjure up the exact words that will make him feel as small and helpless as he made me feel today.

Just then, my door clicks open. I turn to yell at whoever it is, telling them to respect my damn privacy. All that comes out is air. My shoulders bunch up, and anger floods my frozen skin.

The irritation melts away when a pair of bright blue eyes, tanned skin, and beach-blonde hair greets me. I recognize this male from when I first got to the ship. He was talking to the captain. My first thought is that he looks like a surfer.

I can't help when my lips tilt up. He smiles back, turning on what he must think is languid charm.

Oh, this is very good.

Ancient legends told to babies and small children claim my

kind are murderers for our habit of entrancing sailors and drowning them in the sea. Perhaps I can revive the legends... after he helps me escape this place.

As much as I like my uncle, I don't want to be monitored every second I am with him. I would much instead visit the Gates of Hell without my armed escorts.

"Sun is down," the surfer drawls, "do you know what that means?"

My smile freezes in place, and I must fight the urge to roll my eyes. As sweetly as I can muster, I shake my head.

His smile grows wider. "So, it is true. You don't speak."

I don't give him the courtesy of attempting to reply. Not that I can, but still.

After a few more moments of regarding me thoughtfully, he says, "Well, it means that it's time for dinner. I trust you've unpacked all of your things, Madeline. Would you do me the honor? My name is Conrad, by the way."

Conrad's voice is like rancid oil, and it slides over my skin, but I play along. I fully intend to use him to my advantage. As soon as my hand slides into his, I walk upright as smoothly as possible. Like a newborn colt, I stumble down the hall and climb up the stairs to the mess hall.

When we arrive, I'm greeted by an incredibly pleasing scene. Large, thick windows overlook the sun setting over the sea. It's stunning, and the soft, yellow lights that hang overhead bathe the wooden tables in a pleasing glow. The space looks more like a restaurant than a mess hall, even though there appear to be no other females on board. Small lights are embedded in the ceiling, providing a warm light.

Interesting. This boat is so fancy.

Most of the crew is crowded around a cluster of tables that have been unceremoniously shoved together. The captain sits at the head of the table. He's wearing a black shirt unbuttoned a third of the way down his chest, revealing the soft, black curls that grow there. There is the barest hint of a swirling tattoo peeking out, and I'm struck by the oddest desire to find out what it is. One of his elbows is propped against his armrest, and his legs sprawl in front of him.

One of the other crew members is telling a story, and he watches with a critical expression. The punchline hits, and the room erupts in a roar of laughter. Men slap the table and throw their heads back as the bartender makes trips back and forth with flasks.

The captain doesn't laugh but releases an amused exhale as his mouth quirks up into a smile.

Conrad notices me watching the captain and leans in to say, "He's a bit of a bore, Captain Erik."

Erik. I file the name away with the other information I'm learning and nod encouragingly to Conrad. Is it a first name? Surname? It's hard to tell. Humans aren't nearly as efficient at naming themselves.

We are already halfway through the room when Erik notices us. I can't help but put an extra sway of my hips into my wobbly walk. His joyous expression blinks out like turning off a light.

A hush blankets the room as everyone turns to look at me. I wink at some of them.

"What is she doing here?" Erik asks. He's scowling at me.

"You told me she needed to be fed," Conrad says. "The food is here." He is leading me to the other end of the table. I tilt my head playfully towards his shoulder, and Erik's scowl turns into a sneer.

I feel completely at ease until I realize there are only two empty spaces. One is at the other end of the table, and the other is across from the sneering captain. Conrad seems important; he will likely take the space at the head of the table. I pray he does. I don't want to sit across from the captain. My heart speeds up at the thought of having to make eye contact with that dark-haired man sporting a stick up his ass the whole evening. He's made it clear he despises me.

My muscles relax a fraction of an inch when Conrad touches the chair at the end. Then my stomach drops when I realize he is just taking it out for me to sit. He gestures to the seat, "For our guest of honor."

One of the men scoffs. I glance at his scrawny, wind-weathered face. A crisscross scar marks his left cheek. The captain clears his throat, a dangerous sound that sends shivers down my spine.

"Apologies, sir, but you know it is bad luck to have a female aboard," the scrawny man leans across the table as if he can hide what he is saying.

I roll my eyes. I *am* bad luck for them, but not for the reason they think.

"That's enough," the captain says.

"I was just saying—"

Erik's chair scratches against the wooden floor and teeters on its back legs momentarily. He stands and prowls over to the man's chair. He grabs the back of the sailor's shirt in one heartbeat and yanks him into a standing position.

"I said," the irritable captain growls between gritted teeth, "That's enough. I don't like it either, but you *will not* question my decisions." A smack fills the air and a red mark blooms on the man's cheekbone. No one breathes as the sailor tumbles to the ground, falling with a *thump*. The poor man is alone and without help as he scrambles to his feet and hurries out of the room.

A chill skitters down my spine. The captain has made his dislike of me obvious. If I could speak, I would've goaded him at this moment. This feels personal, and I want to see how far I can push him.

Opportunity lost.

I sit in my chair, and Conrad goes to the bar to get two plates of food for us. He smiles warmly when he hands me mine, and I return the gesture with a delicate shrug.

Ugh. I am even starting to annoy myself.

When I look up, the scowl has returned to the captain's face. He watches me with such fierce intensity from across the table. If looks could kill, I would have two holes burned in my forehead by now.

"If any of you touch... *her*, you will be thrown overboard to visit all the Mer females you want. Perhaps they will spare your eyeballs when they feed you to their pets," Captain Erik says, warning his crew.

The rest of the meal passes in complete silence, and the captain never stops staring at me. Surely the others notice, but no one comments on it further. It doesn't take a genius to realize they're afraid of him.

After eating, I allow Conrad to take my arm and guide me back to my room. I'm the perfect, mindless doll for him. He doesn't seem to mind that all I can do is nod and smile when he says something.

He lingers momentarily at the door, but I fake a yawn and slip inside, shoving the door shut. I hope Conrad doesn't notice how much force I put behind it.

I let out a long exhale and stretch my arms, allowing the idiotic smile I'd left plastered over my face to melt away. My fingers loosen the band I'd wrapped around my rib cage to give the loose tunic some form. As I toss it on the bed, one side of the shirt slides off my shoulder, and I slide out of the black legging-like things.

A firm knock sounds at the door, and I roll my eyes. Conrad certainly is persistent. I walk over, wondering if baring so much skin is a bad idea. There's no peephole to check who's on the other side.

If it's Conrad, I'm angry enough to shut him down here and now. He's too eager, anyway—mindless bastard.

I yank the door open, fixing my face in my most withering stare. A pair of brown, black-fringed eyes glare back at me. I take a step back at the intensity brewing within the captain's eyes.

"Did you enjoy making a spectacle of yourself this evening?" he asks, leaning against the door frame.

I shrug, and more irritation builds in his eyes. Pushing this man's buttons is kind of fun. Especially after a night of Conrad's idiotic pining.

"So, you're a mute?" Erik asks, pushing past me and closing the door. I try to ignore how he smells like sea salt as I shake my head.

"No? So what is this, then?" he gestures to me.

I shrug again, and his eyes widen a fraction of an inch. He clenches his teeth, a vein pulsing in his neck. If he were a dragon, he'd be breathing smoke by now.

The thought makes me smile, and my lips tilt into a wide grin. Somehow, he becomes even more frustrated, his nostrils flaring dramatically.

Pushing past him, I grab the small notepad and sit. Scribbling at a rapid pace, I write,

Can't speak. Dad exchanged my voice for legs.

I shove the pad at him. His eyes fly over the text, squinting for a moment.

"What the hell, Princess?" he starts. "Your handwriting is terrible."

It's my turn to scowl. I go back to my pad and draw a quick sketch. Once again, I shove it at him and watch his face expectantly.

For a moment, he looks confused, and then the anger flushes

his face. "Why, you spoiled—" he throws the rough sketch of him with a pirate hat and a giant stick up his ass. I let out a silent laugh so violent that it tips my chair backward.

My heart skips a beat as it falls to the ground, but Erik's hand shoots out instinctively and catches it. I stare up at him for a second, wide-eyed. The look of disdain still coats every one of his features. His mouth is set in a tight line, his eyebrows furrowed as he glares at me.

For a moment, there's a thick blanket of tension in the air as I meet his eyes. It dissolves as he clears his throat and blinks. He relinquishes his grip, and the chair drops back to its proper place as his gaze drops to my bare shoulder ever-so-quickly.

"You will not disrespect me like this again, especially not in front of the crew. They don't want you here. I don't want you here. Stay out of our way, and everything will be fine."

He's already opening the door when I put on a stern expression and salute him. He rolls his eyes and slams the door violently. The frame shudders in his wake.

I stare at it for several minutes. A small, genuine smile tugs at the corners of my mouth for the first time in two years.

5
MY OWN PERSONAL SIREN
ERIK

The following day, I wake up groaning as vicious shards of sunlight shine through the windows of the captain's cabin. I shove my hand over my eyes as though that can stop the pounding hangover from raging through my body. There is a heaviness in my limbs that can only mean one thing.

Last night, things got out of control.

The proof lies on the floor beside me as if I needed more than my raging headache and dry tongue. A curse slips out of my lips as I eye the empty bottle of bourbon that had been my only companion in the early morning hours.

I don't usually drink, especially to excess, but something about the mermaid drives me up the wall. When Conrad paraded her around at dinner the night before, I wanted to reacquaint my fist with his face right then and there.

He's always liked to push the boundaries as first mate, but last night was too far. The last time someone pushed me like this, they ended up with a broken arm and a matching pair of black eyes. Conrad might need a reminder about who is in charge on *The Black Rose*. We are going to have a chat about this.

Today.

Just as soon as I can successfully peel myself off my bed. The ship's steady rocking is usually a comfort, but today, all it's doing is making me feel sicker.

That damn female is ruining my life.

It takes half an hour, but I finally reach the jug of freshwater I keep by the door. I drink as much as I can, hoping it will alleviate the pounding in my temples. Pulling on some clothes, I brush my teeth before opening the door. It swings open on silent hinges, and I snap at the first person I see.

"LaRue, tell the First Mate his presence is required in my office *right now*," I say to the man, barely older than a boy, who happens to be walking by.

He gulps and nods, changing course and scurrying off immediately.

I grin. There's something about flexing my proverbial muscles that always makes me happy. I spent years following other people's orders. It's about time my crew follows mine.

Slamming the door, I shut the blinds before dropping into the chair behind my desk. I steeple my hands, mentally reviewing what I want to say, and wait for Conrad.

And wait.

And wait.

A gods-damned hour passes before the door to my office clicks open and soft footsteps fill my ears. My mood has deteriorated from foul to outright enraged.

"You summoned me, sir?" Conrad drawls. His tone is indignant, and I instinctively stiffen. Clenching my jaw, I crack my neck and glare at my first mate.

"Sit down," I snap, gesturing to the chair in front of my desk. He drops into it like he hasn't a care in the world. It takes everything in me not to hit him for his insolence. "We need to have a conversation about Madeline."

He tilts his head, raising a brow. "Oh?"

"I don't want her to be paraded around the ship. She's not some whore you picked up on the docks. You need to leave her alone."

"Why? Are you interested in her?" he asks, studying me. He picks up a paperweight off my desk. He looks intense as he tosses it back and forth.

I grab it from him, slamming it on the desk so hard that the thick polish cracks beneath the rock. "Of course not," I say forcefully, pinching the bridge of my nose as I count to five in my head before continuing. "You can't touch her because she's not some average female."

"Then who is she?"

"What I'm about to say is top secret." I lean over, my voice dropping to a whisper as I make sure the door is closed behind us. "It can't ever leave this room. Do you understand?"

I stare at the man, not even blinking until he slowly nods. His brows are furrowed, but an interested gleam has entered his eyes. "Yes, Captain. Of course."

"Good." I lean back in my chair and rake my hand through my hair. "Madeline is the Crown Princess of the Ice Mer."

A slew of colorful curses leaves Conrad's mouth as all the blood drains from his face. I've never seen him so surprised, and it takes him a few minutes to regain his composure.

"Did you kidnap her?" he asks, rubbing a hand on his neck. "That's messed up, even for you, man. Shit, Erik—"

"Don't be an idiot," I snap, furling and unfurling my fists. "I didn't kidnap her. Her father has called in his life debt."

I sit back and let the words sink in. Conrad has been with me for years and knows about the unfortunate situation with Henrick. He was the one who tried to talk me out of helping the Angel in the first place, telling me it wasn't worth it.

He was probably right. Look where *that* got me.

"You mean..." Conrad's eyes widen as he realizes what I've been ordered to do. His face pales as he swivels to look at the closed door, then back at me. Dropping his voice, he whispers, "You're going to kill her?"

"I am." I force the words out of my mouth despite their bitter taste. I continue, "Once I do this, I'm free from the King's shackles. I'll have paid my life debt."

Conrad sits back, his blue eyes unblinking as he takes in the ramifications of what I just told him. "So she's a dead woman walking."

I nod. A heaviness came over the room. "But I have to take her away from the Ice Mer lands. Her father has given me specific instructions on what to do."

"Well..." Conrad draws out the word, "shit."

"That about sums it up," I say, shaking my head. The movement causes my headache to worsen, and I stand, groaning. "Gods, I need some coffee."

Nodding, Conrad waits for me to get around the desk before standing. "So, if she's got a target on her back, can I..."

"You are not to lay a finger on her," I command, shoving Conrad back. "Don't you *ever* bring it up in my presence again. Next time, there won't be a warning."

He straightens himself, raising his hands in supplication. "You've got it, Captain. It won't happen again."

"It'd better not. Let's go."

The mess hall is nearly empty by the time we get there, and Conrad disappears to go talk to Jean Luc in the kitchen. I head straight for the coffee, ignoring everyone else. I pour myself a cup, cradling the mug in my hands as the warmth seeps into my bones.

As I am about to sip the steaming hot ambrosia, footsteps warn me that someone is coming. I sigh, knowing that whatever this is, it won't make me happy.

"Captain." Phillips' voice comes from behind me. There is a tremor in his voice as he speaks. "You're needed above deck."

"Why?" I growl. Everyone knows not to disturb me before I drink at least one cup of coffee. I might be an ass, but coffee makes me tolerable.

"I'm sorry, sir, but there is a situation with some of the cargo. We need you above deck immediately."

Cursing, I grab a piece of fresh bread as I follow him. There go my plans for a nice, long, drawn-out breakfast. On my way out of the mess hall, I stop the cabin boy in his tracks. His eyes widen as he looks up at me, his small stature accentuated by his trembling body.

"Sir?" he asks.

"Bring some food to the lady. Make sure she's fed, but don't talk to her."

He nods. "Right away, Captain."

At least one person on this ship understands how to speak to me.

By the time the sun is high in the sky, my stomach is grumbling. The bread soaked up the remnants of the liquor in my system but did little to sate my hunger. I've been stuck above deck for hours, dealing with problem after problem after problem.

Now, finally, I have a moment of peace and quiet.

I head down into the ship's hull and end up in my office, which used to be the ship's formal dining parlor. Instead of fancy parties, it houses the safe where I keep the ship logs, most of the ship's weapons, and the black-market bullets manufactured to take down the largest beings in Aranthium.

Pushing open the door to my office, my lips tilt up in anticipation of my soft leather chair when I suddenly stop. A red-haired sailor is bent over my bookshelves, pawing through my novels as though he doesn't have a care in the world.

"Tell me there's a good reason you're in my private office, Anders." I snarl, not even trying to temper my words.

The sailor straightens so fast he hits his head on the floating shelves I keep behind my desk. "Dammit," he curses, holding a large hand to his head. He turns around, his eyes widening when he sees me.

"Anders, you have two seconds to explain yourself, or you'll find yourself sleeping with the fish." I cross my arms over my chest, glaring daggers at the sailor.

The man joined my crew last year after I picked him up in the Spring Mer territory. So far, he had proven himself to be a trustworthy sailor.

Until now.

Anders shifts, his red hair almost brown in the light. His brown eyes widen as he stares at me, holding a crumpled paper in my direction. "Cap-cap-captain," he gulps, stumbling over his words. "I was just... the lady gave me a note when I brought her lunch, and I thought..."

Strolling forward, I snatch the piece of paper out of his hands.

Is there anything to read on this ship? I've never been so bored in my life.

"So you thought you would go through my personal library for our guest? Without asking permission?"

Anders pales, and I note with satisfaction that he is trembling. "I just thought..."

"That's the problem. You aren't paid to think. And you are paid generously, correct?"

"Yes," he croaks.

"Exactly. You are here to listen to me, not anyone else. I'll deal with this." I wave the paper in the air. "You're not to come in here or associate with Madeline. Is that clear?"

He nods. "Crystal, sir."

Before I can say another word, he turns and runs out of my office. I give up all hope of a peaceful afternoon and stomp toward the Princess' room. She and I are going to have a little chat.

WHEN I SEE her room at the end of the hallway, a piece of paper is stuck to the front of the door. It's fluttering in the breeze from an open window, and when I get closer, I see a crudely drawn picture of...

Me.

There is something scrawled in less-than-splendid penmanship on the bottom of the note. I squint, reading:

If you have a stick up your ass, go away!

Blood rushes to my head, and a roaring fills my ears. With a huff, I tear the note off the door with my right hand. Crumpling the paper, I bang my left fist against the wood. I pound my prosthetic so hard echoes of pain break through the cloud of fury that has surrounded me since I found Anders trespassing in my office for *her*.

"Open the door this instant, Princess. We need to talk."

There is no response, but I know she's there.

"Princess," I accentuate each word with another bang. "Open the gods-damned door, or I'll break it down."

There's a shuffling sound on the other side before the door cracks open, just enough to let me see into the small room.

Helena is staring at me, her pink eyes filled with fury and anger. Her lips are pursed, and her jaw is clenched. A rainbow of muted, deep ocean colors overwhelms me like an icy wave whenever she moves. Her hair is wild and untamed, and she looks like vexation personified. A slight chill snakes from her room.

She tilts her head. A silent, demanding question is in her eyes. *What?*

I shove both notes at her. Helena takes them from me, and her eyes flash with fury before she shuts the door in my face. No one has ever slammed a door in my face before. Her audacity is so overwhelming it feels like my brain is short-circuiting.

It creaks open a moment later, and she hands me another note. Her hands are icy.

If you're going to be an ass, the least you can do is give me a book.

"I don't have to do anything for you," I snap and shove the note back to her. "My only job is to take you to your destination."

She grabs the paper with her frosty fingers and scribbles while holding the paper against the doorframe.

Please.

My first reaction is to say no and leave her to her icy hell, but something about the look in her eyes makes me stop. I grab the door and study her. Her gaze meets mine, and she stares right back, unflinching. Inexplicably, her hand ends up resting on the door just under mine. I stare at those gray fingers, their difference from my skin even more marked than before.

The air thickens, and for a moment, I think she will touch me. Before I can react, she grabs the paper from me and presses her fingers against the word. Only the ghost of an icy breeze meets my hand.

Please.

Oh, dammit.

"Fine," I say through clenched teeth. "I'll bring one to you within an hour, as long as you promise not to pass notes to my crew. They're not here to serve you."

She pinches her lips together and frowns. I can practically see the wheels turning in her head before she nods tersely.

"It's a deal. Goodbye, Princess."

Closing the door, I head back to my office. It will be another long night, and I need a drink.

6

BE SOMEONE WORTH RESPECTING

HELENA

I'm sitting patiently on my bed and hating my windowless room. Getting to the Gates of Hell is not a quick journey. This is the first time I've ever left the safety of the ocean, and I am missing every bit of the trip. I can't see what the water looks like, nor the stretches of land veiled by gorgeous, gossamer clouds. I can only imagine what it must look like as I stare at the wall.

I've seen contraband videos of the land world. I know a little about its culture. Dancing, running, walking. They all seemed so unnatural, once upon a time. Now I am here with two legs, and I can still not do most of the things I had seen.

The captain had told me he would give me a book before he left. Now I'm sitting here, silently cursing that I didn't press further.

I didn't even tell him what kind of book to bring me. He's probably going to send me a maintenance manual.

He would do it, too, just to spite me.

Clenching my fists, I fall back onto the small bed and draw in a long breath. The magic from the ocean is still wearing off. It feels like I am melting in this gods-awful place. My heart longs for an ice bath.

And my tail.

I used to count things when confined to the small room in my sister's house. Tiles, sparkles, shells, seconds, whatever I could. When that grew tiresome, I'd sing to myself. Hallie had hated that.

I look around. The flat walls of this room don't have anything for me to count, and I don't like the thought of training these legs. It feels too committed to this form, even if it is necessary.

Luckily, I had a pen and paper, so there's that. As a bonus, I can leave and go to the bathroom down the hall. Thank the gods, there is running water on this ship. I can't imagine how horrible it would be to have this body and not have access to modern plumbing. I can lock my door from the inside as well. But the captain has made it abundantly clear that he doesn't want me here.

But maybe if I am careful and avoid Erik, I can make this work. Ideas and images rapidly pop into my head, making my blood course through my veins due to all the excitement.

Every idea is more ridiculous than the last, making me grin from ear to ear. The insufferable captain is going to regret agreeing to take me on fast. Maybe he'll even give me a boat when I decide to escape. It has been years since I have had any kind of fun at all. Elva and I used to get into so much trouble. I miss her desperately.

I've felt like half a person in the years I have been forbidden to contact my best friend. And... she's married now. Even if she could contact me, there's no guarantee she would message or call. I've heard that married-lady things usually take up a lot of time. I should remember her as she used to be. Whole memories are better than partial shells of friends.

But... this crew, this captain, is a challenge. He is presenting me with something that I can *do*. I will get under his skin, and it will be the most fun I've had in a *very* long time. The irritated, exasperated look in Erik's eyes is simply too delightful. It is like playing with fire. He reminds me of Elva—both are too serious for their good.

The most exciting part is that he thinks I'm weak. Granted, I'm not the most stable on these legs, but I doubt he would be prepared for my century of hand-to-hand combat lessons with a master swordsman. I'm going to start strength training.

A hurried knock follows a small *thud* outside of my door. I stand up quickly, only swaying slightly this time. When I peek outside, a large paperback book is lying on the floor. I would've squealed if I could've. I glance around, but the hallway is empty. The captain must be reinforcing his hands-off order.

I snatch the book up and close the door as quickly as possible. I'm kneeling on the firm mattress in a second, tangling my feet and legs into the soft, polyester blanket. The book has worn edges and a cracked spine. Whoever it belongs to must have read and reread it.

When I was younger, my father enchanted books for us to read so they wouldn't get ruined underwater. Hallie and I used to write each other notes in the margins, and I wonder if I will find any notes in this story. My fingers brush against the cover, *The Worth of a Man*.

I'd never read this before, but I could recognize human literature when I came across it. The crew seems to be made of only humans, so that makes sense.

Cracking open the spine, I start at the title page. Written in clean, evenly spaced letters is:

Property of Henry Erikson. Keep your filthy hands off, or else!

The "or else" has been underlined twice. I can't help but smile. This must belong to the crew member who I cornered earlier. Human names all sound so similar, though I do like the sound of the name 'Henry.' My mother chose H-names for all of her children.

Eager to do something other than come up with mindless pranks for my dangerous pirate escort, I start the book.

The first paragraph is underlined. *"Humans. What are we? Are we our thoughts? Perhaps our words? Or do our actions, the things we do daily, define us? Leland Allen Porter certainly thought that actions were the key definition until one day..."*

The rest of the chapter details a man who tried his best to be a good person until one day, he couldn't deny the blatant discrimination and exploitation his magical overlords were subjecting him to. He decides that what he has been through and what happens to him is just as important as what he does. It is action-packed and exciting, and I gasp when a bit of romance enters at the mid-way mark.

Together, he and his super-smart partner decide to fix things for humans. I smile. I like the philosophical tone of the book.

IT'S impossible to know precisely how much time has passed with my nose buried in the crook of the book, but my neck hurts, and the words are blurring. I expect my skin to itch without water... but my mortal form doesn't have that problem. The deck above me is pounding with whatever fight training the crew is holding. This book is massive, but my sorry ass is making quick work of it.

I get up, desperately needing to stretch my legs. Perhaps I can find something to eat. I tentatively open the door, checking the usually empty hallway. It appears this ship has a decent-sized crew, so it is odd that I never manage to run into anyone down here.

To the left, there is the bathroom. Directly across from me is another door that I've never seen anyone use, and to the right are the stairs leading to the mess hall. Behind them is where the rest of the crew sleeps. I haven't returned to the main deck since I arrived.

Grabbing my pen and paper, I slip out and stop at the bathroom first. I take a look in the mirror. My gray skin looks pale and unnatural under these lights. My hair hangs in tangles around my shoulders, and I desperately try to comb through it with my fingers. There is a box in the corner, near the shower. Necessity gets the better of me, and I rummage through it, looking for a brush. All I find is a small comb.

It will have to do.

I rake it through my tangles and then tie them into a bun at the back of my head, tucking the ball of hair in. It is loose, and I try to remember how Elva showed me to make it tighter all those years ago. No luck.

Shrugging, I duck back into the hallway, grateful my hair is no longer a disaster. I creep up the stairs and see no one in the mess. Despite the empty room, the distinct aroma of food wafts from the back. My stomach grumbles. I wander through the open area, taking my sweet time looking at the ocean. When the bartender pops out, he sees me, pales, and then hurries back inside.

My brows knit together, and I squint my eyes in the direction the man disappeared off to. *He* must've told them to avoid me. The captain had said that they believe I am bad luck. I scoff. There is no way anyone alive is still that superstitious. I can't believe the irony. Here they are, living and working on this top-of-the-line ship, and they still believe old wives' tales.

Angry, I scribble a note.

It isn't very "respectful" to make everyone hate your guest, you know.

I fold it into the shape of a heart, write Erik's name, and then lick the back and press it to the window until it sticks. *Perfect.*

At the opposite end of the room is a nice, carved wooden door. I would've bet good money that this is the captain's office. I consider going in, but I still have quite some time to irritate him. By my best estimates, we will be on the water for at least a month. Best to leave a few options open for a rainy day.

I spot the stairs that go up to the deck and move up them with the same slow caution as before. When the sunlight hits me and the sea-salt wind fills my lungs, I feel like I am home again for a moment.

My head pops out of the hull. At least two dozen men are moving around quickly. They are shouting orders to each other, and several are brawling in a nearby ring blocked off by crates. I spy the man I had cornered earlier to force him to get me a book. I wave a toned arm at him, and he pauses.

His eyes widen when he sees me, and he hurries forward.

Again?! My fists clench at my sides. This is beyond rude. I am tired of not fighting back, sitting like a good little prisoner. No one else pays me any attention or even notices me, so I sit on the steps and write five different notes.

As I do, I can't help but listen to the men as they talk.

"... new Ice Queen and her husband..."

My ears perk up at the mention of Elva. What I wouldn't give to get to talk to her again. Maybe once I am with my uncle, I can call her.

"Captain is grumpier than..."

"... so many rules."

I seal all the notes the same way as I had with the one in the mess hall, except this time, I write numbers to order them.

Time to get some exercise in. I need to train up these legs.

Once I am finished, I grasp onto some nearby railing and stand. There is no sign of Erik, so I clumsily lope up the stairs and duck behind a stack of crates covered in a faded blue tarp. One of the men walks in front of me, his conversation mostly centered on the fights.

I jump out, lose my footing, and grasp his shoulder. He startles, but when he looks at me, it's as if he's seen a ghost. I smile, stumble, hand him the note, and then dash away.

I repeat similar processes, snaking in and out of obstacles like an eel until they are all handed out. I find that if I crawl, I can move faster. The gods above must've smiled at me because I neither saw Erik nor Conrad. I am surprisingly silent without shoes. All the hiding and ducking around is exhilarating. A smile creeps on my face. My new muscles burn like they have been boiled. Narrowly avoiding the thick, industrial cable that swings down from the mast, I continue running back down the stairs and to the mess hall.

I'm getting the hang of this! My hair whips against my face, my feet connect with the sunbaked surface, and the salty air fills my new lungs.

When the sunshine warms my skin, it banishes all of the frostiness from my icy home. A strange thing happens because instead of heating my skin, my insides feel on fire too. Running is *addicting*.

I trip down the last step, the tiredness finally catching up with my agility. When I hit the ground, my feet stumble. A nearby chair is the unfortunate victim of my clumsiness, and I crash into it. Moments later, the same man from before runs into the hallway. He bites his lip when he sees me again, and I give him a sheepish smile as I sit up.

Allowing kindness to get the best of him, he hurries over and helps me up. He's older but has a gentle face. I like the way the deep lines on his face make him seem like he's smiling even when he's not.

"There we are, miss," he drawls. Once I'm back on my feet, he promptly lets go. "Are you all right?"

I nod.

He smiles, turning away, and I pull out my notepad. I frown because it's starting to run out of pages. He stops, quirking a brow. I sloppily scrawl out,

Thank you.

He reads the small note. When he looks back at me, I mouth the words and bow my head a bit.

His sun-aged lips are tan and covered with brown freckles. They twitch when he smiles. "Would you like to eat?" He gestures to one of the tables near the kitchen.

I nod eagerly.

"Right this way... Madeline? Is that right?"

Bouncing my head from side to side, I shake my hand a bit as if to say, *more or less.*

He laughs at my action and says, "I'll be right back."

Plopping into one of the chairs, I keep thinking that this is my chance to talk to someone who doesn't hate my guts—*cough, Daddy, Hallie, Erik, the list goes on*—and seems like they would listen to me.

While he's away, I write out a list of questions. What's his name, why is he on this ship, and where can I find a clock and maybe some clothes?

A few moments later, he comes out with two plates. He sets one down in front of me, and I greedily look at the breaded fish filets and salad. I dig in, eating quickly.

He looks almost ashamed when he sees how fast I eat. I tilt my chin, chewing in full view and allowing him to feel bad for everyone treating me coldly. I know it's not his fault, but he might chastise the others.

A Crown Princess is still a Crown Princess, even if she can't speak... and no one but the captain knows who she is.

Ready to move on from my meal, I pull out the pad, point to the first question, and then pass it to him.

He looks between me and the pad before reading. "My name? I'm Jean Luc."

I smile and nod encouragingly.

His expression clouds a bit on the next question. "I am here... because my family needs me to be."

It is a very heavy answer, thick with hidden meaning. Unfortunately for my curiosity, it isn't like I can press him without a voice, so I let him continue. Several moments pass with nothing more than the sounds of us chewing in silence.

His frown deepens when he finally looks at the last bit on my list. He wipes his mouth with a napkin and stands up. "Damn, they didn't even give you a clock? I will take care of these two and get back to you at dinner. The others will be down in about a half-hour. Do you want more food?"

I nod eagerly and move my closed fist as if carrying a bag. He seems to understand the meaning and nods. He puts together a small takeaway container of rolls, steamed vegetables, and a small bit of candy. Leftovers in hand, I gleefully head down the stairs to return to my reading.

I finish the rest of the book and shove food into my mouth. The soreness in my muscles is starting to ease. From what I've experienced today, some strength must've transferred over from my tail. But it wasn't like I was strong before I arrived.

My legs tuck under my bottom, and I study the words. At the end of the story, I'm reduced to tears, weeping into my pillow. It is ridiculous. The book ended with a perfectly happy-ever-after, complete with hope and peace.

Human literature is very different from the tragedies I was forced to read as a child. Just as I'm wiping away the tears with my shirt, I realize how bad I smell. I wince and wonder if everyone else who has come into contact with me has smelled this odor.

Being above water is something I have never done. How was I supposed to know how gross I would get? I still don't have any spare clothes, but maybe I can wash and re-wear these. I am used to being waterlogged, after all.

When I wander back to the bathroom, I almost feel lightheaded. It's odd to roam freely. I wandered around for hours, and nobody stopped me, even if they thought I was weird.

Peeling off my clothes, I rummage back through the plastic crate. I grin as I find something I have never used before: soap.

Soap isn't great for scales, which tend to be silky-smooth with natural slime.

The other bottle reads: lot-ion. The directions say to rub it on my body.

Oh... like sea snail mucus! Perfect.

I am pretty sure these are the only things I'd need. When I step into the shower, I turn the water on as hot as possible. I shouldn't like it, but I want to try it. It is too hot, so I crank it to the middle and settle on a medium temperature.

Once the shower head has thoroughly soaked my hair and skin, I open the soap.

Shit.

It smells exactly like the captain. What the hell are his things doing here? And why does he use a body wash that smells like the ocean when he is already *living on the ocean?*

Just as I am panicking and cursing myself, a loud pounding on the door sounds.

"Princess, are you in there?" The captain's obnoxiously irate voice calls through the door, his voice slightly muffled.

I freeze. I have no idea what to do, so I quickly finish rinsing and shut off the water.

"What do you think you're doing wandering around my ship handing out notes?" he shouts.

Well, damn. That didn't take long.

"Did you hear me? Do you think I don't respect you? This has nothing to do with respect. It's not safe for you to be out wandering around. I gave you a book. Isn't that enough?" Erik's voice is full of calculated rage.

I roll my eyes and reach for the disgusting clothes. He is already starting to get under my skin. The prank isn't that fun anymore. I start rummaging for my pen and paper. He's still spewing nonsense, but I can't find my pad. Grinding my teeth, I tear at my hair. I can't think when he's—

"Gods, I forgot you can't even speak. This is the worst..." he drones on.

That does it. I'm so furious, I write on my palm. The writing is sloppy on my skin, but I yank open the door and shove my hand in his face.

Stop yelling, asshole. If you want respect, be someone worth respecting.

Red clouds my vision, and I'm trying to control my huffing breaths. It takes me a second to realize that he has gone red, but not from anger.

Nope. That's all on me.

I look down, my eyes widening as I realize what he is seeing. In my anger, I forgot all about the clothes. My waist-long hair is doing nothing to preserve my modesty. I grab the door and hide my lower half. Water droplets fly around me and glint in the fluorescent light. I stick my tongue out at him and close the door.

Proceeding to hit my forehead with the heel of my palm, I scream silently.

I just want my stupid tail back. Why the hell did I do that?!

I grab my disgusting clothes and then drop them on the floor. They still smell terrible.

I slide to the ground, wanting to cry and wallow in embarrassment, but another knock interrupts me a few moments later. I intentionally wrap myself in a towel and crack open the door. Only my head pops out, and I see Jean Luc standing with a pile of clothes. I'm still blushing furiously when I take them, so I close the door quickly and return to my hell.

I hate that Captain.

I dress quickly, trying to ignore that I smell like him.

7
I CAN'T SLEEP RIGHT WHEN SHE'S HERE
ERIK

It's been two days since Helena hijacked my shower and used my shampoo. I rub my eyes, trying to eliminate the memory of her standing in the doorway, dangerously gorgeous, flushed, and dripping with water from my brain. Not for the first time, might I add.

Yup. Two incredibly long, hellish days. Yesterday, we finally left Ice Mer waters, which means that I am meant to kill her by sundown tomorrow. If she hadn't invaded my thoughts, maybe I wouldn't feel like a paper shredder is working on each of my internal organs. When I informed Conrad yesterday, he nodded before heading off to ensure we were on course. There was a part of me that was angry he didn't try to stop me.

After this, I'm going to need a break. I'm getting too emotional, too involved, and it's affecting my health.

Case in point: my current predicament. I'm sleeping on the small settee in my office, of all places, because the Crown Princess has taken up residence in the room across from mine. My neck has a weird kink, and my legs are sore from being bunched up for hours. I woke up from a less-than-stellar sleep ten minutes ago. Already, I can tell that this day will be a horrible one.

It's all because of her. I don't understand why she is being so damned frustrating. She asked for a book. It was given to her.

Should be enough, right?

Wrong.

She left these notes all over my ship, *and then* she had the gall to use my things.

A small, niggling voice at the back of my head tells me that my irritation is a placeholder for the awfulness of my situation, but I shove the thought away like it's bad sushi. It's best if I pretend that none of this is happening. After all, all anyone else will know is that the Ice Mer Princess disappeared. It's none of my business.

I straighten my collar.

It's fine if I'm mad about people using my things. I'm the captain, and this whole ship belongs to me. I should be able to leave my things wherever I want. If I want to leave all my clothes strewn over the deck, then I will. Should I choose to parade around naked, I will. No one will stop me.

Effectively numbed to reality and confident in my masculine right to my own space, I stand and stretch. I walk into *my* bathroom, shower in *my* shower and then walk into *my* mess hall to have some coffee.

By the time I've finished my third cup of liquid gold, I've reached a conclusion: I'm not going to let some spoiled, bewitching Ice Mer princess take away my freedom. It's not just my life, it's the money too.

The thousands of gold marks that have been wasted in the hands of malevolent royalty should be reserved for those who actually need it. When I think of those who suffer, the humans without homes or jobs, left to the whims of the climate, or superior beings, my stomach roils. For the first time, I am angry enough not to care about the brutal reality. By the time the sun sets tomorrow, Helena will have breathed her last breath. It will be a small price to pay for what I can do as a free man.

Buoyed by the thought of a brighter future, I leave the mess hall feeling better than I have in days. I'm going to spend the day on the deck. I will talk to my men, do my job and enjoy the feeling of the sun on my face.

My plan works for all of three hours.

That's all it takes before LaRue runs up to me on the deck and says, "Captain, there's a call on your FaePhone for you."

LaRue is panting as he extends his hand. He is holding the silver FaePhone like it's a used diaper. It's still ringing, the tune nothing but a set of rapid, high-pitched trills. Instantly, I know who is on the other line. That ringtone only belongs to one person.

I snatch the phone and accept the call by sliding my thumb across the screen.

"Hello?" I say, shoving the sailor aside and crossing to the railing. "This is Erik."

"*Please hold for His Majesty, King Phelix.*" A shrill voice comes through the speaker. Gods-awful waiting room music begins blasting in my ear, and I grimace. I sit through ten minutes of mind-numbing music before it abruptly stops.

"*Erik?*" The voice on the other end of the line is gruff, sending chills down my spine. I straighten, even though this isn't a video call, and I know he can't see me.

"Yes, sir."

"*There's been a slight alteration to the plans.*"

"Your Majesty?" I smack my forehead with my hand. How many alterations can a simple plan have? There are only two parts to this damned plan.

Get out of Ice Mer territory.

Kill the princess.

For the gods' sake, part one is already complete. Now he wants to change it? Gods, royals are such a pain in the ass. There's a reason why I try to avoid them at all costs.

"*I need you to take her to the Gates of Hell before you deal with her. Leave the body there. Once you do, you will be released from your debt.*"

Before I can respond, the line goes dead. I stare at the offending piece of technology in my hand and groan. How could something so small bring so much trouble?

In one fell swoop, this damned trip more than doubled in length. Instead of finishing things tomorrow, I have to take her straight to the Gates of Hell. I bite my lip.

This means we'll end up in Lethe. Banging my head against my palm, I blow out a long breath. The city of Lethe is home to the Daemon King.

It doesn't take a genius to see that King Phelix doesn't just want his daughter dead. He wants to start a mast-cracking war, and he will use me to do it. A swirl of curses leaves my mouth before a throat is cleared behind me. I groan and turn around. LaRue is still standing there, shuffling from one foot to the next.

"What is it, LaRue?"

He has the decency to look frightened as his eyes widen, the whites of his eyes standing out against his terra-cotta skin.

"You-you-you said you wanted us to-to..." LaRue stutters, his hands trembling.

"Spit it out, man, I don't have all day."

"You said you wanted us to stay away from the lady, but I saw the first mate heading to her room when I was coming up here with the phone," he blurts out all at once. I don't even think he breathes. When the words leave his mouth, LaRue steps back and dips his head. "I thought you should know, sir."

There is a roaring in my head. "What the hell does he think he's doing?" I ask.

Fire runs through my veins. Without looking, I know every inch of my skin has turned a deep red as I tremble with fury. My clenched fists shake as I push past LaRue and descend into the hull, barely noticing my surroundings. I'm aware of sailors jumping out of my way, the sound of muffled conversations filling my ears. I don't stop for them, I only have one goal.

Before I know it, I am yanking open Helena's door. It hits the wall with a *bang*, revealing the people inside.

The reality is worse than what I thought.

A shirtless Conrad is clawing at Helena's pants while he leans over her. His other hand is wrapped in her hair, pressing her face closer to his. She pushes her hands against his chest and shakes her head back and forth repeatedly.

His shoulder is bleeding and angry red marks run down his neck. Helena is kicking wildly, trying to push him away. Her legs beat against him weakly. There's no way she can push off a man weighing forty stones.

"No!" A guttural roar fills the room. "Not again."

That's my voice. I don't even remember opening my mouth.

Conrad stops what he's doing. Red floods my vision, and I shove the chair out of the way. I am no longer his captain. I am acting on my basest instincts, and he is the enemy.

"What in the nine circles of hell is going on here?" I roar. I walk over to them, grab him by the back of his neck, and yank him backward until his throat is exposed.

He yells in surprise. "This isn't what it looks like, Erik," he says placatingly, his eyes darting back and forth. His hands are trembling, and I know he is scared.

Helena curls in a ball, her back rising and falling with heavy breaths.

"You should be scared," I whisper in a dangerously low voice to Conrad and throw him against the wall.

He staggers. Good. I grab his arm, yanking him out of the

room. A dozen sailors are standing in the hallway. Every single one is gawking at us.

I glare at them. "Get back to work, *now*."

They scurry off, although I see them glancing back and forth between us. I tighten my grip on Conrad's arm and shove him up the stairs before following him onto the deck.

The afternoon sun has disappeared behind deep gray clouds, and a storm is on the horizon. A frigid wind blows past us as we stare at each other. The water is rough, and the ship rocks back and forth as we stagger on the deck.

"I told you not to touch her." I shove Conrad's bare chest, ignoring the pounding in my ears.

He grasps the railing, trying to catch his footing. Pitiful creature.

"I thought... I just..." He swallows, then continues. "Since *you know what* will happen tomorrow, it would be okay..."

Adrenaline rushes through my body, and I lunge at him, grabbing his neck and pulling him close to me until our noses nearly touch. He's shorter than I am by a few inches, so I stare down at him with narrowed eyes.

"I told you not to touch her," I repeat through clenched teeth. "What about that was so hard to understand?"

"Erik, man, we've known each other for twenty years." Conrad laughs, trying to peel my hand off him. "She wanted it. You should have seen the way she was looking at me. All smiles."

"That scratch on your neck says otherwise." I want to hurt him. The desire to inflict pain is coursing through my body.

He shakes his head, smirking. "You just don't get it."

"I get it just fine," I say, shoving him again. He stumbles, and I crack my neck. "I told you, asshole. She is off-limits."

Conrad laughs, and the sound grates against my every nerve. "You've got to lighten up, man. That's why no one likes you. You've got a stick up your ass about the rules."

I twitch when I hear him use Helena's phrase for me. "Those rules," I whisper, my voice dangerously calm, "are why I'm in charge here, not you. And you will pay the price for breaking them."

Raising my voice back to normal, I circle him, raising my fists. Not for the first time, I'm grateful that my prosthetic functions exactly like my other hand. This isn't the first fight I've ever gotten in, and let's face it, it won't be the last.

Conrad stares at me, his eyes wide. "Shit, man, are you going to do this over a female with *gray* skin? She's not even a human, and you don't—"

My control snaps again, and my nostrils flare as I lunge forward. My left fist connects with Conrad's nose, cutting off whatever he was going to say. The impact reverberates through my prosthetic. I shake out my fist as a loud crunching sound is followed by a heavy stream of blood that gushes down the front of Conrad's shirt.

"Theriously?" Conrad yells. "You broke my noth."

"You broke my rules," I reply curtly.

Conrad wipes his hand under his nose, bringing his arm away, covered in blood. "Athhole." he says. My first mate barrels towards me, swinging out a fist.

I duck. My arm swings out, and I pummel him in the side as he lurches forward. He doubles over, groaning, but he continues charging at me. Conrad's fist catches me on my cheek, and I yell. That's going to be a nasty black eye tomorrow.

"Son of a bitch," I curse. "You're going to regret that."

A crowd of men has gathered in the distance, watching to see if they will get a new leader. No such luck. I *will* win this fight. No one gets away with the disrespect Conrad is showing me right now.

No one.

The ship's rocking causes both of us to stumble for a moment before I lift my right leg and kick Conrad in the stomach. The force of impact pushes him back as I stagger to my feet. He curses, turning around and clenching his fists.

"The only thing I regret ith not doing thith yearth ago." Conrad spits out a wad of blood and saliva. It lands in a glob on the deck. "Thith ith an overreaction. You're too uptight, Erik."

"I am *not* uptight. It's a basic rule of humanity to *only* have sex with people who are enthusiastically asking for it, you disgusting bastard," I yell, running towards Conrad. Before he can move out of the way, I've pinned his body against the railing. My arm is braced under his neck, and the other against his chest. He is struggling under me, but I'm stronger. "I am the captain here," I bite out. "Not you."

Conrad pushes against me, fighting against my grip.

A large wave comes over the side of the ship. Water drenches us both, leaving us dripping in its wake. My heart is pounding. My fists tighten. My whole body is tight.

Just as I think he's about to shake his head and give in, Conrad leans in and whispers, "Captain or not, you and I both know that you anthwer to the Ice Mer King. You're nothing more than an errand boy ethcorting ith bitch daughter."

Under his words, like a hidden current in a river, I hear the violent undertones of the orders I've been given. Orders to kill her. An innocent.

Blood flows to my extremities like crashing waves. Before I know it, my fist connects with his face again and again and again. Conrad yells as the bones in his nose crunch, and he lets go of the railing to grip his face. At the same moment, I hit him under his ribs.

He screams at the impact, his feet losing purchase on the wet deck.

I watch, everything seeming like it's in slow motion, as he

falls onto his back. A brisk wind blows as the ship's gentle rocking becomes more lethal.

The sailor within me shouts a warning to the crew.

Gasping, I lurch forward and grab onto the railing, but it's too late.

A wave comes over the side once more, and when it disappears, the spot where Conrad stood is empty.

My heart pounds.

He's... gone.

Another wave crashes against the boat. A second. A fifth. A tenth.

There is no sign of him.

He's gone. He broke a rule, and now... he's dead. Swallowed by the sea.

Rules are the reasons why what we do works. Rules are why we take... side trips to help those who are less fortunate. They are the structure of everything good in my life. And they are the only thing that can redeem my black heart.

Saving the Mer princess doesn't atone for my sins, but it sure as hell will be a mark on the good side for me.

8
WHAT THE HELL IS HAPPENING?
HELENA

My chest heaves as I stand in the stairwell that leads to the deck above. I cling to the railing, my legs feeling weaker than ever.

Did Erik just... kill Conrad?

One step at a time, I climb the stairs. Then I gaze at the ninth circle of hell. The ocean is choppy, and the sky is rumbling above. Streaks of white lightning snake across the sky, flashing light across the already-lit area. I've never seen a storm before, and this looks terrifying. No one seems to be that afraid, though.

I wrap my arms around myself. The sounds of nature are all that is left because the crew is staring at Erik. Not a soul so much as takes a step. He isn't looking at them, he is still staring over the rail where Conrad fell moments ago.

Before Erik had burst into my room, Conrad had kicked my legs in, causing me to slam onto the bed. My knees still ache, and the metallic taste of the man's blood is still on my tongue from when I'd bit his lip so hard he screamed.

The memory makes a cold shakiness take over my body, and I want to throw up. I am okay. Why does this hurt so much? The tips of my fingers have grown cold, and my heart is palpitating furiously.

Still, no sound comes from the water.

One of the men, Anders, steps up and looks over the railing. When he turns around, his face is fixed in a grim line. He shakes his head once, and the thunder cracks overhead as if in reply.

I lean back against the rail and let out a long breath as I hug myself tighter. I'm happy someone is dead. What does this say about me? That I am finding relief in a man's death? Even though he was going to... to... touch me, I can't believe I am *happy* he is gone.

But I am.

As I get lost in my thoughts, the men begin moving. Some of them glance at me, the bruises already blossoming on my face, before they look away. I recognize their looks. They are ashamed.

I want to scream.

But I can't. Father stole that from me when he put me on this horrid ship. This whole thing is a nightmare.

When Erik turns around, I can't help but meet his eyes. They are cast in shadow by his brow and the downward tilt of his head. His face is almost casual when he looks around and shouts, "Everyone to their posts! This storm will be rough."

I don't understand why he was the one who helped me. He has made his hatred of me clear. So why did he put it aside? There is something underneath his hatred. Something deep. For the first time, I wonder what kind of man Captain Erik is.

A crew member I don't know whispers something to the dark-haired captain. After a moment, Erik responds. He as good as commanded me to get the hell back to my room, but I can't seem to move. My body isn't listening to me.

A phrase snags my attention as one of the men whispers, "Pirate of Death."

The words carry weight, and instantly, I understand. This

kind of thing has happened before. Often enough that the crew is used to it. Captain Erik is just as brutal as any leader in the Northern Courts. I furrow my brow as I watch him disappear without a word. He doesn't care about me, he was just angry. He's an asshole.

Even if he is an asshole, at least he's proven that he won't hurt you.

Just then, Jean Luc comes up behind me and whispers, "It's time we take you back to your room, Maddie."

I turn around and smile, gratefully accepting his arm. The nickname is sweet, and the warmth in his voice wraps around me like a blanket.

As we pass through the mess hall, he ducks inside and grabs a plastic bowl with a lid. On top of the bowl is a crappy digital clock. Just like I had asked him for. Suddenly, a wave of sadness crashes over me, and tears fill my eyes.

Jean Luc's expression grows panicked, so he awkwardly draws me into a hug. I am the first to pull away. Without even saying thank you, I walk down the stairs and stand in the doorway to my room.

The room feels wrong.

I don't feel safe here.

I grab a change of clothes and try the bathroom. This place is more neutral. I turn on the shower as hot as I can and get in. It isn't as unpleasant as the first time I tried it.

I don't want to be freezing anymore. I don't want to be powerless, lonely, or the same female that almost got raped.

The water stings my skin in a comforting way. I wash out the inside of my mouth and scrub at my skin until it burns. This time, I don't even care that I am using Erik's soap. It's almost as if I do it out of spite.

I am finished in less than fifteen minutes, even with trying to drag out the shower for as long as possible. The sadness sneaks in under the door and puts an icy hand at my throat to choke me. I shove it away by drying off and dressing.

The door slams behind me as I try to escape the pain, but then I am greeted by the hallway where Conrad stood as he unlocked my door. My gaze goes to the handle. I wonder what kind of thrill he must have felt when he realized he could take what he wanted from me, and not a soul would know because I can't speak.

I recoil, suddenly sick to my stomach.

There is no way I can stay in that room. My lips pinch shut. I *won't* stay in that room. I turn my back to the horrible memories and go to the room on the other side of the hall. I jiggle the handle. It's locked, which is expected.

Quick, shallow breaths accompany my shaking hands. *Calm down, Helena. You can figure this out.*

I go back into the bathroom and grab the comb. Tears slide down my face. Stacking everything that was in my arms next to me, I finger the teeth of the comb. The bristles could be stiff enough to work, though they are a bit short. Using my sharp canines, I tear several prongs off, and get to work picking the lock. My heart and my brain detach themselves from each other. My mind forces me to continue working, despite the rivulets of salty water sliding down my neck and dripping off my chin.

Not even a drop of magic exists in my veins, so I am left with my sheer stubbornness and panic. It takes me a long time to fidget with the lock, and footsteps and conversations start to come from the mess hall's direction. Sweat breaks out on my forehead. My stomach clenches. My heart pounds.

Come on, I beg the lock. *Work.*

Just as I am about to give up, I feel the mechanism inside of the door twisting in just the right way as the lock clicks.

I scramble to grab my things just as I hear footsteps coming down the stairs. When I enter the room, it is dark. I shut the door, though I still don't turn on a light. My chest tingles, and I am lightheaded.

A curtain-less window is letting in the littlest bit of moonlight. By the light of those moonbeams, I walk through the room and head towards a lush-looking bed. This room is much bigger than my own, and it feels much more comfortable, despite the choppiness of the sea and the sway of the ship.

My bare feet connect with a fur rug, and I continue forward until I hit the bed. Drawing myself up, I locate the side table and clumsily put down the clock, clothes, and book. I cling to the sheets for a few seconds, trying to breathe as deeply as my lungs allow.

You're okay. You are safe now. Nothing happened, I think over and over.

After a few moments, the dizziness passes, but then the shivering starts. I peel off the lid on the bowl and take a deep breath. The broth is herbal and rich. It smells like comfort. I bring the bowl to my mouth and drink. A little bit dribbles down my chin.

It tastes like comfort, too.

It takes no time for me to devour it, allowing the broth, vegetables, and bits of fish to fill my stomach. Warmth spreads from my insides out, and I lean back on the feather pillows. Another bit of me defrosts from the frigid deep-ocean temperatures.

Gods, this bed is comfortable.

I sink back, wrap myself tightly in the covers, and find my eyelids extremely heavy. A warm numbness robs me of my ability to think.

Sleep claims me almost instantly.

I BOLT UP, ramrod-straight.

Everything is all right! my brain shouts, attempting to soothe my raging fears.

Frantically, I pat the covers around me. I see my clothes, remember where I am, and relax. Dread sits like a stone in my belly. I had made it out of last night with little more than a scratch and a few bruises. And my attacker...

It is going to be okay.

In the morning light, I see the room better. A gloriously beautiful bookshelf is along one wall, a fine wooden desk is next to the door, and a leather chair sits in the middle. The room is luxurious.

I bite my lip. The only person who could have a room this fine would be the captain.

Something inside of me had suspected this before I opened the door, but still, I had entered. He never comes down here except to bother me, so I'm positive he wasn't occupying it.

I look at the clock to my right, which reads 8:17 a.m. Still morning. I haven't heard any voices yet, which is hopeful. All I know is that I want to stay away from everyone today. The pitter-patter of rain and the rumbling of thunder is a backdrop as I hurry to the bathroom, take care of my needs, and shower.

Once I'm done, I return to the room and grab a book from the shelf. This one is nothing like the worn paperback at my side. It's leather-bound and has gold lettering. *Love in Times of War.* I widen my eyes. Who knew the captain would like romance?

Before I know it, my eyes are flying across the page. The book is more about politics than love, to be honest, but I don't mind.

When I get to the part where the lovers kiss for the first time, my stomach tightens, and I slam the book shut.

It's too soon after Conrad's lips had invaded my own.

A familiar clamminess covers me from head to toe. My stomach twists. Bile rises in my throat at the memory. Black spots appear in my vision, and I squeeze my eyes shut. I take deep breaths, willing the sensation to pass.

Inhale.

Exhale.

Again and again, I focus on my breathing until the world settles around me.

The storm is relentless, continuing for several hours. I peek out the door once and find food piled in front of my old room across the hall. Gods, after what happened... I never want to step foot in that room again. I grab the food as quickly as possible and disappear once more.

NIGHT FALLS, which doesn't look much different from the stormy gray that I stared at all morning. I've done nothing but stare for the past several hours, drifting in and out of sleep. Earlier, the boat was rocking from side to side so violently that I had to hug my knees to my chest to keep myself from vomiting.

It is so damn awful. I had no idea how cruel the sea could be above sea level. No wonder my father loves it so. His temper is as volatile as the waves currently assaulting the ship.

All of a sudden, a deafening crash sounds from above me. My spine straightens immediately. Something is wrong. Very, very, very wrong. An itch to run up to the deck and see what has happened fills me. Everything slants to the right, and it stays that way.

Then the yelling starts.

Screams sound, and then I hear someone running down the stairs.

"Captain's overboard!" someone yells through the ship's intercom. Notes of fear are laced through his voice.

My blood runs cold. Colder than the coldest rivers in the Ice Mer territory.

How? The word rings in my skull. Before I know it, I am back on my feet, out the door, and I rush to the steps. When I enter the mess hall, people are scrambling around, talking over each other.

The thoughts stand out clearly in my mind. Erik is in danger. Not even one day after he rescued me, he is facing his frail mortality. I blink. I can't let him die, I have to do something.

The speakers on the ship are blaring a list of instructions. I can hear Anders shouting through the microphone.

"*Stay inside! Place towels underneath the doors to help keep things dry. Do not go after Captain Erik!*"

Good ideas... for weaklings. I owe him my life.

As I dart past on shaky legs, people stop to look at me, really look at me, for the first time since I got here. They stare at my pink eyes. The crew sees my blue and purple hair. They watch as I run, and no one makes any move to stop me.

"She's going after the captain!" one of them yells, but I don't turn around.

For a second, their cowardice makes me irritated.

But then, the more profound understanding of what is happening takes over as I ascend the stairs. They don't want their captain to die, but they are bound by ridiculous rules. *His* rules. It's been made extremely clear that disobeying orders has deadly consequences.

A retractable sliding door is at the top of the second flight of stairs. It is sealed to stop the water from coming into the ship. It is airtight, but luckily, it wasn't locked with a key. I grasp at the handle and tug back with all of my might. I need to get out there. Nothing else matters.

I clench my teeth and yank harder, and the door to the deck finally unseals. Water crashes down on me, obliterating my warmth. Nonetheless, it is salty and familiar, even though it burns my eyes and nose as I try to breathe through it.

"Maddie! What are you doing?" Jean Luc calls after me. I'm already scrambling onto the slippery deck when I turn to look at him. Even if I could speak, I'm not sure I would have responded.

As I rush toward the side, one of the men helps me tie a rope around my waist. I nod my thanks, and he shows me how to untie it once I'm in the water.

"Surely you won't let her go after the captain? She can barely walk," Jean Luc yells above the wind. Fury leaks into every word.

"If she doesn't go, who will?" the sailor responds. "Captain deserves more than his anal retentive rules."

The real question becomes... Why do they care so much?

My reasoning is fueled by desperate need. I need to find and save him, just as he saved me from Conrad. Then I will be free of his debt, and we can both go our separate ways once my journey is complete.

Glancing to the side, I see a sailor in a room with thick glass walls. Anders is surrounded by dozens of black boards filled with lights and buttons. The hierarchy of this ship is confusing, but it appears he has replaced Conrad as the first mate. Anders doesn't look up while the lightning cracks around me. The electric currents in the water will probably be very dangerous.

Erik, my mind calls as the sound thins out, leaving a series of lingering reverberations. If I don't try to save Erik now, he will die.

Over and over, I chant the words in my mind as I slip and slide against the deck. My legs still ache from what Conrad did to me. What he was trying to do. What Erik saved me from.

The boat is still significantly tilted, and I run to the side. I slide the last five paces and ram into the railing. My hands connect with the metal. My skin burns and tears against a jagged screw head. I am desperately trying to avoid falling.

Such a short amount of time has passed since I heard the first emergency cry, but the sea is wild. She takes no prisoners.

I scan the roiling ocean. The choppy waters have become nothing more than cutting green-gray waves. Several of the crates are bobbing violently up and down. Realization blooms, and I understand what has happened. He must've been around the mast and checking the crates when a large wave crashed over the boat, tilting the hull and taking cargo and captain in its wake.

I focus on those crates in an attempt to follow the direction of the waves. There are at least a dozen scattered on the churning surface. They vary from light-colored wood to rust-red metal. The metal ones are bobbing like dead fish above the water.

If I were with Elva, the huntress would tell me to stop looking so hard and let my brain weed out the odd movements that don't fit. She isn't here, but I try it anyway. I unfocus my eyes, and then see the black figure clinging onto a red crate bobbing in the sea.

The sight of him is pure relief. It feels like standing under a warm stream of water in the shower or drinking fresh tea. The feeling is new and utterly confusing.

My legs wobble as I climb over the railing.

"*Madeline, please return to your cab—*" the voice over the intercom begins to drone, but I don't hear the rest as I launch myself into the water. Anders has spotted me, but he is too late.

When I break the water's surface, it feels like someone has

paralyzed me. The rope is rough and cuts against my skin. The cold is so intense my joints lock up with reminders of home... only now my body isn't built for the ice. Instantly I am thrown back and forth through the waves while my teeth chatter. I realize just how minuscule I am, how powerless I am against the raging force of the sea.

Something inside of me humbles for just a moment.

I search for any Ice Mer power, but Daddy hasn't asked the gods for my birthright power. I get nothing until I wear the crown. Untying the rope, I propel myself in the general direction of the rust-red cargo crate. It is becoming less visible by the second. I must be coming to terms with this new mortal form because even though I lack a tail, my body still moves in the same lithe way through the water.

Speed I didn't know I could achieve makes my blood pump through my veins and warms my chilled body. The rain is falling again, pelting my skin as I pull myself up on top of the crate. Immediately, it dips, so I slide back into the water and use my hands to guide myself closer to Erik.

The waves seem to help more than hinder me. When I finally reach his side, I grab onto Erik's leg, my webbed fingers a very odd comparison to the wet denim he is wearing, and pull with all my might. He doesn't budge.

I can't tell if he is still alive. He has no gills, and the constant bobbing makes it impossible to see whether or not his chest moves.

I want to scream, but, of course, no sound comes from my mouth.

I pull again, this time anchoring my legs against the side of the crate and using their pitiful muscles to help me pull. Slowly, the captain inches across the ridges on the edge. Little by little, he moves, and then all at once.

When he finally slides into the water, I am gasping for

breath. Relentless seawater sprays my face from below as torrents of rainwater drench me from above.

Growing up, I always thought water was water. As a Mer, it was my life force. As much as part of me as I was a part of it. That is no longer the case. It turns out that water is not your friend as a mortal; it is thicker and more sinister—a carrier of death and doom.

Water can be frightening in ways I had previously only associated with my father.

I pull Erik close and pray to any gods who will hear me.

Even if I haven't been granted power, and what little I might have had is stripped away in this form, help me. Help us. Please.

I think of the Ice Mer King—of my father—and I think of his parents. I don't know their names... but surely they will hear me. They have to hear me.

I stretch out my webbed hand and mouth a hoarse incantation. To my shock, my hand sends a ripple. My fingers tingle. Even though I am mute, the ocean has passed on my call.

When Erik's warm shallow breaths tickle the base of my throat, my breath hitches. I tell myself it is just because I am glad for the proof he still lives. But that doesn't explain the warmth in my stomach.

Moments pass, and then a salmon shark arrives. The little magic that miraculously tore through me has now left me exhausted. My heart stutters, fear running through me as I doubt whether the small shark will be able to pull us both. When I grab onto the dorsal fin, the surprisingly powerful creature shoots straight toward the ship. I can barely hold on as we shoot through the water like a bullet.

Erik's body is cold, but somehow it molds perfectly to my own. Do all men fit this well? One thought of Conrad makes my body lock up.

When we arrive at the ship, the deck has evened out. I search frantically for the rope, but it's nowhere to be seen. My stomach seizes, but it releases as I see a small lifeboat being lowered. It is a terribly dangerous move in the still-tumultuous sea, but less dangerous than sending someone down to get us. When I scan along the ship's surface, I spot Jean Luc.

Relief, warm and comforting, floods me just as my limbs weaken further. Exhaustion is a heavy weight, pressing down on my limbs, and I can barely keep my head above water.

For one second, I consider giving in. I could let my head bob under the surface and let this body shrivel. Surely the crew would be close enough to grab Erik. It is not as though anyone would miss me. My father sent me away, Elva has been cut out of my life, and most of these men don't care either way.

In a funny way, it would be like returning home.

Before I can continue down the path of these deadly thoughts, a sailor begins to yell at me.

"Get in!"

Another screams at me, his face red with anger, "He needs heat! Hold him closer!"

I realize that neither of them are angry at me. They are angry that Erik almost died. Hands grab at me, and all thoughts of death vanish. It's strange how deeply ingrained the desire to survive is. My brain sees the outstretched hands as invitations. I help lift the unconscious captain into the boat before I wrap myself around him as best I can. Our chests are pressed together, and I can feel his heartbeat. I turn to see the shark disappear below the surface again.

"Thank every god that has ever looked down upon us that you were here, Maddie," the angry one says.

Again, more warmth. It feels like a blow to the heart.

The boat hitches, and then we ascend. When we reach the top, one man asks, "Would you like help?" I nod, and then his warm hands are around me. It's getting harder to stay awake now that my body knows it's safe. The sailor pulls me out, and two more men grab Erik.

"Get the captain below deck," one of them barks. "Immediately!"

Jean Luc comes over to the captain and then looks at me. "Are you all right?"

I nod weakly, grasping at his words to make sense of them.

"Can you walk?" Jean Luc asks, and I nod again. "Good. Anders and I will take you to your room."

Exhaustion is tugging at me. I am so tired, and my heart pounds inside my chest. I lean all of my weight against Anders as we walk down the stairs. He lightly lays a towel across my shoulders. I hear the sliding door shut, sealing off the rain from the deck, and then feel my blood pumping through my veins. It warms me much better when I'm not fighting against the chilled ocean.

We approach the hall, and I lull against Jean Luc's shoulder. When I realize where we are, I stiffen and remember that I've spent the last day and a half in Erik's quarters. Ander's and Jean Luc are speaking, but it is hard to keep up with precisely what's being said as they fumble for the right key only to find the door still slightly ajar. There is a collective pause as the men holding Captain Erik draw their brows together.

"That's odd," one of them mutters.

No one looks at me as Anders crosses to the other side and opens my door. Just like that, I am wide awake. The too-fresh memories of what almost happened in that room assault me. The seawater in my stomach revolts.

My knees buckle, and I throw up all over the floor. Two of the men grunt in disgust, several of them side-stepping my mess. The sweet, acidic smell fills the air.

"Anders, help me," Jean Luc starts, "You two, go get something to clean this. You okay, Maddie?"

I'm still looking at the ground, my arms cradling my head when I lift one hand and give a thumbs up.

"Be with you in a moment, dear," the kind cook mumbles. "Let's get Erik inside."

"I'll take care of Maddie," Anders says.

"I've got it, just get the captain into bed and get rid of those clothes," Jean Luc replies.

Erik's door swings open further, and I know they will find me out. All the evidence of my stay is strewn over the room. They are going to be furious. Their kindness toward me will be spent.

Especially Jean Luc. He'll know it was me.

My bowls are still stacked there, next to some of the clothes he gave me.

"What the hell is this?" Anders starts.

"Just move that stuff over there," Jean Luc says.

Tears sting my eyes at my careless mistake. Now I will be locked in the room where...

I don't have time to finish my thoughts when a warm hand rests on my back. "Maddie, I am going to get you clothes. Why don't you go clean your face." It's Anders.

I crawl to the bathroom, using the doorknob to pull myself up and go inside.

Taking my time, I peel off my wet clothes and hang them beside the shower. When I step in, I meticulously scrub my skin, hair, and mouth.

I leave feeling stronger. There are new clothes tossed into the sink next to the door. I grab them and change. When I walk out, the men are almost done cleaning up the mess in the hallway.

Both of them smile at me before returning to their task, and Jean Luc stands outside the captain's quarters. I catch him staring at the open door to my room.

"I know what happened with Conrad. I'm sorry," he says, his eyes downcast.

Why isn't he getting angry with me? Why isn't anyone angry? I rub my eyes.

"I understand why you want to stay elsewhere, but you can't be seen in the captain's quarters. I would take your room, but I don't think you'd like a cot in the kitchen." I shake my head, and he laughs a bit. "What can I get you to make this place okay for you again?"

That question is... thoughtful. It takes me a moment to think of something. Then, I look around for something to help me illustrate my point. Seeing nothing, I take his hand and pull him into the room. I point to the blanket on my bed and make puffing motions as if to say I want something thicker, warmer, heavier.

He seems to understand because he walks back into the captain's room and returns with one of his down comforters. I nod.

He hands it to me, grasping my hands. "You are safe now, Maddie. I will make sure of it."

The gentleness in his voice makes me want to cry all over again. He helps me throw the luxurious, velvety comforter over my bed, and when he leaves, he hugs me.

"Everyone is thankful, you know. The crew can't speak to you, but they are grateful for what you did."

I nod in his arms.

"Gods, you look like death. You need to sleep now." Slowly, he releases me and slips outside. "I will check on you tomorrow."

The door closes, and I lock it.

When I turn out the lights, the monsters stay in their corners. At least for tonight.

PART TWO

9

THE UNTHINKABLE
ERIK

My head feels like hammers are being thrown around in my skull, and a chill has settled in my bones. I crack open an eye and fling my hand around, grabbing my FaePhone and holding it a few inches from my face. Fumbling with the button on the side, I stare at the screen.

10:09 AM.

Who wakes up at 10:09 am? It's so unorderly. The date tells me I've slept straight through the night, which is unlike me. The near-incessant urge to check on the ship is at odds with my human desire to sleep for eight hours at a time.

The brightness of the phone is overwhelming. It causes my head to ache even more. Squeezing my eyes shut against the onslaught of bright light coming from the window, I instinctively wrap my arms around myself, only to make two discoveries at once.

First, I'm naked. That wouldn't be a huge concern, except that I have no memory of shedding my clothes.

Second, I'm not on the couch in my office. I stretch out my

bare legs, the fluffy down comforter laying over me, covering me fully. This feels like... *my* comforter.

In *my* room.

Which I haven't been staying in because of *her*. Because of the guilt.

All of a sudden, everything comes flooding back. Jolting upright, I press my hand to my forehead as I groan. Visions of the day before flash in front of my eyes, one after the other.

The storm. A giant green wave came over the side of the ship. A strike of lightning snapped the cables holding crates in place. Cold. Water so cold, it was paralyzing.

Even now, from the warmth of my bed, a shiver runs down my spine as I recall the water's frigid embrace. It had been sweetly lulling me to my death.

My crew has strict instructions. During a storm, the priority is the safety of the majority of the crew. While this might not be the case on all ships in Aranthium, it is on mine. The moment I became captain, I made it clear that on *my* ship, if something were to ever happen to me, they wouldn't put themselves at risk for me.

After all, who is there to mourn me? On good days, I'm an ass. On bad ones, I'm a murderer.

Not even my work is unique to me. If I were gone, someone else would take up pirating in my absence. No one will miss me when I'm gone.

It's much better to lose one person than an entire crew. Many of my sailors have families. Parents. Wives. Children. People who would mourn their passing. People who will remember them when they're gone.

I have none of these.

So when the wave washed me off the ship, I knew that it would only be a matter of time until the gods of the sea claimed me for their own. It was fitting, I thought. I lived by the sea, and so I should die by it as well.

Then Helena did the unthinkable.

This female, whom I have sworn to kill, risked her life for me. Clinging desperately to the shipping crate, I watched, wide-eyed, as she flung her body over the railing.

The echoes of the ship's intercom had been faint in my ears, but the splash her body made as it hit the water seemed to reverberate through my soul.

I had tried to remain alert, but the frigid waters of the Northern Sea had seeped into my very human bones so quickly I could barely breathe. The last thing I remember before passing out was glimpsing her lithe gray body as it bobbed towards me.

Then I fell into the darkness. Obviously, she must have made it to me and brought both of us back to the boat. She saved me.

Shit.

How could I kill someone who saved my life?

There's only one real answer to that question. And it came well before yesterday.

The weight of what exactly this means settles on me, my stomach cramping as I bend in half. My entire body aches as I lay back on the pillows, rubbing my temples and wishing I could erase the last day of my life. Between Conrad and Helena, things have really gone to hell in a handbasket.

As I contemplate ways to travel back in time, a hesitant knock comes on the door.

"Who is it?" I say. Damn. My voice sounds weak to my own ears, my throat raspy as I force the words out.

"It's me, Captain. I've brought you some food." Jean Luc's voice is hesitant, which isn't a surprise. I'm not known around the ship for being a morning person. Nonetheless, the prospect of food intrigues me.

"Come in," I reply rather eagerly. I pull the dark blue

comforter around my hips as I settle into a seated position before donning a black sweater to ward off the chill.

The knob twists, and true to his word, the sailor is standing with a tray laden with a steaming bowl and something that looks like bread. My stomach grumbles at the sight, my mouth salivating. Jean Luc hurries over and places the tray on my nightstand. I was right- he even brought me a freshly baked baguette.

"Thank you, Jean Luc."

He nods but doesn't move from his spot by my bed. Instead, the sailor stands with his hands clasped in front of him, his thumbs twisting together. A beat passes before I realize he wants something.

I narrow my eyes, "Anything else, sailor?"

The man shifts from one foot to the other before opening his mouth. "It's the lady, sir," he says.

Groaning, I bang my head against the headboard, shutting my eyes against the pain. "Of course it is. Can it wait?" Peeking open one eye, I see Jean Luc pursing his lips and shaking his head. I sigh, running a hand through my hair. "Go ahead. What do you want to say?"

"We all know you're a strong leader, Captain Erik. Fair and respectful, and of course, we would never question you. I would never dare to tell you how to run your ship," he starts.

I fight the urge to roll my eyes at his flattery. Of course, I'm fair. It's how I've always lived, by the rules. That's why I'm still here.

I wave a hand, "Go on."

"Madeline wasn't in good shape last night, sir. I thought you should know."

I narrow my eyes. Since when is he on a first-name basis with Madel—I mean, Helena? My fists clench as I fight the desire to attack the man for his forwardness with the Princess. How dare he be so familiar with her? The only thing that stops me is that he doesn't know who she is.

Conrad was the only other person who did, and now he's dead. I'm sure many women will be mourning his passing. I won't be. Not after what he was going to do. The thought of my former first mate sours my mood even further.

I growl, "Is that it?"

"Y-yes sir," Jean Luc stammers.

"Good. Thank you. You may go."

Jean Luc looks like he wants to say something else, but after he looks at my scowling face, he closes his mouth. The cook nods, walking backward out of the room before shutting the door behind him.

It's official.

This day is not going to be a good one.

Sighing, I demolish the tray of food Jean Luc brought for me. If I have to deal with Helena, I might as well do it on a full stomach. The stew is delicious, filled with deep and fragrant spices. The fresh baguette is the proverbial cherry on top of this meal.

Half an hour later, my stomach is full. Ready to face the day, I've located a pair of gray sweatpants and pulled them on. My legs are wobbly, and every movement seems to drain me of more and more energy. It's like I'm walking through thick mud, and moving even an inch feels like a mile. By the time I've pulled on a pair of running shoes, I need to sit back down on the bed and catch my breath.

At that point, I would've given anything to have some of the natural healing abilities of the Were shifters.

Considering this was my first time nearly drowning in the sea, and hopefully my last, I'll file that knowledge away under 'things I don't need to know' and continue with my life.

After having caught my breath, I stand. Holding onto the footboard, I wait until my legs feel sturdy before letting go.

Taking a deep breath, I take one step, then the other. Everything seems to be working, so I head out of my room.

I knock on Helena's door, trying to fight down the irrational irritation I feel. It's not her fault I was given an impossible task, and it certainly isn't her fault that she's a good person. This would have been so much easier if she had been cruel. Leaning against the door jamb, I keep pounding until I hear a scuffle from the inside.

I say, "Open up, Princess, I know you're in there."

A few moments pass before a white piece of paper is slipped under the door. I bend down and pick up the note. There are two words on it, scrawled in Helena's horrific handwriting that is not what I ever expected to see from a Crown Princess.

Go away.

"Nope," I say, shaking my head even though she can't see me. "Not going to happen, Princess. We need to talk. I'm going to stand here for as long as it takes. I assume, at some point, you'll need to use the restroom. I'm happy to wait."

Silence.

Of course. I expected nothing less.

I've never met someone as stubborn as me in my entire life. My mother, gods be with her soul, used to call me her little stubborn octopus. She would tell me that when I was a toddler, I would latch onto her legs and refuse to let go. She used to tell me that I would hold on tight, gripping her leg as she moved about the house.

I don't remember that. I don't remember most things about my parents anymore. But my mother was right. I am stubborn, and in this, I will not give up. I need to talk to Helena. Today.

My head rests against the door, and I rally my strength as I wait in the hallway. I can hear her moving around inside the room. My shoulders slump, and I swallow as I lower my voice.

"Princess," I say. "I'm serious. We need to talk."

Nothing. As the seconds tick by into minutes, I begin to believe that I may have met my match in this Mer. I have never met any being, human or otherwise, who infuriates me like this female.

It's getting harder and harder to sort through my anger. I'm angry at myself for being put in this terrible position. I'm angry that I have to hurt this innocent woman. I'm angry at Conrad for his horrible actions. I'm angry at her for ignoring me.

But the worst part is that I know the anger isn't all I feel. It's a mask for the deep shame that wracks my heart. And that, more than anything else, angers me.

Because I never used to feel, and I was happy being numb.

Sliding down the wall, I cross my legs and lean against her door. Sailors pass by and give me questioning looks. In response, I glare at them. None of them has the guts to stop and ask me what I'm doing. They just walk around me, hurrying to complete their daily tasks as though I am not doing something completely out of character.

Finally, after what seems like an eternity but is probably more like forty-five minutes, the door creaks open behind me. I brace my hands against the frame, tilting my head back to look at her face. Her pink eyes are narrowed, and her lips are pursed as she looks down at me. Our gazes meet, and for a moment, it feels as though all the air is sucked out of the hallway. Something foreign stirs within me.

Eventually, she scribbles something on a scrap of paper and drops it on my lap.

Well? What was so important that you had to block my door?

The word important is underlined twice, and for some

reason, it kindles fiery emotions that lick against my insides. I push myself off the floor and brush my hands on my pants as I stare at her. The room behind her seems so tiny. I grimace.

Images of Conrad on top of her, touching her without her permission, play on repeat in my head. It's like a bad song that I can't get out of my head. I curl my fists, my knuckles turning white as I fight the urge to hit something.

"Let's talk in my office," I say, avoiding her eyes and turning around. "It's bigger."

Lines bracketing Helena's mouth dissipate as she lets out a long breath. She hurries down the hallway towards my personal office. I watch her walk and note that every time we pass a member of my crew, they dip their head toward her. She leaves a trail of smiles in her path.

Soon, we are both in my office. I've claimed my seat behind my desk. The comfort of being in my personal space is helping to ease my emotions. It also helps mask the fact that I'm exhausted.

Helena doesn't sit. Instead, she walks around and runs her fingers down the spines of my books. Her delicate touch is respectful and gentle, and for a moment, I wonder what it would be like to have her touch my face like that.

I shake my head in surprise at the stray thought, watching her move. She ignores me completely, her attention fixated on the books.

"Princess, will you *please* take a seat?"

She turns and looks at me, raising a brow. I can practically see the wheels turning in her mind as she tilts her head, studying me. Her lips curve into a smile, and she walks towards me, swinging her hips as she moves. I'm a bit shocked at the way she so easily changes expressions. It's as if the fear I saw so clearly etched on her face when Conrad had been touching her never existed.

How is she okay with everything that happened?

Helena heads for the chair on the other side of the desk, but she doesn't sit. Instead, she leans over, removes papers from my work pile, and sets them in the available seat.

Then, as if she hasn't a care in the world, she sashays over and slides onto the edge of my desk. Her legs are dangling over the side, dangerously close to mine, as she stares at me. She smirks, and my nostrils flare.

I raise myself off the chair, placing my hands on either side of her, and lean in close.

"Princess," I growl.

She stares at me, her eyes glinting with a challenge. Something strange happens because as we stare at each other, everything fades away. The danger, the anger, and the horror of Helena's time here all disappear. I grip the desk on either side of her. The wood where the lacquer has faded away is rough under my fingers. I can't help but notice the way her body fits perfectly between my arms as I box her in.

Her shirt is sliding down one shoulder, and my eyes are drawn to that bare patch of skin. Never has a shoulder looked more tantalizing than it does right now. I had been wrong to think she was fragile, and I marvel at the fact that this female was able to save us both yesterday.

Suddenly realizing *where* I am looking and *who* I am looking at, I blink. It takes actual effort to drag my eyes up to her face. Those pink eyes are wide as they meet mine, and I am still locked in an orbit around her. Helena parts her lips, her tongue flicking out over the bottom of her mouth, as her eyes stay on mine. Everything within my body tenses as I lean in closer, cutting the distance between us in half.

Helena doesn't move, her eyes watching me carefully as I draw nearer and nearer. Her breath catches, and she lifts her hands—those strange, webbed hands. We both watch as she grabs my shirt, pulling me towards her.

"Are you all right?" I ask gently.

She freezes, and her hand falls away. Very slowly, she nods, and one of her webbed fingers traces over my hand.

Two things become abundantly clear in this moment. The first is that somewhere along the way, Helena has become very important to me. The second is that I must be insane. Absolutely, certifiably insane. Because this isn't just any random female. And I am not supposed to be feeling this way about her.

I close my eyes, taking a deep breath, before reopening them. *Everything is changing.*

"What are you doing on my desk, Princess?" I ask. The words come out sharper than I had intended. Just like that, the moment is broken.

She flinches, and something akin to sadness flits through me. Her face hardens and becomes expressionless as she raises a shoulder and pats the desk, as though saying, *I'm sitting, just like you wanted.*

"You and I both know this isn't what I meant when I asked you to sit."

She glares at me, and after a moment, I sigh.

"I wanted to... thank you for yesterday." I practically choke on the words. They feel like chalk in my mouth. However, I need to say them. She did save my life, after all. Personal feelings aside, I know that I would have died if it wasn't for her. "Truly, thank you. You didn't have to do that."

A long moment passes before she nods. She reaches over and grabs a piece of paper, scribbling on it.

You're welcome. We're even now.

Then, without even waiting for a response, Helena hops off my desk. Ducking under my arms, she walks to the bookshelf and points at a book. It takes me a moment to catch up with her. My mind is still stuck on the almost-kiss.

She despises me. I've done everything possible to avoid her before her father forces me to kill her.

That's simple. This, what just happened between us, is not simple.

I ask, "You want to borrow a book?"

She nods eagerly, her eyes lighting up.

"Sure, go ahead," I say, sighing as I run my hand through my hair. *Why not complicate the situation further?*

She pursues the shelves briefly before grabbing a novel and heading out the door. I watch her leave before collapsing on my couch.

I am so screwed.

10
WHAT'S A SHOWER?
HELENA

I shoot up from my shallow sleep. My chest is heaving, and I am fighting the urge to throw up again. Sweat has drenched my sheets, so I tear them off and toss them in a pile.

Luckily, some kind soul returned my clock to me after my little escapade in the captain's quarters. It reads 3:58 a.m.

Gods! I tear at my hair and shake my head.

Sleeping is becoming increasingly more difficult. The last week spent in my room has been one isolated, hellish experience. The cold is seeping into my wet clothing without the blankets. The shivering is getting unbearable. It doesn't take me long to decide to go shower. Hopefully, the hot water will help.

The violent shaking doesn't subside until the steam is so thick in the small bathroom that I can hardly see.

Erik's soap is still here, and I notice that a bottle with a thick, creamy goop has been added to the pile of toiletries. I pick it up.

Conditioner.

I've seen commercials—illegal ones, of course—but I've seen them. This is for hair.

The hot water is just to the point of burning my skin as I squeeze the bottle, and a pile of nice-smelling stuff comes out. I don't know what the hell this scent is. Where I come from, we use our noses to find our next meal or scout out danger. There's nothing dangerous about this…

At least, I don't think there is. Unsure exactly what to do, I just plop the conditioner onto my head and start moving it around.

It feels nice on my scalp.

The monotony of the rubbing, combined with how relaxed I am starting to feel, causes my mind to wander. The dream, the experience, all come crashing down on me.

The impact on my legs causes them to buckle, and I am shoved onto my bed. Hands tear at my clothes as I bite and scratch. My attempts are met with laughter, followed by the same hands clamping down on my thighs and moving up towards the apex between my legs.

He smiles up at me, and I want to throw up.

"Don't be such a bitch, you'll be dead soon anyway," Conrad leers.

I open my mouth, try to scream, try to do anything, but I am still frozen. The absence of my voice is agonizing, and I start to cry—

Reality snaps back. I raise a trembling hand to my cheek and find it damp. I've started to cry in real life. Tears run down my face, mingling with the water from the shower. I've dropped to my knees, and my arms are wrapped tightly around me as I squeeze myself into the corner of the tiny shower.

Get up, Helena. GET UP! I yell at myself, trying to will away the sweat that has reappeared.

I cannot move, I cannot breathe. The pressure is building so intensely in my chest that I feel like I am moments from exploding.

A loud knock cracks through the small room. A jolt makes my spine go pin-straight, and I realize the water has gone cold.

Shit... There's only one other person I know who uses this bathroom. I have no idea how long I've spent in this place.

I rinse as fast as possible, noticing that the conditioner on my scalp isn't coming out very easily. I resolve to leave it be.

Being interrupted this early in the morning wasn't on my pathetic agenda, and once again, I am left without a change of outfit. *Damn, strike three.* I wrap myself in a towel and open the door. The leftover steam billows out into the hallway. Captain Erik is slumped against his doorway, eyes closed. They snap open moments after I look at him.

His pupils dilate ever so slightly. Just as quickly, they narrow.

"Gods, did you even leave any hot water?" He waves a hand in front of him arbitrarily as if he can force the fog to evaporate.

I am still shaking, and I am sure queasy terror is written all over my face.

His expression softens as he really looks at me. It's as though I am watching the venom peeling off his face, layer by layer.

"Good morning," he murmurs in his least offensive tone. Something flickers in his eyes.

Pity?

I steel myself and force a casual, odious look on my face while wiping away every bit of Conrad's presence from my mind. This human will learn his lesson for daring to pity the princess of the icy seas.

Erik's head cocks to the side a bit. He senses this shift, too. After all the hours I've spent near him, I recognize the new mood blossoming on his chiseled features. It's amused irritation.

The need to do something—anything—to go back to hating me is strong.

He says, "Don't you have anything else to wear?"

The captain's eyes flick up my body. The look is far longer than would be considered appropriate. If we were back home, he'd already be shark food. I throw him a look that I hope says, *I wasn't expecting company.*

He smiles as if he understands me. The pity is still there, though.

Shame heats my cheeks, and I can feel my eyes getting damp. Damned human. I turn and open my door.

"Wait—" Erik starts.

I pause, my hand on the door.

"Did you finish the book you took last week?"

The one about a human man obsessed with killing a leviathan, which probably didn't exist? I want to retort. But thanks to my father, I can't say anything. Instead, I tighten my grip on the doorknob and nod.

"Good," he says.

I don't have anything to respond to that, so I hurry back to my haunted room.

Just as the door is about to close, he adds, "If you want another one, all you have to do is ask."

The door hangs open slightly, and I turn back to look at him through the crack.

A wicked expression clouds his face as he continues, "That is if you can ever figure out how to speak again."

I bite my tongue so hard that I taste blood. He is right. I can't respond. I'm learning that being in close proximity to Erik is to be incensed by his cruelty, his pity, his amusement at my pain, and the misplaced veneration by his sheep-like crew.

He shrugs. "Or you could ask me nicely in one of your notes, and I might oblige you."

I grit my teeth and slam my door. I will never, in a million years, write him that note.

SLEEP NEVER COMES, but my malicious creativity brings something better. After the shower, I spend the rest of the morning bowed over Erik's precious book. My pencil is like a sword, and I am a warrior reading the text while writing in the deadliest, most spiteful words I can conjure in the margins.

Now finished, I thumb through the pages. On the title page, I have drawn my signature stick-up-your-ass stick figure. I grin to myself. *This is art.*

I get up, slide my feet into my shoes, and go to the door to his bedroom. His muffled voice comes from inside.

"... *dammit!*" he shouts, and his footsteps come close to the door.

I freeze, book still in hand. Not feeling confident enough to run away, I raise my hand as if I were about to knock just as he opens the door.

Stormy eyes filled with dark emotion stare back at me. I take a step back at the rage coming off him in waves.

"I can't help you right now, Helena," he says harshly.

I cringe at the use of my name. The book is still pressed to my chest. I flip it down, passing it to him with the title up. For a second, a glimmer of worry sparks in my brain. What if I made a huge mistake trying to piss him off today?

"Thank you," he grinds through clenched teeth, taking the tome. He spins on his heel and tosses it on the bed. I'm too relieved to be appalled at him for what he could've done to that expensive leather binding.

He turns back to me, his whole face downcast, as he shuts the door behind him. "You need to stay in your room today."

What? No. I look around frantically for a paper to write that on.

"Nope, this isn't negotiable. You need to stay in your room today if you want me to keep you safe," he says as he brushes past me.

My hand lashes out and grabs his arm. He whips around, eyes burning with the heat of a thousand flames. "What part don't you get about staying in your room? Gods, you are like a parasite. I can't entertain you all the time."

The words sting. *Damn*, I think.

I don't let him see the rest of my anger as I barge into my room, sure to slam the door so hard that the frame rattles.

Sinking onto my bed, I let out a long breath and start closing my eyes. The shadows return. I had forgotten for several hours they existed.

Instead of shutting my eyes, I roll to the floor and start exercising. One hour passes as I curl my chest to my knees repeatedly.

Another hour goes by. I'm doing push-ups this time until my limbs are so tired that they are quivering with every movement.

The shadows dance around me, watching me strengthen my muscles. They wait for my moments of weakness to wrap me back up in the iciness I've known my whole life. The only reason I've started to thaw is... Erik.

My eyes go wide as the realization hits me. I roll onto my back, staring at the ceiling. Sweat trickles down my forehead and chest. I heave out a breath. This realization is alarming.

I can't begin to feel things for a man like him. He is *dangerous*. Deadly. And there is the little, itty-bitty issue of the hatred between us.

Right then and there, I decide that there is no way in the nine circles of burning hell that I am staying in this room. I am past the point of giving two shits what "commands" Erik gives, anyway. I'm not part of his crew.

Luckily for me, I have a full wardrobe of sailor attire. I wipe my temples and don a baggy shirt, loose pants, and boots. Pulling a cap low on my head to cover my unusual hair, I head out the door.

First stop, food.

And then?

Then I raise hell for the captain.

II
GARRET THORN
ERIK

Lifting my coffee mug to my lips, I study the Vampire sitting across from me through narrowed eyes. As if his non-human status isn't enough to make him stand out, his all-black suit and tie make it clear he isn't part of my crew.

We're sitting in my office, the crew having been warned not to disturb us under any circumstances. They know the drill. Whenever Garret Thorn, the Enforcer, shows up on the ship, my crew makes themselves scarce. I don't blame them.

The Vampire's very being oozes danger and brutality. He is six feet six inches of pure muscle and death, but that's not even his greatest weapon. Those would be the razor-sharp canines that slide out every time the League is displeased.

Most Vampires in Aranthium try to blend in, but not Garret Thorn. He doesn't even attempt to hide his differences. Hence the suit and tie.

The marking characteristic that makes Thorn stand out is his violet eyes. No other Vampire on Aranthium has them. They are piercing in their intensity, seeming to look into your very soul.

Not only that but when he smiles, his canines seem to gleam in the sunlight. I swear he chisels them into fine points.

Garret Thorn is known in Aranthium for two things: his cruelty and his predisposition for enjoying barely legal women. Rumors abound about the trail of drained human women that seem to follow him, but every time Thorn is reported to the authorities, the charges mysteriously disappear.

Even in cities claiming anti-Vamp laws, unlike the Northern Court, where Vampires can run wild, he gets away with literal murder. Though, they say his body count has lowered in the past fifty years or so. His job protects him from his past now that he is "reformed." Instead of hunting people for sport, he chases those who refuse to play by the League's rules.

The Vampire in question is currently bent over in his chair, his short chestnut hair catching the sunlight as he studies a list of figures I've shown him. Everything my crew and I do is marked down in that ledger. Well. Mostly everything. Certain private trips are left off, but I can't have anyone know about those.

I've been told at one point before the League was formed, pirating was a much simpler endeavor. The League of Pirates is just a bunch of thugs. They operate out of the Consortium, which has several locations throughout Aranthium. The League collects "dues" to ensure the waters remain "safe."

The day before he retired, officially passing the mantle of Pirate of Death down to me five years ago, my predecessor Barthalamew had locked us in his office to reiterate the danger the League posed.

"The League will drop in from time to time. They always come unannounced," he said over a glass of Aranthium's finest whiskey. "You must always be ready, boy. They take their job of keeping the waters safe very seriously."

"Safe is a relative term," I had said to the old man. "We're pirates, for the gods' sake."

"Even so, lad," Bartholomew had said solemnly, his graying hair falling into his eyes. He rubbed a hand down his face, past the scar that marred his features. "You must never cross the League. They have arms in places you would never imagine."

Of course, I had agreed. It was not like I had a choice. But I know the League is a farce. They claim to keep Aranthium's waters safe, but what they do is make sure to pad their pockets without doing any of the hard work of actual pirating.

Realizing I've drifted off into a sea of memories, I shake my head and take another sip of my coffee. The Vampire didn't seem to notice that I had zoned out. He is muttering to himself, his fingers running down the ledgers carefully. Every once in a while, he pauses to tap some numbers into his FaePhone before continuing his perusal.

It's been eight months since Thorn last showed up on my ship. Eight glorious months.

I should have known the League would decide to visit while I had the Ice Mer Princess on board. Why not? My life is a shitshow, and Fortuna seems to enjoy throwing one thing after another at me.

The Vampire continues his perusal of my pristine ledgers for another ten minutes before he finally puts them down. When he looks at me, his violet eyes seem to stare right into my soul. I'll never get used to the unnerving glare of Vampires.

"Take me above deck," he says in a silky, smooth voice meant to make me feel at ease. Thorn pushes himself to his feet, baring his fangs at me in something that looks like a smile and a sneer had a baby. His entire body is a weapon, and an involuntary shudder rips through me at the sight of his fangs.

Vampires are the only beings in Aranthium that are made, not born, and as such, they have always made me feel uneasy.

The Enforcer looks like he is in his mid-twenties, but I know he is at least six centuries old. Pirates have been talking about this particular Vampire for a very long time.

"Are you coming, Captain?" Thorn's voice is smooth as he runs a finger over my desk, but there is an unmistakable edge.

"Of course," I reply, pushing myself to my feet as I make a show of looking around. "Where else would I go?"

The Vampire stares at me for a moment before bursting out into raucous laughter. He slaps me on the back so hard that I stumble momentarily.

"You're funny, Erik," he says, choking on his laughter. "I don't remember you having a sense of humor."

Forcing a smile, I open my office door and poke my head out. The hallway is empty. Thank the gods, Helena has listened to me for once and is staying in her room.

I don't want to consider what the Enforcer might do to her.

THE SUN HAS DECIDED to grace us with its presence after a week of constant clouds and rainstorms. The waters are calm, which is probably why the League decided to visit today, of all days.

They've never shown up during a storm. That would mean they actually would have to work.

Averting my gaze from the Vampire's glittering skin, I keep an eye on him as he inspects crate after crate. Even above deck, the crew is giving us a wide berth. They are going about their duties mechanically, keeping their distance as the League's enforcer inspects everything.

He turns to me, his brows furrowed as he counts the crates.

"You're missing some cargo," he says carefully. "What happened?"

"We had a storm about a week ago. Lost some cargo. Better that than lose the ship," I reply. My hands are behind my back, and I'm leaning against the railing as I study him.

He harrumphs, his fingers tapping on his leg. "Did you lose any people?"

"Conrad. My first mate," I say after a moment. "He fell over the edge."

It's a slight alteration of the truth, but only the crew and I know what really happened to Conrad. I know I can trust them to keep their mouths shut about Conrad and our other... extracurricular activities.

"Shame." Thorn's tone is dry and uncaring. I can tell by his emotionless expression that he doesn't give a damn about our loss. The life of one human means absolutely nothing to him.

Typical Vampire.

Finally, we get to the last crate. He pries open the lid, his eyes lighting up as he takes in the contents.

"Where did you get these?" He asks without turning. Reaching into the crate, he pulls out a handful of enormous white pearls. Sifting through them, he pulls out an especially large pearl the size of both his hands put together.

It takes everything inside of me not to yell at him to be careful. That pearl is worth more than this entire ship. Which means something because this ship cost me millions.

"The Ice Mer," I say icily. "We picked them up less than a month ago."

He raises a brow. "From the Finfolk? Interesting. I've never known them to enjoy dealing with humans in all my years."

I force myself to shrug. "I guess being the Pirate of Death has its benefits."

There's no way in hell I'm telling this man about my deal.

The pearls are my cover for having gone into the underwater city. Even my crew doesn't know the real reason we were there.

And they never will.

King Phelix is nothing if not exceedingly careful. Gods forbid anyone ever traces him back to the murder of his daughter. It would mean trouble, even for him.

As far as my crew knows, we stopped in Aqualis to pick up the pearls for my buyer in Angel's Landing. She's discreet and human. The two main qualities I look for in business associates. But now that King Phelix is forcing us to go to the Gates of Hell, I had to call her and tell her to meet us in Lethe instead.

That unpleasant conversation took place yesterday. To say my contact had been less than thrilled with the changes of plans would be an understatement. However, after a reminder of exactly *who* she was dealing with, she agreed to meet in Lethe instead.

For a higher cut of the money.

Of course.

Thorn rolls the pearl around in his hands for a few more minutes before tossing it back inside the crate. Tension that I didn't know existed leaves my shoulders as he slams the lid of the crate shut and grabs his FaePhone. He begins tapping on the screen for a few moments, snapping a picture of the manifest, before putting the phone back in his pocket.

"Anything else you need to show me, Erik?"

The Enforcer has already gone over our manifest, finances, and most of the ship. His helicopter is flying above the water, with special floats designed to allow his pilot to land on the water.

Almost done. I'm going to need a stiff drink after this.

"Nope," I reply instantly. "That's it. Of course, we will transfer the League their dues once we have completed our transactions on land."

He nods at me, baring his fangs in my direction. "Good man. We wouldn't want to have a chat, would we?"

Shivers scuttle down my spine, but I manage to choke out a 'no' even as I think of the last Pirate who was caught withholding information.

Captain Longsmith, by all accounts, had been an exceedingly cocky pirate. Seventeen years ago, he had apparently refused to continue working with the League. Two days later, he and his entire crew of thirty men were found drained of blood. Their corpses were discovered piled on the deck of their unmanned boat, floating at sea.

The warning was clear as day. Pay your dues. Or die.

I'm about to lead the Enforcer away from the crates so his chopper can pick him up when, out of the corner of my eye, I catch sight of a sailor wearing baggy clothes peeking out from behind a crate and watching us. My jaw clenches as wisps of purple and ceruleum hair swirl in the sea breeze. Delicate gray hands quickly reach up and tuck them in, but it's too late.

I've seen her.

It takes every bit of composure I have in me to look away from Helena and return my attention to Thorn. His gaze has returned to his phone, but within seconds, he snaps it back to me. At that same moment, Helena stands from her perch and slinks closer to us. The crew seems to have noticed her, but no one says anything other than a few eyes watching her.

I try to catch her eye, to tell her to get out of here, but she doesn't look at me. She has that infuriating look of amusement about her.

She thinks this is a joke.

Blood boils through my veins, and my nostrils flare. After this, she and I will have a long talk about the importance of doing what you're told.

If Thorn doesn't see her, that is.

"Where will you be going after the Gates of Hell?" The Vampire's voice breaks my concentration, and I swing my gaze back to his. His purple eyes are bright, and the sun is right above us now. His skin is glistening and making it difficult to concentrate.

I speak slowly, ensuring I say precisely the right thing. "We are unsure at this time. We may return to the Northern Court in time for the Winter Solstice. I've been hearing rumors about the parties hosted by the new Queen's Consort."

"Ah yes, the new Winter Queen. I've heard of her pacifist husband." Thorn laughs as if pacifism is a joke. "She's not the only one who is part of the rumor mill." Thorn glances at his FaePhone, clicking around momentarily before pulling something up. "An interesting video was brought to our attention just a few months ago."

I swallow, shifting on my feet. "Oh?"

Thorn nods as a wolfish grin appears on his face. He holds up his phone, pressing a few buttons before a hologram appears in the air about it.

I grab onto the railing, holding tight as my stomach plummets. I can guess what I'm about to see.

Fuzzy black and white security footage is projected in the air. Instantly, I know this isn't *The Black Rose*. The deck of this ship is wooden and old, nothing like my modern boat. But that's not what draws my attention.

No, it's the five people kneeling on the ground.

"Tell me where it is." A deep voice thunders through the air as someone large looms over the trembling group.

Silence.

The male cocks his gun, the sound echoing through the night. "Will anyone here speak?"

There is no response.

"You leave me no choice." Five seconds pass, then ten, before a gunshot fills the air. The four remaining victims scream as the fifth falls to the ground, lifeless. The victim's blood seeps out from under them.

The male with the gun kneels before the second person, who is sobbing. "Tell me."

"Never," the male on the ground says bravely.

Another gunshot. More blood. Screams.

"How about you?"

Silence. Deafening, absolute silence.

Then, a whisper. "It's in the safe. I know the code. I'll take you there myself."

"Good." The male wielding the gun turns and walks through the blood. He glances up at the security camera and winks.

I swallow, shutting my eyes.

"Quite the show you put on there, eh Pirate of Death?" Thorn sounds pleased with the video.

"They were flesh traders," I grind out. "Children. Human and Angels."

Thorn shrugs, pressing a few buttons before the projection disappears. "They had bills to pay. So do you." The Vampire's callousness sends shivers down my spine, but he doesn't notice as he continues to speak. "As soon as you know where you're going, send us a message. We wouldn't want to lose track of our best pirate, now would we?"

"Of course not." I wave my FaePhone in the air, hoping that somehow, Helena didn't see the video the Vampire had projected. "I'll send you a message the moment I know."

"Good man." Thorn hums, pressing a few buttons on his phone before he shoves it in his back pocket. A few moments later, his chopper dips towards the ship. I watch as the Vampire takes a running jump before launching himself into the air and landing perfectly in the center of the open door.

Damn Vampires and their inhuman agility.

The chopper's blades are exceedingly loud, the sound drowning out everything around me. I fight the urge to block my ears. Instead, I force myself to watch as the black helicopter rises higher and higher.

Once the chopper is little more than a speck in the sky, I sigh and rub my hand over my neck. My shoulders ease as I continue to study the swirling blue sea all around me, the waves crashing against the side of the ship. With each passing moment, life begins to return to normal around me. The crew starts chatting again, their laughter filling the air as they continue their day. Everyone is more at ease now.

Except for me.

Because I have a princess to deal with.

Taking a deep breath, I try to compose myself before turning around to find Helena. I don't have to look far. She is cavorting with a small group of sailors, her shoulders shaking in silent laughter as they seem to share a joke.

The sight infuriates me. The leash on my temper snaps, and I see red. Clenching my jaw, I stomp over to her. Instantly, the mood in the air shifts as everyone takes a step back. My men gaze at the floor, avoiding me, but it's too late.

I saw them.

"Get back to work," I snarl.

There are murmurs of assent as the sailors suddenly find somewhere else to be. Their voices are overly loud as they talk about changing the course slightly so we can make it to the Gates of Hell a day early. My sights are set on the female before me.

Reaching out, I grab Helena's wrist and pull. Hard. "Come with me."

She struggles to wrench her arm out of my grip, but I don't let her go. I'm too incensed to even look at her right now.

She hurries behind me, her free hand smacking me repeatedly on the back as I lead her below deck. On another day, I'd admire the way she never gives up. She is fierce. But not today.

We don't stop moving until we reach my office.

"Sit down." I shove her past the threshold. Crossing my arms in front of my chest, I wait for her to do as I say.

And wait.

A minute passes, then two, as she purses her lips and shakes her head. Her pink eyes flash as she silently hisses, baring her teeth at me.

Blood rushes to my face as I clench my fists. I turn, smashing a fist into the wall. It's a poor conduit for the brunt of my anger, but it will have to do. I yell, "Gods, Helena! You just don't get it, do you?"

She stares at me, her eyes wide as she tilts her head and grabs a notepad. Ripping off a piece of paper, she scribbles a note and shoves it in my general direction.

Get what?

Crumpling the note and throwing it on the ground, I run my hands through my hair as I turn around.

I hiss, "Thorn."

She stares at me blankly.

"The Vampire. The one who was just here," I say, my voice dangerously quiet. "He would have killed you. Probably me, too. You don't play games with the League. They are *dangerous*. Even for people like me. Why couldn't you just have stayed put like you were told?"

She shrugs. Shrugs!

Another note.

I didn't want to.

"You know what? I don't care what you want anymore," I say. Grabbing her arm, I pull her out of my office. "You refuse to be anything other than a problem, Princess. It's time you finally learn your place on my ship."

I don't even register the walk to her room. In the back of my mind, I know she's fighting me every step of the way, but I don't care. She keeps putting herself in reckless danger, and I'm tired of having to watch out for her every moment of every day.

I didn't want this female in my life. I didn't ask for any of this.

Before I know what I'm doing, the door to her room is open. Shoving her inside, I slam the door behind her. Leaning against the door with all my weight, I pull the knob as she pounds against it. Her knocking is frantic, like drums banging against the door, and she is clearly putting her entire weight into fighting against the door.

"I can do this all day, Princess. You should've listened to me. I know you're mute, but I thought you had some brains in that pretty little head of yours."

A couple of sailors pass us by. Their faces turn ashen when they get a look at my face. The moment their eyes meet mine, they hurry down the hall. Their whispers reach my ears as they pass, walking around me like I might hurt them.

"... angry..."

"Give the captain his space..."

Space won't fix me, but they don't know that. It's this female that's the problem. Well, she will just have to stay in her room until she learns her lesson.

A few minutes into my vigil, a white piece of paper slips under the door. It pokes me in the leg, and I bend over to pick it up.

Please let me out.

"No."

Settling in for a long day, I slide down the door and lean against the wall. The sound of her frustration is like fuel to my fire.

Finally, this female will learn that everyone on this ship listens to me for a good reason—so they can be safe. Minutes pass, and the door rattles behind me as Helena continues her relentless attack on the piece of wood keeping her prisoner. For a woman who can't speak, she certainly is loud.

Eventually, though, the sounds stop. The silence feels deafening after her onslaught against the door.

For a moment, I think she's given up.

Just for a moment.

Then, a crash sounds from behind me. I'm on my feet in an instant, ripping open the door. The shattered remains of a wooden footstool lay in pieces at my feet. She stands there, wielding a broken leg like a dagger, and she snarls at me. She doesn't care about being safe.

Bending down, I gather the other pieces of the stool in my arms before tossing them into the hall. They clatter, rolling away with the gentle movement of the ship.

Pulling myself to my full height, I point my finger at Helena.

"Keep your little weapon if it makes you feel better," I seethe. My head is pounding as the desire to hit something, anything, rips through me. Helena just stares at me. Her face is paler than normal, and her brows are pinched together. Any fool could see that she is upset. But it's not enough. Not yet.

I continue my tirade. "No matter what, you will get it through your gods-damned mind, Princess. This is my ship, and you will do as I say." Stepping closer, I look her dead in the eyes as I say the one thing I know will hurt her the most. "I bet your father wishes you died instead of your brother."

Slamming the door, I barely glimpse the hurt on her face before I stomp away to get someone to clean up this mess.

Good riddance.

12
DON'T BE AN ASSHOLE JUST BECAUSE I'M CURIOUS
HELENA

In the hours after Erik's temper tantrum, I have remained in my room. I'm curled up in a ball on my small bed, clutching his velvet comforter as his words play on repeat in my mind.

The voices of several crew members float through the thin door. "Vigilante," they whisper as if I can't hear.

That word. Are they talking about Erik? How could that son of a bitch be someone who lies and cheats to save others? I scoff. I can't believe it. He is so horrible to me. Besides, even if they are right, it doesn't change the fact that Erik is an asshole.

The short fibers of the velvety fabric show trails along the quilted patterns as I scratch my fingernails into the cloth. It's calming.

I've long since stopped crying tears fueled by white-hot anger. Now, all that's left is the familiar burn of a cluster of embers in my stomach. How dare he have anything to say about *my* life or *my* father?

The worst thing of all is that the captain is right. His words were terrible and potent and true. The truth always stings the most.

My father loved his son and brought him up as his heir. Perhaps he would've even begged the gods to bestow a gift worthy of a DemiGod on Henrick. Stupid, horrible, depraved Henrick. No such supplication was made for me.

Being the daughter of the Ice Mer king is meaningless. *The daughter* of the Ice Mer king is meaningless. I am meaningless.

My stomach rumbles, and I am drawn from my agonizing self-pity party to the necessity of food.

I grab a pencil and pad and go to the door. My hand hovers over the simple aluminum knob. If I try to open it and it is locked... something will break inside me, I can feel it. The effects will not be good for anyone, least of all me.

My body trembles and a flash of cold makes my stomach lurch.

Do it, Helena.

I don't move. I am frozen in place.

Just do it. Not knowing is worse than knowing. At least if you know, you can figure out how to deal with it.

The air that rushed into my lungs is stinted, freezing the inside of my nose. I lay my hand down and turned. The knob gives way easily, turning in my hand. The way it has a dozen times before.

Life floods back into my cold limbs, and the shaking stops everywhere except in my stomach. I still feel somewhat weak. To my left, there is a guard. With a flash of a bald head, he jerks around to look at me.

I put my hands on my hips and stare at him.

The middle-aged, wrinkly sailor gruffly says, "Maddie—Madeline. I've been stationed here to... well, I'm supposed to watch you."

I raise an eyebrow in response.

His eyelids squeeze shut as he recites his orders. "Watch Madeline. Make sure she doesn't go anywhere she's not supposed to, especially if there are visitors. If I do not, I lose my balls." He makes a choking sound, and his eyes fly open. "I—er—mean, milady," he bows just a little, "I will lose the ability to perform in a... hobby I very much enjoy doing."

I throw my head back and laugh. The silence of the act has stopped feeling strange to me.

The man has turned positively crimson. I can't tell if it's his embarrassment that a woman laughed at him or that he was crude in front of "a lady." His misstep makes me feel so much more at ease. All the anxiety melts away and slides back into the shadowy corners of my room.

Putting pencil to paper, I write him a fast note.

Noted.
Your balls are of the utmost importance to me. What's your name?

The crimson becomes purple as his eyes flick back and forth across the words. The sight is hilarious.

"My name?" he stumbles on his words. The man looks like he might faint. "I'm Fr-fr-freddy."

I loop my hand with his arm and appreciate the clean scent that wafts towards me. The men's cleanliness makes this trip a whole hell of a lot more pleasant. I shudder to think about what the crew might smell like on a ship that didn't have working showers. Clearly, there is another bathroom for the crew. Thank all the gods for small mercies.

I gesture to the stairs, and Freddy escorts me to Jean Luc for something to eat.

Walking into the mess hall, I'm focused on one thing: food.

The mess hall smells so good that I don't see anyone in front of me until my face collides directly with something warm and utterly unmoving. I stumble back in surprise as a shooting pain erupts in my nose. The impact causes a shock to pass through my teeth. Glancing up as I hiss, I see Erik's dark eyes staring back at me. The captain's face fills with panic, and Freddy gasps loudly at my side.

My hand flies to my face, grabbing my now-throbbing nose. I am too busy pinching the bridge of my nose to listen to what commands the captain barks at Freddy. The pain in my nose is now accompanied by a copious flow of blood. My head snaps back as I try to staunch the flow when a damp dish rag is thrust in my face by Erik.

I can feel the weight of everyone in the mess hall watching me. I grab the dish rag and descend a few steps to escape their obnoxious stares. The cool rag feels good against my nose, and I lean against the wall. My eyes burn holes in Erik's face, which is now twisted with worry and regret.

I am cursing viciously in my mind when he dismisses Freddy and comes down to stand in front of me. I don't take my eyes off him for one second, though the rag is now beginning to soak through with blood.

He opens his mouth and then closes it. And then opens it *again*. I roll my eyes just as he says, "I'm so sorry."

Erik reaches out, and I swat his hand away. I glare at him silently. *Really?*

Nodding, he reaches into his pocket. "Really."

I turn to leave when he holds something out for me.

He says, "No, wait, take this."

I stare at the FaePhone he has placed in my hand. It's the same one I watched him using earlier. Finally, I look back at him. I make it clear with my glare that I don't want his pity gift.

"It's easier for you to write with."

Swiping up to unlock it, I notice the lack of a password. And background. And apps. It's basically a shell of a phone. Suddenly, all the anger melts away when I open his messages. There is one chat available.

With Anders...

Interesting. The captain's room is richly decorated, which shows his depth of personality—as much as I hate to admit it. But his phone? Where I can see how he interacts with others?

He is bland as sand.

I close out the messages and open the notes, hyper-aware of how Erik watches my every move. He still uses the stock background image, for the gods' sake.

My finger pads clumsily across the letters on the phone as I type:

> YOU ARE A REAL ASSHOLE. ALSO, WHY ARE THERE NO PICTURES?

I pass his bland-ass phone back and watch him read the message. There's something different about communicating with people through the written word. Their reactions are less guarded this way, and I get to see every emotion in real-time.

His stupid, worried face goes from a twinge of anger to surprise and then lands on an emotion that causes a school of guppies to have a racing contest in my stomach. I suck in a breath of air, which incites a wince.

"First, stop the name-calling. No one else here so much as calls me by my first name." He pauses, hesitating on the next answer. "Pictures of what? The ocean? There's plenty of it to look at out there. It existed before we did and will continue to exist once we're gone."

I smirk. Now, *that* sounds like something I'd read in one of those philosophical books on his shelf. My hand shoots out and steals the phone again.

He considers for less than half a second. "Nope."

But then his eyes lock on mine, and like witnessing a light turn on in his mind. He sees something in me at that moment.

We stare at each other, and he watches me adjust the rag against my nose. The air has become thick with a new kind of tension. Holding my gaze, Erik does the unthinkable and moves closer.

The space around us is alive with electrical charges. Thoughts fall away as my senses heighten. His hand comes up, presumably to touch my face, and my skin tingles at his nearness, anticipating his touch.

"I really am sorry," he whispers again as he shifts a corner of the rag to wipe away blood on my cheek. Violent power envelops us. I look down, expecting to see sparks dancing in the air between us, but there is nothing there. Still, the energy remains. I would be scared, except this power is different from what my father is capable of. This kind of power is intangible and magnetic. A part of me craves the sensation of his skin on mine. It coaxes me to lean into him.

And that's the thought that scares me.

So, instead, I do the next logical thing. My hands fly out and shove him hard.

He makes a muffled sound as he crashes back into the wall and loses his footing. A series of loud *thuds* follow him as he somersaults down the stairs. Not wanting another lecture or another heated fight, I bound back up the stairs into the mess hall.

The entire crew is there, and they all turn their heads to stare at me. It's clear I've become their dinner entertainment. I'm still covered in blood, and I'm breathing a bit rapidly from the surge of emotions.

"Everything okay, Maddie?" Jean Luc says from behind the bar. He doesn't outwardly say it, but I see him search behind me for Erik.

I shrug slightly too enthusiastically just as Erik's furious footsteps thump up the stairs. I tense, not allowing myself to look back.

Anders stands up from the table, "Cap—"

"She pushed me," he half-shouts. He's at my side now, and I steal a glance. He looks very disheveled, and his hair is a mess. I fight against a smile that's threatening to surface and make this situation ten times worse.

"Madeline, I will see you in my office," he grinds as he wraps his hand around my elbow.

No one speaks as he drags me into the room at the back of the mess hall. He slams the door after we pass through it.

"Sit," he hisses.

I remain standing and place my bloody rag on the polished wood. With my nose functioning more normally, I try not to notice how nice this office smells. How much it smells of him. I also try to ignore how much that scent relaxes me.

There should be nothing relaxing about the Pirate of Death.

He lets out a strangled sound. "Fine! You win."

I tilt my head, watching him carefully. Waiting to see what exactly I won.

Erik throws his hands up, and I shift uneasily. "No more bitchy notes scattered around my ship, no more pestering my officers."

My stomach is in knots now. I can't read what he intends to do. If we're being honest, I'm expecting him to call for another chopper to take me away. Instead, he pulls out a drawer on his wooden desk with enough force to nearly break it. He rummages around and then grabs a white cardboard box. I glimpse several more, just like it lying side by side.

This man must be made of money.

"These," he starts, noticing my nosiness, "are burner phones. I buy them so that I can throw them away later. I'm giving you one. It will work well enough. You can have mine and Jean Luc's number in case you need something."

He sits down, and this time, I follow suit. I watch as he holds the side button to turn it on and then begins typing. He's so focused on filling in whatever information he wants to that he doesn't see me swipe his phone and take a quick selfie of half my face and him staring down at the phone. He looks like a total idiot.

I do, too, kind of.

His eyes flick up at me, and I quickly hide my hands under the desk. He lets out an irritated sigh. Erik holds out the phone, and I reach to grab it with my free hand when he snatches it away. "You get this on one condition: stop the attacks."

I nod enthusiastically. He seems placated.

"All right, this is a piece of shit. But it's yours." He hands it back to me and starts cleaning up the boxes. I stealthily punch my new number into his phone and attach the stupid picture of us as the contact photo. I put his phone back on the desk and stand.

"Are you happy?" he asks, barely able to keep the irritation out of his voice.

I flash him a grin, open the door, and run out.

"*Madeline! You left your damned bloody rag!*" His muffled shouts follow me through the door, but I'm already halfway to the bar where Jean Luc is. I open my crappy phone and find his number.

My steps stop abruptly. His contact info reads, "Not-an-asshole Erik." I roll my eyes.

> Me: No. It's your fault. You clean it up.

Now I'm at the bar. I set the phone down next to the glasses when it buzzes again. Jean Luc is still talking to one of the other crew members, so I check the phone.

> Not-an-asshole Erik: I thought you agreed to stop the attacks??

> Me: I refuse to be held accountable for promises made under coercion.

Another loud crash sounds, and I'm starting to get tired of the captain's dramatics. I am mustering up the courage to tell him when his office door opens.

"I did *not* coerce you," he shouts across the room.

The following moments are deathly silent as the whole crew stops what they are doing to stare at him. He clears his throat, his cheeks turning pink. "What I meant to say is I don't coerce you all to be here. Get back to work."

He slams the door behind him. One of the sailors, I don't know his name, says, "What the hell is wrong with him?"

A chuckle comes from behind me, and I turn to see Jean Luc. I scowl at him as I shove the phone in his direction.

"Must be something about the recent upgrades to the boat," he says through his laughter as he reads the text.

I get my phone back from Jean Luc and decide to send one last text.

> Me: Only assholes slam doors like that every two seconds.

13
BREAKFAST AND TRUE CRIME
ERIK

"**S**ix years ago on the Summer Solstice, Melinda Johnson, a twenty-seven-year-old Were was in the small kitchen of her first-story apartment in Port City. She was washing the dishes when her FaePhone went off with an alert of an escaped prisoner nearby.

"By all accounts, she sent a screenshot of the alert to her wife with the caption "check this out" before returning to the kitchen. Two minutes after the text was sent, records show that the alarm system in her home was tripped when—"

When what?

My phone starts vibrating in short bursts on my desk right before a loud *ping* breaks through the final remnants of my concentration. As if that wasn't enough, it's followed by two more *pings* in rapid succession.

Instantly, I know who is to blame for interrupting my true crime binge.

My nostrils flare as I slam down the ledger I had been working.

"Seven times," I mutter, reaching for the offensive phone.

"Seven gods-damn times. How much can one female have to say?"

Pointedly ignoring the gods-awful screensaver Helena put on my phone, I swipe up and see what was so important that she had to interrupt me again. My last message has been clear.

> Me: I'll be working in my office this morning.

Meaning: Leave. Me. Alone. Let me work in peace. But she clearly didn't understand the message.

> Princess: What are you doing? I looked for you this morning but didn't see you.

> Princess: You're not on the deck either. I checked. You should be out here. The sun is shining, and the birds are out this morning.

The third text isn't a text at all but rather a blurry, out-of-focus picture of Helena with her fingers held up in the international peace sign. I can make out Jean Luc standing behind her, his expression one of wary amusement. Just as I'm about to reply, *another* text comes through. I groan, scrolling down to read it.

> Princess: You missed the most incredible breakfast. Jean Luc made beignets.

It is true. I had missed breakfast. On purpose. Last night, I had been tossing and turning in my bed when my phone pinged at 2 a.m. I had picked it up and squinted at the screen with bleary eyes.

> Princess: What is there to do on this ship at night?

I was up. Sleeping never came naturally to me, and once I was up, that was it. I hadn't been in the mood to chat, let alone learn why Helena had been awake at such an ungodly hour.

For all I knew, she had woken up, sent the text as a joke, then returned to sleep.

How infuriating. That word sums up our relationship. Infuriating. Frustrating. Vexing.

A few hours later, I had given up on all pretenses of sleeping and wandered into the mess hall. I had been determined to have a good day. Work had been piling up in my office over the past few days, and I had finally decided to deal with it. That was the downside of being the captain. There was no one else to do your work for you.

The only person in the mess hall this morning had been Jean Luc. He had been bustling around in the kitchen, the aroma of something delicious wafting through the air.

Even after twenty years, I don't know much about the man. He is a man of many secrets, but one thing is certain. He knows how to cook. The modern appliances on *The Black Rose* only make his job easier.

"Morning, Captain," he had said, a grin on his face as he popped out of the kitchen. "Bit early for you, no?"

I had grunted a reply that sounded somewhere between "yep" and "don't care" as I poured a copious amount of coffee into my thermos. It was going to be a long day. I could feel it in my bones.

Jean Luc had studied me for a moment before raising a brow. "Maddie showed me the phone you gave her yesterday. That was kind of you."

Slamming the lid on my thermos, I turned on my heel and glared at the chef. "I just did it to get her off my back. She's insufferable."

The sailor tilted his head, watching me carefully. "I've known you for a long time, Captain, wouldn't you say?"

"Yes," I grunted.

Jean Luc had served the previous Pirate of Death before I took over the mantle. He was one of the few men I had kept on the crew. He was loyal and trustworthy.

"I like Maddie," he said, focusing on the cutting board before him.

"Good for you." I ran a hand over my face.

He continued to chop, the sound echoing through the empty mess hall. "I like you, too."

"Is there a point to this conversation?" I bit out between clenched teeth.

Chewing on his cheek, Jean Luc considered me for a moment. "Nope. Just wanted to let you know what I see."

The sound of chopping filled the air as we stood there, watching each other.

"Okay, then," I said, slamming the door as I left. My mood thoroughly soured, I had stomped back to my office, where I had remained ever since.

For an entire two hours, my day had been peaceful.

I had binged three consecutive episodes of *True Crime Aranthium*, my guilty pleasure. Full of caffeine, I started on the mountains of paperwork I had been putting off for the past month. Payroll for my crew, etc.

Things had been going peacefully. Until 8:02 a.m.

That was when Helena had woken up.

I know that because she had texted me the second her eyelids had fluttered open. Three hours have passed since then, and she has sent me over ten messages.

Ten.

I haven't even sent ten texts in the past two months. How can one being have so much to say? Gods. It isn't even lunchtime yet.

Groaning, I rest my forehead against my palm as I consider the slew of texts on my screen. An exasperated sigh leaves my lips as my fingers fly over the keyboard. Pressing send, I slam my phone down on the desk. Threading my fingers, I rest my forehead on my hands and consider the text I just sent.

> Me: Not hungry.

I let out a low breath as I yank open one drawer, then the next.

"Come on," I mutter as I rustle through the drawers. "There must be something in here to eat."

After inspecting the third drawer, I groan as I bang my head against the desk. All I have are some oat protein bars.

This is not exactly the feast I was hoping for. Peeling back the wrapper, I chew on the grainy bar before turning my podcast back on. The breakfast bar tastes like sawdust, but anything is better than dealing with Helena right now.

Leaning back in my office chair, I force out thoughts of the irritating female as I close my eyes.

My mind drifts as the hosts of *True Crime Aranthium,* Jenny and Ansel, finish talking about the gruesome murder of Melinda Johnson. She was killed by a Daemon who had escaped from the prison in the Gates of Hell, but the DaePolice never had enough to charge the suspect. The Daemon only served two years for his escape from Blackwater Prison before being allowed to go free.

Two years.

"Typical," I mutter under my breath as the closing credits roll. Yet another murderer roaming free in Aranthium. Daemons get away with everything. The haunting memories of female screams flit through my mind, and I sit up abruptly as my heart begins to pound in my chest.

Push it away, Erik.

Rubbing my prosthetic on my head, I turn off the podcast and focus on my meditative breathing.

You are not there any longer. You are safe. They can't hurt you.

Repeating the mantra in my mind, I focus on breathing in and out. Slowly, the screams become nothing more than a distant memory. A wisp of nothing more than a nightmare.

Once they are gone, I shake my head and scroll through my FaePhone to download the next episode of the podcast.

Just as Ansel, the perkier of the two hosts, is diving into the explanation of the episode—apparently, this one is about a Warlock, a Pixie, and a torrid love affair gone wrong—my phone dings *again.*

Berating myself for my moment of weakness, I pick up my phone. "You just had to respond to her and open the door of communication, didn't you, Erik?"

> Princess: I have a question for you. 😊

Staring at the phone in my hand, I blink. What in the nine circles of hell is this? Who sends this crap?

Did adults even use emojis?

My fingers fly over the screen faster than they ever have before. I hit send before I can even re-read what I've written.

> Me: This better be good. You're interrupting my work.

Three dots appear on the screen, and almost instantly, three *dings* come from the infernal piece of technology in my hand. I resist the urge to throw it against the wall, instead watching as one text after the other appears on my screen.

I would love nothing more than to silence my phone, but I can't. Rule number 654 of the League of Pirates: Captains must be accessible no matter where they are in Aranthium at all times.

> Princess: I didn't know work meant listening to true crime podcasts. Do you use them as research?

I growl in irritation.

> Princess: You're very angry for a human. Want to talk about it? I've been told I'm a very good listener.

Two more minutes pass as I stare at the screen, dumbfounded. I am... speechless.

> Princess: That was a joke. Because I'm a mute.

I slam down the phone and stalk to my door. What the hell is she doing? Something else strikes me at the same time. How does she know what I'm doing?

She must be nearby.

Yanking open the door that leads into the hallway, I'm not at all surprised to see Helena tumble headfirst into my office. A sheepish look crosses her face as she blinks up at me from the floor, her phone clutched in her fingers. Hands on my hips, I glare into the hall.

Anders is standing a few feet away, his face beet red as he opens his mouth.

"Anders," I say, running my hand over my face. "Since when does 'watch Madeline' mean allow her to eavesdrop outside my office?"

"Well, Captain," Anders's face is turning purple. "She was very insistent."

"How can she be insistent?" I roar, red spots clouding my vision as I gesticulate wildly. "She doesn't even speak!"

"She—"

Ding.

I tighten my grip on the phone, my eyes widening as I stare at Helena. She's ignoring me, her fingers flying over the phone. I've never seen anyone type so quickly in my life.

> Princess: See? I was right. You have an anger problem.

Don't blame him. I can be very persuasive.

Rubbing my temples, I groan. *Persuasive*. More like invasive.

I haven't had a moment of peace since this female came into my life. She has invaded my thoughts, my ship, my time. Now, it seems like even my office isn't mine anymore.

After a long moment of silence, my phone dings again.

> Princess: Is there therapy for felons? You should consider it.

That's it. Fury rolls through me as I stare down the hallway. My voice drops, "Get out of here, Anders."

For a long moment, the sailor doesn't move. He looks between Helena, who is still lying on the floor, and me. I can see the conflict warring on his face.

"Go!" I yell.

He runs away, his footsteps clattering down the hall.

> Princess: You should be kind to him. He's afraid of you.

That's it. I get down on my knees, crouching in front of her. Waiting until her eyes meet mine, I snarl. "Everyone should be afraid of me, Princess. I'm the Pirate of Death."

She shrugs, her pink eyes wide as she studies me. Without even looking at the phone, she sends another text.

> Princess: You don't scare me.

A moment passes where I can't do anything except stare at the words. They stir something deep inside of me.

How can she not be afraid of me? She saw my first mate get pulled overboard by the sea, and then she watched me leave him there. A man I had known for twenty years. She's seen the people I work with. She saw the video Thorn showed.

From where Helena landed on the floor, her long, wavy hair has fanned out all around her. Her wide pink eyes watch me, and before I realize what I'm doing, I reach out and run my hand through the strands. It's silky and smooth and unlike anything I've ever touched before. She shivers, her mouth opening in a soundless gasp.

Then, the guilt comes crashing down. I lied to her. Her father sent me to kill her, for Fortuna's sake.

Withdrawing my hand as though I've been burned, I grab my phone. I can feel the weight of her gaze as I type out a message and send it to her. The moment she gets it, her eyes narrow before she huffs.

Pushing herself up onto her elbows, she glares at me before rushing over to the shelf and grabbing a book. Without a backward glance, she takes the book and her phone and leaves my office.

Long after she's left, I pull out my phone and look at the last message.

> Me: Leave. Me. Alone.

A twang of regret flies through me, but I squash it down.

THE REST of the day passes by in a blur. Helena leaves me alone, and I push through my work. But something is off. No matter what I try, I can't help but feel like I'm missing something.

I try listening to my podcasts, but even the tale of a serial murderer and his eventual arrest don't bring me joy. Every two seconds, I expect to hear my FaePhone chime. It never does.

By the time dinner rolls around, I've given up trying to work. I head into the mess hall, keeping my eyes peeled for Helena. The crew keeps trying to engage me in conversation, but my efforts are half-hearted at best.

All through dinner, I pick at my pot roast and sautéed vegetables. My mind is so wrapped up in itself that I barely taste anything. I keep glancing around, my brows furrowed as I search for a now-familiar head of wavy hair.

It never appears. The mess hall feels emptier than normal, the atmosphere heavier than it has been for days. With a jolt, I realize what's missing.

Helena's silent laughter. The way her shoulders shake at a joke, and her eyes light up. Half an hour into the meal, my phone dings. I pull it out so fast, I almost drop it onto my plate.

My stomach drops when I look at the screen, letting out a breath I didn't know I was holding.

> Jean Luc: Maddie asked to eat in her room tonight.

I stare at the phone in my hand as a pang wrenches through my stomach. This is what I wanted. So why does it hurt so much?

Helena never reappears. The next day, Jean Luc informs me she's asked to take all her meals in her room.

My phone remains silent, and my mood worsens with every passing second. The sailors keep their distance, and no one talks to me all day.

I'm alone. Just like I wanted. I get my work done, but there is no fulfillment in it.

Even the coffee tastes bitter on my tongue.

A glance at the navigation system tells me we'll be at the Gates of Hell in a week. What should have brought me joy instead just makes me feel... lonely.

I usually like being alone. Quiet time makes me happy. I thrive on solitude. Being alone is easy. And yet, every time I think about the future after she's out of my life, everything looks gray. Helena has brought life aboard this ship.

She is not simple, or quiet, or easy. She is infuriating, irritating, and intoxicating. Helena is bad luck.

And I miss her.

My eyes fly open as something pulls me out of my dreams. I blink, rubbing the last vestiges of sleep from my eyes as I look around the room. What could have woken me? Waves lap at the outer walls of the ship, the sound a comfort after countless nights at sea. My heart beats steadily. It's dark, the only light coming from the moon shining through the window, but as my vision adjusts, the doorknob turns.

Who would dare?

I sit up in bed, watching in fascinated horror as the door swings open.

This has never happened before. I'm torn between anger and complete fascination at the person who would trespass upon my privacy in such a blatant fashion.

The door opens, the dim light of the hallway casting a soft glow around the feminine figure standing before me.

I should have known.

"Princess?" I whisper hoarsely.

It's her. She's dressed in a long white rail nightgown, and her hair is in a thick braid down her back. Glassy eyes meet mine as silent sobs wrench through her. Her hands clench at empty air, and she's shaking.

"What are you doing?" My eyes land on my prosthetic resting on the nightstand, but her head jerks up before I can move to put it on.

She stares at me for a moment, not really seeing, before taking one wobbly step forward, then another. As soon as she is at the foot of the bed, she climbs on, climbing on her hands and knees towards me.

Her face is shining, and wet tears stream down her cheeks. She is shaking uncontrollably.

"Oh, Helena," I murmur. I've never seen her like this. Completely and utterly unguarded.

Beautiful.

Without thinking, I push several pillows behind my back before wrapping my right arm around her. Drawing her against my chest, I run my hand up and down her back while murmuring nothing in particular into her hair.

My mother used to do the same thing when I was young.

Soon, her shaking slows, and the shuddering gives way to low, deep breaths. Then, impossibly, she falls asleep.

On my bed.

With.

Me.

What can I do? Her head is against my shoulder, and I don't have the heart to move her.

The waves lap at the side of the ship, and I stare at her. One minute passes. Five. Ten.

Eventually, I realize I'm not going to move her. I can't.

Instead, I draw the blanket over us both. There's a strange feeling in my chest, and it takes a long time to realize what it is.

I'm not lonely anymore.

14
THIS IS NOT MY BED
HELENA

Before my eyes open, while I am just barely reentering consciousness, I know where I am.

I mean, his scent is everywhere. The ocean breeze mixed with sunlight. I inhale, drinking deeply from the air. When I open my eyes, Erik is nowhere in sight. I've moved overnight, and now I am on the opposite end of the bed. The covers are barely rumpled on the side where I presume Erik slept.

The man doesn't have an arm! What the hell?

I don't know how I hadn't noticed this before. Until I saw his prosthetic resting on the side table, I had no idea.

Curiosity fills me. How did he lose the limb? Does it hurt?

He isn't here, so my questions remain unanswered.

Letting out a long breath, I drag myself out of the depths of the lush covers and lean back against his beautiful headboard. My cheeks flush as I take stock of the events of the last several days.

No way in hell had I harbored any secret intention of coming to his room. Once I was left alone with my FaePhone, I tried to call Elva.

The only number I knew was disconnected.

The overwhelming wave of sadness and disappointment had caused me to reach out to Erik. I had texted him, thinking he wouldn't respond. My jaw had gone slack when he answered.

Gods above! He answered.

I press the heels of my palms into my eye sockets as I remember how shamelessly I had flirted with him in our messages. Little guppies wriggling in my stomach as I remember how the corners of my mouth tugged at every reply.

The high I had gotten from his attention had lasted until last night. Instantly, my thoughts darken as I recall the night before. Even though I'd exercised the entire day, restful sleep eluded me. When the nightmares began again, I had awoken in a silent scream, feeling like I couldn't breathe. Survival instinct had caused me to lose all sense.

In the light of the morning, I try to tell myself that I had come here because his room was the closest. The truth is that he had saved me before, and deep down, I was sure that he could do it again.

Disgusted at how drastically my feelings have changed toward the arrogant, pain-in-the-ass pirate, I tear the covers off of myself and slide out of his bed.

What is wrong with me?

I don't like the pirate. He's an ass.

Standing on two feet, I scowl at his room.

The tension still doesn't subside, so I ball the velvety soft fabric in my hands and throw it onto the ground.

The soft *thud* it makes as it lands brings a smile to my face. It gets even wider when I realize this will piss him off.

That makes me grin.

An angry Erik is one I can deal with. Besides, there is something about irritating him that makes me feel better. It enlivens me, this addicting feeling. I like getting a rise out of him and making him break the aloof, unreachable persona he puts on for his crew.

A wiser person might have considered that I have some daddy issues.

I am not wise or analytical.

Instead, I throw a pillow onto the ground.

Whatever strange feelings I had after spending a night in his bed slowly dissipate.

Thank the gods.

I throw another pillow.

The bedcovers soon follow. Then another pillow. A fourth.

He's going to hate this.

Fabulous.

I realize I might look ridiculous, but honestly, *mental* and *health* aren't typically used in the same sentence in the Ice Mer courts.

Another pillow thuds against the door.

Discomfort is still threading through my thoughts, and I'm quickly running out of pillows to throw.

This won't do.

I need to do something else. Something... more than a pillow. A horrible, repulsive idea pops into my brain, and I can't resist. Traipsing to the bookshelf, I traverse the sea of covers, barely tripping and grasping at the bookshelves for stability.

Panting lightly, a wicked grin spreads across my face.

I gently slide a paperback book off the shelf and hold it in my hand, wondering if the inanimate object can forgive me for what I'm about to do.

Just as I'm opening the book, the door opens tentatively. It's as if the person on the other side doesn't want to disturb anyone who might be sleeping.

Almost immediately, the door drags over a corner of the cover and is halted by a super-plush pillow. Erik's face pops into the room.

"What," he shoves the door open a bit more, "*the hell*," he pauses a second to jiggle the handle so that he can squeeze his large body in, "have you done, Helena?"

His eyes make contact with mine. My cheeks heat, and I blink my underlids to piss him off. The book is in my hands, barely open.

His focus snaps to the book in my hand. "Helena," he warns. "Put the book down."

My toes curl. He is furious with me. It's written all over his face.

This is what I wanted. This is the type of relationship he and I have. I do not care about him or his things.

He steps towards me, and my instincts tell me to run. There is no kindness in his face as his lips twist into a sneer. "Are you listening?" he says. "Put the book away."

I shake my head defiantly and snatch a hardbound book. He reaches for me as I rip the dust jacket off. His hand swats at mine, and the dust jacket tears.

The *rip* it makes is like ice, causing me to freeze.

Erik lets out a strangled cry and grabs my shoulders, pushing me back into the wall and causing the book to fall.

"What is wrong with you? What are you doing to my things?" he whisper-yells. His eyes gleam with fury.

Perfect.

Now, I just need him to return to despising me, and life can return to normal.

I stare back at him with clenched teeth. It is nice to have things back to how they used to be—before I had shown him my utter, despicable weakness. I am a coward unworthy of my crown, seeking affection from a dangerous human man.

His grip tightens as he shakes me. I continue to stare into his eyes, baiting him. He will hit me soon, I am sure of it. I just need the blow to come, and the spell will break. Once it is, I can stop needing him so damn much.

There is darkness in his voice when he speaks. "Why are you destroying my books?"

Anger and self-loathing course through my veins. Unable to stop myself, I twist my head and bite him.

"What's gotten into you?" he roars, snatching his hands back. Red indents mark his hand from my teeth.

Immediately, I miss the contact, and the voice in my mind murmurs, *You have gotten into me.*

I spit on him, and he makes a disgusted sound.

A head pops into the office. Anders. Excellent. "Sir, is every—"

"Get out!" Erik roars. He whirls around to throw a book from the shelf.

Anders disappears as the book hits the space where his head had been a moment before.

Good. I stare at Erik, hoping he'll do something to break the spell. Hit me. Hurt me. Just... make things go back to the way they were before.

I silently goad him as he turns back around.

A part of me relaxes, awaiting the blow that will surely come. I have taken things too far. I flinch when he extends his fist. Except, he doesn't touch me.

"Type," he commands, thrusting the phone in my hand. His eyes are wreathed in shadows.

Snatching the thing, I glare at him and type out exactly what he can go and do to himself. His brows furrow as he reads my message, and then he grinds, "Get out of my room."

My heart lands in my stomach like a stone plopping into shallow water. Erik turns around, wades to the nightstand, and grabs my phone. I barely catch it when he tosses it to me. "Get. Out," he repeats.

I oblige and hurry away. Each step causes me to feel worse. He didn't even hit me. I cross through the open threshold, and the door slams behind me.

Wrapping my arms around myself, I cringe. Not wanting to see anyone else, I walk back into my room and slam the door. My back connects with the door, and I slide down.

The loss of the severed connection echoes throughout my body. It is worth it. It is my price for my reckless attitude towards him.

It's truly incredible how long I can stay staring at the wall.

My tear-stained cheeks have long since dried, and my hair lays in limp tangles around my face. The bland white wall in front of me is as empty as my brain.

I'm trying to keep my mind quiet, so I don't tumble down the bottomless pit I had spent more than an hour in after returning to my room. The thoughts had been dangerous, and they scared me. It is much better to be blank and emotionless, like the wall. That wall is the clean slate I am begging for inside.

A life with stability, loving parents, siblings, and friends. Friends whose current, verified contact information I can have on my phone.

A clean slate was what I had been before I'd been stripped of my voice and nearly assaulted. And... just like that, I am falling back into the abyss.

The tears return, and I squeeze my eyes shut against the pain.

I don't want to be the Crown Princess, I don't want to be heading to my uncle's Daemon empire. I'm not ready to prepare for becoming a queen. Everyone knows I will fail miserably at the role.

The whole time I have been on this boat, I have been shoving these thoughts and burying them under a pile of other shit. Now, less than a week and a half before we dock in the Gates of Hell, I have to face my future.

I consider taking my father's throne and all the birthright power that comes with it. I imagine I will become a fearsome being of cruel authority, just like him. Quick to punish, slow to listen.

Henrick was the one who had that role down pat. I suppose a bit of that exists inside me, but I find the more time I am forced to listen, the more I enjoy it. Enjoying living and not just objects is relatively new for me.

Most of the joy I have found in my life can be reduced to Elva and this ship.

My face crumples. If I enjoy it so much, why did I hurt Erik? I ran around, throwing and breaking things like a child. What the hell is wrong with me?

The intrusive thoughts come back. I see myself walking out of my room and up the stairs to the deck. When I reach the rail, I climb over it and throw myself into the churning sea.

The tears come harder, and I hate the thought. I want to look away and distract myself, but my own mind is poisoning me. Red-hot self-hatred is a whirlpool that causes gooseflesh to pebble on my arms and tighten my lower back.

I look up, staring directly into the cool, fluorescent light. I wish for anything to distract me. *Please, gods above, just anything.*

A tense moment passes before a familiar vibration buzzes next to my hip. I look down.

> Not-an-asshole Erik: Hey

I blink. I've never been a particularly spiritual being, but I can't stop the word *miracle* from passing through my brain.

The FaePhone fumbles in my fingers as I unlock it and stare at the message. Three dots pop up below it, and I stare at those, too. A menacing thought pops into my mind. What if what comes next is more anger? I deserve that after how I acted.

A very long message appears.

> Not-an-asshole Erik: If you disrespect me like that again, I will personally see your removal from my ship once and for all. I will not stand for disrespect, and I have been made painfully aware that I look like a simpering ass allowing you to do whatever you wish with me.

I wince. All of this is merited.

> Not-an-asshole Erik: However, I recognize that some of the recent things you've gone through have been traumatic. As such, despite my initial reactions, you deserve kindness. What happened to you was wrong, Helena. If you promise not to break any more things, I can arrange for you to have a cot in my room and you can stop sleeping in the same room you were attacked in.

Tears sting my eyes. I can't believe what I am reading. My fingers are flying, trying to type out a thank-you-I-don't-deserve-this text when the dots reappear.

> Not-an-asshole Erik: Oh, and when we get to the shore, you are replacing my books.

I let out a sob and a laugh at the same time.

> Me: You've got a deal.

No response. That addictive fire ignites in me once again.

> Me: Sooo… how long do I have to wait until I can come back?

Seen. No response. I tap my fingers on the ground and allow the phone to lock.

> Not-an-asshole Erik: Helena, I'm working. I can't be distracted by you anymore today. You can go in whenever you wish. In fact, it better be clean before I get there.

I grin from ear to ear, grab his comforter from that horrible, uncomfortable bed, and dash across the hall.

It may be a bad idea to put myself close to him. It feels like playing with fire, but I am tired of the lingering cold.

Maybe a bit of fire is what I need.

15
DISTRACTIONS
ERIK

Rubbing my palms against my eyes, I groan into my hands. This day is dragging on, and I've been staring at the same bill of goods for the past two hours. No matter how hard I try to focus on my work, my mind keeps returning to the infuriating female on my ship. I cannot get her out of my head.

She's supposed to be cleaning up the mess she made in our room—in *my* room—while I get some work done.

But instead, here I am. Sitting in my office, thinking about her.

This lack of productivity is infuriating. I pride myself on being a hard worker and completing things on time. I run a tight ship, and my men respect me for it.

Not for the first time since I sat at my desk three hours ago, I glance at my FaePhone. Swiping up, I stare at the last text Helena sent me. It's accompanied by a selfie of her holding a glass globe filled with swirling white flakes. Her pink eyes stare at me through the phone, her brows raised as she intently studies the globe.

> Princess: Why do you have this? It's not very terrifying

I've just been staring at the message since it came in. Time after time, I've tried to type out a response, but nothing seems to be right. In the end, I just decided not to respond. After all, what would I say?

Oh, hey, Princess. That globe you're holding? Yeah, be careful with that. It's the last thing my mother gave me before she was brutally murdered.

That is not going to happen.

We are drawing nearer to the Gates of Hell with every passing moment. Where I'm supposed to kill Helena and dump her body.

A roaring fills my ears as potent, overwhelming rage rushes through my body. I clench my fists as visions of lifeless pink eyes flash before me.

The more time I spend with Helena, the more I realize I am screwed. Totally, completely, one hundred percent screwed.

It's not like the female is perfect. Far from it, in fact. She is maddeningly exasperating. Helena is rude, obnoxious, spiteful, and makes me angrier than I have ever been in my entire life. The problem is—and it is a problem—she is also smart, beautiful, spirited, and full of life.

In the short time I've known Helena, she has blown me away with her perseverance despite the crap life has thrown her way. She pushes me in a way no one else has ever dared. She doesn't see the Pirate of Death when she looks at me. She just sees *me*.

Helena has breathed life into me.

And there's no way in the nine circles of hell that I will ever be able to bring myself to kill her.

Which means I'm going to be on the run for the rest of my

very short life. I'm guessing I'll have a week, maybe two at best, before the finfolk catch up with me.

Then why are you spending your limited time doing paperwork?

The thought echoes through my mind, and I drop the pen I've been fiddling with on my desk. Why *am* I doing this?

I think through the obvious reasons. It needs to be done. It's my job. No one else will do it. These are all valid. But whenever an argument reaches my mind, another one pops up to counter it.

You could be doing something better with your time.

Before realizing what I'm doing, I've picked up my phone. My fingers are flying over the screen, typing out a text.

> Me: Hey.

I click send before I can talk myself out of it and slam my phone back on my desk. Slouching back in my chair, I try to focus on the papers before me when my phone dings almost instantly.

> Princess: Hey, back.

Two seconds later, three dots appear on the screen. I bite my lip, watching them intently. A moment later, another message appears.

> Princess: I thought you were working? Or maybe you're just binging true crime again?

I smirk, settling into my chair as my fingers fly over the screen.

> Me: Who says true crime isn't work? Maybe I am just doing some research.

> Princess: Spill the beans, Pirate of Death.

A laugh spills out of me, shattering the silence of my office. Her humor is so... unexpectedly dark. I can't even remember the last time I laughed. My lips tilt up as I respond.

> Me: That's classified information, Princess. It's rude to kill and tell, you know. 😉

The rest of the afternoon flies by as we exchange messages, talking about nothing and everything. Helena tells me about life in Aqualis and her best friend, Elva. I tell her about my obsession with true crime and what it's like to live on a boat all year round.

By the time dinner rolls around, I know Helena's favorite color (turquoise), her favorite food (chocolate), and her favorite hobby (reading, no surprise there). My mood is better than it has been in years, and I leave my office whistling. The aromatic smell of Jean Luc's signature stew permeates the ship and beckons me to the mess hall.

As I approach, boisterous laughter fills my ears. My curiosity is peaked, and I push the door. It flies open, banging as it collides with the wall, and the laughter abruptly stops.

In the middle of the room, Helena sits on the table, a crowd of sailors standing around her. As one, they turn and stare at me. A few of the smarter sailors pale at the sight of my face and back away from her. She simply raises a brow and smirks at me. The sight makes my nostrils flare.

And there goes my good mood.

"What's so funny?" I ask, putting my hands in my pockets and sauntering to the table.

Silence is my only response.

"Anyone?" I growl.

"Well..." Anders begins to speak, his face whiter than a sheet of paper, when my pocket vibrates.

Throwing up a hand in the air, I yank my FaePhone out of my pocket.

> Princess: I was just telling the boys a story, that's all. No need to go all Pirate of Death on them.

Clenching my fist at my side, I raise a brow. "Move," I bark.

Feet scurry on the wooden floor, chairs shuffling as the men quickly find seats. I glare at them, and miraculously, they all find something interesting to look at on their plates.

Walking over to Helena, I place my hands on either side of her before leaning in close. "The 'boys,' as you called them, Maddie, are busy. I would ask that you refrain from regaling them with your stories in the future."

Tilting her head, Helena purses her lips as she studies me. Her fingers start flying over the keyboard without even looking at her phone.

> Princess: Is that an order?

"Yes," I bite out between clenched teeth, running my hand through my hair as I fight to keep my voice down. The last thing I want to do is give my crew something to talk about. "It is an order."

> Princess: Too bad I'm not a member of your crew, so you can't order me around. You sure are cute when you're angry, though.

My nostrils flare as blood rushes to my face. There is a roaring in my ears that is hard to ignore.

Cute.

I am six feet five inches, two hundred and thirty pounds of

terrifying flesh. A vein pulses in my neck, and my eyes bulge as I glare at Helena. Her shoulders shake in silent laughter as she giggles, my phone buzzing in my hand once more.

> Princess: See? You're all sweetness beneath that hard, grumpy shell. Basically, you're a cinnamon roll. 🌀

Just like that, all the warm feelings from earlier are well and truly gone. They've dissipated into thin air. In their place are all the reminders of why Helena and I are a bad idea. She pushes all my buttons, she doesn't respect me, and she distracts my men.

> Me: That's a donut.

> Princess: They don't have a cinnamon roll one. Take it up with the Summer Fae.

It takes everything in my power to turn on my heel and march out of the mess hall. I hear the crew calling after me, but I ignore them as I head to my room. My sanctuary.

It isn't until I'm twisting the doorknob that I remember.

I told her she could sleep here.

Groaning, I pound my head against the door jamb. How could I have been so stupid? In a moment of weakness, I had suggested the cot. At the moment, it seemed like a good idea. Now, though, the realization of what it means is setting in. I can either return to sleeping in my office or deal with it. With her. The thought of another night on the uncomfortable furniture hurts my back. That's not an option.

It looks like I'm stuck with Helena in my personal space.

This will not go well.

NOT WELL IS AN UNDERSTATEMENT. I spend most of the evening dreading Helena's arrival, knowing it will be a matter of time before she walks through my door. At first, I pace the room, double-checking that she returned everything after her tantrum this morning. Nothing is out of place except for the cot against the wall.

I begrudgingly admit she did a good job tidying up. Even my books have been returned to their rightful spots. She even alphabetized them. I run my fingers down each spine before continuing my circuit around the room.

After about an hour, the pacing loses its appeal. I refresh my phone a dozen times to see if she's messaged me.

Nothing.

Pinching my lips together, I tap my fingers at my side. I feel trapped. Knowing that Helena will be coming at some point this evening has completely destroyed any chance of peace I might have had.

Eventually, I run out of patience. Grabbing a towel, I stalk out of my room. Mumbling under my breath about the female that has me all up in knots, I head into my bathroom and turn the water on full blast. It takes a few moments, but soon, steam is billowing out of the shower. Relief fills me as I shed my clothes, dumping them on the floor.

The moment the hot water hits my skin, tension melts off me in waves. Shutting my eyes, I focus on the steady pounding of water on my back. With every passing moment, I feel more like myself.

She's just a female. You are a pirate. *Don't let her get to you.*

After a few minutes, my mind is clear, and my resolve is firm. I will not let Helena take over my room.

It's easy enough, I reason with myself. *Just be strong. Relegate her to the cot and let her know her place.*

Emboldened by my shower, I dry myself off with the towel before I pull my clothes back on. My resolve to be strong lasts up until I reach the door. The moment I push it open, something *floral* hits my senses.

"What the—"

My voice trails off as I shove open the door and see a large white candle on my nightstand. Its flame is burning bright, casting long shadows on the wall. Helena is sitting cross-legged on my bed, her hair unbound and hanging around her in waves, with a book in her lap. I can't help but notice how she's made herself comfortable in my room.

"What the hell is this?" I ask. Stomping into the room, I glare at Helena. Without even looking up, she messages me.

> Princess: Do you mind? I'm trying to read here.

My eyes feel like they're about to explode out of my head. "Why is there a candle in my room? I don't *like* candles, Helena. They pollute the air."

She looks up at me, her mouth twitching as she sends another message.

> Princess: I've heard that only psychopaths hate candles. They smell good. If you must know, I got this one from storage.

Rubbing my hand through my damp hair, I groan. I don't have the energy for this. I huff, "Fine. The candle stays, but for the love of the gods, will you read on your bed, please?"

She raises a brow, and for a moment, I think she will argue

with me. She inhales sharply as the space between us diminishes before pushing herself to her feet and staring at me.

Clutching the book to her chest, Helena skirts around me. We almost touch. The space in my room was tight before adding the cot, and now it's cramped. The air itself feels electrified. As she moves, our eyes never leave each other. It's as though we are the only two people in the entire world.

It feels like an eternity passes in the blink of an eye as she reaches the cot. My heart is hammering in my chest as I watch her bend down and pull the blanket over herself. Our gazes are still locked, and for a long moment, neither of us moves.

Eventually, Helena drops her eyes and dives back into her book. Despite myself, I am entranced by her every movement. How her lips silently move as she reads, how her fingers trace the path of the words down the pages. It's as though every single letter gets her full attention. Watching Helena read is the most interesting thing I've done all evening.

Realizing I'm staring, I drop down onto my bed and grab my own book off the nightstand. For the next two hours, we read together. The only sound in the room is the flipping of pages, the sound as soothing as the lapping of waves against the ship.

By the time the clock reads 10:00 p.m., my eyelids are growing heavy. I dare a peek at Helena, only to see that her book is lying flat against her chest and her head is resting against the pillow.

Shutting my own novel, I slip off the bed and walk over to Helena, pulling the book off her chest and placing it on the shelf beside her. Drawing up the blanket, I tuck it around her before stepping back. Asleep, Helena looks... peaceful. Calm. Young. And even more beautiful than ever.

Pulling myself away from her, I blow out the candle and turn off the lights before heading into my bed. As sleep draws near, my last thoughts swirl around Helena.

I can't get her out of my head, and for the first time, I don't want to.

16
NOT SO DIFFERENT
HELENA

*T*oday *is going to be a good day.* I repeat the mantra to myself as I walk towards the mess hall to pay Jean Luc a visit. The enticing aroma of breakfast is already spreading through the ship, and my stomach grumbles.

I pass a few of the crew members on the way up. They each glance at me quickly before hurrying away. *Odd.* It's as if I am carrying a hulking sword.

The crew is usually pretty chill when Erik isn't around.

The mess hall has a few stragglers from the morning meal, who quickly clear out upon seeing me.

What the hell?

I pause. This entire situation has got Erik's name written all over it. Clenching my fists, I stalk to the bar and sit down loudly.

Jean Luc appears from the kitchen a few moments later. He sees my expression and grabs a notepad. He still prefers it when I write to him.

"What's up, sweetheart?" he probes gently.

I roll my eyes so hard my under-lids blink involuntarily.

Jean Luc nudges the paper towards me ever so slightly, and I start scribbling as fast as I can.

No one will talk to me. Everyone left when I got here.

The lines around his eyes deepen as he squints slightly while reading the sloppy script. I scribble a hasty *"Erik did this"* underneath. His eyes widen with understanding. He looks back at me.

"Maddie, I think you'll find that you did that all on your own," he says. His voice is gentle, but my nostrils flare. "Love, simmer down. First, everyone is heading upstairs for our weekly PT. Next, think about it for a second: where did you spend the night?"

The cold shock of realization settles in. I stayed in *his* room last night. And everyone knows. News travels on this ship faster than I had ever imagined.

My face flushes, and I tilt my head down to cover myself with my hands. I hadn't considered the consequences of staying with him in his room. Honestly, I was just so grateful to get out of my damned room and away from those nightmares, consequences be damned.

"One of the crew saw you go to his room last night," the cook continues quietly. "It's been all anyone can talk about this morning. They don't trust you."

A silent huff escapes me.

Gods, that makes horrible, terrible sense.

Of course, they are afraid of me. The crew is terrified of him, and now they think we are sleeping together. I let out a loud breath and look up to see that Jean Luc has crossed around the bar. He places his hand around my shoulders and pats lightly. It's a comforting gesture and one I'm not used to.

"This trip will be over soon enough. We don't have much more than a week before our estimated arrival in the Gates of Hell." Jean Luc's familiar, lilting accent comforts me.

He has become a friend.

But I don't want to hide away anymore. I don't want to be written off as the captain's lover... or whore.

In two clumsy movements, I grab the paper and write:

I need to do something to fix this, and I need your help.

He eyes the note and then looks at me warily. "What do you mean?"

The corner of my mouth curls despite my roiling stomach. Clutching the pen, I start writing.

HUMANS TEND to do one of two things in Aranthium; they either worship at the feet of other races, clinging to them for their wealth and power, or hide out. The world is dotted with human settlements where they do gods-know-what. Since coming aboard this ship and reading that same book from the mysterious crew member, Henry, I have learned they have book presses.

The only thing that the Northern Courts care about is that these groups of humans hate us. In the centuries past, there had been a joint effort to weed these little hate-filled groups out and exterminate them. New treaties imposed upon the world have made that illegal.

This was when the Northern Courts separated their government from the rest of the world, built a wall, and took matters into their own hands.

As far as I know, there are no more humans to speak of in the North. Either that, or they have gotten better at hiding.

Living with Erik's crew has been an almost anthropological experience for me. The most unsettling discovery is that humans can crave pain and revenge to the same degree as the Ice Mer.

While they laugh at my jokes and tolerate my presence, it is easy to see that not all of them welcome me into their ranks. And now they think I slept with their captain. I'm sure my presence in Erik's room only confirmed the suspicions that several had the moment I stepped onto this ship.

Today, I will show them what I am capable of. I will use these gods-forsaken legs to carry me to victory. The weeks of strength training in my room will pay off; I will demonstrate how easily I can dismember them limb from limb.

Erik locked himself in his office early this morning. Jean Luc told me he had informed the captain that today would be the crew's weekly PT.

Now, on the flat surface of the deck, I stand barefoot. I'm grateful that some sort of artificial plastic coats the deck instead of wooden planks. It's amusing, really. Such a modern ship for such a dastardly pirate.

Pant legs and sleeves have been cut off my clothes to create acceptable fighting attire. The men already have their own exercise clothes. The smell of warm Lycra mingles with the salt of the sea.

The sun shines overhead with burning ferocity.

A makeshift fighting ring is marked by the crates, and the ship's railing isn't far away. The thrill of such a dangerous setting crackles in my bones like lightning. I am already in the ring, ready to begin.

The rest of the crew listens to Jean Luc's instructions. Some eye me warily; others watch me with scowls or an unspoken hunger.

Oh yes, this will be good.

Anders steps up next as the "first" officer. To be honest, I still don't really understand the ranking situation here... not since Conrad.

For the first time since that night, a cold sweat doesn't

break out on my brow. I'm still not exempt from a reaction, however, and a thirsty rage shrivels my heart. The horror of that night has turned from fear to rage, and it's a welcome switch. Fear is debilitating and can send me running to a cruel man's cabin.

Anger enlivens me and makes me want to rise to my station.

I'll hold onto that anger for the rest of my days.

Anders shoots me an uncomfortable glance as he walks over. He's finished organizing the men. They have been arranged in a row.

"Well-er-Maddie, the way this works—" he starts, but I hold up a hand. They've explained it to me before.

"All right. So," he stalls uncomfortably, "we've paired you with the second engineer, Francois. There are 24 crew members, including the captain. I've been informed he won't be fighting today, and of course, we need the medic on standby. There will be five rounds of pairs until we find the end. Jeffrey will sit out two rounds to fight the last winner. He's the only man ever to beat Erik, so he gets that right."

I nodded, sizing up the hulking man who is standing on the deck with no shirt. He stares at me with a look of indifference.

A short, squat man comes forward. The man, Francois, is not much shorter than I am, actually. But I see exactly what this is. They've sent the weakest among them to gauge my ability.

I let out a silent snarl and glare at Anders.

The short man doesn't seem afraid, although he definitely should be. He seems put out. I narrow my eyes. He doesn't want to be here and doesn't care about the outcome of this fight.

He doesn't anticipate much damage. He will pay for that.

Anders stands to the side of the ring and says, "Remember the rules. No head shots; don't hit hard enough to incapacitate; you win once the other player has been down for more than ten seconds."

I grit my teeth when the men start to count down from five and beat out a drumroll on the crates. My skin is itching to begin.

Silence prevails once the men finish counting down. I allow myself to focus in a way I haven't since the last time I really fought... before Henrick died. The man stares at me. He clearly expects me to make the first move. His arms have come up in a lousy fighting position and he starts circling around the ring. The waves lap loudly against the ship.

Stop playing around, I warn him with my eyes. He doesn't heed me, so I punish the sailor. A few men groan when my left arm hooks right into the man's nose. My arm strikes like lightning, something near impossible with water resistance. The crack is louder than I expected. Underwater, such sounds have layers, traveling at a much slower rate to my ears. Here, I live in the impact.

I grin, cracking my neck.

Francois yells and stumbles back as he grabs at his face. Blood is pouring out faster than he can staunch it. He spits out curses that would make most women blush, biting his tongue when the nastier ones directed at me are about to come to the surface.

The wounded sailor makes a move to exit the ring, but I'm not done. The rules say he has to be down for ten seconds. And I know how much the captain of this ship values rules.

Using my inadequate legs, I sprint over while Francois' back is turned and knock him down, face first. My knee is still pressed against his back when he starts yelling, "Yield! YIELD!"

My mouth curls in disgust. He is weak, and he underestimated me. I stand up, daring the sailors to say a word. I look each one in the eye, letting them see how restless I am, how the fun, silent siren has been replaced with one whose future birthright power could end them all with half a glance.

There is no sound, save the second engineer spitting blood

and grumbling about how "barbaric" these training sessions are as he walks over with the medic.

My blood is pumping through my veins so fiercely, I want to fight again. That was barely a morsel, and I am half-starved. Anders sees the hunger in my eyes, but he shakes his head. I have to force myself to get out of the ring as the next fight starts.

I watch the men, placing silent bets with myself on who will win. I'm almost always right. Except for when I see one of the men who carried me and Erik the night of the storm. The crowd has warmed up, and the cheers cut off his name. He is thin, almost gangly. He appears more academic than warrior.

His brunette hair is cropped and his facial features are sharp in a pleasant way. His smile stretches across his face arrogantly, despite his stature. For some reason, I think of Henry's notes in his worn book. Perhaps this man is him.

My lips quirk up.

When the sailor's opponent, a man corded with far more muscle than him, saunters into the ring, I almost feel bad for him.

And then the lanky sailor beats the much larger man in less than ten minutes by ducking around the ring and jumping on his back. From my semi-secluded place near the crates, I clap slowly. As I stand there, the hairs on the back of my neck prickle. Without turning around, I know a presence that I am beginning to recognize well comes up behind me.

"See something you like?" Erik asks gruffly. "You don't seem like the kind of female to praise subpar fighting."

My hair is tied in a messy bun and the sunlight has been warming my skin, but the sound of Erik's voice slides over me like a cool breeze.

When I don't acknowledge him, Erik continues, "What are you doing here?"

I turn around and raise a brow. His face is unreadable. I turn back around.

"You didn't answer my message..." he says casually, leaning against the crate next to me.

I am still watching the next round when I shrug and pat my empty pockets. A twisted glimmer of satisfaction fills me when I realize he must be staring at my ass.

I'll never know his true reaction because he still doesn't shut up. "Imagine my surprise when I heard the words 'Mer-bitch' outside my door. I mean, what a title."

I clench my fists at the name. The next round finishes, and everyone breaks for twenty minutes to get water or tend to wounds.

Our casual proximity turns awkward as the crowd dissipates. Knowing that everyone thinks we are sharing a bed makes me want to shove Erik away. This isn't going to help the rumors. There is nothing keeping us in the same space, so why haven't either of us moved? Some part of me expects Erik to be mad, to tell me to get below deck, but he doesn't.

In the end, it's me who leaves first. Or tries to, at least.

Erik's hand darts out, grabbing my wrist. I stare at his fingers wrapped around my arm. He follows my gaze, dropping my arm like he's been burned before saying, "I've been wondering when you would finally join in here. You couldn't possibly be the Crown Princess and not have some sort of fighting skills."

Without my phone, I feel helpless. I just smile back at him. Part of me hopes he will go back to his office, especially because I am up first for round two. The thought of him watching me fight feels uncomfortable—intimate, almost.

My luck is shit, though, because the twenty minutes end and Erik and I are both still standing in the same spot. When the man I've dubbed Henry walks by, I flash him a smile. I have high expectations for him now. Erik notices, and he frowns.

That reaction sparks something within me. Is he... jealous?

I turn the thought over in my mind as I get ready to fight again. This time, I've been put up against a man who is much more adept than Francois. This fight lasts more than twenty minutes instead of less than five.

Erik's dark gaze remains on me the entire time. I feel the heat of his gaze when I duck, roll, and punch. He watches my form with blazing intensity. I wish I could stop the fight and scream at him, but giving Erik any more attention would only reinforce the crew's ideas.

My thoughts distract me, and my opponent takes advantage of the situation. He lunges and swipes my legs out from under me. Disgruntled, I land ass-first on the ground. My mouth connects with his forearm on the way down. The crowd cheers while I wipe blood from my split lip.

For the love of Fortuna.

The rage propels me to kick his gut with said legs, and pin him to the ground with my elbow pressed into his sternum. He isn't hostile and smiles up at me while we lay there.

I let out a silent laugh. Erik passes me an alcohol wipe when I exit the ring, and I silently wish for him to go away. I'm getting tired, and he is so aggravating.

The remainder of the round passes quickly.

And then the next one.

Finally, we are in the fourth round. When *Potential-Henry* walks into the space, I grin. Erik watches with a scowl.

After three grueling rounds, I've finally made it to the semi-finals. Only one more fight to go before I face their champion. I have no thoughts of losing now. I *will* win. It's no longer just a want, but a need coursing through me.

I ease into a fighting stance before Potential-Henry, the sweat from previous fights dried against my skin. Soreness makes me wince, but it's not enough to stop me.

The man flashes me a charming smile when the counting is finished and then we are off. The other fights were fueled by my rage, but by now, the anger has cooled enough for me to enjoy the process. The other fights were therapeutic, this one is artistic expression.

We dance around each other, throwing calculated shots. Unfortunately for him, Potential-Henry doesn't have my stamina. He slips up, and doesn't protect his right side well enough. I duck under his arm, and bounce up inches from his face.

"Shit," he whispers as his brown eyes widen, and I land a punch to his chest. He falls and holds his hands up in submission.

This time, the men grunt and cheer their approval. I can't tell if it's from actual acceptance or just because they know I am about to be throttled by Jeffery, the mountain of a man.

They announce another break and I notice Erik has disappeared. Part of me is grateful. His gaze is heavy and unrelenting, causing me to make mistakes.

Jeffery waves at me from across the boat. The medic is tending to the hulking man's broken finger from his last fight. I analyze him. He has gotten more time to rest throughout the day, but I think that injury might just give me enough purchase to win.

The twenty minute break passes quickly, and I walk into the ring first. The scowls and smirks from the men appear in equal quantities throughout the crowd. I ignore them all, and turn back to the ocean. A breeze comes in from the shore and I spread my arms wide, basking in the coolness.

Then the chatter quiets down. Even the breeze seems to still.

"Are you sure—" Anders asks hesitantly.

Before he can continue, he is cut off with a gruff, "Take this.

Jeffery is injured. If he breaks another finger, he will be useless with the masts."

I freeze, drop my arms, and whip around. My breath catches in my throat as I stare.

Erik stands before me, naked save a pair of SummerTec exercise shorts. His body is corded in tan muscle. He looks... good. Really, really good. A dark black tattoo is scrawled across his chest, and there are inked bands on his arms and thighs. They are beautiful, poetic lines that twist together in waves and flowers. Beneath the flowers are skulls, each image telling a different story. I wish I knew each one.

His hands are wrapped with black tape, and that reminds me why we are here. I blink, trying not to ogle him so noticeably. But, the crew sees everything.

Godsdammit.

Erik turns to the men. He chuckles darkly, saying, "Can't let a female win against all of you, can I?" He shakes his head and the men lap up his attention. "Always protecting my crew's honor."

They adore this side of him, I think while crossing my arms. They lavish in his swagger, in his power. He makes them feel like they can win. Maybe that's why they think he's a vigilante.

A familiar, bitter taste fills my mouth. I will not fall victim to his forced charm. My hearing muffles as the crowd finishes chanting their count-down.

Erik is close to me, far closer than any of the other fighters dared get in the beginning.

"Ready, Princess?" he smirks, far too low for anyone else to hear. That sets me off and I lunge forward.

Far too late, I realize I've fallen into his trap. He steps to the side and trips me. I tumble more gracefully than the last time and look up into his shining eyes. The burn in my stomach, thighs, and arms only intensifies. A smirk still ghosts his lips. I roll over and get back onto my feet. Cracking my neck, I switch to being defensive.

I meet his smirk as if to say, *You are going to have to attack this time, asshole.*

He tilts his head. *Message received.*

He comes at me, and I throw another curved punch at his chest. He moves and my arm hooks around his neck, bringing us chest to chest. Less than half a second passes before I shrink back, pulling my arms in tightly to my core once again.

Our audience fades away, and all I see is Erik. This is no longer a fight. This is war. It is a slow and tantalizing battle of wills. Every punch is a caress, every kick a step in a dance only we know. Sweat is pouring down my face and his body glows in the sun.

I refuse to be distracted, but he still manages to duck, grab my legs and pull me into the air. I realize what he intends to do when it's too late. He is already in the perfect position to throw me on the ground flat on my back.

Erik is still fresh, and this is my fifth fight. It's clear he wants to win dirty. I throw my weight around, causing him to kilter over to the side and fall instead. I land on my feet.

He yelps and jumps back up.

The dance continues. Duck, punch, swipe. Duck, punch, kick. We move in threes, like a waltz. The deck is our ballroom, the sun our chandelier. The music of the wind billows around us as we continue to fight.

My chest is heaving now, and air hurts as it comes into my lungs. The anger is returning. It helps me see an opportunity for a quick win. I dance to the back of the ring, putting unwanted space between us.

The captain analyzes me, his brow furrowed. In his face, I see he is trying to understand whether or not he should follow. Before he can decide, I rush forward and run into his shoulder.

He tumbles to the ground with an *oomph*, but not before he can grab me.

We fall together, his head in the crook of my neck and a charged electricity licks my core. My body responds to the nearness of him in a dangerous way. My stomach twists and my skin feels like it's on fire.

I hear a low rumble sound in his throat against my chest as we both lay, heaving. He can feel it, too. The raw, primal energy in the air.

I swallow hard when his mouth presses to the side of my throat. Gasping, I still as his lips open just barely enough to press his teeth into my skin.

He murmurs, "Defeat never tasted so sweet, Princess."

The tickle of his breath along my jaw is light, and yet I can't suppress my shiver. My hand twists in Erik's long hair for a moment before I try to save us both by slamming my other fist into his gut. He pulls back from my neck, roaring in pain and clenching his side as I roll off of him.

I can stand.

I can win this now.

But then I look up and see Anders' face. He looks defeated. This is the price of winning the war. I don't really know how much the crew saw of the sensual bite, but I refuse to destroy Erik's relationship with his men. It seems like it might be the one good thing he has in his life.

Unrolling my body, I lie flat against the ground. I let the crew see my feigned weakness and heaving breaths.

Erik brings himself to his knees and then stands. He stares down at me with so much fire in his gaze, I fear actual flames have begun to lick their way over my skin.

He presses his foot onto my chest and I can't help the jerking motion with which my hand flies up and grasps his ankle. My breath catches as I meet his eyes.

The crowd cheers, happy to see their beloved captain defeat the invading female.

My hand lingers, my fingers brushing his leg hair lightly for a moment. His eyes don't leave mine as he spits out, low and venomous, so only I can hear, "How dare you?"

My legs shift uncomfortably in the aftermath of being so near to him. I smile and let my hand fall away.

17
FIGHT ME
ERIK

Red spots fill my vision as thick and heavy rage rolls through me. I stare at Helena through narrow eyes and clench my teeth. It takes everything I have not to lunge at her and shake her shoulders until her teeth chatter. Force her to fight me again. Tell her I don't accept her defeat.

Instead, I shove down my anger and bite my tongue while enduring slaps of encouragement on my bare back from my men. I listen to the scores of laughter and jeers of male superiority that come from them as they dismantle the ring and get back to work. The crew is jubilant, as though they had beaten Helena themselves.

Happiness is the godsdamned furthest thing I'm feeling, despite glimpsing it this morning with Helena in my bed and my book, nestled next to her. Such a strange, fleeting emotion.

All I can think about is when Jean Luc had informed me the men would be doing their PT like they always did during this time of the month. I had texted Helena, thinking she would respond right away.

When no message came through, I had resigned myself to

working in my office when I overheard one of my sailors talking about the "Mer-bitch". Emerging from my office, I slammed the door shut behind me.

"What has Maddie done, Whitehall?" my voice had been eerily calm.

The sailor had taken one look at my face and tried to back-pedal his comments. "She is fighting the men above deck, Captain."

I ignored how he cradled his arm and the blood leaked from his nose because the knowledge that Helena was above deck had been a beacon, summoning me nearer. When I first saw her standing by the side of the ring, a surge of anger mixed with worry so potent ran through me that I had to physically hold onto the railings to stop myself from pulling her back to our room. What in the gods' names had she been thinking, taking on my crew? They could have killed her.

Then I watched her beat the shit out of one man, then the next. It was... unexpected. Another layer was peeling back from Helena, and she was showing more of herself to me than she ever had before.

I learned something about her today, watching her fight in the ring. There was anger deep within her that called to me. It resonated with the decades-old rage that lived within me. One that I hid from the world. We recognized each other at that moment, and anger bound us together in a way few could understand.

Despite my best efforts, I couldn't tear my eyes away from her as she fought. She might have been the most aggravating woman I'd ever had the displeasure of meeting, but one thing became clear on the deck of my ship today. She was strong. Strategic.

I had ripped off my shirt and wrapped my hands. I *had* to know what it was like to have her sole attention focused on me.

More than that, I wanted to see who would come out on top. To feel her skin once more. I wanted to know whether this tension was just in my head or if she felt it, too. And, for Fortuna's sake, static seemed to crackle between us every time we touched. I was surprised the entire ship hadn't caught on fire. The sun spotlighted her before me, gilding her entire form like pure gold as she moved in tune to the rhythm of my heart.

And then the illusion vanished. She lost to me *on purpose*. The very second I realized what she had done, it was like someone had dumped a bucket of seawater on my head. How *dare* she?

"Captain?" Anders' voice breaks through the fog of my anger. I'm still standing on the deck, staring at nothing. Emptiness takes over, pulling me from the reverie.

"Yes?" I say. My voice is curt and sharp, and I don't do anything to mask my anger.

The sailor shifts on his feet, holding my FaePhone between two fingers like it is going to burn him. I had shoved it at him before the fight. "I thought you might want to know that a message came in for you while you were... indisposed."

For the love of the gods. Is it Helena?

"Why the hell are you looking at my messages?"

Anders' brows raise to the top of his head. The sight would be comical if I wasn't in such a pissy mood. "I-I just," he stutters.

Sighing, I run a hand through my sweaty hair. Anders hands me a towel from the pile, and I start to dry off. I dry my hand on a nearby towel. "I'll deal with that while you make sure the men get back to work."

He nods, handing me my phone. "Right away, Captain Erik."

Grunting a response, I tighten my fist around my phone and head to the shower. If she wants to talk about what happened, then she'll have to wait until I'm ready.

THIRTY MINUTES LATER, I've washed off the sweat from the fight. Pulling on black sweatpants, I grab a plain, black t-shirt and yank it over my head. I chug a glass of water before collapsing into my office chair.

"Rip off the bandaid." I give myself a little pep-talk and set the glass down. Unlocking my phone, there is a message for me, but not one that I was expecting.

> Unknown: Update on the cargo.

A pit forms in my stomach as I stare at the text, reading and re-reading it. Four words. That's all it takes for reality to come crashing down. I've already made up my mind. I won't be doing what the King is asking of me. But... if I don't play along for a little longer, there's a chance he sends his Elite after us.

And that, more than anything else, is the thing that has caused me so much inner turmoil. Those ancient, high-speed swimmers were proven through blood and brutality. They'll tear me to shreds and kill my entire crew in retribution for my actions. My sailors' faces flash before my eyes as I stare at the message. They are my responsibility. Their lives matter, even if mine doesn't.

When the King finds out that Helena is gone, I hope my crew will have disappeared like fog on a sunny day. I will stay behind. They have a much better chance without me and my Fortuna-cursed life.

> Me: The cargo will be disposed of before we reach land.

I press 'send', and almost instantly, three dots appear on the screen. Dropping the FaePhone on my desk, I stare at it. My back is stiff as my eyes are glued to the three dots. One minute ticks by, then two, before a short burst of vibration shakes my desk.

> Unknown: You have one week. Send a photo of the body and destroy this phone.

There's no use responding to the message, so I toss the phone on my desk before banging my head against my hands.

This entire day has been a shit show. Between the fight on the deck and now *this*, it's just been a reminder that my life is short. The sad reality is... I probably won't even live to see the end of the month. My fate was sealed the moment I saw that damned Mer prince.

If only I had known that his sister would torment me as well. As if on cue, someone knocks on my door. The sound reverberates in my skull.

"I'm busy," I shout.

There's no response, but the knob slowly turns. Irritation rises in my throat but is stifled as a white napkin is thrust into the room and waved about. Lithe gray fingers hold onto the fabric. My phone dings and I snatch it up.

> Princess: I come bearing chocolate beignets and coffee. Truce?

Instantly, my whole mood changes. If I'm going to end up in Tartaro anyway, why the hell not indulge a little? Even men on death row are usually offered one delicious last meal. I could get over my anger if it meant touching her soft skin again. Even the thought has a pleasant warmth running through me.

"Come on in, Princess."

Moments later, the door swings wide open. Helena holds up a finger before bending down and giving me a prime view of her glorious, heart-shaped ass. I forget to be mad about her throwing the fight.

She's changed and is standing barefoot in the hallway, wearing a pair of form-fitting leggings and a soft gray t-shirt. She must have showered after me because her hair is in a wet knot on top of her head.

There's a tray resting on the floor, laden with a coffee pot and two mugs. The platter of promised beignets sits in the middle. I remember the manners my mother pounded into me before she died. My chair scrapes on the floor before I hurry over to the door. "Let me, Helena."

She stares at me, raising a brow before stepping back and gesturing towards the tray. Bending down, I make sure to take my time and give her a show. It's heavy, and the aroma of the coffee is enticing.

Placing the tray on the table, I straighten. The hairs on the back of my neck tingle, and I know Helena's standing right behind me. If I turn around, I could wrap my arms around her and pull her flush against me. She would gasp silently, her cheeks would flush, and I would kiss her until her fingers wove through my hair.

Instead of stealing the moment, I stop myself and say, "So, you threw a fight. *You lied.* Didn't think I could handle losing to a woman?"

A long beat of silence passes before my phone vibrates.

> Princess: You needed the win more than me.
> Your men needed you to win.

"Did you even consider that I wouldn't want you to do it?" I whisper.

> Princess: I honestly thought it was a good idea.
> I overheard some of the men talking.

"And... ?" I'm not even phased by the strange conversations we have anymore. Seconds later, her response appears.

> Princess: The men were talking about us.

That catches my attention. Turning around, she's still so close. The image capturing her lips with mine passes through my mind again. What's one more mistake? I'm already going to the deepest, darkest circle of hell, and my self-control is waning. I take a step forward, closing the distance until our lips are hovering above each other. My voice is quiet, "What are you talking about, Helena?"

> Princess: They think we're sleeping together.

The image is sweet. Humans and sirens were compatible, and we would both walk away from that night happy and satisfied. I would make her pant, and she would scratch my back.

My mind races. I told everyone she was off-limits. I've never messed around with a female in front of them; we've always been focused on the work. Killing people who need to be killed, taking what other people need.

I have rules. They know that—and they shouldn't be saying shit about me.

I don't realize I've said the words aloud until my phone vibrates. I step back, and glance down at it. It's shocking how good she is at texting without looking.

> Princess: Well, I don't think they trust me.

Rubbing my hand over my face, I exhale. It has been imperative for my crew's own safety that they don't know why she's here. I can't change that. Regret that I have put so many people in this position pulses through my veins.

There is something else below the bitterness that I can't quite put my finger on. But it makes all my muscles tighten as I think of anyone degrading her. I can't help it—I am protective of her.

Sliding my phone back into my pocket, I raise my gaze to meet hers. It's as though all the air has been sucked out of the room. Raising a hand, I watch as my fingers brush Helena's cheek. Her skin is as soft as my forbidden dreams had promised it would be. She leans into my fingers, pressing herself into my hand as a small, soundless sigh leaves her mouth.

"Is it so bad, the idea that you might be with me?" I ask. My voice is gruff, and I draw near to the female I had once resolved to kill.

Helena's breath catches as her hands fist together in my shirt. She watches me for a long moment, her pink eyes wide while a decision flits through them.

I wonder when I've become so in tune with Helena that I'm able to understand her facial expressions just as she closes the distance between us. My heart is pounding in my chest, my lungs tightening as we draw nearer to each other.

Determination darkens Helena's eyes, and I smile. They're a swirling fuchsia when she pushes herself onto her toes.

Before I can do more than inhale, her lips press into mine. She is forceful and warm and utterly feminine. She tastes exactly how I thought she would. Like salt and chocolate. My new favorite flavor.

Moaning, I wrap my hand around the back of her neck, pulling her against me. She softens even further in my arms, melting into me. We are a tangle of tongues and teeth, my hands sliding down her back and around her ass. She bucks when I give a little squeeze. Then she bites my lip just hard enough to hurt.

I'd been wrong—even in my dreams, Helena didn't taste this good.

Soon, too soon, she draws away from me. Emptiness rushes in to take her place. She watches me, her eyes crinkling with silent laughter moments before vibrations rush through my leg. They jolt me back to reality.

> Princess: Always promises with you.

A chuckle rises up within me, turning into a belly laugh before I draw Helena against myself once more.

Her lips are addicting. She is better than coffee, podcasts, and anything else I've ever enjoyed. For her, I will throw out all the rules. I will destroy anything that stands between us. Right here and now, I vow to myself that I will enjoy every moment of my life right until her father kills me.

18
I DON'T KNOW HOW TO DO THAT
HELENA

P*raise Fortuna.* That is the first thought in my mind when the morning rays filter in through Erik's window, bathing us in sun-soaked joy. I stretch, and feel the weight of Erik's leg wrapped over my hip. He holds me tight, as though he is afraid I will leave him.

When I think of the night before, my blood rushes so loudly in my ears I can barely hear his breathing behind me. He had kissed me so deeply, so passionately and I had kissed him back. I *bit* him. It was as good as being laid naked before him.

Except, the moment his hand found its way beneath my shirt, I had frozen. All the ease and passion I had been feeling earlier had dissipated, leaving me a statue. My mind had known that Erik wasn't Conrad, that I wasn't in danger—at least, not in the same way. But my body cared little for my brain's rationality. I had turned from flame to Ice, and I had shaken while I cried in his arms.

He had pulled me against his chest. It was as if Erik had known what was running through my brain. The problem was... he didn't really know. How could he?

His eagerness ignored my inexperience. Romance had always been off the table for the King's daughter. Surely Erik had an inkling of what King Phelix was like. But, how could he know that I was truly afraid of my father's wrath? I'd never even been on a date. If I had slept with someone, what little worth my father saw in me would have been swept away by the vicious eddies of the ocean.

Even thinking about it now causes me to become paralyzed in terror.

Inch by inch, I peel Erik's arm away from me and roll out from under his leg. He is so peaceful, so deep in his sleep that he doesn't even stir. I run a mental finger over the tattoos scrawled over his chest. In the early morning light, they look even more intriguing than they did on the deck.

Looking at him, watching him, fills me with longing. It tugs at my heartstrings, and *almost* makes me want to stay.

Almost.

But it is foolish to throw a kingdom away for a man. If my father finds out that I was ever here, he might just have me assassinated, and give my crown to Hallie just to spite me. Besides, who's to say that Erik won't use last night against me? He knows my greatest weakness and that terrifies me. It almost renders everything else void that we've been through because he is a man and he can hurt me.

I tug my sweater over my shirt and pad upstairs to the kitchen. Jean Luc is already cooking breakfast. I exhale a mouth full of the savory-scented air. Gods, he is a good cook.

"Maddie," he calls when he pops out from the door to the kitchen.

I tense, unsure how to not be awkward in this situation. Finding no better course of action, I cast him a tentative wave.

His expression isn't stern, but it's a far cry from the usual friendly smile he gives me. He looks pensive. "Maddie, I want what's best for you. And I know what those men said affected you. I just don't think it was the right decision to beat half of them within an inch from death."

I cross my arms defensively.

"Ah, my dear," he rests his elbows on the bar. "You really do remind me of my wife. She was always so convinced that she had to earn respect from every person who looked down on her."

My eyes turn to the floor and I consider leaving. I really don't want to hear what he has to say.

"She was wrong then, and you are wrong now," he says. "You do not earn the respect of those who aren't fit to lick your boots. You leave them be. Let them live their miserable, bitter lives. Otherwise, you lose what is so precious about you—your spark, your vitality. My Morna didn't learn that lesson until it was too late. But you... you still have a chance to change the way your life is going. Listen to me, Maddie. You are better than them. Let their words roll off your back. It's not worth it."

It's still just the two of us in the mess hall, and I feel tears pricking in my eyes. The urge to toss myself on the wooden laminate floor like a crumpled-up piece of paper sounds better by the second.

How does Jean Luc know so much? He seems to know exactly how I'm feeling all the time. How can he ever understand that my entire life had been spent trying to earn the approval of a man I wouldn't hesitate to decimate in real life? King Phelix is the worst sort of being, but he is still my father. Somewhere in the hundred years of lectures on the importance of family, that much had stuck in my brain.

Between last night and this morning, I am feeling too vulnerable. It makes me want to start hitting people or stabbing them.

My webbed hand flies up just as Jean Luc opens his mouth to

speak once more. Hurt flashes in his eyes at my dismissal just as I turn around and stomp up the stairs. The fresh, salty air invigorates me, and I no longer feel like the walls are closing in.

I wander to a secluded spot on the deck, near where the fighting took place yesterday. I am surrounded by cargo, a small pocket of peace just for me. The feeling of the cool metal against my skin grounds me. The ocean, which usually stretches out in every direction, is blocked straight ahead. The water is more choppy here, behaving like a lover scorned.

Not for the first time, I think about how I will be the one to command it soon enough. When I take my father's crown, the birthright power will flow through me and irrevocably connect me to the sea.

I am the granddaughter of the old gods. But even still, they hated my father after the rebellion. They limited him like a dolphin on a leash. Many consider the Ice Mer's kingdom too large... but it is a mere shadow of what it once was. I was not yet born when the rebellion took place. Perhaps, if I do well with Uncle Aidoneus, the gods will bestow me with the full rights meant to be endowed to the Merfolk crown.

The early morning sunlight is fading as more and more mist billows up from the water. An unexpected chill sweeps across the waves and bites into my hands and feet.

And then the mists curl in obedience to the wind. It's as if the waters want me to follow them—to show me something.

I suck in a breath as the first view of the Gates of Hell fills my vision. The jagged black mountains split the thick, gray fog and threaten to pierce the heavens like the ancient weapons of warmongers.

Sweat collects in my palms, and a tremor starts in my knees. It's just as the story says. The gods only leave this region alone because they fear *him*. They would be fools not to. The King of the Daemons lives there—the man who single-handedly decides the fate of us once we die. Second in power only to the King of the Angels. Both uncles whom I have never had the pleasure of meeting.

"There you are," a deep voice says. The timbre of it makes the hair stand up on my arms. It is the voice that accompanied me in hot kisses and feverish dreams.

Fixing my face into a playful mask, I turn around. I have no desire for Erik to see my fear once again. Not again. I whip out my phone and take a picture of Erik scowling at me. The smile that it evokes is genuine.

"Why did you leave?" Erik asks. His voice is soft, something I only ever see between us. "I missed you."

I swallow hard and the same fears from before bubble to the surface. I've let him in too far. He can hurt me worse than anyone else. He watches me as I type on the phone.

> IF YOU KNEW HOW TO PLEASE A WOMAN, YOU MIGHT ALREADY KNOW.

My stomach flips, hoping he doesn't sense my false bravado as he reads the message. I hate how I can feel so torn between pushing him away and pulling him close.

Erik's face clouds when he reads my words, and I am left in awe for the second time in moments. Half-concealed by the mist, he looks like a water wraith sent to drag me into the depths of the sea. My scowl falls away. Looking like that—tall, dark, and handsome—I might just go with him willingly.

"Ah, Princess. You wound me," he whispers. He steps closer as I press myself harder into the railing. In a way that only Erik can, he puts his hands on either side of me and leans in. I retreat, my back bending over the rail. Heat spreads through my core and I am desperate for him to touch me again. Traitorous body. "You have no idea what I am capable of."

My toes curl. Every inch of my skin tingles in anticipation.

I've never felt so aroused, so alive.

End it, I remind myself. But all thoughts evaporate with the space between us as he draws me in. When his lips meet mine, my brain empties of all rational thought. We are lost in each other, kissing in the fog.

The protective cloak of the mists makes me abandon all semblance of self-control, and grab at him with the same force that he grabs at me. Something hits the ground with a *thud,* but it's soft enough that I can't bring myself to care.

I want more, *and* I want to run. I want to dive into the water and extinguish the fire Erik has lit inside of me. I want to burn for eternity with him by my side. He makes me *want.* He makes me feel powerful. Power and strength overcome loneliness, giving him more power than I should.

A silent giggle escapes my lips as I imagine changing Erik's contact picture to the mist wraith shot from moments before. His new name would be "Pyromaniac."

Erik draws back when he feels my laugh on his lips. "What?" he asks. A smile tugs at the corners of his mouth and amusement glitters in his eyes.

How in the nine circles of hell am I ever going to walk away from this?

Our lips barely brush against each other again when a shout breaks the silence.

"Captain?" Anders calls. "Has anyone seen Erik?"

With lightning speed, the captain steps back and straightens his clothes. I am left there with frizzy hair, and my sweatshirt twisted around in a weird way.

I try to fight it, but I touch my fingers to my swollen lips. His eyes follow the movement as he says breathlessly, "Coming!"

"Captain?" Anders asks again.

"I said 'coming', man," Erik calls back, vigorously tucking in the shirt I had untucked moments before.

"Right, it's just, we are nearing the port and the water's riddled with rocks. We can't find the map of the larger rocks," Anders says.

Erik pulls at his cropped hair and lets out a guttural sound. "I told you: look in the drawers on the left of my desk. It should be in the bottom drawer."

Just like that, Erik disappears in the mist, and the voices fade. I am left alone on the deck of his ship, staring at my foreboding future.

But, even though I am terrified, I cannot deny that there is an undercurrent beneath the fear. As if the way to my uncle's tower is paved in gold-gilded destiny, I *know* that is where I am meant to be. The Fates are known for being impossible to understand, but they are guiding me now.

I can only trust that I will not end up dead at the bottom of my beloved sea. Either by the hand of my human lover or malicious family. When I make to leave my position by the railing, my foot connects with something and the object slides across the polished deck. I look down and find Erik's FaePhone at my feet.

Hmm. That must've been what fell.

When I pick it up, the motion makes the screen light up. My hand flies to my throat when I am greeted with an artistically taken picture.

It's a picture of me... sleeping in Erik's bed.

Shit. No no no no.

I unlock his phone to take down the picture. I don't want anyone to see this. My fingers fumble across the glass. Before I can go back, the screen changes. I find myself in the messaging app.

My eyes scan the thread between Erik and "Unknown."

My vision tunnels as I read each word. Heat envelops me, pounding in my ears and burning my throat. Cargo.

What in Fortuna's hell is this?

He thinks he can exact justice on me like those people he thinks he's helping. I am going to rip out Erik's throat and watch as life leaves those dark, stormy eyes.

19
YOU BETRAYED ME
ERIK

Yanking the drawer so hard it comes off the track, I pull out the cursed map.

"Here," I say. My voice is gruff as I shove the map at Anders. "Right where I said it was."

"Sorry, Captain," the sailor starts, but I push past him. I don't want to hear his excuses right now. Not when Helena and I were finally getting somewhere on the deck, only to be interrupted again.

The night before, all tension had waned from my body as Helena's webbed fingers left a trail of goosebumps along my back. Even thinking about how she had traced my collar bones with her lips causes my heartbeat to pick up. All I had wanted was to get closer to her—eliminate every inch of damned space that still existed between us. We had fallen asleep in each other's arms, and my chest had felt like an ever-expanding universe. I was making room for her in my heart.

Imagine my surprise when I woke and realized she had slipped out of our bed before I woke. *Our* bed.

Shaking my head, I run my hands through my hair. When did

things become *ours*? I don't do *ours*. Cursing under my breath, I shove my way into the corridor. This whole situation has become such a huge mess, and I don't know which way is up. I never used to feel things like this. I never used to feel much at all. And that was the way I liked it. So, I took a picture of her sleeping. It was a spur-of-the-moment idea. Something spontaneous.

I don't do spontaneous. Now, in the light of day, I am wondering if she will hate it. She was angry enough with the idea that my men thought we were together.

And that thought, the reality of our situation, is like a bucket of cold seawater dumped over my head. It extinguishes the fire beneath my skin instantly. Some semblance of control grabs ahold of me. I can't let Helena pull away, not over something as stupid as a picture. Reaching for my phone, I wonder where she is. If she'll let me kiss her again.

Gods, that would be marvelous.

I check one pocket, then the next. By the third, I am downright panicking. My heart is pounding in my chest, my hands growing clammy as my search turns up no results.

Shit. Where is it?

I know I had my phone with me when I left my cabin this morning, but now...

The deck.

My stomach twists into knots as I lurch off the wall. I become frantic as I rush towards the deck, shoving past my crew as I take the stairs three at a time. In the back of my mind, I hear the men talking to me, but I ignore them.

If someone else finds it first, it would definitely upset Helena.

If the Ice Mer King found it... I shake my head, pushing the thought aside. Gods, why did I have to be so idiotic?

I try to calm down. Maybe the gods are with me, and my phone fell into the sea. That would be a stroke of luck.

Throwing open the doors onto the main deck, I careen forward at the same moment that a large wave rocks the boat. Grabbing onto the nearest railing, I turn and sweep my eyes over the deck. I don't see Helena anywhere.

Come to think of it, not a single thing looks out of place. Maneuvering around the crates strewn about the deck, I walk past several sailors as they shout at each other.

"Hold steady..."

"Wait!"

"... starboard..."

Ignoring the men, I crouch where Helena and I were standing not twenty minutes ago.

My phone is not there. Everything looks perfectly normal. Scurrying around on my hands and feet, I lift ropes and check under canvas tarps.

Nothing.

This could either be very good or very bad.

Knowing my luck, it's probably the latter. Sitting back on my knees, I visually sweep the area one more time. Still no sign of the phone.

Just as I get back on my feet, footsteps approach from behind. I stiffen. When no one speaks, I clench my jaw, and slowly turn around.

Instead, my eyes widen as the scent of seawater fills my nose, moments before a flash of blue and purple hair fills my vision. Then, a loud *crack* sounds as a fist slams into my face. Stumbling back, I wipe the back of my hand across my throbbing mouth. It comes away red. Raising my clenched fists, I shake my head.

"What are you doing, Helena?" I hiss her name under my breath, dodging as a right hook comes for my face.

Her pink eyes are bright with fury as she ignores my question, barreling into me. We crash into a crate, the wood splintering beneath us. The force of impact forces us apart, and she rolls away from me on the deck.

"Stop it," I whisper-yell, but she doesn't listen. "Did you find my phone?"

She nods, narrows her eyes, and then rushes at me. Helena drives her fist into my side, barely missing my kidney. My body twists left, but she just gets angrier. If she could talk, she would be screaming by now.

The crew surrounds us, and a few men start shouting. I ignore them. My focus is solely on the female in front of me. My crew's words are muffled as though they are underwater.

Helena relentlessly lunges at me again and again.

Just like before, we dance across the deck, but this time it isn't for practice. She is furious, and there is only one thing I can think would cause her to act like this. Over and over, I block her hits, my fists clenched as she alternates between jabs and kicks.

"Let's talk about this," I beg, raising my arm to block her punch. "I don't want to hurt you." *As if I could.*

She shakes her head, her eyes flashing as she swings out her legs. I jump aside, but I'm not quite fast enough to evade her kick. Her foot lands in my stomach and I wheeze, doubling over at the impact.

"Helena, please, let me explain," I hold up a hand, trying to catch my breath, but she completely ignores me. "You're mad about rumors, right? Look, I took the picture because you were just so beautiful. I'll delete it, I promise. It was a mistake."

She reaches behind her, her mouth pressed into a grim line as she pulls something long and silver out of the waistband of her pants. My eyes bulge as I realize what it is. Instinctively, I take a step back to keep a healthy distance between us. I had resigned myself to being killed by the Ice Mer King's men. But this. This was something I *didn't* see coming.

"Captain," Anders' shouts, his voice sharp and clear in the misty air. "Are you all right?"

I shake my head, keeping my gaze locked on Helena's. Her entire body is vibrating as anger leaks out of her pores, but she doesn't try to hit me again. "Get the hell out of here."

"Are you sure?"

I twist, meeting his eyes for a second. "Leave," I bark.

That split second costs me. I swing back around, my fists raised, but there is nothing but empty air in front of me. I tense, but before I can do more than straighten my back, a hand locks around my neck. Helena yanks me against her, her forearm jabbing into my throat, and I put my hands up in the air.

Helena is much stronger than anyone—including myself—has ever accounted for. She walks us back, her arm firmly around me, and I claw at her.

"Helena, please," I choke out as my airway tightens. "Listen to me."

Her arm is trembling, but she doesn't stop. With each second that ticks by, I struggle to breathe.

"I don't want you to get hurt," my voice is raspy as my vision begins to blur. "If you kill me, you'll die." She doesn't know about the deal. About what her father has planned. Helena is safer with me, but she refuses to answer, tightening her grip. I try to wrench away before the last drops of air leave my body.

"Is this about the picture?" I try one more time.

Helena stiffens, her grip loosening for one blessed moment. Gasping, I draw in deep breaths of air. Tilting my head back, I watch as she shakes her head back and forth, seething.

I rack my mind, trying to remember what else could be on the phone besides the picture. It's not like I have a lot on there. Besides the ship, I basically don't have a life.

Running down a mental list of what she could possibly have

found, I try to pull her arm off my neck. It isn't as tight as it was, but it's still there. The crew is watching us, ready to attack.

Podcasts, texts from the crew and...

Gods damn it all.

"Wait," I pant, my heart pounding as it strains to keep me alive, "did you see my messages?"

For a long moment, there is no response. I wonder if she even heard me as her grip tightens once more on my neck. It is tighter this time. Worse than before. The blade glimmers in her other hand, and I know this is it.

Helena's pink eyes are filled with fury as she nods once. It's as though the bottom of the ship has fallen out from under my feet. Suddenly unsteady, I wobble while I shut my eyes for one brief moment. I don't pray to any gods. They won't hear my prayers, anyway. My lungs are tightening and black spots appear before my eyes as each breath comes further and further apart. I won't last much longer now.

"Helena," I whisper, "I can explain. Please."

Suddenly, the pressure is gone. Gasping, I drink in deep breaths of air as oxygen rushes into my lungs. Twisting around, I stare at the woman who will be the death of me. She is panting just as much as I am, the knife still firmly in her grip. I take one step back, then two.

Around us, my sailors are on standby. "I told you all to leave," I order in a stern voice. They do as they're told. When they've moved far enough away, I reach out a hand to Helena. "Can we talk?"

She stares at me, her brows raised. I don't know why she doesn't lunge again. I can hear the unspoken words hanging in the air. *You're talking now, aren't you?* The fact that she hasn't stabbed me yet is a good sign, and I take it as permission to continue.

"I didn't have a choice. I'm sorry," I repeat, feeling like the words are inadequate.

Helena waves the blade in the air as she crosses her arms in front of her chest. The blade glistens in the sunlight. Her very aura is menacing as fury radiates off her in waves.

"This would be easier if you put the knife away," I venture, trying to get her to calm down. In response, she simply takes a step closer to me. "Or not," I say, backing up into the railing. "It's okay. Let's just talk. Can you give me back my phone?"

She huffs, reaching into her pocket and tossing the phone at me. I barely catch it before it flies over the edge of the ship. Flipping it over in my hands, my fingers brush up against broken glass.

"What the..." My voice trails off as I take in the state of my phone.

The once-pristine screen is completely covered in dozens of fractures. The glass is rippled, as though it's been stabbed repeatedly with a knife.

Just as I'm about to toss the broken phone into the sea, it dings. It's a miracle it still works. My heart cracks as I read the name through the shattered screen.

> Helena hates Erik: I read everything. You have two minutes to explain.

I tighten my grip on the phone. My skin stings, and I look down to see a trail of blood dripping down from my right hand. A ragged exhale leaves me as I raise my gaze to hers, ignoring the sting from my cut.

"You're right. Your father wanted me to... take care of you, but I've already decided I am not going to do it. I didn't tell you because..." my voice trails off. I sigh, running my prosthetic hand through my hair.

Behind me, the crew is shouting orders as we slow down.

Beyond the ship, buildings are beginning to appear out of the fog. My heart pounds as we draw near to the ports of Lethe.

Swallowing, I take a step towards Helena. She eyes me warily as I continue, "I didn't tell you because I didn't know how, Princess. At first, it was because I was trying to put distance between us. But then, you forced your way into my small, orderly life. You've ruined everything in the best way. And now... I can never go back. I decided not to kill you, please believe me."

A moment passes, then two.

> Helena hates Erik: No.

My heart drops into my stomach, and Helena shoves the knife back into her waistband. She snatches the phone from my grasp before launching it into the air. We both watch it fall in a smooth arc before it lands in the water with a splash.

"Helena." I reach for her, but she turns around and sprints across the deck. For a moment, it is as though I am frozen in place. The sailors stop and gawk at her, their expressions matching mine as she grabs onto the railing.

The moment her hand connects with the metal railing, the spell is broken.

"Wait," I call out, running across the deck towards her. My feet slide, but I keep going. "Helena!"

Pulling herself over the railing, Helena turns around and makes a rude gesture before falling over the edge of the boat.

"No!" I shout. My breath catches in my throat as I rush to the edge of the deck. My crew stares at me. I am blinking rapidly, and my neck and shoulders are so tight that I can feel tendons pop out. There are still at least ten feet between us and the dock, but the water is still. Unmoving.

Almost as though she didn't fall into it.

I stay there for several minutes more, staring but no longer seeing. I tear my gaze away from the water, and my eyes sweep over the docks. Crowds of sailors and merchants swarm the port. An Angel with stark white wings wearing a black suit holds a clipboard as Mer, Were, humans, Angels and Daemons all hurry about the damp cobblestones. I take note of the pointy ears on beings that almost look human.

The sounds of the city grow louder by the second as we approach the dock master.

Running to the end of the ship, I grip the railing and I lean over the edge. The stench of unwashed bodies, overripe fruit, and smoke fills my nostrils. Below, workers rush to help secure *The Black Rose*.

But I'm not watching them. I'm looking far off in the distance, where a flash of blue and purple hair weaves through the gray streets. I grasp the railing, my legs giving out as relief surges through me.

Seconds later, she's gone.

PART THREE

20

LETHE
HELENA

I didn't kill Erik.

A feeling twisted low in my stomach, warning me I would regret that decision for the rest of my life. I should've killed him... but when I saw his face, all I could think about was how much he made me feel safe despite being ordered to kill me.

By my father.

Could Erik fake such gentle protectiveness? He's so damn confusing.

My vision blurs, and my body aches while I walk along the docks of Lethe, the capital city of the Gates of Hell. Most of Aranthium looks at places like Lethe or Olimpie with awed fascination. They come to lay their wills at the feet of the two demigod children of the Elementals: Aidoneus and Raphael.

My uncles.

The air has changed to something more sulphuric than what the blessed ocean had provided during my passage across the sea.

I hurry across metal-reinforced wooden walkways and into

the mess of buildings. The simple variety of people makes me feel disoriented and paranoid. Bulky Weres walk side by side with lanky vampires. A fortune-telling Warlock sits on the corner with his Fae partner. Even humans walk freely up and down the streets.

I silently curse every single one for their ability to live leisurely lives. *Their* fathers aren't trying to have them killed.

The different smells, body shapes, and skin colors overwhelm my senses. My front teeth dig into my lip as I consider how sheltered my life has been. I have never left Ice Mer territory. In fact, save for Hallie's estate in Liqure or Erik's ship, I have never been anywhere.

A Mer with legs is absolutely not a common sight, yet I am warranted no more than a few stray glances. I am not news. I am no one to these people. The thought fills me with a new sense of determination as the ground under my wet, bare feet changes from wood to concrete.

I break free from a particularly aggressive crowd of people crossing the street like a fish breaking from its school. Such a fish would die in nature... community is needed. But these people are not my community, and I am seeking safety from my own family.

The buildings are passing by in a blur as I desperately try to walk downtown. Everything else is secondary to getting to the historic square where my Uncle Aidoneus's tower rises high enough to commune with his brother, the King of Angels. I can only hope that the family I have never met will take care of me better than those who raised me.

This city is the perfect combination of the ancient world and contemporary life. The twelve-story high rises stand tall next to ancient temples and government buildings. If I look hard enough, I can recognize our land's five significant historical periods.

Above me, Angels are swirling through the gray clouds. Their wings are all variations of metallic colors from bronze to brilliant pure gold. I am lost in the clouds with them when I run face-first into a being in front of me.

The sensation of leather snakes across my cheek as I pull back. Enormous black wings fill my vision, and my jaw drops like a dumbfounded child.

"Sorry about that," the Daemon male says with a smile. His hair is cropped short, and he is wearing fashionable athletic garb.

My jaw snaps shut, and I glance awkwardly to the left. I shake my head. He doesn't stop staring.

He says, "It's been a long time since I've seen a Mer with legs. I didn't know your folk still did that with those new aqua chairs."

I shrug, feeling more uncomfortable by the minute.

"Oh! No voice, right?" The corners of his red eyes crinkle as he smiles. I can't believe he knows this.

This is normal? I desperately want to ask him questions. I'd love to know about an aqua chair and where I could find my uncle's tower, so I nod encouragingly.

"Got it. Believe it or not, I've worked with many of your kind. My name is Toth'toros, but you can call me Todd." Todd extends his black hand between us, and I stare at it with a raised eyebrow. He lets out a laugh, "Come on, legs. It's your lucky day, I'm one of the least shitty Daemons in the King's employ."

At the mention of my uncle, I grab his hand and shake hard.

"Och," he says with humor gleaming in his eyes. "Take it easy, Siren."

I frown at the use of such a violent name. I don't want him to get the wrong idea. When he starts walking again, I jog alongside him. He is easily three heads taller than me.

"So, in the ancient days, the Merfolk used to give up their voices to follow their lovers on land. I can't say I know exactly what those relationships looked like, but I know that they used to use the walls of their home to write their messages. I think a few of them are still preserved in one of King Hades' museums."

Get to the point! I want to yell at the Daemon. Is he so arrogant that he is content to converse with himself? Or maybe he is just being polite. It is honestly hard to tell.

Without finding another solution, I grab his elbow, and he stops. When he looks at me, he appears confused. I mimic writing in the air vigorously.

The confusion persists. He's like a giant gulper shark. My hands fist and rest on my hips as I consider stealing his phone from his overly tight shorts. I can make out their outline from here. Erik would never wear shorts so casually in public.

I shake my head, pushing thoughts of that traitor away.

"Oh!" he says at last. "You need something to write with."

I nod as a laugh fills the air and grates against my patience. Todd says, "I was considering carving some symbols into one of the older buildings."

I just stare back at him.

He continues, "That's why I told you that story."

My hand flies up and smacks loudly against my forehead before I can stop it. I try to apologize with flailing gestures, but he smiles and passes me the phone.

THANK YOU, AND SORRY.

My hands are clumsy and sweaty, making my typing take a veritable eternity.

I NEED TO GET INTO KING HADES' TOWER.

As he reads, his expression tightens, and he pockets the phone. "Nope."

Then he's walking once again.

His bluntness startles me, and I'm back to jogging at his side.

"Sorry, legs. I can't let some *rando* near the King. Who do you think you are?" he asks. His voice is much more guarded. At this point, I am close to running. I want to shout at him and tell him exactly who I am and what he can do to himself for talking to me like that.

But he is simply too fast. He disappears into the thick, motley crowd of beings ahead of us, and I am left behind panting.

The worst part is that he is right. I have no birthright power, no token or seal from my family and no voice. Who in their right mind would let me near a king looking the way that I do?

Defeat bubbles up inside me, and I follow my short shadow. Hours pass, and the clouds darken as night falls. The violet darkness mixes with the neon lights, and a coldness chills me to my bones. My clothes are barely dry, and I have no place to sleep.

My stomach growls, and the reality of my desperate situation crashes over me. I am useless. I am lost. I am unwanted.

If Erik were here, he could vouch for me.

The unbidden thought gets pushed far down under all of my other feelings. Erik betrayed me. He is dead to me. The only person who can save me now is myself.

After hours of walking down narrow streets, open air caresses my skin and causes it to pebble.

I look up to find an enormous square. My eyes widen as I look to the middle of the open space and see the expansive statue depicting the gods with the King's Tower in the back. The massive obsidian building comes to a point which is shrouded by clouds. Black, crystal windows add to the architectural beauty of the place, but no light shines through. Even in the darkness, it draws the eye.

It is ominous and radiates pure, deadly power.

Please, gods. Do whatever mystical stuff you do... give him a nudge to come and find me.

No response comes. Serious effort goes into tearing my eyes away from the tower, and I only make it a short distance before my gaze returns to the statue. Even in the evening, the city is bustling with life. I move forward with an inconspicuous crowd and head to the sculpture. The closer I get, the more I am impressed with the white rock that seems to glow from within.

The stone is alive, somehow. It calls to me from across the distance, but I am sure I have never seen it before.

The bottom level depicts male and female Mer. My brows furrow. They are huge, presumably some of the gods I am descended from. On their backs is a large, round shield where another group of gods and goddesses stand. Their forms are significantly smaller. Instead of bearing this group with their backs, they lift them easily with their hands.

Tour guides buzz around us, their tinny microphones projecting their annoying voices throughout the square.

"You there, sir Were, what do you see when you look at the gods?" one of the guides asks. She is a human woman with short black hair.

"Amazing," he breathes. "They are Were!"

The woman smiles thoughtfully. She says, "Not quite," just as a dozen other people chime in, swearing that the gods are of their own species.

"Quiet, folks, quiet. It is a magical enchantment. King Hades has left us with reason to believe that the gods are represented through the lens of the onlooker. The Warlock who created this in 104 A.E.D. was made famous by his rendering."

Their voices soften as I gravitate away from the crowd.

Several moments of my study pass before I realize one of the gods on the top tier has been blown away. The jagged edges of the ruined art jut out in an ugly way.

It is my father. Phelix. The other two take on the forms of different species. Both bear glorious wings, one of an Angel and the other of a Daemon.

I study the features of the Daemon from a distance. He is

handsome and far more familiar than Todd. A steadying breath fills my lungs, and I allow my gaze to float back down to eye level. That is when I see the plaques positioned all around.

The first one, written on a golden plate, reads, "Kiara and Dror: The Primordials." The name is unfamiliar to me. The circumference of such an enormous masterpiece is mind-blowing, and it takes me at least five minutes to see the next one.

"The Primordials begat the Elementals."

My brow furrows. I am not new to reading, and Daddy paid for extension education, but I have never heard any of these names.

These *Elementals* must be my paternal grandparents. My father never allowed us to call them anything other than the gods. I knew their hatred was mutual, but I didn't realize the lengths each side had gone to erase the other.

As I round to complete my circular escapade, I near the final sign.

"Fortuna cursed her children for the sins of their fathers. After the birth of Phelix, she withdrew her golden pen and wrote upon a tapestry with their blood:

One would rule the skies, giving birth to the seraphim,
One would rule the land and all things below it,
One would govern the waters until he lost them.
The price for the power would be a fated queen rivaled to the dark desires of their hearts.
One would love all but his wife,
One would marry well and watch her die,
And one would find himself wed to a woman who could suppress the power of the gods."

My mind scans what little I know of Raphael and Aidoneus. I barely had any idea who their wives were. I think of my mother, who had died birthing Hallie. Perhaps my father had been a kind, doting partner once when she was alive. That would make the second prophecy about him.

Then, I spot the round collection of columns around the place. Each space creates a circular pantheon. The moon is high in the sky, but I barely notice the people slinking off to their dinner reservations and hotel rooms. This is my family history, and I am ravenous to learn.

Immediately, I spot the water god. I hurry to his statue, taking in the striking features of his face. Like the other Primordials and Elementals, he presents himself as a Mer to me. My breath hitches as I look at his name. *Adrian, God of all Water*.

Sadness bubbles up inside me as the yearning for family takes hold. I hug myself tighter, trying to gather Erik's sweater around me for warmth.

I wipe away foolish tears as I look at the others. *Terran, God of all Land. Aearan, God of all Air*. Their faces are handsome in a cruel, unfeeling way. I cannot tell if that results from how the artist captured their likeness or if I am glimpsing their temperament.

I pause at *Fortuna, Goddess of Fate*. My Grandmother. Her rich, black scales shift colors, just like real ones. Another pang of loneliness resounds in my chest. It feels as though I have been robbed of the truth regarding who I am over some feud my father started long ago. It's almost as if she winks at me as I stare, so I quickly hurry away.

A strange addition to the Pantheon comes into view. *Miranda, Wife of Hades*. Then I see the text that makes my blood run chill despite the scorching heat emanating from the ground below Lethe. "Buried in the year 2020 A.C.E. Our good queen. *Departed from this world too soon, a casualty of the rebellion.*"

The gears in my mind start to turn. The people called her good... and she was dead.

That means that the second prophecy about the demigods' wives wasn't about my mother, it was about her—Miranda.

Which means...

I shut my eyes tightly before I finish the thought, *Which means that my mother was more powerful than Phelix. And my father had my mother killed, just like he tried to have me killed.*

Hot, angry tears pour out of my eyes as my body shakes. I am torn between wanting to remove my bastard father's head from his shoulders and curling up before the statue dedicated to my aunt. The kindness in her eyes makes me wonder if she would've liked me.

The thought is ridiculous. Gods and demigods have no room for tenderness.

But she wasn't a goddess, just like my mother wasn't. Just like I am not. She could have been something entirely different. She could have taken me shopping for dresses not made by royal tailors and showed me how to paint my nails or gossiped about mindless things.

"I am sad I never knew you, Miranda," I murmur to the empty air.

When the moon is high in the sky, and exhaustion seeps through my bones, I am reduced to a defeated lump of emotions. I resign myself to the fact that I cannot get in to see my uncle tonight. Tears spill down my cheeks as I wander to a secluded corner of the square covered by a metallic roof.

There is nowhere else to go. I lay down on a bench and tuck my knees in as tightly as I can. I will sleep here tonight, and tomorrow... tomorrow I will find Aidoneus.

21
LEFT BY ALL
ERIK

It takes five hours and forty-seven minutes to dock the ship and oversee the unloading of the cargo.

I know this because every minute feels like an eternity, and I spend several eternities staring into the crowded docks, trying to glimpse Helena. The bustling sounds of my crew chattering behind me fill my ears, but my men aren't talking to me.

That's good.

I'm not in the mood right now. Helena would have known that. She would have taken one look at my tense shoulders, how I am gripping the railing with white knuckles, and sent everyone away before invading my space. She would have sent me some stupid text that plastered a smile on my face despite everything else. Helena would have made me feel something more than my sodden clothes and the salty air.

At least I have my impending death to keep me company. It's not like I plan on just rolling over and letting King Phelix's men kill me like a dog. But I'm also a realist. And a human, which is basically a death sentence in Aranthium. I used to think we were incredible, noble even, until my ninth birthday.

Gods. That lesson has haunted me ever since that fateful night. Twenty years have passed, but standing at the bow of my ship as the brisk wind blows past me, I am transported back into my nightmares. The sounds of the dock fade away, becoming something much more sinister. I've learned my lessons. Given the chance, anyone can and will betray you.

I am all too familiar with betrayal. Death. Violence. Echos of horror remain in my mind to this day. Shudders rush through me as the gods-awful sound of tearing flesh fills my ears. I shake my head, trying in vain to clear the memories and put them back into the box where they belong.

Instead, my mother's screams echo through my mind as she pleads for her attackers to end her life quickly. If I close my eyes, I can hear the Daemons chuckling as they close in on her. Their laughter sends shivers down my spine.

Whimpers, echoes of the boy I was, are trying to escape me. I shove them down brutally. I had wanted to help her, but she had made me promise not to come out, no matter what I heard.

It was the last thing she had ever said to me. At that point, my father was already dead. They had taken him out quickly. A liability, they had called him in their low, deep voices. But they had taken their time with her.

She had been beautiful. Not in the way that every boy thinks his mother is beautiful. No. In a people-stop-in-the-streets-to-stare-openmouthed-at-her beautiful. She had been stunning for a human. Tall, with long, windswept, wavy golden hair that had flowed down her back. She'd had a face that made you realize Angels weren't the only celestial beings in our world. That's why the Daemons had targeted her in the first place.

Rubbing my palms against my eyelids, I try to shake the memory of that terrible night. It's not working. All I see is the darkness of the small closet. I'm lost in the memory, becoming that boy once more.

I'm huddled in a ball, shaking. Screams surround me, coming from all sides. They are ear-piercingly loud and filled with pain. So much pain. Something wet and sticky slides under the door, coating my skin. If I open my eyes, my hands will be painted red.

Tremors wrack my body as I remain in that small, confined space for hours. Long after the screaming has stopped and my tears have dried up, the door slides open a crack. I blink, then slit my eyes as I look up. An older man with a worn face grimaces in my direction. He has a scar running from his forehead down to his chin.

"I'm not going to hurt you, boy," he says softly before pulling me to my feet. "Close your eyes. You don't need to see this."

The scent of copper, urine, and bile fills my nose as he hauls me out of the closet.

Past and present collide as the scents mix the aromas of the port of Lethe. My stomach roils within me as I fight to regain control.

Push it down, Erik. Get a hold of yourself.

It takes a few minutes, but finally, the memories of the last time I saw my parents disappear from my mind.

I might not have been able to fight when I lost my family, but now, things are different. I am different. I plan on bringing as many Elite down with me as I can. I'm no fool. I know I won't be leaving the Gates of Hell alive. It was either me or Helena, and there was no way I could ever do it. I would have let her kill me on the ship if I thought the crew would have let her go.

It's good that she left because she is better off without me. We both know that. All I bring is death and pain. She was too far out of my league, anyway.

Shaking my head, I stare off into the horizon. By the time the crew has unloaded the last of our cargo, the sun is dipping below the vast city before us.

"Captain?" Anders' voice comes from behind, his footsteps quiet on the deck as he stands beside me.

"Go ahead," I say. My voice is gruff to my ears after such a long silence.

He coughs into his arm before staring out into the growing darkness. "Everything has been unloaded, sir. I've made sure it will make it to its proper destination."

"Good." I supervised unloading the pearls, ensuring they got into the correct hands a few hours ago. "Thank you, Anders." I turn from him in blatant dismissal, but he doesn't move. A few minutes tick by in silence. Clenching my jaw, I sigh. "Was there something else?"

Anders shifts from one foot to the other. "It's about Maddie," he starts hesitantly, "What—"

Snarling, I grab him by the collar and lift him off his feet. His eyes bulge as I tighten my grip on his shirt. "Don't you ever mention her name to me again. She's gone. As far I'm concerned, she never existed."

"But..."

"No!" I yell. Tossing Anders onto the deck, I watch with narrowed eyes as he sprawls onto all fours. I step towards him, clenching my fists as Anders gasps for air. The sailors are all watching me warily.

"This goes for all of you," my voice thunders through the night air. "Never, ever, speak her name aboard this ship again. Don't talk about her. Don't even think about her. Break the new rule, and the next man to utter a word to me about her will find themselves feeding the fish at the bottom of the sea."

Silence. Below us, the sounds of the market grow louder as the day ends. People are trying to get one last deal in before they head home for the night.

Shaking my head, I stride towards the gangplank. Throwing my bag over my shoulder, I strap my gun to my side and slide a long knife into my boot. Francois brought them up for me earlier. Turning around, I stare at my crew. They're good men and don't deserve to be caught up in what is coming to me.

"Good. I see you understand me," I say. "Now, I have some things to take care of. Don't wait up."

Throwing my satchel over my shoulder, I join the throngs of sailors and merchants who are still milling about. The sounds of chatter overlay the constant shouts of working males and females as species of every sort mingle with each other. No one even glances at me as I stroll through the crowd.

Here, the Pirate of Death isn't out of place. They know to look for the man who leaves a brawl with one man drowned and another with a slit throat.

This is my stomping ground. I've been to this city that never sleeps many times before and know exactly where I'm going. Pushing through the throngs of people, I hurry into the darkened streets beyond the docks before my executioners come.

THE CITY of Lethe is not for those who are weak at heart. It is a place where people go to forget and be forgotten.

As I hurry through the darkened streets, the sounds of the city absorb the way my feet clatter on the cobblestones. I rush past the well-lit parts of town, the newer buildings with their fancy security cameras and well-to-do Angels and Daemons, towards my old stomping grounds.

I make a point to avoid the Gods' Square. I've never liked that creepy place, and the presence of so many species makes my skin crawl. Besides, there was an Oracle from Fortuna's temple spouting nonsense the last time I was there. She grabbed my arm, shaking me as I tried to walk past.

"Heed Fortuna's call, young man, before it is too late," she had crowed into my ear, tugging my arm with surprising force. "One day soon, you will be asked to make a choice. You may think of yourself as evil beyond repair, but your heart is good."

"Excuse me?" I had asked, incredulous.

The Oracle had pressed a withered hand to my chest before continuing, "Listen to your heart. It will tell you what to do."

I shake my head, scoffing at the memory of the Oracle's words. The following week, I read she was found dead in an alley. Cut up like a piece of meat. I think they even covered her unsolved murder on a podcast.

Shivering, I quiet my brain and focus on walking so I didn't think about my heart. Or Helena. Where she might be. What she might be doing. If she found somewhere to sleep.

Just call me Reckless Erik.

A dark chuckle escapes my lips, but it's quickly silenced as I catch sight of a couple embracing in a darkened alley. They tense when they hear my footsteps and turn around.

Roars fill my ears when I get close enough to make out their faces. A tiny female is squirming underneath a much larger male, pushing at his chest and squealing under his filthy hand. The pointy ears sticking out from under her bright orange hair immediately give her away as Fae. Probably Autumn Court. A vision flashes through my mind of Conrad leaning over Helena, and red spots fill my vision as I growl.

The Daemon male pinning her against the wall looks up at me, and his eyes flash red in the darkness, highlighting the horns pushing through his blond locks. His black, leathery wings fill the alley as he snaps them open.

I ask, "What the hell are you doing?"

The Fae bites her lip and looks between the two of us. She spits something out in a tongue I don't understand, her wide eyes flitting between the Daemon and myself.

The Daemon says something to her in another language before he grunts, pushing off against the wall and blocking the Fae from my view with his wings. "Get out of here," he addresses me in the Common Tongue.

I refuse. "No."

He stares at me, shaking his head incredulously. "Do you have a death wish?"

I stand tall, bracing myself as my legs spread. The adrenaline coursing through my veins is sweet and addicting. My calling card is well known, but I can't tell if I want to slit the man's throat or shoot him and throw his body into the ocean.

"Last warning, Daemon," I say calmly. "Leave, or I'll kill you." My fingers brush up against the cool metal of the weapon against my side as I study the Daemon. He has at least a foot on me, but I've got him beat on muscle.

The Daemon raises a brow. "Are you challenging me, *human*?" he asks. He says the word like he believes I'm a piece of garbage.

"Yeah," I calmly reply. Killing others has never been hard for me, especially when there was a good reason. Caging a woman against an alley wall and pawing at her clothes while she protests definitely falls into that.

The monstrous male in front of me stalks towards me. "If I win, you'll be dead, and I still get her."

I bite my lip, considering his words. "Okay." He has no idea who I am.

The Daemon takes two steps, falling into the light cast by a nearby streetlight, and it takes everything I have not to cower. My previous assessment had been wrong. He is at least two feet larger than me and significantly bulkier.

Great.

I clench my teeth and crack my neck before raising my fists. The sound of his chuckle echoes through the near-empty streets.

Footsteps approach, but as soon as the Angel gets a look at what is about to go down, they launch themselves into the night.

I scoff.

Of course, no one else wants to get involved. That's the Gates of Hell for you. Taking a deep breath, I pull my gun out of its holster. The weight is heavy but not unpleasant, and it feels comforting in my hands. The weapon is loaded with black-market bullets specially made to incapacitate and kill even the biggest species in Aranthium.

At least, that's what I was promised. This will be my first time putting them to the test.

The Daemon sees my gun and scoffs, "Is that all you have, human?"

He towers over me, his lumbering bulk casting dark shadows around us.

"Nope," I say. Pulling the knife from my boot with my free hand, I cock my head. "I don't need anything else. I will kick your ass for touching her without her permission."

He raises a brow before shrugging. "It's your funeral."

Then, without warning, the Daemon lunges towards me. He whips out his hands, and there are giant claws where I could have sworn his fingers were a few seconds ago. I leap backward, thanking all the gods for my nimble feet as I shift around him.

The Daemon and I spar for a few minutes. He advances towards me, and I skirt around him. The female Fae stands against the alley wall, her eyes wide.

Everything else fades away as my focus narrows in on one thing: saving this female. I couldn't save my mother. I tried to save Helena, but instead, I lost her.

But I *can* save this female.

I swipe at the male with my knife, but he deflects my attack. We travel down the alley, leaping over broken glass and wooden crates as we stare each other down.

Seconds become minutes, and still, no blood has been drawn.

"Let's hurry this along," the Daemon says. The words are garbled as long fangs lower from his gums. He rushes towards me and kicks out his legs, sliding on the wet cobblestones. I jump away from him, but something blocks my fall. I land on my back, pain rippling as I scramble backward.

My heart is pounding in my chest as adrenaline rushes through me.

Raising my gun, I narrow my eyes and aim where I think his heart should be. The Daemon lifts his taloned claw, presumably to rip out my throat, and I know I only have seconds left if I'm going to do anything. The female Fae has begun screaming. Her screams are ear-piercingly loud and distracting.

Adding to the growing cacophony of the night, my finger presses down on the trigger. The gunshot echoes through the alley. For a long moment, I don't know if my bullet hit true.

Then, the Daemon roars. The sound is unlike anything I have ever heard before. His taloned fingers grasp at his chest as black, sulfuric blood leaks from the wound.

Well, there you have it. I'll be sure to leave a good review for the bullets.

The dying male screams, but instead of collapsing, he lurches towards me with frenzied movements. I scramble backward, but a crate blocks my escape. A searing pain rips through my shoulder as I roll away from the Daemon before my fingers brush the cool metal of my gun. Raising the weapon, I unload the magazine into the male's chest. My ears are ringing from the gunshots.

Pushing myself to my feet, I stand over his body. My heart is pounding, and every breath feels too shallow as black blood covers the ground around me.

Eventually, the female stops screaming. The Fae says something to me, but her words are muffled. It's as though she's underwater, and I am disappointed that I won't be able to throw the Daemon to the water's salty embrace, too.

I lift my gaze to her, but suddenly, everything feels wrong. There's not just one Fae in front of me anymore but two, then four, then eight. They're reaching out for me, their voices muffled as they point at my shoulder.

One touches my skin, sending a searing pain through my body. Someone screams before a thick liquid is forced down my throat.

Darkness is calling me, and I give in to its welcoming embrace.

22

SLEEPING ON BENCHES
HELENA

Voices are swarming around me, pushing past the quiet of the imageless dream that has taken over my subconscious. Suddenly, I'm awoken by a small Were child poking my nose. I jolt up and stare at his furry face. There is a peak in the middle of his hairline, and his brows are furrowed in a darling way.

Ian and Giselle cross my mind as I study the boy. My brain is a minefield, and Erik has given me the wings to fly over the dangerous thoughts that threaten to explode on a whim. I squint in the scorching sunlight and swat at the child, trying to get him to go away.

"Mommy!" he squeals. "She's all right, I checked!"

A bewildered Were mom rushes over and grabs her son's arm. She looks mortified as I sit up on the bench and rub at my face.

"Sorry, miss," she says before dragging the child away. She whispers, "What did I say about talking to people on the street?"

My mouth twists into a grimace, and I try to adjust my

appearance to make me look less haggard. *What in Hell's Sweet Gates am I going to do?*

It is still early morning, but people are crammed into every square inch of the square like sardines. Every muscle in my body protests as I stand up and stretch. Yesterday, no one so much as glanced at me, but today, people shoot me dirty looks with unveiled disgust.

I bare my teeth at them in a silent snarl.

My attention travels back to the King's Tower. It is only a matter of time before that traitor Erik reports back to my oh-so-dear Daddy Phelix, and my father sends his Elite Mer after me. If they catch me, the death I will suffer at their hands will be neither quick nor kind. I shudder, smoothing out my wrinkled clothes.

Knowing my father, it is likely that when his men are done with me, there won't be a spoonful of my soul left to go to the After Life.

I knot my hair behind my head and force myself to focus. One of the main problems with my last attempt to get to my uncle's tower was that I looked like a dead shrimp. If I look the part of a princess, I will get through those gates.

The thought takes hold, and I nod, a small smile creeping on my face. Yes, this could work. A plan forms, piece by piece. To look the part, I will need to shower. Perhaps a dusting of cosmetics... maybe luxury clothes.

The thought sends a thrill through me. Before my imprisonment, I was very stylish in Aqualis, but there are some designer brands I've never had the privilege of using. I long to see the inside of Le Baba Morgaine Couture.

Emboldened by my plan, I head into the city. Thoughts of Erik threaten to creep into my mind, but I shove them aside.

I *will not* think of him.

THE MORNING HAS WASTED away with me stalking outside of Fortuna Fitness. I'm staring through enormous glass windows, my mind swirling as I figure out how to get inside without raising suspicion.

This was the first gym I happened across in a five-block radius. I had no desire to waste more time looking for a new one when I was sure the wards would be cast over every peppy threshold leading to the locker rooms.

A very toned Daemon female stands behind the desk. To describe the expression on her face as "glowering" would be an understatement. When there are no patrons to greet, she just stands there with her arms behind her back. Her focus and dedication to keeping those who have not paid out is impressive. If she took that work ethic to Daddy, I am confident he would hire her to help with the frontiers of Aqualis.

The enormous, circular building boasts three floors filled with various exercise equipment. Perhaps I would enjoy coming here under other circumstances. The diversity of this city makes me long for the ability to live here and relax under the safety of the King of Daemons.

Beings filter in and out of the gym over several hours. I am lounging at a gentrified cafe on the corner, watching the building while nursing a leftover cup of coffee abandoned by some businessman who took one look at my disheveled appearance and thought the worst.

It is pathetic, but I don't care. Coffee is delicious, and this one has the perfect, equal part ratio of cream, caramel, and caffeine.

As I sit there, I can't help but listen to the people sitting next to me. A pair of Winter Fae holding a FaePhone between them with wide eyes.

"Malinda, I'm telling you, the new Queen is amazing. Without her, we would never have been able to come to Lethe for our vacation. Just look at this phone. It's incredible!"

The other Fae scoffs. "Listen to you, talking as though you know the Queen personally. Wilhemina, I know the closest you've ever gotten to her is watching her monthly addresses on TV."

Wilhelmina crosses her arms, pouting. "Well, it's not like you know her any better than me..." her voice trails off as the two women pay their tabs and go on their way.

A Summer Fae with a fancy FaePhone is hurrying along at an alarming pace. "I need the reports yesterday, Patricia," he barks. "I'm sorry, I'm on edge. Just need a quick swim."

The Fae fumbles through his ratty gym bag and produces a small gym card. I stare at the luxurious metal card hungrily. That card is what stands between me and a shower.

"I said I was sorry, Patricia!" he yells. His voice is frantic now, and I smile as a furious voice reaches a volume loud enough for me to hear several feet away. In defense, his hand flings up, and the card goes flying.

His pleas for forgiveness are unsuccessful, so he turns and stomps away to wherever he came from. People continue to move down the sidewalk a hundred miles a minute. The card stays on the ground, forgotten and shining in the hazy sunlight.

No one so much as looks down. The card is calling me like a beacon, summoning me. *Use me*, it says.

Oh, how I want to heed its call. Looking one way then the other, I push myself to my feet. My fingers itch as I walk over to where the card lies on the ground, like a dead fish on a beach.

The metal card is cool in my hands, and I allow hope to fill up my insides. It is cut short when my gaze returns to the large glass doors and see the Daemon's green eyes staring straight ahead. They watch my every movement.

Damn.

Pacing back and forth is such a lame response, but it's the only one I've got. I wander around in circles, weaving through the crowded streets and trying to remain unnoticed by the thing of nightmares inside the gym. I pretend to look into unremarkable stores filled with conservative, business-related fashions.

At last, the effects of my hyper-sweet coffee begin to wear off, and I am left with a slight headache. My body isn't used to how much sugar they use on land. I sit on an empty bench, putting my head between my legs. Minutes pass as I stay like that, suspended in my own thoughts.

When I look up, what I see causes me to blink. I find a thoughtful-looking human man in place of the hulking Daemon inside the gym. For a second, his dark hair and tanned complexion make me think he is Erik.

I can't contain the gasp that escapes me. Nor can I stop the rush of fury that floods my whole body because, for a moment, I feel relieved that he has finally found me. Something is reassuring about the pirate.

Curse my weak heart and my soft brain. It's not him. You don't want to see him. He betrayed you.

Apparently, my heart and my head aren't listening to each other because the memories of Erik's kisses still send warmth through my body. Despite his betrayal, I yearn to be held by him.

I must deal with those cravings because I don't want to see that pirate again. My resolve is firm as I stand, ready to take a risk I wouldn't have dared with the previous employee.

My hair is twisted up on my head into a crappy bun, and I straighten my clothes. Squaring my shoulders, I force myself to muster confidence and charm before strutting through the doors.

The place smells like chemical cleaners. Ducking my chin into my chest and looking up through my eyelashes, I walk up to the attendant and smile. He is sitting down.

The Daemon female would never.

My hands make a show of searching my pockets for the fancy card I already know is there. When I withdraw it, I dangle it in the air between two fingers and feign an air of arrogance. The man looks me up and down appreciatively before smiling.

"Welcome to Fortuna Fitness! I see you're one of our VIP members, so how about we just skip over the scan? We value our members here," he says. Too-white teeth are revealed under thin lips. "Let me mist you down with a quick spell so you don't have any trouble with the wards."

Up close, I can see the small earpiece he wears. His tight-fitting clothes speak to his apparent addiction to protein shakes and hustling. However, he seems kind enough and eager to please. I nod graciously and wait as he sprays me from head to toe. The mist feels strange and tingly as it settles on my skin.

"Never seen a Mer with legs," he says casually, and I smile. I notice a business card for the gym and grab a nearby pen. I scribble,

thank you for your help.

When he picks up the card to read it, I am already walking down the hall. With every step, I pray to all the gods above that the man doesn't get a whiff of this cursed land-bound body.

I faintly hear him say, "Wait, I'm sorry. I'm new here! Could you sign in?"

I ignore him and keep on walking. Moments later, someone else comes to the desk and distracts him. The space behind the front desk is enormous and filled with dozens of machines, which all appeared to be designed in such a way that would inflict pain. It makes me very uncomfortable.

I walk briskly past neon-colored nylon and squeaky, foam-soled shoes. A breath of relief whooshes out of me when I spot the female lockers. It's good to know that I won't have to traverse three levels to accomplish my mission.

The thought of a warm shower and cleanliness propels me forward. The inside is lined with something resembling marble, and everything is slightly heated. The luxury of it all shocks me. Flashbacks of the ship's bathroom cloud my vision and fill me with nostalgia. I shove those feelings so violently that I wince at my gruesome methods.

There are few females in the place. Feeling desperate not to be seen in a bunch of old men's clothes, I peel off the things from Erik's boat and throw them in the trash. I walk naked to the showers, and not even one person looks up from lacing their shoes or tying up their hair.

The showers are individual, thank goodness. The white tile is also heated and brighter than the matte black lockers in the next room. The whole area is coated with a foggy cloud of steam. When I turn on the hot water and step inside, it feels like I have left my body.

How in all of Aranthium could I ever go back to cold water when such niceties existed on land?

Complementary soap and conditioner dispensers are installed in square indents on the wall. They smell generically like something fruity. It is such a delicious scent, and I'm delighted I'm starting to recognize peaches and strawberries. When finished, I grab the enormous heated towel rack and wrap myself up tightly.

The only problem now is finding clothes. I stare at myself in a fog-resistant mirror, wondering if there is a way to make my towels resemble fashionable clothing. I exhale, exasperated, as I tear the terrycloth from my wet hair.

It is no use. Even in Lethe, a woman clothed in towels would draw too much attention.

It is time to commit even more heinous acts than stealing a forgotten key card. I will need to steal clothes and ensure their owners don't see me as I leave.

A group of six women are still chatting as I leave the showers, staring at some sort of bruise one of them had acquired on her leg. I narrow my eyes, taking in my surroundings. A discarded gym bag lies unattended on the floor, its owner nowhere in sight. I suck in a breath as I spot a piece of red fabric sticking out haphazardly. Taking a deep breath, I know what I have to do.

I grab the clothes, and I run. As I move quickly, I shake out the fabric, disappointed to find it's some sort of red leotard. It's definitely not what I was going for. But beggars can't be choosers.

Way to stay under the radar, Helena.

A pair of flip-flops have been abandoned near the showers. I snatch those, too.

Pulling the clothes on under the towel, I walk back to the open floor. Pulsating music comes from one of the rooms, but my eyes light up as I take in the bright red exit sign next to it. I suck in a breath, adjust the tight fabric that has ridden up my rear, and walk as fast as possible.

Glancing in a large window, I watch as men and women gyrate against long metal poles, following the lead of a lithe Spring Fae. The female is wearing a headset, barking orders as she swings around a pole. No one pays me any heed. My stolen outfit isn't out of place here.

I press both hands on the push mechanism of the emergency exit, and a trio of shocks echo through my hands. I grit my teeth and continue through the door even as an alarm starts. Everyone panics, coming out of rooms with shocked expressions. Others emerge from locker rooms half-dressed. A few steps out of the gym, I hear a shout from behind me.

"Hey!" someone yells. "That bitch stole my clothes!"

Shit.

Giving up all pretense of calmness, I start running. I throw my card on the ground as I pound down the sidewalk. I hear the shouts of angry people and feel the gust of sweaty bodies running past.

One of my flip-flops is threatening to separate and break as I run. But still, I move. I don't want to be caught and labeled as a thief. That *certainly* won't endear me to my uncle. I ignore the cries behind me as I dart into the crowd.

I continue down the street until my footwear is well and about to collapse between my toes. Seeing no other option, I slip into a narrow alleyway and press my back against the wall. I can only hope the mass confusion and running beings will suppress my scent long enough to catch my breath and find another way out of this mess. At least I no longer smell of Erik.

23
LANGUAGE BARRIERS ABOUND
ERIK

Everything around me is black and fuzzy. My head pounds with the force of a thousand waves as the scent of bleach fills my nose.

Where am I?

I search my memory for any idea of what happened to me, but things are suspiciously blank. Groaning, I pry my aching eyelids open.

Brightness assaults my vision, and I squeeze my eyes shut, my retinas screaming against the sudden attack of artificial light. Stretching out my fingers, I feel something cold and hard beneath me. It's frigid to the touch, and a cool breeze washes over my bare skin. Naked and vulnerable is not what I want.

I reach out, my eyes still squeezed shut, towards my bottom half. My hands encounter fabric, and I exhale, *relieved*.

Being kidnapped is one thing. Being stripped naked against my will is another thing entirely.

"Hello?" I croak, my throat sore and raspy. It aches as I force the words out. "Is anyone there?"

A rustling comes from behind me, and I instinctively push

myself onto my elbows. Or at least, I try to. A searing pain rushes through my shoulder, and I drop back down. Opening my eyes again, I squint in preparation for the bright light I now know is there.

I'm in a small, sterile room with white walls. There appears to be a window on one side, but it's covered in a thick, black curtain. My curiosity is peaked, but before I can further analyze my surroundings, the female Fae from the alleyway pops into my vision. She blows out a breath, the line between her brows disappearing as she looks me over.

Now that it's not pitch black, I can see her more clearly. I was right. She is definitely an Autumn Fae. Her bright orange hair reaches her tiny waist, standing out from her pale features, unlike Helena's much darker hair. The points of the female's ears are covered in green tips that match her eyes. Her clothing resembles something my mother would have worn in the cooler weather despite the heat of Lethe.

The Fae reaches out with her tiny hands, pressing and prodding against my bare shoulder, which causes a fiery burn to rush through me. I yelp.

She makes a soothing sound with her tongue, reaching behind her. On instinct, I pull away but relax when I see a large tub in her hands. She holds it out to me, a questioning look in her eyes. I nod, dropping back onto the table. Seconds later, a soothing relief pushes away the pain as she applies a cream to my shoulder.

For the first time, I really notice her hands. Her touch is warm, but it's nothing like Helena's touch. Memories of the Mer Princess cupping my face, running over my jawline and through my hair, play through my mind. Their pain is deep, breaking my soul in a way I didn't know was possible. The thought of the Crown Princess is like a spear through my heart, and I grimace.

The Fae notices my movement and stops her ministrations. She looks at me with a questioning look in her eyes.

"It's fine," I say gruffly.

Her brows furrow, but she continues applying cream to my shoulder before wrapping a bandage around it without speaking. The silence is good. It's right. Silence will serve me well until the Elite come for me. I know I only have so much time before Phelix's men find me.

That's why I need to get out of here. Wherever *here* is, I don't want to endanger anyone else with my existence. Especially not someone as kind as this Fae, who was willing to take me in when I was clearly injured.

After a few minutes, she steps away, gesturing to my shoulder as she begins to speak. The musical lilt of her voice reaches my ears, but her words don't make any sense to me. My brows furrow, and I wonder if I hit my head in addition to hurting my shoulder.

"Wait." I hold up my hands as I stare at her in confusion. My brain is having trouble catching up with the words coming from her mouth. "Slow down. I can't understand you."

She pinches her brows together, her hands waving in the air, as she starts talking even faster. Her words wash over my ears, but I still don't understand what she says.

"I don't know what you're telling me," I say. My voice is sharp as I try to get her to stop. "I can't understand you."

The Fae steps closer, gesticulating wildly, as she seems to reiterate what she said.

"Please," I repeat, "slow down."

She just keeps talking over me. Her pitch increases as she points at me, then at the door, then at herself. Her words are complete and utter gibberish to my ears. Panic begins to set in as my heart speeds up. Ignoring the burning in my shoulder and chest, I shove myself into a sitting position. The tiny bed creaks its displeasure under my weight.

"Slow down," I repeat, rubbing my hands on my temples. The urge to pull my hair is strong as I try to get this female to hear me. To understand me.

All of a sudden, a wave of awareness hits me. Like a dagger to my heart, understanding I had no desire to have floods through me. It's almost laughable how much this situation mirrors another one with a stunningly beautiful... nope. I shake my head.

I will *not* be going down that road. I feel utter despair, but I refuse to think about *her* anymore.

Raising my hands, I shove myself off the bed and onto my feet. The floor is ice-cold as I approach the woman, extending my hands. "I don't know what you want from me."

The female steps back, and words start flooding out of her at an even more rapid rate. Her eyes widen to an impossible size as she reaches a higher decibel than before.

The Fae is working herself into a tizzy, her cheeks turning bright red as she talks, and her anxiety is rubbing off on me. My hands are clammy as I try to calm the woman down.

A hysterical female is the last *thing I need right now.*

"Stop it!" I bark. My tone is sharper than I intended, and I wince as the female immediately ceases speaking.

She takes a step back, then another. Her face pales as a tremor rushes through her. At that moment, I realize how much larger I am than her. There's a mirror behind her, and I try to see myself from her eyes. I'm a massive, bare-chested human man with dark tattoos scrawled over my body. My hair is messy, and the circles under my eyes are pronounced in a way that I'd expect from a corpse.

It's not surprising she is frightened of me.

"Shit, sorry. I didn't mean to scare you." I hold up my hands in supplication. She watches me warily, and I try to lower my voice. "I'm Erik. What's your name?"

She shakes her head before erupting in another stream of unintelligible language.

Pinching the bridge of my nose, I breathe as I try to figure out what to do. My precious rules won't help me here. What good are they if I can't even communicate with the person right in front of me?

"Please," I say again, tapping my chest and speaking more slowly, "My name is Erik. What is your name?"

Another stream of words rushes out of her mouth as she crosses her arms and studies me intently. Then, her eyes light up.

"Do you finally understand me?" I ask, excitement lacing my tone. "I need to get out of here. Can you help me?"

She shakes her head, babbling incessantly as she rushes out of the room.

Great.

A groan escapes my lips as I look down at myself. Wearing pants and nothing else isn't ideal, but I also need to leave this room. I'm halfway out the door when I realize I'm forgetting something.

My satchel.

I can't leave without it. It has everything I need in it. Turning around, I look around the small space. Other than the bed and mirror, it's completely bare.

"Where is it?" I mumble through gritted teeth. "I need my gods-damned bag and my weapons."

As if in answer, footsteps pound down the stairs. I clench my fists at my side, focusing on the open door. In rushes the Autumn Fae, but she isn't alone.

A large, burly male is walking beside her. He's clad entirely in black leather, and his hair is shorn into a mohawk on the top of his head. His ears are rounded, and his eyes are as black as the night. His face is as stunning as a piece of art, too angular and chiseled to be flesh. He walks towards me, his lips curling up to reveal fangs as he runs a finger down one of my tattoos.

The Vampire says something in the strange tongue, which causes the woman to laugh. I bristle, pulling away from his touch.

"My name is Erik," I repeat. I feel like a broken record. I'm trying to keep the frustration from my tone, but it's difficult. "I'll get out of your hair as soon as I get my things. Do you know where they are?"

The Fae and Vampire launch into a rapid conversation. I'm completely lost, following only their expressions and the way they move their bodies.

The male steps towards the Fae, his eyes flashing as he crosses his arms. She nods, pointing at me and then at herself before miming long talons running through the air.

The Vampire pinches his lips, turning to stare at me. I can feel the heat of his gaze as he observes me. I fight a shiver as his eyes travel from the top of my head to my bare feet. He says a few short, clipped words as he stares at me.

I refuse to cower in his presence.

Then, the Fae starts speaking again. I watch as she turns and rushes into the stairwell. She comes back a moment later with her hand clasped around that of a much smaller child. If the boy were human, he wouldn't be older than five or six. As it is, his pointy ears mean he could be older than me, for all I know. Based on his bright orange hair, I'm guessing the female is his mother.

The woman opens her mouth again, and another volley of words comes flying at me. She is gesturing, and the boy keeps looking between us. The Vampire steps between me and the boy, his gaze hard.

I quickly decide this child is my best bet for leaving here

alive. "Please," I try again, moving my hand across my chest and miming, putting a bag over my shoulder. "My satchel. I had it on me before. Where is it?"

The female stares at the boy expectantly. He steps forward, clearing his throat.

"My mother..." he stops, staring up at the female. Relief floods through me at the sound of the Common Tongue. The boy's voice is accented, his words clipped, but I can understand them. "She says you don't understand her?"

"Thank the gods," I say hurriedly, crouching to look into the boy's bright green eyes. "You can understand me, right?"

He nods.

"I don't know what they're saying. Can you ask them where my satchel is? My weapons?"

Confusion crosses his face as he shakes his head. "S-satchel? I don't know this word."

I want to hit my head on the wall. I have no idea how Helena did this for so long. If I see her again, I will... no. I won't see her again. She made sure of that.

Sighing, I pull my attention to the family staring at me. "My bag?" I make the motion of putting it over my shoulder again. "I need it."

Understanding fills the boy's eyes. He turns and rapidly starts speaking to his mother. All I can do is sit back and wait as the three begin speaking.

After a few minutes, the boy turns back to me.

"We have your things," he says, "but my father says you can't go."

"What?" I yell, pushing myself to my feet. "I won't be kept prisoner."

The boy turns, talking to his father. Then, less than a minute later, he starts again. "No, not a prisoner. My father says you are... honorable guest. You save my mother, yes?"

I nod grimly. "Yes."

The boy grins. "Then you are a guest." He grabs my hand and pulls me towards the door. "Come. You can shower, then we will feed you."

"What about my things?" I growl through clenched teeth.

"They are upstairs. Come."

Mollified, I follow my unexpected translator. A new plan is forming in my mind.

Shower. Eat. Get my stuff. Then, I will finish my business in Lethe and put my things in order before death catches up with me.

24

STEALING AGAIN
HELENA

L e Baba Morgaine, Le Baba Morgaine, I chant silently as I climb up fire escapes and rush around buildings. The hot metal burns my skin, sweat drips from my face, and I like the way it feels when the wind blows through my hair. Thank the gods, no one is chasing me now. I look less like a weirdo when people see me jogging in my ridiculous outfit.

I feel drunk with anticipation to find clothes. I used to have beautiful things in Aqualis. Stylish, good-quality contraband that I only risked wearing when Daddy wasn't home.

Thoughts of my tyrannical father make my gray legs pump faster.

The high-rise apartments around me still look relatively nice but not as opulent as Fortuna Fitness. I need to find the portion of the city that screams "Money!" if I am going to find clothes worthy of a princess.

I climb higher, pulling myself up old metal stairs attached to the brick-and-mortar buildings. The sheer height makes me feel dizzy. I have never been this high up... ever. Height isn't really an issue in Aqualis. When I look down, my stomach lurches into my throat.

Breathe.

An old Daemon female pokes her head out of one of the double-paned glass windows. "Get the hell away from my home!" she shouts. Her black hair is spilling out of a messy bun not too different from my own.

I keep running.

The woman continues, "I'm serious, ingrate! Get away from here, or I'm calling the DaePolice!"

My pace speeds up. I'm running as fast as possible. Every time I look down, my stomach lurches with uncomfortable terror. Even if I could have, I wouldn't have responded to the irate female. I am not hurting her or anyone else—I am trying to save my own life.

I pull myself up. *Only three more stories till I reach the roof.*

"That's it! I warned you!"

I tune out her screaming.

Self-preservation is still a good enough reason to keep moving. It is the reason I've made so many questionable decisions. I've stolen before and will likely have to steal again. If I don't, I will die. That is a good enough reason to pilfer expensive goods.

Right?

Some moral compass that I didn't know I possessed points me in the opposite direction. Still, the physical exercise necessary for scaling a wall makes it much easier to ignore my principles simply because I don't have the time to listen to the call of morals.

Daemon woman has stopped screaming, and worry quickly settles low in my gut. Not only are my muscles screaming, but now my body is racing against the efficiency of the DaePolice. Their speed depends mainly on how efficient a ruler my uncle is, whether or not he appoints good leaders or simply his insufferable friends, like my father.

The war inside my head takes my attention away from the burning in my arms and legs as I grip the decorative gargoyle crowning the top of the building. I push out rough, scalding breaths and prepare myself to vault over the edge of the sculpted creature and onto the hopefully flat surface of the rooftop.

When the moment comes, it carries a fresh dose of fear. Cold sweat beads on my forehead as my stomach clenches. Vertigo takes over in the same instant I am heaving myself upwards. Gulping, I look down at my hand. In this body, I am so... mortal.

The realization that I could be moments away from death fills me just as my hands grow slippery with sweat. With a terrified cry, I lose my grip. The stone scrapes my hand raw as I tumble down. I barely manage to grasp onto the lower foot of the ominous-looking beast.

My legs dangle half over the rust-red fire escapes and half into the open air. My heart is racing so fast that I fear fainting.

Stop, I command myself.

A familiar flame alights in my stomach. The same one caused me to jump off Erik's ship and flee for my life. This fire, the one Erik awoke in me, is the one that propels me forward in my own miserable life.

I will not yield to death simply because I don't want to.

It feels impossible to get more breath, so I rely on my rage to give me strength. After conjuring the face of Conrad, I gain an inch. My mother's painting in Aqualis flashes before my mind, and my other hand is on the statue. Hallie, Henrick, Daddy... their faces are all swirling together as I recall their abuse, their lies, and their manipulations.

The crowning jewel to my diadem of fury comes into view: a carmine firestone encasing Erik's betrayal. The man I had begun to trust and feel safe with was meant to be my murderer.

And like a foolish young Merling who didn't understand the way of the world, I had trusted him. I had trusted his salty kisses and muscular arms. I had trusted the curve of his lips and the honesty in his brown eyes. He made me care for him, all the while betraying me in the shadows.

He made me look like a gods-damned idiot.

All these thoughts coalesce and create a hideous monster. Armed with boiling blood and a broken heart, I successfully pull myself over the top of the stone creature.

The wall is taller than expected, and I fall flat on my back. Beneath me is some kind of lounging couch, which satisfies my body's demand for softness. Without it, I am sure I would've broken several bones.

I'd choose tender, deep purple bruises over broken bones any day of the week.

My body protests as I straighten. The couch-looking thing is deep-seated and easily enough for ten people to perch on at once. The fact that it didn't break denotes good quality and a strong base. Music is playing somewhere close by.

My heart races as voices reach me from the other side of the partitioned room. My hands grow clammy as I focus on drawing myself back together in record time.

"... this is the last time," someone says in a husky tone.

It's met with a female voice saying, "You don't mean that."

"Don't I?" the low voice asks. "My-my wife—"

"Has her own lover. I can show you proof, remember?"

My relieved exhale mingles with the wet sound of their kisses. It makes me roll my eyes.

Unfaithful bastards. Why would two people be together if they have no desire to be together?

They continue to volley scandalous words back and forth. I drag my gaze over the rooftop. My breath catches in my throat as

I spot a mink blanket draped over a polished wood chair. The simple, elegant design whispers "expensive."

Could I really have been so lucky? Did all of the buildings have luxurious penthouses on top of them?

The music must have been loud enough to mask the sound of my fall. I pad over to the partition made out of thick, black fabric. The white pots and vibrant green plants seem at odds with the desolate landscape of the Gates of Hell.

I lean in and hear more kisses and a few growls. Slinking over to where the partition ends, I peek over... and find another partition. The light makes it possible to just barely glimpse two forms moving together, becoming one. I scoff. For all the male's complaints, he certainly doesn't seem unhappy about his current situation.

In the face of such blatant wealth, all my guilt over thievery evaporates. I scan the rest of the roof, searching for stairs leading me to the apartments below.

The clock for the DaePolice is still ticking, and I don't want anyone pounding on the door while I am slipping into someone else's clothes.

My eyes catch on the domed building that must house the stairs to go down, and I do a triumphant dance inside. The only problem is that bolting across the way will put me in the amorous couple's direct line of sight. And a red leotard is not exactly inconspicuous.

It is a risk I will have to take. I screw up my courage and run. I run like I haven't been running for hours before. Holding my breath for as long as possible, I try not to make any more sound than necessary.

I've just ducked under the cover of the walls when I hear, "What was that?"

"What was what?" the female replies breathlessly.

"Something red over there."

Fabric rustles, and I hold my breath again. As quietly as I can manage, I move down the cool, marble tile steps. I only make it down two when the male says, "I promise you, I saw something."

My heart is pounding in my chest, my lungs tight. He is much closer now.

"You are paranoid. Maybe it was a bird," she offers.

"A bird, Luella? I know you're not from here, but seriously? These skies are inhabited by Daemons and Angels, nothing else." he scoffs. The tone in his voice makes me flinch. He's a condescending bastard.

Then I hear Luella stand up. Dread coils in my stomach. *No, no, no.* If she leaves, then they will both go downstairs. My plan will be ruined before it even begins.

"You're insufferable, you know that, Dragnium?" Luella spits.

His footsteps halt. "I thought you liked that about me."

"Absolutely not. You are despicable, and I wish I had never laid eyes on you my first night here," Luella says. Her voice is rising.

"But Lue—"

"—don't you dare. I have been ensnared in your trap long enough. I take back what I said earlier. Go downstairs and wait for your wife," she says. I start down the stairs again, taking them two at a time.

Luella continues her tirade, "Go back to her expensive jewels," my breath hitches, "and her bitchy designer clothes!"

My mind is reeling. I am near the bottom, where the door to the apartment lies open. Both of those beings are assholes, but I appreciate the information.

I won't even need to set foot in a store! No security and high potency wards—just a man and his overpriced penthouse. A slow grin creeps along my face. I'm sure this male won't have any protection except on the doors and windows. I can work with that.

Luella is still screaming at her presumably Daemon partner when she lets out a little yelp of excitement.

He makes a guttural sound. "Your excitability has always done it for me, Lue."

She laughs. "Ugh, this is why I can't stay mad at you."

I blush at the way her voice sounds. The noise of their resumed lovemaking fades away as I rush into the apartment. Guilt for the Daemon's wife bleeds into all my emotions. Having been betrayed recently, I didn't want other women to suffer the same heartbreak. Especially not when I could do something to let her know.

I stop dead in my tracks when I reach the TV room. On the long, pristine white couch sits a chimera. I've never seen them in real life, and it looks far more imposing than I had ever imagined. The creature's long fangs poke out under its furry lip. A panther's head is mixed with a serpent's tail and a small hippogriff's body.

That long, serpentine tail flicks back and forth as it eyes me. Cold sweat begins to bead up along my spine. It isn't as if I can use my voice to soothe the beast, so I must use my demeanor. My mind races with all of the useless facts I have learned about chimeras in the past.

It takes a few moments—seconds that feel like hours—but eventually, I remember. Chimeras communicate through feelings and thoughts. That's why they make such good houseguards—they can sense ill intent and warn others off.

My heart is beating fast enough to burst out of my chest. If I am going to reassure this creature that I am not worth killing, I need to calm down. Forcing myself to breathe, I keep my eyes on the chimera as deep breaths move in and out of my lungs like waves on a turbulent sea.

I put my hands out, extending my palms so the beast can

smell me if it so chooses. When I take a step forward, it bares its teeth. A low snarl rips from its mouth, so I cease all movements. With elegant grace that only an animal such as this can achieve, it slinks over to my feet.

Then, my mind flashes back to a book belonging to the mysterious Henry. That book with a philosophical tone, authored by a human. Some of the notes in that book's margins shine before my eyes like the neon lights of the Gates of Hell.

What is the measure of a man? Why, it is his actions that define him coupled with the intentions behind those. If the gods cannot equally weigh both in their hands, then they are not gods worth worshiping.

For some reason, these words spike an idea. Instead of focusing on my death at the hands of this chimera, I think about my fear of dying at my father's hands.

I let my betrayal pour out of my skin like ink from an octopus. I see the chimera pause and let out a deep breath. It soaks up all of the pain, fear, and anger. Behind all of that... there is no ill intent, only a scared inner Merling. I think of my father, of Hallie, of Erik. For a few wretched moments, I give life to the pain that has haunted the deep recesses of my soul.

The creature pads over to me. I have no way of knowing whether or not this will work. It might still judge me as worthy of being its lunch.

I hold my breath while the silky black fur touches my ankle. I inhale, and the chimera nuzzles my leg. Instantly, I want to cry. It takes a moment to realize that the stuttering sound isn't a growl. It's... what's the word? *It's purring.*

Without hesitation, I reach down and scratch the fur on its head. I'm hesitant to touch the feathers because I don't have enough experience with such creatures to know whether or not they would like it.

Sea creatures don't like being scratched at all.

The purring continues as the mid-sized chimera rubs against my legs. A sense of calm washes over me, and I realize the incredible creature is a telepathic empath—meaning it can also return emotions.

Surprising, salty tears stream down my face as the pain ebbs away and is replaced with a sense of peace and protection. I allow myself to lean into the illusion for a few moments before I move again, only to be interrupted by a new image that flashes in my mind. I gasp. The mental picture is of a silver bag with a chimera printed on the front nestled on the top shelf of a cabinet.

My head swings down to look at the beast, and it licks its lips. I run my hands through my hair desperately and look around. I have no idea where this food is supposed to be, much less how to get there.

Upon sensing my confusion, the chimera breaks away from my legs and trots to a door on the other side of the house.

I pray to every god in the pantheon that the amorous couple above won't descend in the coming moments. When I push against the door, it swings open on well-oiled hinges, revealing a spacious kitchen with black tile and chrome appliances. The sight would've brought Jean Luc to his knees. I spot the cabinet I had seen in my mind. When I open it, I instantly locate the bag.

One glance at my new friend tells me that this is the one. I grab it and find that my fingers barely brush the bottom of the metallic bag. Locating a stool, I place it in front of the cabinet and carefully step up. When I wobble, I grasp onto the cabinet handles in front of me. They hold firm, thank the gods.

I grab the pouch and set it on the ground. The cabinet is wide open, just like the bag. Then I think of clothes. As the chimera munches, it flashes me back an image of a hallway leading to its owner's closet.

Such a traitorous creature to help a stranger over its own family.

I love it.

I give the chimera another scratch, which elicits a purr, and head out of the room.

With the mental map from my new friend, I locate the closet in less than a minute. I freeze when I walk in. Clothes line the racks from ceiling to floor. Garment bags hang in pristine condition, nicely zipped up, and puffed out with the promise of luxury fabrics inside.

My hand trails along the rainbow of colors and textures, and I feel like I might die. *This is much better than any department store.*

Magazines long lost to decay under the sea swim through my memories. My brain hurts from so much mental communication and rigorous memory recall. Then, I find precisely what I am looking for: The Princess of the Angels. She is wearing a white cashmere suit. It has structured shoulders and wide-leg pants.

Biting my lip, I look for something that might match that description. The sound of zippers accompanies my anxious breaths. Each passing second grinds against my nerves. It's enough to make me crumble inside of myself and ignore the sweating of my palms.

If these people have anyone check these rooms after I leave, my scent will be everywhere.

Come on, I beg in my mind. The chimera appears at the closet door. It sends me an image of a DaePolice car at the base of the six-story building.

My hands grow clammy, and I desperately tear through the clothes.

At last, I unzip one of the cream-colored garment bags and find a pale pink suit. Instinctively, I know that's the one. When I slide it on, the style doesn't exactly match what I pictured, but it fits me well enough. I grab a pair of sunglasses from the accessory shelf and two white stilettos. I'm sliding them on when the chimera growls.

Shit. I clamor as I straighten the clothes and hurry outside. I am a mess in these heels, but they look like something a princess would wear.

As long as I don't break an ankle. I'm hurrying to the door just as a knock sounds. My blood chills to the exact temperature of the Ice Sea.

I'm out of time.

25
TYING UP LOOSE ENDS
ERIK

My translator's name is Zephyr. He informs me over a delicious fried lamb and quinoa meal that Jasper, the Vampire, is not his birth father.

I think I could have figured that out on my own. They look nothing alike. However, to avoid upsetting my hosts, I bite my tongue.

In between bites of food, Zephyr takes the mantle of conversationalist upon his shoulders. He tells me he and his mother, Calista, immigrated to the Gates of Hell four years ago, escaping a difficult situation in the Autumn Court. When they arrived in Lethe, the Vampire had taken them both under his protection.

"Jasper is very kind," Zephyr continues before launching into a story about how they first met the Vampire.

As the boy speaks, I take in my surroundings. We are eating around a small circular kitchen table, the prevalent theme of the retro kitchen causing me to be thrown back to a time I had no desire to visit. The cabinets, the fridge, and even the stove are all varying shades of orange, speaking of a time in the past when, apparently, people didn't have any aesthetic taste at all.

I nod as the Fae boy speaks, sipping my water as I try to figure out how to get out of here.

"It was kind of Jasper to help you," I say absentmindedly. My damp hair drips onto the collar of my new black sweater. It's an indefinite loan from Jasper. I asked for my shirt back, but Calista told me, and Zephyr translated, that it had been completely destroyed after the Daemon attacked me.

Zephyr smiles, continuing to speak. "Especially since—"

Before Zephyr can continue, a quick spurt of what I've decided must be some dialect of Ancient Fae comes from Calista. Her face is hard as she glares at her son. Zephyr slams his mouth shut and sends me an apologetic glance.

"Sorry, Erik," he mutters around a mouthful of lamb. "Mama says I can't tell you anymore."

"It's okay," I say. The food is fantastic, and I feel more alive now than I have since Helena leaped off the ship. "Please tell your parents thank you."

Pushing back my plate, I stand and bow deeply at the waist. It's probably an overreaction since, judging by their living conditions, this family is middle-class at most, but the last thing I want to do is step on any more toes.

At this point, I just want to make sure I get out of here before the Elite find me. I wish I had already left. More than that, I wish Zephyr hadn't given me their names. I'll be damned if they get killed because of me.

I take a step towards the door, but before I get any further, Calista's voice reaches my ear. A stream of language erupts out of her, and Zephyr hurries to grab onto my hand.

"Mama says it's not safe," he translates quickly. "The DaePolice are looking for you. Because of..." Zephyr swallows, his eyes growing wide as he whispers, "The murder."

I groan. I had forgotten about that. But even so, my clock is ticking.

It can't be helped. Crouching, I look Zephyr in the eye. "I'm sorry. Tell your parents I am very grateful that they helped me. But I don't want to put them in danger. I must leave."

I wait as the boy tells his parents what I said. His mother looks worried, but Jasper pushes back his seat. It groans as it moves, and the sound echoes through the tight space. He comes over to me and shakes my hand. His voice is low as he speaks.

"He says he understands," Zephyr says after a moment. Then, waiting for the Vampire to speak again, Zephyr translates as Jasper walks out of the small kitchen. "Follow me. Your things are in the other room."

A sigh of relief escapes my lips as I hurry out the door. I follow the Vampire into a small living room with a ratty couch on one end and a tiny flatscreen TV on the other. The large male bends down, and the sound of metal opening reaches my ears. I shift on my feet, catching a glimpse of a metallic door.

Moments later, he turns around. My satchel looks laughably small in his hands. My gun and knife are lying on top of the bag.

The Vampire steps forward, extending my bag towards me as his brows furrow. "Here," he says in broken Common Tongue. "Thank... you... save... wife."

My lips turn up as I bow my head. "It was nothing."

Zephyr translates, and Jasper shakes his head. He shoves my bag in my direction. "Not... nothing." Once his hands are free, Jasper launches into a loud stream of Ancient Fae. Unable to do anything else, I wait for Zephyr to translate.

"He says he owes you a great debt. If you need anything, please let him help you. You have saved my mother, and for that, he is eternally grateful."

Nodding, I bite my lip. After a moment, I reach a decision.

"Okay," I draw out the word, putting my satchel over my shoulder. "I suppose there is one thing he can help me with."

An hour later, the roar of Jasper's motorcycle is all I can hear. Every other noise has become nothing but buzzing as the electric sound of this death machine rings in my ears. Maybe it's because I've spent most of my life on the water, but every single time the motorcycle dips around a corner, I see my life flash before my eyes.

As we take an especially sharp turn, my hands tighten around the Vampire's middle.

When he had shown me his bike earlier and motioned for me to get on the back, I had almost backed out of the whole thing.

Reluctantly, I accepted the helmet he offered me before holding on tight as he took us out onto the busy streets. Now, the burly Vampire is expertly weaving through the late-afternoon traffic. My grip hasn't loosened since we got on the road, and I'm just holding on for dear life.

Thank the gods Calista's medicine seemed to have miraculous properties because my shoulder isn't hurting anymore. On the flip side, my stomach is moments away from losing all the food I ate earlier.

I don't think anyone is following us, but Jasper isn't taking any chances. He is zipping around the slow-moving cars and trucks as we travel through Lethe.

My teeth feel like they're seconds away from falling out, and if it wasn't for my impending death, I might feel more concerned about the state of my previously fantastic dental hygiene. As it is, I'm praying to all the gods that we make it to our destination in one piece.

There's no blood left in my face, but at least it isn't painting the road.

The curses of our fellow motorists are drowned out by the sound of the engine. The roads through the Gates of Hell are not uniform. They keep alternating between more modern pavement and ancient cobblestone roads.

The motorcycle is fast, which I appreciate. Jasper clearly recognizes a man short on time when he sees one. I don't know how much Zephyr understood of my situation, but it's clear by the way the Vampire is driving that he knows that time is of the essence.

The King's Tower is visible as we drive through the city, which is both modern and ancient. The giant structure looms over us as we race through the streets, casting its long shadow over the city. It stands sentinel as we veer towards our destination.

I look up, watching as Angels and Daemons alike soar through the skies. Everything in Lethe is so... normal. So regular. People are going about their days as though nothing is amiss.

The sounds of the city are overwhelming after spending so much time on the water, and a part of me wants to just shut it all out. For a moment, I give in to the numbness pushing at the back of my mind. I let everything filter through me, like water through a sieve.

I give myself five minutes. Five minutes to be numb. To give into the emotions rushing through me. To let the intense regret that I've been feeling push its way forth. Five minutes to remember that for a few short weeks, I felt like things could have been different for me. For the first time in my life, I had thought that maybe, just maybe, I was redeemable. That I wasn't doomed. That there was more to life than just pirating.

Scrubbing a hand over my face, I close my eyes. Instantly, I see Helena in my mind's eye. I wince as she glares at me, her bright pink eyes sparking with anger as she taunts me. I give myself five minutes to feel.

Then I lock up those emotions and throw away the key. Damn Helena. Before her, I hadn't known I was missing anything.

Now, it's as though a hole exists within me, and it has her name written all over it. If I can warn her uncle before she's killed, then I will have done what I can to repent.

WHEN JASPER PULLS TO A STOP, he removes his helmet and raises a brow. He doesn't even turn off the motorcycle as he waits for me to dismount.

After handing him my helmet, I dip my head. He returns the gesture before sliding the bulbous thing onto the side of the bike. I turn around with one hand on my bag and the other hanging at my side.

My eyes widen as I look past the bustling sidewalk at the ancient building before me. Long, tall steps lead into the structure, and marble pillars support the front.

I step forward, intent on my destination when someone shoves me to the side. My hand tightens on my satchel as I stumble backward. Reaching a hand, I steady myself on a lamppost as I glare at the male before me.

"Watch it, human."

The speaker, a Warlock with glowing eyes and long violet hair, stalks past me. He says something to his companion, a green-haired Witch, who cackles in response.

My blood boils, and I clench my fists at my side. I make a rude gesture that Helena would be proud of, cursing the Warlock under my breath as I ascend the steps. My feet pound as I take them two at a time, leaping towards the top.

"What's the big rush?" a female asks. I hurry past her, not even stopping to look at her.

The cold metal of my weapon presses into the small of my back when I lean against a marble column, staring out into the city of Lethe. It is a comfort in the intense heat. From here, I can barely make out the vivid blue of the sea. The water calls to me, but I don't heed it. Instead, I focus on remembering what I came here to do. My chest tightens as faces flash through my mind. Clenching my free hand at my side, I shake my head and push off the column before opening the glass door.

"Welcome to The Consortium," a Pixie flutters by my ear, her voice annoyingly high-pitched. I clench my jaw as I step inside. Instantly, a frigid air washes over me as I enter the ancient building. "How can I help you, sir?"

My eyebrows raise as I take in the female fluttering before my face. She's no bigger than my hand, with translucent wings that remind me of a bat. "I need to see Yardley."

The Pixie nods, her gaze sweeping over me. She places her hands on her hips, her silk gown bunching under her fingers as she studies me. "And who should I say is here?"

"An old friend," I force the words through clenched teeth.

The Pixie hovers before me. Her face is pinched as she presses a few buttons on her watch. Her brows furrow as she squeaks out, "Just a moment, sir."

A gilded clock shows the time at the far end of the spacious entrance. "Dammit," I mutter, strolling past the Pixie into the building. It's later than I thought it was. I'm halfway across the marbled floor when the Pixie's voice catches up to me.

"Sir! Sir! Please wait in the lobby."

I ignore her.

"Excuse me, sir. This is highly irregular. If you'll just give me a moment to see if Yardley is free..."

I turn the corner into an empty hallway. The second we leave the lobby, my hand snaps out and grabs the Pixie around the middle. I pull her close to my face as she struggles. She throws dust at me, but I easily duck away.

"Listen to me, you ethereal irritant." I tighten my grip around her middle, and she gasps. "Be a good little messenger and tell Yardley that the Pirate of Death is here for her."

The Pixie's face drains of color as she stutters. "You killed someone again?"

I nod, releasing her as I elaborately bow at the waist. "At your service."

She gulps, her wings fluttering furiously as she looks me over. She raises her ashen face to mine, her eyes impossibly wide as she nods. "Yes, sir. Right away, sir."

"That's better."

"Yardley is ready for you, sir," the Pixie says as she curtsies in the air, suddenly polite.

Nodding, I shove open the door. It bangs against the wall as I take in the space. Floor-to-ceiling windows cover two of the four walls, and an enormous desk fills up more than half the space.

Prowling over to the large mahogany desk, likely compensating for something, I grab a seat and drop into it. "Hello, Yardley," I say through clenched teeth.

For a moment, there is no response. Then the office chair creaks as it turns around.

"Erik," a strong, aged voice says from the chair. "I thought I told you never to return."

I tap my fingers on the desk, willing myself to remain calm. "I wouldn't have returned if it wasn't an emergency."

The tiny, wrinkled woman in the chair looks up at me with wide orange eyes. "You killed another prince?"

Crossing my arms, I shake my head.

"You slept with a vampire's partner?"

I growl.

"Shit, did you visit the Were—"

"It's not important."

Yardley tsks, wagging a finger. Her gray hair shakes as she moves. "Now, now. You know that's not how the Consortium works. You agree to honesty, or you get nothing."

"Fine," I grumble. "But we might be here a while."

"Good. I love a good story." Her lips open in what I think is a smile. Her gap-toothed smile is peppered with yellowed teeth, and I fight a shudder. Pressing a button on her watch, she waits as a holographic image of a different Pixie appears.

"*Yes?*" she says. The Pixie's voice is tinny.

"Julietta, I am not to be disturbed."

"*Yes, ma'am.*"

Seemingly satisfied, Yardley presses another button on her watch. Suddenly, a black mist appears over the glass windows. Once the panes are entirely covered, she steeples her fingers and turns back to me. "Now that we have some privacy, my boy, tell me why you're here."

Settling in, I begin my tale the moment after she helped me sort through the trouble I'd caused with the crown prince of the Mer. At the end of my story, Yardley leans back.

"So," she says, tapping her fingers together. "You were sent to kill King Phelix's daughter, but you developed deep feelings for her instead?"

"That's what I said," I reply. Crossing my arms, I lean back in the chair while she continues.

"And now you're being hunted by the Elite because you, the legendary Pirate of Death, one with a slit throat and one drowned, couldn't kill one female."

The last word comes out of Yardley's mouth as a snort as she erupts into raucous laughter. My eyes bulge, and I clutch the arms of the chair as she dissolves into hysterics.

"What is so funny?" I ask through clenched teeth.

"You were kicked out of here the last time for your violent tendencies," she says between pants for air. "The irony of the situation is incredibly hilarious."

"Not. To. Me." I clench my teeth, rubbing a hand over my face as I force myself to take long, steady breaths.

Yardley places a wrinkled hand on her chest and gasps. "Yes, yes. Of course. So, I assume you need me to do the transfer?"

My shoulders loosen as I nod tersely. "Yes."

"Do you have a recipient in mind?"

"I do," I reply. Pulling my satchel over my head, I drop it on the desk. It lands with a *thud*. "I have everything right here from when Barthalemew left me the ship."

Piercing orange eyes meet mine. Yardley's mouth sets in a firm line. "Are you sure, Erik? Once this is done, it cannot be undone."

"Do it."

An hour later, I calmly walk out of the building without my satchel. My fingers twitch at my sides as I take in the setting sun before I turn into a dark alley.

Now, I'm ready.

26
I OWN THIS PLACE
HELENA

There isn't time to hesitate, so I grab the knob and contort my face into an irritated sneer. Two thumps from the roof above assure me that no one is coming down soon.

I was, and am, a snobby royal. I can absolutely play the part of an affluent, disgruntled homeowner. I only pray they don't ask for identification. My left hand settles on my popped hip while my right leg extends outward and ends at the elegant point of my white stiletto.

My suspicions about the visitors being the police are instantly confirmed when I spy two large, menacing Daemons through the small peephole in the door.

The door swings open with a vicious yank, and I catch it swiftly, just before it hits the wall. The two males take in my haute couture suit and my nasty expression. They glance at each other uneasily.

Inwardly, I scoff. Size really doesn't dictate ferocity, it seems.

"Ma'am," one of the Daemons says. He dips his enormous head and studies my face with yellow eyes.

They take my lack of response as confirmed irritation. I mean, I get it. Only someone incredibly sure of their innocence would dare to ignore a uniformed officer.

"Sorry to take up any of your time, but there appears to be a report of a break-in. One of your neighbors—a Mrs. Haginni—reported seeing a female climbing up the fire escape."

I raise an eyebrow. A thump sounds above me, and the Daemons glance at the roof.

The Daemon who spoke shifts his weight from one foot to the other. His wings rustle, and I hone in on that movement. His partner, sensing the discomfort, tries in his place, "Mrs. Haginni couldn't identify the exact species that she saw—"

Thank the gods for that!

"—but just that she was wearing a red bikini—"

Leotard. Another thump.

"—with bright yellow hair."

I roll my eyes. This makes them even more visibly uncomfortable, making me feel icky inside that someone would have this amount of power just by having the *illusion* of wealth. I mean, my father is wealthy, but I am not. I have virtually nothing to my name.

My chimera friend slinks to my side and rubs its head against my pink knee. The visible shock on the nervous one's face at the pet sets in just as another thump knocks above.

"We are sorry to take up your time, so we'll get to the point: Did you see anyone that matched that description? We came here first since she said that the suspect was climbing towards the roof," the nervous one says, eyeing the pet.

I shake my head and scratch the chimera's ears.

"Very well, ma'am. If you notice anything—" I slam the door in their faces. I press my back to the door and slide down to the floor.

I pray that the thumping above doesn't stop and that they fill in their own conclusions with... whatever the hell was happening on the roof. A few more moments of silence tell me nothing deterred the cheating bastards above from their afternoon romp.

I collect my abhorrent leotard and flip-flops while straightening my round sunglasses. Images of a nearby bathroom guide me so that I might fix my unbelievably frizzy hair.

Thanks to my new friend, the help of a flat iron, and some red lipstick, I am much more presentable in three minutes than I was earlier. Twisting this way and that, I look at myself in the mirror.

I look like the picture of wealth. I hope I look good enough to be a princess. Nibbling on my lip, I realize I need something to write on. I no sooner think about a pad of paper before the telepathic beast trots over with a piece of paper and a pen.

A pleasant emotion fills my chest. More pats and scratches are the only reward I have to give, but she receives them eagerly. After writing a simple note that says,

Your husband is cheating with Luella.

I pocket the pad and open the door. Once again, I pray that the DaePolice are gone.

As I walk through the door, something akin to a meow sounds behind me. My feline friend is waiting at the threshold.

Come on, I say silently. I've already stolen a lot of shit. What's one whole-ass chimera?

Images flash through my mind that make me weak at the knees. The chimera waited at the door for hours. Its owner ignoring it. The chimera standing at the window, unable to leave.

I draw in a deep breath as understanding floods through me. It cannot leave the home. It is meant to protect it. Only permission from its owner will signify its freedom.

The reality makes me cry... this beast is trapped by people who care little for her safety. I know how that feels.

I draw her into my arms as silent tears drip onto the fur on top of her head.

I promise I will come back for you.

I close the door, and the last image the animal sends me conveys her feelings perfectly. It is her owner, the faceless beauty with a cheating husband. In the middle of the picture is a list with only one name: Cebe. She leaves me her name.

The chimera is afraid, sad, and lonely.

Me too, babe. Me too.

The sound of my heels clacking against the tile stairs helps to drown out my thoughts as I head to the King's Tower.

BLISTERS ARE FORMING on my feet as I walk through the unbearable heat toward the shiny black building that presumes to pierce the sky. It is liberating and terrifying all at once; all it would take is the owner of this suit to spot me near this house for me to be called out and plopped into whatever kind of jail cell they use in the land of the Daemons.

Anytime I spot a bike rack, I find myself trying to inconspicuously grip the metal bars to steady my wobbly feet. People are staring at me now. My new look has given me new visibility. Some of them snicker when they see my unsure footing. I will be in trouble if I don't figure out how to get myself together before I get to the Tower.

If Cebe had stayed with me, undoubtedly, she would be walking alongside me and helping me with my death march.

If I cannot gain an audience with my uncle, then I am shit out of luck. I'm becoming used to how the feeling drains out of my fingertips and toes when my anxiety heightens. In a show of false confidence, I assume a more suggestive pose with my body by pushing out my chest and clasping my wrist with my other hand behind my back.

It's impossible to resist twisting the smooth, cool metal of the bracelet around my skin.

My natural sense of direction doesn't fail me. Soon, I am back in the same square as before. It is cloudy, and thunder rumbles ahead. The heat is becoming heavy and oppressive, and the air is filled with humidity. Nothing like this ever happened underwater, and it's completely new to me.

I hope I can make it to my destination before the rains fall. My pace slows as I consciously make the effort to soften my steps and transform my gait into something more akin to belonging on a runway than a drunken being stumbling from a bar.

As I pass through the enchanted statues depicting my family's history, I wish I knew what they *actually* looked like over what they had been presented to me as. I want to know whether Fortuna's eyes really held the ghosts of kindness.

The opposite end of the Pantheon boasts a walkway protected by rows of Daemon guards of all genders. There are velvet stanchions separating the tourists from the truly elite few. The peasants from the royalty.

I sneer at the thought. My whole purpose in coming here is to hopefully appeal to a man who is not like my father in any way, shape, or form. If he is the same flavor in different packaging, well...

I stop myself there. There is no reason to sabotage my plan before I give it a proper chance. My hands are coated with sweat as I make a mental list of everything I need to say to my uncle.

Schooling my face with a look of indifferent condescension, I pat the pocket where the note about my identity is stashed. I feel the artificial gleam fill my eye, and I widen my stride. Crossing to the space where two exceptionally strong Daemons stand at attention, I remain looking forward and bored.

A crisp hiss of paper against cloth sounds as I take out the note written on nice stationary and fold it into thirds. One of them holds out his hand as I place it delicately in his palm.

All of my princess training happened underwater. I hope it shows through as I wait for him to read. Once finished, he looks up from the note and gives me a good once-over. I wink.

His eyes widen as he turns to his impassive partner. "Says here that she is the daughter of Ice Mer King Phelix. She's requesting an audience with King Hades. Do you know anything about this?"

The other snatches the note and reads it over. "No, we better go ask Toth'toros."

That name.

For the love of Fortuna.

"I'm one of the least shitty Daemons in the King's employ."

Wariness floods my body. If I run away now, it will absolutely imbue suspicion into a pair of already paranoid alpha males. My elbows press into the sides of my body, trying to make me appear smaller.

One of them does a sharp about-face and marches into the Tower.

"First time in the Gates of Hell?" the one who remains asks.

I shake my head.

He smirks. "Oh yeah, you can't speak. Got it."

The moments drag on as we wait for the other Daemon to return. My eyes stare forward, but don't really see any of my surroundings. One visitor to the square stops to take a flash photo of me.

My lips compress. They don't even know who I am, they just want to remember that one time they saw a supposedly famous person in a very ancient place. They don't know that the picture they took on their crappy, bottom-tier camera could be worth millions in the right hands.

I am a wanted female.

An ache has started in my shoulder blades from how tightly I hold my posture. Finally, the other Daemon returns. Tension brackets his mouth, but thank the gods, he is alone. I am sure Todd remembers me.

When he reaches us, his eyes flash something that looks like a warning to his teammate.

"You are to come with us," he says. His voice is neither hard nor gentle, but at least he hasn't arrested me on the spot.

Maybe this will actually work.

I stop sweating as the feeling slowly returns to my hands. When I start traipsing around in these ridiculously high heels again, I feel confident. The walkway to the Tower is lined with a black marble fountain that runs all the way up to the doors. Small lilies dance atop the mirror-like water. It really is lovely.

For as fearsome as everyone claims Uncle Aidoneus is, he has excellent taste. The gold-trimmed crystal sliding doors open for me with a satisfying swiftness. I step through and immediately feel the heat dissolve into cool, air-conditioned luxury.

All sense of security evaporates when I see Todd waiting for me. His jaw is tight, his eyes flashing as he says, "We meet again, *Legs.*"

One of the other Daemons grabs my hands and yanks them together behind my back. My jaw wrenches open in a silent scream.

"Didn't think I would recognize you, did you? I detest scenes, which is exactly what would have happened if we had apprehended you out there. I figured it would be much easier to bring you inside first."

I struggle to yank my arms back when something cold is jabbed into my neck. My eyes widen before I lose all control of my body.

"Don't worry," the Daemon Toth'toros sneers. "I have a cell fit for a princess."

27
PICKING FIGHTS AND POLYGRAPHS
ERIK

"Can I get another?"

I slam the empty shot glass on the bar top, resting my prosthetic hand on the counter. My fingers brush at the dirt and grime, and I suppress a shiver of revulsion.

The quiet din of conversation surrounds me, but I don't pay it any attention. I've been here for three hours, and my mood has steadily deteriorated. When I first entered the bar, I felt like getting a drink before leaving. But then I realized I had nowhere to go. No Helena to see. No real friends in the city anymore. I didn't even have my ship.

I was alone and waiting to die.

So I gave up on my one-drink plan. Instead, I dove into the pit of anger and rage that had been simmering within me for the past twenty years.

The bartender turns around and smirks. His gray brows rise, and I feel his gaze dragging over me. I bristle at his obvious assessment.

"Are you sure you can handle another shot, *human*?" he asks.

Disdain drips from his voice, and his gray wings rustle behind him as he approaches. His eyes flicker with amusement. The male positively towers over me.

"Don't say that word like it's an insult. It's small-minded," I say through clenched teeth. With my other hand, I reach into my pocket.

The Angel tenses, his wings snapping together as he widens his stance. My mouth twitches as I slap a stack of bills on the counter.

The bartender's position loosens as his lips form a wolfish smile. "Ah," he nods. "I see."

His eyes gleam as he takes in the stack of cash. I can practically see the dollar bills in his eyes as he tilts his head. The way he realizes that he could make far more than the hundred dollars I've already paid him. His greed is understandable, but I clench my teeth.

I pick up the cash and put it back in my pocket as the Angel dips his head. His voice is silky smooth as he asks, "What can I get you, sir?"

"Another shot of Liquid Fire," I reply firmly. "Keep them coming."

The Angel nods, his greed winning out over his disdain. He turns his back, and the clanging of bottles tells me all I need to know.

A low whistle comes from beside me. "Damn, Erik," the man next to me says. His stool creaks as he twists in the rickety seat. He elbows me, and I twist to glare at him. He sips his beer. "What's with all the cash?"

"It's been a good couple of years, Smith," I reply.

The old acquaintance had walked into the bar an hour after me and had claimed the barstool to my right. He tried and failed to start numerous conversations, and eventually, he realized I wasn't here to talk. We've been drinking in silence ever since.

Until now.

Smith raises a brow, making a show of looking at the pocket where I put the cash. "That looks like more than just 'good'."

I shrug. "If you have to know, I was at the Consortium earlier. It's an advance from Yardley."

Smith raises a brow. He places his arm on the bar top, resting his chin in his hand. "Interesting. Want to tell me what it's from?"

I shake my head. "Nope."

A high-pitched laugh comes from the other side of the bar, and I turn. A pack of seven Weres, male and female, are crowded around a booth on the other side of the bar. They're laughing over a FaePhone, their eyes lighting up as their chatter grows louder.

One of them looks up and catches my eye. A languid smile spreads across her lips, and I see a question flit across her expression. I blink. I know her—*knew* her. We'd met in this same bar. I remember quick, rough touches. Fleeting, meaningless kisses. Her apartment is on the next block.

But now, as I look at her, I feel nothing. Exhausted, I shake my head. She turns her back on me. A mix of relief and self-loathing vibrates my chest.

At this point, I've given up. I've done what I needed, and now I'm just waiting.

The Angel turns around and places the shot I ordered before me. Nodding, I grab it and toss it down my throat. True to its name, the alcohol burns as it runs through me.

"Another," I demand. The Angel complies.

By the third shot of Liquid Fire, my head is foggy. I lift my hands in the air, and the feeling is similar to wading through water.

A vision of bright pink eyes appears before me, and I groan. Rubbing my temples, I slam the empty shot glass down.

"Barkeep," I yell, beckoning the Angel back over. "Something stronger."

A hand lands on my arm. "Maybe you should slow down, Erik," Smith says. His voice is laced with concern, and I bristle.

Clenching my jaw, I shake his hand off me. "You're not my babysitter, Smith. In fact, as I recall, you're nothing more than just a washed-up pirate who makes a living selling black-market goods in Lethe because he couldn't make it on the sea."

Smith lurches back, his brows furrowing as he clenches his fists at his side. He makes a face. "What the hell, man?"

"I'm just calling it like I see it," I say. The watery sensation is getting heavier by the moment.

A vein pops in his jaw as he watches me with narrowed eyes. "I thought we were friends."

"Nothing good comes from being friends with me," I say. My voice is low as I groan. "I used to think women were bad luck on boats, but you know what?"

He shakes his head.

"I was wrong. It's me. I'm the bad luck. Ir-ir-irredeemable." I slur, pushing away from the bar. Slapping a few bills on the table, I stumble before pulling myself upright. "Do yourself a favor, market-boy, and forget you ever met me."

"Fu—"

The bell at the front of the bar chimes, and Smith's voice drops off into thin air as all the blood drains from his face. My back stiffens, and the hairs on the back of my neck prickle.

Just like that, I'm stone-cold sober.

All sound floats away, except the faint melody of *Thought You Were the Fae for Me* by *The WereRaiders*. The music is completely at odds with the tension thickening the air.

My shoulders tighten, and I reach into the waistband of my pants. The cold metal of my weapon is reassuring.

Turning around, my eyes widen as I take in the three large,

gray-skinned males with seaweed green hair who are standing in the doorway of The Midnight River. Their blue, pupil-less eyes are steely, their jaws firm, as they scan the seedy establishment. Their hands are empty, but a quick glance at the black leather they're wearing tells me they're each armed with multiple weapons.

"Shit." My jaw strains while I watch the Angel. His hand slips under the bar, his muscles tensing for a moment before he steps back. The faint gleam of a red, blinking light comes from under the counter. "Dammit."

Curses continue to slip out of my lips as my mind jumps ahead of me. I'm calculating my chances of getting to the back of the bar before these thugs decide that everyone in here is better off dead.

It would probably take me fifteen seconds to get out of here. But the way the largest male is eyeing me tells me exactly how low my chances would be of making it.

Slipping my hand into my pocket, I grab the wad of bills and press them into Smith's hand. "It's been nice knowing you, man. Sorry about the crap I said."

He stares at me. "What the hell are you doing, Erik?"

I wipe my mouth, trying to get in control of my slightly foggy senses, and shrug. "This is between the Ice Mer King's men."

His brows furrow. A dozen questions flit through his eyes, but before he can ask them, I've turned away. Raising my hands in the air, I saunter past the slack-jawed patrons of the bar towards the males and then tilt my head toward the exit.

"Gentlemen," I say lightly. Now, Reckless Erik is firmly in control. "Why don't we take this outside?"

The males stare at me, and then at each other. It's clear my willingness is a surprise to them. They use their fingers and palms to sign rapidly at each other. After a few moments, they turn towards me. The largest one opens the door, while the other two step aside.

They watch me warily.

I walk out slowly, carefully. The moment the humid evening air washes over me, a strange sense of calm overcomes me. I'm ready for this. I've accepted my fate. Better me than Helena.

She is worth *everything*. Her soul isn't dark, and I know her uncle will care for her. I've done everything I can to protect those I care about.

Taking a deep breath, I widen my stance and prepare for my final stand.

This is it.

In the space it takes me to breathe, I grab my gun and pull it out in a practiced movement. In the next breath, I click off the safety as I jump backward. My grip on my gun is steady as I aim it at the leader.

The three males tilt their heads, their eyes glimmering in amusement. I can practically hear their thoughts as they watch me. *Idiot human. He thinks one gun can save him from the three of us.*

"How can I help you, gentlemen?" I ask. Sarcasm drips from my words as I walk backward. I glance around, taking in the dim streetlights providing pockets of illumination against the darkness of the night. For a long moment, silence is their only response.

They snarl, coming towards me, when suddenly, one of them stops. He holds up his hand, his head angled to the side.

It takes a second before I hear it, too. Sirens, faint at first, fill my ears. They are growing louder by the second. My heart pounds when I realize the bartender must have called the DaePolice.

I keep my gun drawn as I evaluate the scene in front of me. Exchanging quick glances between each other, one of the Elite reaches into his jacket. The streetlight shines on something metallic as he draws out his hand. Above us, I hear the flapping of many wings. It sounds like a flock of birds is about to descend.

Very violent, deadly birds. Ones that have little care for human life. The DaePolice.

Making a split-second decision, I squeeze the trigger. The rapid sounds of gunshots shatter the silence, and seconds later, screams erupt from inside the bar. At the same moment, there is a stinging sensation in my left side.

Cursing, I place my hand on my side before turning and ducking down a dark alley. The sirens have become an incessant beat in my head, and the pounding of wings in the air is adding to the symphony of the night.

Footsteps pound on the cobblestones behind me. Keeping my hand on my side, I dart around garbage bins, wrinkling my nose as my eyes water.

"Stop that one!" a loud voice yells from behind me.

"Almost there, Captain," someone else says. This voice comes from… above me.

Shit. Shit. Shit.

Before I can even look up, steel-like claws attached to human-esque hands grip my shoulders. I try to rip my arm from them, but suddenly, the ground is five feet away. Then ten. Then I can't look down without feeling terrified. Buildings that loomed above me become nothing more than tiny dots as I struggle against my captor's iron grip.

Bile rises in my throat. "Let me go," I shout, thrashing. My side aches, but I shove away the pain.

He laughs. Gods-damned laughter fills my ears. Red fills my vision as I struggle against his strong hands.

"Do you have a death wish, human? Be still," he snarls. The hands around me tighten, and somehow, we start moving even faster.

The world below me becomes a blur. The flapping of wings is all I hear. I shut my eyes and pray for a quick death.

No one hears my prayers.

Of course.

"You can open your eyes now, weakling."

The same voice as before is taunting me as my feet make purchase on solid ground. I fall, my legs unable to support my weight as I collapse onto all fours. Pebbles cut into my hands as I am filled with an overwhelming urge to kiss the dirt-covered cobblestones.

Wincing, I open my eyes. My side burns, and I glance down. My black sweater is matted with blood, sticking to my side.

Two things strike me at once.

I first realize I have no idea where in Lethe these Daemons have taken me. Then, it solidifies that I am in deep, deep trouble. A dozen DaePolice stand before me. Their expressions range from apathy to downright disgust.

Not far from where I'm currently lying, the three gray-skinned males kneel with their hands behind their heads. A pile of weapons is nearby and behind the Daemons... I swallow, my eyes growing wider by the second. A tremor overtakes me before I can tamp it down. At least now I know where I am.

The problem? I probably should have just let them kill me at the bar. Death would have been a mercy compared to what I will face here.

My eyes sweep up the massive obsidian tower, the immense structure reaching high into the night sky. I gulp, shifting onto my knees, as I stare at my captors.

One of the Daemons, presumably the captain I heard talking earlier, steps forward. "Take the Elite inside. Keep them separate."

I start, "Wait, I'm n—"

"Shut up," one of the Daemons says before drawing his hand back. My face reels from the impact, and I see stars as black fills my vision.

My head pounds against my skull as I blink. My eyes struggle to adjust to the bright light swinging in front of me, and a moan escapes my lips.

"Welcome back," the Daemon says. His black wings are spread behind him, taking up most of the room. Everything about his posture screams relaxation as he leans back in his chair, eyeing me.

"Where are we?" I snarl. My eyes widen as I take in my appearance in the mirror behind the Daemon. My black hair is a mess, and a trail of bright red blood has streaked down my face. I'm no longer in the black sweater, though. My brows furrow, and I see a white bandage peeking out from beneath the generic white t-shirt they must have put me in while I was unconscious.

The cop tilts his head, his eyes studying me as he ignores my question. He gestures to my side. "You're welcome for that, by the way. Our surgeons used some laser tech on you. You'll heal within a few hours. Be as good as new."

"Why?" I ask.

"We need you to be in good shape before we interrogate you. There are laws in the Gates of Hell, you know."

Interrogate.

"I mean, why am I here?" My neck itches, and I go to draw up a hand, only to have my arm snap down. My gaze drops, and I take in the electric cuffs and chains binding me to the table.

A laugh escapes the Daemon as he jolts towards me and bangs his hands on the table. I flinch but maintain eye contact with the male.

Eventually, he speaks again. "A member of the Elite asks *why* he is in custody? I should think the reason is fairly obvious. You and your pack of murderous mates left a trail of bodies a mile long all over Lethe. You lot are a menace to society."

"I'm not a member of the Elite, man," I shake my head, raising my hands as far as they'll go. "*They're* hunting *me*."

"Likely story," he scoffs, crossing his arms. "If you're not working with the Elite, I'm a Pixie. We have reports from inside The Midnight River that you said, and I quote, 'This is between the Ice Mer King's men.' Did you, or did you not say that?"

Groaning, I bang my head on the table. "*Damn*. I did say that, but I didn't mean I'm one of them! I'm serious. They are here to kill me. If you hadn't picked me up, I'd be dead now."

The Daemon narrows his eyes. Disbelief is written all over his features. "Is that so?"

I nod. "It is."

He taps his fingers on the table, watching me closely. He bites his lip, his dark eyes staring into my soul. "Tell you what. If you agree to take a polygraph, we can clear the air right here."

My stomach sinks. Every true crime aficionado knows that there are two rules everyone should follow:

1. Don't murder people.
2. Never, ever, ever agree to a polygraph test.

Sighing, I stare at my reflection in the mirror. Well, I break rule one every other week. I might as well go ahead and destroy number two. If it means I can get closer to the Daemon King, to Helena...

"Okay," I mumble. "I'll do it."

The Daemon's eyes light up, and his lips peel back from his teeth, revealing two very long canines. "Perfect," he growls.

I'm throwing out all the rules now.

"How old are you?" the Warlock says. He stares at me from across the table, his brows raised.

He types on his computer, the polygraph machine, nothing more than two white wireless dots attached to my heart and my head.

I reply, "Twenty-nine."

The Warlock nods, still typing on his computer. The interrogation room seems a lot more cramped with the newest additions. I swallow, looking around the room. The same Daemon from before is now standing in the corner, his arms crossed as he glares at me.

"What brings you to the Gates of Hell?"

"Tourism," I joke.

The Warlock glances up, his eyes flashing purple. "Lies," he hisses.

The Daemon's wings snap, and I tense. "The next time you lie, human, you'll lose a finger. Understood?"

I swallow. This was definitely a mistake. "Understood."

The Warlock repeats his question.

"I made a deal," I say through gritted teeth. I'm staring at the logo on the back of the Warlock's computer, avoiding their eyes.

"Who did you make the deal with?" my interrogator asks.

Pursing my lips, I shut my eyes for a moment. "The Ice Mer King."

"Truth." the Warlock says. He looks up, his eyes snapping to mine for a second before he continues. His voice is sharper than before. "What was the deal?"

I shift in my seat, staring at my lap.

"Answer him!" the Daemon barks, slamming his fist into the wall. Dust billows in the air as the plaster cracks.

"I owed him a life debt. He wanted me to kill his daughter. If I did it, I would be free."

The clacking of the keyboard is the only sound. Seconds tick by into minutes.

The Daemon is the one who speaks this time, his voice dangerously calm. "Did you do it?"

Visions of Helena's smiling face appear before me. My heart constricts in my chest. "No. I didn't."

More tapping.

"Where is she now?"

I blow out a long breath, shrugging. "I don't know. Somewhere in the city, I presume. Safe, I hope. Helena will die if they find her."

Just then, there is a banging on the other side of the mirror.

The Daemon stills before pulling out a FaePhone from his back pocket. I watch as he reads something once, twice, then three times.

His expressions change so quickly that it's hard to interpret. He goes from being annoyed to confused to afraid. The Daemon looks up at me, his eyes flashing. It takes the Daemon two seconds to be at my side and another to release me from my bindings. He grabs my arm, pulling me with him.

"What the hell, man?" I try to yank my arm away, but he's too strong. "Where are you taking me?"

There's no reply. Instead, he loosens his grip on me just long enough to grab something from his back pocket.

A cold sweat appears on my neck when I realize what it is.

I really start to struggle then. My heart hammers as I wrench my arm away from him. I shove the cop aside as I run towards the door.

Something black is pulled over my head before I can take two steps. Black fills my vision as I claw at the material covering my face, but it's useless.

"Stop fighting," the Daemon says roughly. "You're just going to make things worse for yourself."

He grabs my arm once more, and I have no choice but to follow as he leads me to my doom.

The polygraph was a very, very bad idea.

28

LETHE'S UNPREDICTABLE WAY
HELENA

Lethe is a mix of ancient and modern, primitive and advanced, crude and sophisticated. I have spent little time in this wonderland, but it radiates an aura of unpredictability. Nothing like Aqualis, where the choices lie between being beautiful, classic, and uniform or being destroyed.

Luckily, the federal prison in The Bedrock District isn't gauche. Far from it, in fact. While I am isolated in a cell, kept away from the other prisoners, the area is sterile and orderly. White walls, white floors, metal furniture. And yes, said metal furnishings do include a seat-less toilet. The wards have been cast with such a heavy hand that I can taste them in the back of my throat, bitter and foreboding.

My stolen outfit was confiscated upon arriving. Everything I own fits into small plastic bags with a pressed seal. I've traded Le Baba Morgaine for a plain, gray jumpsuit. Its fit is baggy, and the grayness is a dull insult to my vibrant skin tone.

No food has been left near my cell, so an invitation to the cafeteria has been extended.

A cell fit for a princess, my ass.

My bunk is a thin mattress with scratchy sheets and springs so prominent they bite into my back as I lay down and look at the ceiling.

This, I think, *is familiar.* It reminds me of being in Hallie's home. I smile despite the tears that threaten to slip out of my under-lids. In that lonely room, with my horrible sister and her clueless husband, two little angelfish had come to whisper secrets and stories under the crack in my door.

Who would whisper to me in the silence now?

I let that melancholy thought drag me under into the tides of sleep.

Nightmares swarm the eddies of my subconscious. Hallie, Henrick, my father, my mother... their faces flash before me and dart away towards some mysterious abyss. The water of said abyss is black and impenetrable. My heart aches.

The terrible flavor mixes with a savory smokiness that is impossible in the soggy depths. Erik comes. He fills the space around him with his large, menacing personality. The taste of him both sates me and drives me mad with hunger.

It is hard to tell exactly when my dreams mix with reality, but eventually, my eyes flutter open upon hearing a key turning the lock to my cell.

An involuntary spasm jerks my body upwards, and I anxiously stare at the generic, bulbous knob. One of the Daemons must finally be ready to take me to eat.

I abandon all attempts at straightening my crumpled jumpsuit as I hop to my feet. The figure that walks in... is not who I expected. For a moment, I think I must be hallucinating.

The back of my knees knock against the bed, and I nearly tumble ass-first onto the cot again. My cell is instantly filled to the brim with large, fluffy wings. Like most of the city of Lethe, the prison is made to accommodate wings.

These wings, however, are far more stunning than anything I had previously seen. Their elegant arcs protrude from the middle of her back, fade from angelic white to corn yellow, then soft pink, and finish with a flourish in a vibrant cerulean blue.

Her wavy, black hair complements the pale rosiness in her cheeks and slanted eyes. A soft smile graces the loveliness of her heart-shaped face. A sweet, rose-scented breeze accompanies her entrance, and I can see the sheer brute force of Todd towering behind her.

"Helena?" she asks in a calm, bright voice. Her clothes mark her as a business female. The fitted turtle-neck tank is robin egg blue to match her wings. I can barely make out two slits that must tie underneath her wings. The tank is accompanied by a modest, knee-length black pencil skirt and black pumps. The Angel clutches a leather-bound tablet in front of her.

Her presence is reassuring, and I forget to respond. She asks the question again.

Yes, I nod quickly.

"Lovely," she says. "My name is Phaedra. I will be taking you to King Hades. If you would please follow me?" The longer she speaks, the more I can discern her voice's bright, wise quality. I wonder exactly how old she is. If I had to guess, she must be at least a century older than me.

I eyeball Todd warily and stay put. Phaedra notices this and frowns.

Her wings snap open, obscuring Todd's view and casting a

brilliant light throughout the room. It isn't magic. The light is just *her*.

She smiles once again. "I apologize for any trouble the DaePolice have made. I assure you, we did not know who you were. Now that your identity is confirmed, you will be taken to your uncle. Toth'toros is only here because he is one of the king's most trusted men."

I stare at her, unblinking.

One of her hands drops from the tablet and gestures out the threshold of the door. "Shall we? Don't worry, we shall go for your clothes presently."

I purse my lips, but I follow. It's not like I have many options.

Todd walks behind us, his wings on full display. His black sunglasses and black suit mark him as death incarnate.

"I know you can't respond, but I need to tell you how sorry I am for all of this," he whispers quietly. "I really didn't know who you were."

I continue to look straight ahead and blink back the surprising moisture in my eyes. Apologies are not things I am used to hearing.

None of the other prisoners so much as come to the front of their cells. Their dwellings are different. They are open to the hallway, save for their bars. They remind me of animals left on display, which I dislike.

Though, it is more humane than home.

We don't even have prisons in Aqualis, just torture houses and arenas. I almost laugh. Death or torture. Those are your only options. The Northern Courts are *not* known for their kindness.

Phaedra's scent is powerful. Its brightness seems to enliven the colors around her. But even the power of the sweetness isn't enough to work out the knot that sits high in my stomach or the heavy sadness I carry from seeing Erik in my dreams. I wonder if

I'll ever think of him without the shooting pain that rushes through me at the sound of his name.

We arrive at the lockers where the inmates' personal belongings are stored, and I squint. The blinding fluorescent lights are a far cry from the dim cell. Phaedra nods to my *bodyguard*, and Todd leaves the room with a tense smile.

"I can take you to one of the bathrooms on the other end of this level of the prison, or you can change here. I assure you, I can hide you from any camera," she says. Her wings flap open, and her bright blue eyes writhe to life with electricity. Pure, unadulterated power fills her as tiny bolts of lightning dance over her skin.

In answer, I unzip my jumpsuit and peel it off. I don't really give a shit if they see me in my scratchy sports bra, but Phaedra casts some sort of net around the room. The lights go dark, along with everything else.

It scares me to see such power. It reminds me of my father's seaweed-green magic.

In a hurry, I dress. It would be helpful if my mortal legs hadn't robbed me of my Mer instincts. It makes me wonder what else my legs may have taken from me.

When I am finished, Phaedra seems to instinctively know. The shocking web of light stops instantly, like a power outage, and the room is bathed in the familiar ghastly artificial green-white.

"You look stunning. Let's go."

The Angel opens the door and waits for me to walk through. Todd still stands at attention, but I can't tell if he is watching me from behind those thick, black shades.

My eyes narrow at him. I want him to know that I do not accept his apology. In fact, I hope he knows how angry I am with him for not believing me and then arresting me. But he remains as still as a gargoyle and only falls into step once Phaedra and I walk out the wards that protect the world from the deadly criminals that supposedly reside inside these walls.

WHEN THE SOUND of mine and Phaedra's high heels clack against the polished granite floor, everyone looks up to greet us.

An impressively stylish Daemon with slicked-back red hair sits behind the reception desk. He has a Bluetooth headset curved elegantly around his ear. I can hear him with perfect clarity when he glances up at us and says to some unseen person, "They're here."

His face is arranged into a professional smile, and he goes so far as to come out from behind the semi-circle reception desk. Everything in here is black, gold, and green. It should make me feel like the walls are closing in, but it feels more like the vast unknown of staring up into the night sky while camping in the mountains.

Not that I've ever done that. The closest I've come is watching forbidden videos. It turns out that once you start watching short, fifteen-second clips on the internet, they are a hard kind of drug to quit. Who knew?

The closer we walk to the desk, the bigger the receptionist's smile grows. I wonder if his cheeks hurt from the exertion of such a ridiculous expression.

"Welcome, Princess Helena!" he shouts.

I wince. His voice is way too loud.

To add to his painfully cloying presentation, he bows deeply. His wings are tucked so tightly against his back that I almost miss them. They are smaller than others, more like an eagle than a bat.

"As the first official member of King Aidoneus Hades's personal enclave to meet with you, can I just say we are honored to at last host one of the members of our esteemed king's estranged brother's family. We—"

"Orith, honestly, give it a rest. I am Hades' personal assistant." Phaedra's dismissive words cause the male to freeze. He stands there, hands tucked behind his back and jaw slightly askew as we walk by. The wall that hides the elevators from view is thick white-veined marble. In a place like this, it is likely solid stone.

The elevators appear to be crafted of gold. And... for all my time as a princess, I can't tell if it's just gleaming polished brass or not.

When we step onto the elevator cart, the enchanted walls reveal themselves. Despite the gleaming metal, we can see through the doors. We shoot up at a manageable speed. I watch as floor after floor of workers pass before my very eyes. Some have sleek, high-tech computers, while others have massive tables dedicated to drawing and designing.

One floor is full of people wielding small brushes and dusting off ancient-looking artifacts, but the last two are filled to capacity with... objects. Rugs, paintings, vases, pottery from the Old World.

I press my face to the glass to look closer, but we are speeding up too quickly. We reach the top level with a startling ding.

The shiny, gold-colored doors slide open, and we step out. As if we are in some sort of world outside of Aranthium where everything is turned upside down, it is darker the closer we get to the sky.

The blackness permeates through this office, and I can feel how large everything is—I just can't see it. It is like looking over the cliff of a seamount and into the depths of the midnight zone in the ocean.

Light simply doesn't reach this place. My senses tingle; I know creatures live here. Some are lethal, others are kind, but the only way to find them would be with light. Spherical spell lights line our path, only to be swallowed up before I can glimpse our surroundings.

Todd and Phaedra walk with ease, even casting appreciative glances at what is hidden from my eyes. How?

A voice slices through the pitch-black room. "Helena, welcome to Gates of Hell."

Leaning back in a tall leather desk chair, the Daemon King sits. His unnatural, electric green eyes stare at me. A few spell light orbs cast his silhouette into view, and I suppress my shudder.

I can barely see the fine cut of his business suit, the elegant form of his ears, and his smooth brushed-back curls. What causes me to involuntarily swallow are the bat-like wings that sweep the space on either side of him and the horns protruding from the high point just above his temples. They are tall—they reach upwards and curve out and in, like an hourglass, until they peak at the top and point to the heavens.

Sweat coats every inch of my skin, and my clothing weighs against me. I nod, sure that he will see me and understand. My fingers stretch outwards, reaching for something to write with. To explain myself.

The voice that could rumble the earth beneath my feet speaks again. "I understand you cannot speak," he says. He moves one of his large hands and flicks a long finger. "I believe I can remedy that. I have provided an aqua chair for you so that we can return your voice."

Todd emerges from the shadows. He is pushing an elaborate chair that contains sloshing water. It has wheels attached to either side and an electrical mechanism clearly meant for steering it on one armrest.

That same, menacing hand glows gray-blue in the spell light, and the Daemon King gestures for me to sit. There is no way to deny the will of this being. I gulp, crossing to the aqua chair. I can't imagine hesitating, yet I do when I look down at the water.

I can't just change myself back to fins. If I could... well, things might be different right now.

"Ready, Helena?"

I flinch at Phaedra's warm voice, but I nod.

My uncle's eyes glow with energy, and pure power flows out of my uncle and down into my throat.

It burns.

Like fire rushing through my veins, it feels like the heat of a million shooting stars is pouring through me. I claw at my throat. My skin feels like it is being scalded and peeling off of itself. A horrible sound fills the room as I sink to the ground and try to curl into a ball. I just want to minimize the agonizing pains shooting through my body.

"*Please stop, please stop, please,*" a voice shouts.

It's my voice. My raspy, tired, unused voice.

Phaedra kneels next to me and puts a hand on my back. She murmurs a few words, but I can't hear her over the keening sound coming from me. As she touches me, a warmth spreads through my body, healing me from the inside out. My breathing slows, my chest eases as all traces of pain vanish. My breathing steadies as Todd scoops me up and sets me into the chair.

My fins... *my fins.*

They are back. My beautiful scales, my delicate fins. They curl around themselves, and I sit back in the seat. The water is warm in the most delightful way. It surrounds me, lapping up against me like the embrace of an old friend.

"Are you all right, Princess?" Todd asks gently.

My hands touch my cheeks and come away wet. I am crying. I take a deep breath to stop the panting. "Yes," I say. A sob wracks my chest, soaking my stolen suit's fine, cashmere jacket. In the place of my legs, I see my beautiful tail.

"Don't worry about your pants, Princess Helena; I have taken care of them with a spell," Phaedra says. She turns to the king, her beauty enhanced by the room's darkness. "Your Highness, I believe she has proved herself not to be a threat."

"A threat?" I gasp. Everyone looks at me. My hand touches my lips. I am not used to being heard. My eyes travel to my uncle.

He is staring at me, the tips of his steepled fingers pressing into his mouth. At last, he says, "Very well."

The king lets out a long breath, and the blackness around me fades.

Nothing is like what I first thought. My uncle's desk is stacked with books and papers. Scattered trinkets clutter the corners. Bookshelves and paintings line every inch of the office, save the roof-to-floor window that gives the most breathtaking view of the Gates of Hell.

Creatures do live here, but none that I can name.

I suck in a breath and savor the taste of cinnamon. "It's beautiful," I breathe.

My eyes lock back onto Uncle Aidoneus and find that he is not as he appeared either. Gone is the frightening businessman, and in his place is someone I'd love to get to know. The cut of his suit jacket is indeed fine, but it is a soft tweed pattern. Crimson, black, and cream cross-cut through the navy blue fabric. He wears a white button-up situated under a gray knit sweater.

He stands, revealing the black, horned crown that sits upon his brow. Part of it comes down his nose, separating his stunning eyes. My uncle's hair is styled, his white curls set back into the look of what one might imagine of a book collector.

"What in the nine circles of hell..." I whisper. When everyone around me reacts to my thought, I realize I've said it aloud and curse again. "Sorry. I am not used to this speaking thing," I explain awkwardly.

Phaedra smiles encouragingly, and I spy my uncle cast one loaded glance at her. The intensity behind the look makes my brows furrow. *This is a man who is still mourning his wife?*

I instantly shove the thought away, relieved I hadn't foolishly spoken it aloud.

"Helena," my uncle says as he stands and straightens his sweater with one efficient tug. "Before you begin. Would you mind explaining this?"

Todd crosses to a carved dark wood door and slips inside. We all wait for him, but sounds of a struggle ensue. I shift in the water, anxious to see what's on the other side of that door.

The stale air thickens with grunts of anguish, and an ear-splitting crash echoes through the chamber. Todd strides out from behind the veil, gripping Erik's collar in one hand. The tortured soul is dragged along like a ragdoll until he falls at my feet.

My mouth gapes open as I recognize his face. My uncle laughs, and not in an unkind way. "You've both made quite a mess trying to find each other," King Hades says.

I move closer, feeling Fortuna's presence fill the room with a rumbling chant. It's as if Fortuna foretold this moment and scripted it to be played out with heavy music instead of sorrowful tears.

The man I cared for kneels with his head hung low, bowing before me in solemn acceptance of defeat.

"Erik?" I say tentatively.

His head snaps up, and he studies my face. More tears slide down my cheeks. He looks like a ghost. A horrible ghost who betrays people who care about him. Heat and sorrow combine to create something potent and unwanted.

"Speak, mortal," the king commands. All of his intimidating nature returns in a flash.

Erik ignores the king. He looks at me and studies my face. At that moment, it is as though there is no one here but the two of us. "Helena."

I hate him for the way my name sounds on his tongue. I hate him for the way I feel when he speaks. It's as if I've been holding my breath, and his voice is sweet air. My body relaxes in a way it hasn't since I last laid in his bed.

"Why are you here?" I demand.

29
STAY WITH ME
ERIK

The sound of Helena's voice is like a siren's song. It is as light as air, as deep as the sea, and edged with a current of violence that sends shivers down my spine.

This is the Crown Princess of the Ice Mer in all her glory.

And *she is* glorious.

Her strong, chiseled features stand out in the spell light. Something about her is different from the last time I saw her; she carries herself with poise in a sophisticated way.

In her Mer form, Helena looks like regal authority.

I can't believe I *kissed* her. That she let my unworthy lips brush hers. She let me touch her. I feel like I'm frozen in time as I stare at Helena. My eyes are wide, and my mouth opens and closes like a fish.

"You're beautiful," I whisper hoarsely.

She blinks. "Erik, I asked you a question." Helena's voice —*her voice!*—is harsh as she pushes the wheels of the aqua-chair. They glide smoothly over the tiles.

"Why. Are. You. Here?" she asks again.

I am dragged back into reality. "It's not exactly a choice I made, Princess." Lifting my still-bound hands, I gesture to the Daemon behind me. "They brought me in. Rather roughly, if we're being honest."

Helena looks at the Daemon. "Is this true?" she asks.

The Daemon nods. "Yes, Your Highness. Three members of your father's Elite were apprehended trying to..." his voice trails off.

"Inflict permanent and irreversible harm to my very human, very fragile body." I fill in the blanks. The restraints around my wrists bite into my skin as I turn and glare at the Daemon. "Bat-boy over here and his men picked me up before I could finish taking them down."

The Daemon looks at me, his brows practically hitting his hairline. "You think you would have walked away from that fight?"

I shrug. "Maybe. I didn't have anything to lose."

"Why are the Elite hunting you, mortal?"

The voice comes from the other side of the room. It immediately draws my attention, and I swivel my head towards the speaker.

Intense power swirls around him as he pins me with his vibrant green eyes. It feels like the air before a lightning storm. Instantly, I recognize the male from press releases. My throat dries up.

"I... they..." I stutter. Shaking my head, I try to get a hold of myself. "Sorry," I say. The words are gruff as they come out of my mouth.

"Yes, human?" the Daemon King's voice booms through the room.

Swallowing, I train my gaze on the woman standing behind Helena. She appears to be a better bet. Her lips are pinched in a straight line, but her eyes... there is compassion in her eyes.

"Give him a moment, Aidoneus," the Angel says, her voice chiding. "The poor man is clearly having a bad day."

The King studies the woman, something flickering in his eyes as they seem to be engaged in their separate conversation. Then he nods, leaning forward in his chair and resting his head on his hands while he waits for my answer.

Closing my eyes, I take three steadying breaths. When I open them again, my head is clearer. I look directly at Helena.

"Years ago, I saved an Angel from the former Crown Prince's clutches." I begin.

My eyes remain locked on the princess while I go through the story, from the life debt to her father's order to kill her. When I come to the part where I decided I wouldn't kill her, Helena flinches.

That minuscule movement destroys the tiny pieces still left of my heart. I want to go to her, hold her. But I can't comfort her.

So, instead, I just push through the story as quickly as I can. When I am done, I turn to the King and say, "And then your men picked me up."

For a very long moment, the only sound in the room is breathing. My heart is hammering in my too-tight chest as Helena slowly comes closer.

"Are you telling the truth, Erik?" she whispers, her pink eyes locked onto mine. I see a flicker of compassion in them, and something like hope flutters to life in my chest.

I hold her gaze as I say, "I am."

She breathes, her words little more than air. "You knew he would send his Elite after you, and you still decided to let me go?"

I nod, my chest heavy as I pull up my bound hands. "Helena, you are... important. To your kingdom, to the world. To me. I swear, I was just stringing him along until I could get you safely to shore. I had planned on telling you, but..."

She sighs, rubbing a hand on her face. "But I found the messages."

"Yes."

"I may have overreacted just a touch." She winces.

My brows raise. "Just a touch? You stabbed my phone multiple times and tried to kill me."

A laugh boomed from behind us. A quick glance at the King confirms the laughter came from him. He covers his mouth with his fist, his eyes sparkling with mirth.

Phaedra chuckles, her wings fluttering behind her as she places a hand on Helena's shoulder. "Overreactions are a family trait, I think," she says to no one.

"I agree," the King says before turning to the princess. "I am glad you made it here in one piece, Helena."

Helena's lips twitch as she tilts her head towards the Daemon King. "Thank you, Uncle." And then she rolls over to me. "Erik?"

My name is a prayer and a plea on her lips. My breath catches in my throat, and for a moment, I don't know what she will do.

Her eyes sweep over me, starting from my knees and rising to my face. The moment our gazes meet, everything else seems to fade away. Every movement of her face, every catch of her breath, every twitch of her mouth means something.

"Yes, Princess?" I breathe. It's a plea that I feel in the very depths of my soul.

Those incredible lips open as she reaches down and brushes my hands with hers. "You were willing to die for me?" she asks. Her astonishing voice is barely a whisper.

"I still am," I murmur, my voice gravelly.

A cough comes from behind us, destroying the moment. Helena's head snaps up. "What do you plan to do with him, Uncle?"

The Daemon King purses his lips, the light catching off the

black crown resting on his forehead. He shrugs, staring at my still-kneeling form on the floor. "What we had planned doesn't matter anymore. What do *you* want us to do with him?"

That's the real question. My head begins to pound as Helena looks back at me. For so long, she's been forced to follow others. And now that she's in control, I have a feeling that I know what she'll say.

She and I both know I'm not good enough for her. I'm not good at all. The dark stains on my soul are as black as a starless night. I'm a very, very bad person. Not only is she nothing like me, but Helena is the Crown Princess of the Ice Mer. A brutal race that values violence above all else.

I know the kinds of laws she follows.

Steeling myself for the inevitable rejection and forthcoming death sentence, I drop my eyes to the floor.

This is it. She'll seal my fate, and that will be the end of me.

A strange sense of resignation fills me. My life will finally be over. Three decades of not being enough. Of just bobbing along the currents of life, trying to do good while knowing I could never be noble. Numbness fills me.

I'm sure they have heavy penalties for treason here in the Gates of Hell.

"Let him go," Helena says quietly. Her voice breaks through my reverie, and I jolt backward.

"Excuse me?" I sputter, raising my eyes to hers. Surely, I misheard her.

She meets my gaze, her mouth twitching. "King Hades, I ask that you spare this man's life."

"The decision was always yours," he replies instantly. The King of the Daemons steps forward, waving a hand at the male who brought me in here. "Toth'toros, you heard her. Remove this man's bindings. He is free to go."

"Yes, sir."

When my hands are liberated, I rub my thumbs over my wrists. The skin is bright red, and I will definitely have a bruise tomorrow. But it's better to have a couple of bruises than be dead.

"Thank you, Uncle," Helena says. Biting her lip, she looks between me and her uncle. "If it's okay with you, can we have some time to talk?"

The King nods, waving a hand at the winged woman. "Of course. Phaedra will show you to a room."

The Angel turns and flashes a pearly smile at us. "Right this way, please."

A FEW MINUTES LATER, Phaedra pushes open a large brass door. Her wings flutter behind her as she turns, her gaze sweeping over us. "I'll have them send up some water bottles. In the meantime, please make yourselves comfortable."

Head held high, Helena dips her head ever so slightly. "Thank you," she says, wheeling herself into the room. The area is decorated with shades of gray and green, and large furniture modified for Daemon wings fills the space.

Phaedra puts a hand on my arm. Her nose twitches slightly, her large wings tight behind her as she makes a show of studying me from head to toe. "There's a shower in there, too, in case you were wondering."

A loud snort comes from inside the room, but when I look at Helena, her face is blank. Everything but her twinkling eyes are impassive.

"Thanks," I mutter. "I'll keep that in mind."

Once the Angel has disappeared, Helena comes back to the door. A wry grin spreads across her mouth. "Are you coming, Erik?"

The authority with which Helena speaks is unfamiliar to me. Seeing her, hearing her speak, and watching her step into her metaphorical royal shoes is arousing.

My entire body is tense, like it was the first time we kissed on the ship. As soon as that thought appears, I push it down as far as possible.

This is not the time for feelings like that. Just because Helena spared my life doesn't mean she forgives me. It doesn't mean we are anything.

"Yes," I say. "I'm coming in."

I pause in the entryway. This is a *massive* suite. I could easily fit four or five of my bedrooms in here. My jaw falls open, and surprise must be written all over my face because Helena laughs.

Her laugh.

Her laugh.

I was wrong before when I thought her voice was the most beautiful thing I had ever heard because her laugh is like when the moon first appears in the night sky. It is rich and boisterous and full of life. It sparks something within me. My muscles clench as warmth pushes away the cold numbness I have surrounded myself with for my entire life. Her laugh takes a sledgehammer to the last vestiges of anger, desperation, and despair that remain within me.

I can feel my entire body rearranging itself to the tune of that sound. No longer am I simply Erik, Pirate of Death, soon-to-be-dead at the hands of the Elite. No longer am I empty. With that laugh, I feel a part of myself that has been so broken begin to knit itself back together. With every passing second, I feel myself becoming more.

I feel.

Right then and there, I know I will do *anything* to hear that laugh again. One isn't enough. How did I live before I heard her laugh? It is full of life. She is full of life. She *brings* me life.

But then her expression is serious once again. "Erik, sit down," Helena says, gesturing to a gilded couch.

I obey her command immediately, and an awkward silence fills the air. I look at her, and she looks at me. For a very long moment, neither of us speaks. Then we both open our mouths at the exact same time.

"Erik, I nee—"

"Princess, wha—"

We both stop.

"You first," she offers, reaching over to put her hand on mine. I stare at our hands for a moment, reveling in the touch before wrapping my hand around hers.

I nod. "Helena—Princess. We need to talk."

She nods, her hand twisting in mine. I don't let go. Another piece of myself knits itself back together as we sit there together. She says, "I agree. You start."

Exhaling, I run my free hand through my hair. "Where do I even begin?" I murmur.

"How about the moment when you decided you weren't going to murder me?" her voice is sharp, and it cuts through my thoughts.

"Okay. That's a good idea."

Biting my lip, I stare behind Helena's head as I shift on the couch. A TV stretches across the back wall, the screen larger than anything I've ever seen. Still-life images flash across it in slow progression. I recognize some of them, but others are utterly foreign to me.

"Erik?"

"You have to know that I never wanted to kill you."

"Oh? Good to know. You didn't *want* to do it," she says. Sarcasm, thick and heavy, drips from her words as she stares at me. Her eyes narrow, and a muscle flexes in her jaw. "Now that I know that, you're instantly forgiven. Sure, you plotted with my father, took me away from my family, kept me on your ship, isolated me, and were getting ready to kill me. But it's okay since you didn't *want* to do it."

I return her glare. "You make it sound like I had a choice. I didn't, not really."

She yanks her hand out of mine, her eyes flashing as she snaps, "Erik. There is *always* a choice."

"Is there, though? People like to say there is always a choice, but they never clarify that some choices are shit."

Huffing, she waves her hand in the air. "Explain it to me."

Taking a deep breath, I flex my hands. "Most of my life has been decided by other people's choices."

A long moment passes as Helena simply looks at me. Her jaw is tight as her eyes sweep over me. "What are you talking about, Erik?"

I rub the back of my neck, avoiding her gaze. There's an image of a snow-covered mountain on the TV screen, and I watch it as though it's the most interesting thing I've ever seen. "I mean, not everyone has a choice. Do you think I chose to have my parents murdered in front of me? That I chose to lose my hand? That I chose to be taken in by a pirate and trained to be his replacement?"

"Wait, what?" Helena demands. "What about your parents?"

Shit.

"Just forget about it," I sigh. "I didn't mean to say that."

"But you did."

I stare at the TV and shake my head. My ragged breathing is the only sound in my ears.

"You don't owe me any explanations," she says. "But I want

to know because I care about you. If you don't want to tell me, then you can leave. I release you from your guilt and accept your apology. We don't mean that much to each other, anyway."

Something within me snaps at her words. Memories I've pushed away for years rush to the surface, and I turn toward her, my heart pounding. "You want to know what happened?"

She nods once.

"They were murdered by a pack of Daemons when I was nine. The pack stalked my family and killed my father so they could... *assault* my mother. They assaulted her like that son of a bitch Conrad wanted to do to you. And then when they were done with her, with my mother... Madeline was..."

She blinks, and the blood drains from her face. She is clearly too shocked to speak. I get it. What do you say to a story like this?

"I listened as they tortured her for hours on end." My eyes close as the litany of jeers fills my ears. Saliva pools in my mouth. I don't want to vomit, so I close my eyes and continue, "I stayed in a closet and listened to everything. Everything." I take a deep breath, pushing through the rest of the story. "Helena, I was so scared, I pissed my pants. I didn't leave until an older man came and rescued me. He brought me onto his ship and gave me a job as his cabin boy."

She is so still; I would think I was seeing things if the water from her chair didn't ripple around her torso. "That's how you became a pirate?"

I shake my head, my gaze distant as I stare straight ahead. "Yes. The only *choice* I was given was to stay in my destroyed house with the mutilated bodies of my parents or go with him."

Helena breathes, her inhale sharp as she touches my cheek. The contact feels like an electric shock. "Your mother's name was Madeline."

I realize what I revealed a moment too late. I blink, "Helena, I—"

"Is that why you reacted so strongly when you found Conrad trying to rape me?" she swallows, her voice low. "You gave me her name. Madeline. And I had no idea at all. Erik, that... I'm so sorry."

I turn away so that she can't touch me, and I drop my head into my hands. "I think that's when I realized I couldn't do it. When I saw Conrad standing over you." I rub furiously at my eyes. "How do you think I was trapped into a life debt?"

"I-I don't know..."

I say sharply, "I saved one of the women your brother was going to use for his pleasure and then dispose of."

Helena actually gasps.

"Come on, don't tell me you didn't know he was a monster," I glare at her.

"I was glad when Nathaniel killed Henrick. I've never told anyone that before." She sits up straighter, but a storm rages in her eyes.

"Then how can you—you, who of all people, has lived a life just as helpless as mine— how can you sit here and tell me that we all have a choice?!" I yell.

She tries to stand up and then splashes back down. "How dare you—" she starts.

I held up a hand and cut her off. "I see you, Helena. I see what you've been given, and you deserve better. What your father wanted was wrong, but this isn't just about me. If I chose to say no, my entire crew would be punished. There are... people that I help. People that rely on the services I provide."

She tugs at her hair, her cheeks red as she shouts, "I was wrong!"

I freeze. Her chest is heaving, her eyes wide as she continues, "I was hurt and betrayed, and I was—am—wrong."

I stare at her. Words have escaped me.

"You make me so frustrated. I can't think straight anymore.

I'm relieved to see you, and yet I'm so mad that you did this. I'm furious with my father. Did you know he killed my mother?"

I blink. "No."

"As long as we're dishing out screwed-up backstories, you should know I can go toe to proverbial toe." The color has returned to her face, and the purple flush on her skin looks lovely.

There is something intoxicating about this moment. I scoot closer. She looks so beautiful, so vulnerable, I can't control the passion roaring in my veins. I cup her cheek. I mean to be soft, but I need her to look at me.

"How about we don't? How about we... help each other for once? I'm tired of fighting you. You know everything now, and whether I stay or not is your choice."

She reaches up, her webbed hand touching my wrist. She melts into my touch, her eyes fluttering closed while she pants.

"I don't know. I already saved your life." Her words are labored, and they stab me straight in the heart. I drop my hand away, and she flinches.

Snarling, I push myself off the couch. "I will be one of the many villains in your story, then," I say. I'm halfway to the door when she stops me with her voice.

"*Wait*," she cries out.

I freeze.

"I'm a villain, too," she yells. Her voice is awkwardly loud like she doesn't know what she will say next. "In my father's story, I am the villain. I let my brother die."

I don't move; I just listen.

"There will be people with incorrect ideas about who I am, who you are. Seeing you walk away... I can't do this. Don't leave me."

Tears are burning in my eyes, but I am straining her words.

"Please," she whispers. Her voice is thick with agony and crying.

I blink against the emotion. "Why do you want me?"

Silence.

Deafening silence.

I repeat myself, louder this time. "Why do you want me?

"Because-because... because you make me feel safe, villain or not. I need that back."

I whip around. The way she looks at me, her eyes wide and her lips open, stirs something within me. The pieces of myself that I just laid bare begin to come together. I feel... peace.

My voice is hoarse as I whisper, "I'll stay."

I cross the room in three long strides, falling to my knees before her chair. She's trembling, and I hold her tightly despite the water. Pressing my forehead to hers, I murmur, "I don't want to fight anymore."

She clings to me, shuddering breaths racked with quiet sobs. I know I shouldn't be doing this. I'm a pirate, and she's a mermaid. But at this moment, I don't care. I just want to hold her, to be close to her. A part of me is relieved that she wants me to stay, but another part is terrified at how much I need her.

It's a miracle when her lips capture my own with fierce passion. Her desperation and need for me are clear in how she presses herself against me. My hands roam over her back and arms. She moans softly as my tongue brushes against her lips, and she parts them, letting me in. I explore her mouth thoroughly, savoring every taste and every sound she makes.

Then she pulls back, taking in my soaking shirt. She straightens her own top and clears her throat. "I'm not ready to do this again yet."

I put space between us. "Whatever you say, princess." This was to be expected, things being as complicated as they are between us. Tonight, I would work for every touch of her skin. I would do whatever she wanted.

Because whether she knows it or not, I am hers.

30
MOVE SLOW
HELENA

Erik is reclining on the leather couch in front of the TV. His feet are tucked under him as he lounges. An open book is balancing on his leg.

I've never felt more strange. Was it really just two hours ago we were screaming at each other? Sobbing like idiots? How do two beings go from that to... this?

I splash the water around the scales on my waist, keeping them hydrated so they don't itch. I put on a trashy show, *The Real Life of Pixies*. Elva had once mentioned it to me.

Erik glances up from his history book on the Goddess Fortuna, and his nose scrunches. "I don't understand how you can watch that garbage?"

"I don't understand how you have access to such peak, prime-time entertainment, and you don't want to watch it," I retort.

He watches the Were shoot her lover, and he gasps. A grim smile comes over Erik's face as he says, "Excellent. Exactly what should happen to cheaters."

I laugh. I can't help it. "So violent, pirate."

He glances from the corner of his eye at me. When he catches me staring, he returns quickly to his book.

The episode stretches on. Soon, Erik's book lies forgotten in his lap, and he is completely engrossed.

"I think the most unrealistic part of the show is that a Vampire who looks like that has no one interested in her," he gestures emphatically to the figure on the screen.

"Oh? I thought you weren't interested in all nonhuman species," I say, lazily drawing a watery circle on the armrest of my chair.

That makes him snap out of his hyperfocus on the television. He shifts his legs and stands, the book falling to the wayside, his attempt at reading completely abandoned.

"Why is that?"

"Because you have an all-human crew," I say. My voice has gone quiet, shy, even.

He kneels before my chair in seconds, bringing us to eye level. My breath catches when he leans forward to brush a few strands of hair from my eyes. "I thought it would be obvious by now... my preference is whatever you are. Mute or lame, angry or soul-splittingly happy, I would rather be with you."

The same nervous weight in my stomach forms when his hands trail down the side of my face and brush against the sensitive skin on my neck. I blink as he leans forward. Have I really forgiven him enough to be doing this? My body and heart say yes, and my mind seems to have taken a holiday.

"Wait, I think it would be best if I bathed," I say hastily.

He backs away and raises an eyebrow. "You are literally sitting in a self-filtering tank?"

"My hair," I blurt out.

"Ah, yes. Perhaps I could help you?" he asks. His voice has dropped an octave, and his brown eyes are dark with desire.

My throat goes dry.

"With your hair," he clarifies.

"I can wash my own hair. I am easily three times your age, boy." My voice is harsher than I intend, and I flinch.

Despite how sharp my words are, he smiles. "That's my Helena," he whispers huskily. His hand trails over my fingers. "Then I will stay here."

Why do his touches feel like licks of flame against my bare skin?

"Thank you," I say dumbly and roll away. I spy the king-sized bed, one that I won't be using. The room is expertly decorated, just like everywhere else in the King's Tower. The high ceilings have lovely, antique light fixtures, but the floor is adorned with lush rugs with colorful patterns. The expensive wood furniture is a gorgeous, rich brown color. They remind me of Erik's eyes.

The fluffy white bed dressings invite me for a restful sleep, which I know would turn my scales into a dry, scratchy mess. I wonder where I will spend the night and whether or not Erik will be there as I continue my journey to the bathroom.

The black and gold tile makes my heart stop. A tub large enough to comfortably house four people with wings is in the corner of the vast room. I roll over and spy the brass water fixtures and the temperature gauge on the side of the tub to control the water and temperature levels.

My eyes widen. King Aidoneus certainly knows about luxury.

I grasp onto the lip of the enormous tub and start to lift myself in. I certainly can wait while the water runs…

Or I can ask Erik to help me.

My body becomes a rolling contradiction. A burning fire of a thousand suns fills me, yet my hands are cold and clammy.

Am I ready to *be* with Erik? My inexperience is undoubtedly something he doesn't share… or is it? How does one talk of such things without bursting into flames?

I growl and tug at my hair. Then I remember that he possibly might hear me from the other room. I look at the fitted tank top I stole and then gaze at myself in the gilded mirror—another priceless antique. My face is flushed, and my hair is wild. My hands descend from my hair and then press into my burning cheeks. The coolness from my palms feels good.

I am a gods-damned Ice Mer. Since when do I find such pleasure in the heat?

My mind is screaming and pulling me in a dozen directions. I want to run away from here, and I want to pull Erik inside this room with me. Without allowing myself any more time to be a coward, I roll out of the tiled room and into the living room.

The TV is still on, and Erik is sitting on the couch, looking deflated. When he notices me, he smiles. It doesn't reach his eyes, making me feel even worse. I watch him try to put on an air of casualness, but I can see the ghost of sadness behind his eyes.

"So..." I start. What the hell am I supposed to say? Come fill the bathtub? Do I want him to fill the bathtub? No, I want to taste his mouth and feel his calloused hands scrape across my skin.

"What's up?" he says lightly, interrupting my thoughts.

"Can... you help me?" I settle on the question, pointedly ignoring the image of him doing much more than that as it skirts through my thoughts.

He's on his feet in a flash. "With pleasure." Erik rests his hands on the back of my chair. "May I?"

I swallow. My stomach feels like a hundred tiny fish have taken up residence within it. "Yes."

As we undergo the infuriating trip to the bathroom, one that feels like I've already taken it a thousand times, he asks, "Why don't you use the control for the chair? You know it's automatic, right?"

I stare at the joystick warily. "Too easy, and as much as I hate to admit it... I am getting a bit tired of all the gadgets."

He laughs and gives me goosebumps. It's such a sexy sound. *Or maybe I just think he's sexy? Maybe I'm overthinking this.* A blush paints my skin purple.

When we enter the bathroom, my anxiety blossoms in the air and fills the room. I'm pretty sure it could stop a bullet.

He walks over to the faucet and places a hand on the tap lined with a blue ring. "This one?"

I shake my head. "I'd prefer it to be more warm."

He nods and twists the red handle. The sound of water rushing through the pipes gives me a small reprieve. Erik is as cool as the sea. He is the picture of relaxation as he stands fiddling with the tub, adding sweet-smelling salts to the bath. I cannot peel my eyes from him, my heart pounding.

Erik turns to me, smiling softly. "Would you like help getting in?"

"Yes, please."

He ducks and wraps his hand around my waist. The other arm slides under my fins and hoists me easily against his chest. My lungs are screaming for air, and my heart races when our faces come close.

"Can I kiss you again?" he breathes. His breath smells like coffee.

"Yes," I say a little too quickly.

This kiss is gentle, filled with the sound of running water. He kisses me as he walks us backwards. It is as though I weigh nothing... *clearly a man of experience.*

I struggle to keep images of the mysterious, faceless... *other* women from my brain as he lowers me into the warm water, my back facing him. The water laps against my tingling skin, and I bite my lips to keep down the little noise that threatens to escape me.

"I've waited for several weeks to be in a place where we could be alone like this," he admits in a gruff voice. "Where we could be together without anyone listening."

I wring my hands together. What if he isn't actually interested in me... he's just a womanizer? When his hands brush the thick strap of my turtleneck tank top, I freeze. Distrust has extinguished the fire.

"Helena," he says gently. "What's wrong?"

I suck in a breath. "I—This is hard for me."

"Why?" he asks. His voice is so gentle.

"You know why."

He tilts his head. "Because you haven't ever been with a man before?"

"—Any male," I shoot back, the purple in my cheeks and ears intensifying. At least my position allows me to avoid looking directly into his eyes. "Two days ago, I was angry enough to murder you. And now you want to make love to me?"

"Princess, that is the sweetness of affection," he reaches out and brushes a lock of my hair behind my ear. "Love is tempered by passion."

"Do you have a passion for killing things?" I ask, and his eyes cloud over. What I really want to dwell on is the way his lips form the word love, but that is foolish.

"Death is necessary for survival. Sometimes it is kinder to kill some people," he says carefully.

"Kinder to who?"

"To their victims. Victims of any kind of abuse; emotional, physical, mental..." His words trail off, and I remember his mother. Madeline. He's got some sort of vigilante justice in him.

Is he a murderer... with morals?

"Sometimes I wish I'd never met you," I admit. The words slip out of me unbidden. As soon as they are out, I'm surprised by how light they make me feel. Honesty tastes delicious on my tongue. My time with Erik will never be anything but colored in guilt if I don't tell him exactly how I felt.

He doesn't speak for several minutes. And then he stands and gestures to the water, "Can I join you?"

I blink, shocked by how forward he is. I bite my lip, "Yes." I do want it, even if I also want to cry and slap him.

The sound of clothes hitting the ground come from behind me, and my heart races so fast that I fear I might faint.

His long tan leg appears in my peripherals, and—thank the gods—he's wearing his boxers. He lowers down, but instead of sitting, comes in front of me and balances on his knees.

"I have never regretted knowing you. I've behaved like a brute. I understand why you might feel that way. But you have ignited this spark..." he swallows. "You have ignited this spark of life inside of me. Your very presence in my life has taught me things I never knew were possible."

He doesn't touch me, and I bite my lip.

"Erik, those lines sound fine enough to be tucked away in your mind, memorized through repetition," I say, forcing down the sensation of wanting to throw up. He has the audacity to look confused. "How many women have you been with before me?"

Understanding makes his eyes widen. "H-Helena, that's not really important."

"I beg to differ."

"Do you trust me?" he asks.

"Yes." *No.*

How do you get past the awkwardness that comes from seeing so much of someone's demons? How can I get over my insecurities?

It's as if he hears the thought as clearly as I do. "Don't lie to me, please. Send me away if you don't want me, Helena. If I never have anything more than the joy of your presence in my life, I will accept that. But please, Princess, don't let any more lies or secrets come between us."

Moments pass, and unbidden tears fall down my cheeks. He's spent so long being closed, aggressive... growly.

This new version of him is surprisingly gentle and soft. It makes my heart sing. "You hurt me, Erik. Gods, every part of me wants to forgive you... but it's hard. I want you; want you to kiss me, to touch me, to teach me about romance, and to make me forget the lies. But I don't know if that will work, and it is scratching my insides out. If I give you too much of myself, and then you walk away to someone else, I fear I might break. I would shatter into a million pieces. I have no desire to be a notch on your bedpost, a story only to be shared with your friends."

Once the words are out into the world, I feel lighter still. Either Erik will know it all, and accept me anyway, or we will stop whatever this was before I lose too much.

But he doesn't run, he doesn't even look away. He draws nearer.

"Is this all right?" he asks. His face is near enough for his breath to tickle my lips, and my tail has slipped to the side to make space for... him.

I breathe, "Yes."

He stays and takes my hands, bringing them out of the water and pressing them to his forehead. Water droplets cause lovely ripples in the bath. The dark curls in his chest glisten with the water, and his tattoos seem even more vibrant than they ever had on the ship.

"I don't want to talk about other women. There have been few, and none of them meant even a fraction of what you do to me." he admits as his eyes stay on the water, "But I promise Helena, I will spend the rest of the time I am near you trying to regain your trust."

My heart soars, wanting to believe him, but my brain sinks

like a stone. I give voice to the thoughts swimming around in my mind. "Erik, I don't think I can make love to you... for my first time... feeling like this."

He finally looks at me, his eyes dark. "Then allow me to work for it in kisses."

I flush again, but this time from anger. "I know where kisses lead," I snap. Conrad, Henrick, and the Ice Mer King all taught me the dangerous nature of men.

He raises his hand to silence me. "A kiss can just be a kiss. And lead nowhere else until you are ready. Please, let me kiss you, Helena. Let me wash away every memory of the horrors you've experienced, every bad thing to come between us. Let me show you something I am starting to realize with alarming clarity."

Every cell in my body vibrates to the sound of his promises. Soon, my brain ceases to advise me at all. "What are you coming to realize?" I pant.

"That what I feel for you is rare. Though I have lived a shorter life, I can't help but think we are somehow in the same place with our souls. I can recognize this, Helena," he says. He takes a deep breath, raising his eyes to mine. I lurch back at the intensity I see within them. Dark storms swirl within his eyes as he says, "I love you."

His words steal my breath, my thoughts, and my control. I launch forward, wrapping my arms around him, and sigh as our lips come together.

At last.

Our kisses are sweet, and he laughs. "Is this your way of returning my feelings?" he says as he lowers his mouth down my jaw and to my neck. One of his deft fingers hooks around the collar of my shirt and pulls down to slide his tongue against my skin.

I gasp and pull away. He stops immediately and respects the

distance I've put between us.

Erik whispers, "A kiss is just a kiss."

I nod, my gaze on his lips. "You're right, but... what if I want more?" My mood is mercurial, and I hate my ever-changing temperament. It's been a way to protect myself from my dangerous life for too long. When beaten into obedience, I changed what I could control—but I can't do that anymore. Now... it's time to learn to move on.

He laughs and comes nearer once again. "You control the pace. I will be a willing participant."

This time, it is me who places his hand on the hem of my tank top and guides the fabric up. After awkwardly pulling it over my head, Erik just stares at me for a moment, eyes trailing across my lace bra and breasts. Then he takes my face in his hands. "You are beautiful. You always have been."

I blush with embarrassment as I mumble, "So are you."

He kisses me again, and my burning skin demands more. Grabbing his hand, I place it on my chest, my heartbeat hammering against his palm. He takes the hint and massages my breasts, eliciting soft moans from my lips.

"You are the greatest treasure I've ever known," he murmurs back before kisses trail down my neck, his hand moving to cup my breast through the lace of my bra. I gasp and arch into his touch as his lips travel down my body.

Then, he pulls back when I am panting and swirling with need. The water droplets glisten on his bronzed skin, and I am hyper-aware of him. Without another word, he leads me to the deeper section of the tub so that I am no longer sitting. "Let me help you wash your hair, now."

I blink. "You want to stop?"

He smiles. "I want to go slow."

My broken heart is lying with two halves in my chest, yet it seems ready to be filled. As he lays me back gently, my hair is submerged in the pool. Slowly, his hands detangle the strands. He reaches for one of the glass bottles of soap. A delicious scent fills the steamy room as he works the shampoo into my hair. As his fingers move around my scalp, I moan.

There are too many sensations. I feel like my body might explode. I can't help the way my tail flips above water. He walks around me and kisses me while the suds melt out of my hair. And then, as quick as an eel, he returns to the space above my head and works all of the water out. From some hidden place, he retrieves a comb and works a thick, sweet-smelling conditioner into my locks.

"I don't think I've ever been so relaxed." I sigh. "Is it safe to ask where you learned this?"

"I'll be honest, I've never been with a woman long enough to learn anything." he chuckles. A mischievous smirk takes over his features. "But you remind me a bit of a cat. And my parents had one of those. It also enjoyed being pampered."

I laugh. "I remind you of a cat?"

The chimera flashes before my eyes, as does my promise to return for her. With my uncle's help, I might still be able to do that.

"Erik," I whisper. The combing stops, and he spins me around to face him.

"Yes, my Helena?"

I blush. "I—"

Just as I am about to voice my feelings, an explosion loud enough to penetrate through the thick tower walls sounds all around us. The bath rumbles, and several bottles fall to the ground and shatter completely. I scream, and Erik wraps his arms around me like a shield.

"What the hell is happening?" I screech as the tub continues to shake.

"We need to get out now!" he shouts over alarms and

rumbles. In moments, his pants are on, and he's scooping me into my aqua chair. I feel safe and helpless at the same time as I look at my tail. There is no way I can do anything more than cower with my bottom half like this.

"Erik," I say.

He starts racing out of the room, pushing my chair. He doesn't hear me as he jerks a shirt down over his head, hiding his gloriously sculpted chest.

"Erik!" I shout. He finally looks at me. A feral look of protectiveness washes over me. "I need my legs. Take me to my uncle."

Before I finish, he's already shaking his head. "No, we need to get you to safety."

"I need you to take me to my uncle," I grind out through clenched teeth.

He pauses. "Fine."

When we reach the living room, he grabs clothes for me: a shirt, pants, and expensive tennis shoes that must have been delivered while we were in the tub. He rolls me out the door, only to find Phaedra in the hallway.

"Princess, Captain," she nods, only a trace of terror flashing across her features. "I'm so sorry. We need to get you to the King." Phaedra looks at how I am only wearing a lacy bra. "Can I offer you a jacket?"

"I'm fine," I snap.

We follow her into the elevator as it zips upward. Another explosion sounds. It is much smaller than the last one, but it's still enough to make me flinch. Erik wraps an arm around me, and Phaedra wrings her hands together.

When we step out, the chaos is streaming on the television. The screaming is unbearable.

I cover my ears and double over. The dizzying sensation of still moving while my eyes are squeezed shut makes me want to vomit.

"Helena," a powerful, ancient voice says.

When I look up, the King's casual style has vanished. My uncle is covered from head to toe in tactical gear, a large gun strapped onto his hip. His black crown stands out in a lethal way, and his eyes are pure green. Red sparks fly off his body, casting a smoky haze around him and his enormous wings. He is death personified.

"We need to get you to safety, Helena. I have a car waiting for you—" he glances at my state of undress.

"No."

"What? It isn't safe here. It will take time to contain everything."

My voice is filled with false bravado. "I said no, Uncle."

"Helena," Erik says gently.

I take a breath, allowing the realization that bloomed the moment I saw the extent of the destruction to settle within me. "My father did this."

I don't need Uncle Aidoneus to acknowledge my words. They ring true. My uncle is silent, his gaze locked on mine.

I let out a bitter laugh. "I don't know how he knows I'm not dead... but who else would be insane enough to pick a fight with the Daemons? If he did this, it means his team of Elite is here. I must send him a message: I will kill every last one he sends after me."

"Princess, it isn't safe." Phaedra glances at the King when she speaks. The strange connection between them is alive and well.

"No, she's got a point," my uncle says. "Her father *is* behind this. His Elite *are* running through the streets as we speak."

I square my shoulders. "Give me back my legs. Erik and I will kill them all."

"We will?" my lover says.

I smile up at him. "Yes, we will." I turn back to my uncle. "I need my legs and my voice. Erik and I will need to communicate."

My uncle's mouth compresses in a tight line. "That's not possible. That's why your father couldn't do it. The magic doesn't work like that... you get one or the other. There is a price."

"Then give me my legs. I will go alone."

Erik starts. "You will not. I am still coming," he insists, looking at my uncle. "I understand her just fine without a voice."

King Hades' gaze studies us for a long moment, and my stomach roils with anticipation for what waits outside. "It would seem so." Aidoneus pauses. "You would do that for a city you have no ties to?"

"You would risk my father's wrath for harboring me?" I shoot back. He nods. "I thought so. We are family. Regardless of whether or not we have history."

My hands shake, but my sentiment rings true.

"Yes," my uncle says finally. His gaze flits over to Erik. "If you survive this, I will grant you a boon. I cannot give you both a voice and legs... but perhaps I can offer you something of far more value."

"*When* I survive, I will come to claim your offer. We will see you soon."

"See you soon? Phaedra and I are coming."

Phaedra and I. So casual for a business relationship.

We smile at each other, and we all watch as the green magic snakes around me once again. This magic is... far kinder. Instead of ripping, it gently replaces. It lifts me into the air, turning gently, and then sets me down.

When the transformation is complete, I am fully clothed.

"Let's get a handle on this shit show," the king says as he snaps his fingers. Instantly, the King's Tower disappears from view.

31
A TRAITOR
ERIK

The second my feet touch the cobblestones, my legs crumple beneath me. My stomach is in my throat, and my entire body feels like it has been torn apart into a thousand pieces and then put back together again. As far as I'm concerned, I never want to do that again.

"What in the gods' name was that?" I ask, turning to glare at Helena's uncle. We're standing on what must usually be a busy street, surrounded by the eclectic mix of old and new buildings that make up Lethe. Right now, though, it is deserted. Everything is eerily empty, and the city looks nothing like the one I had ridden through earlier.

I only see massive black tanks driving through the streets marked with the DaePolice logo on the side. A siren wails in the distance. A voice keeps repeating three phrases amplified through dozens of hidden speakers. *Remain inside. Do not come out. The King will keep you safe.*

The warning sends shivers down my spine.

The tower is visible just behind us. Somehow, we have gone

from the elevator to being outside in the time it took me to inhale.

The Daemon King has the audacity to bite back a laugh, his eyes sparkling with mirth despite the current state of his city. He shakes his head, eyeing me. "Don't tell me you've never Transposed before, Captain?"

Shaking my head, I push myself to my feet and cross my arms. "Never. Nor do I ever wish to Transpose again." I snap. Remembering who I'm talking to, I cough into my arm. "But thank you, sir."

The King smirks, but another blast shakes the city before we can say anything else. The sirens continue to wail, and a dozen DaePolice run out of a building down the street before simultaneously launching into the air. Their black wings mix with the smoke from the city, creating a terrifying visual.

"Shit," I reach down and wrap my hand around Helena's. Tugging her to stand beside me, I keep our hands intertwined. "That definitely didn't sound good."

"It's not. We have to go," the Daemon King says. He snaps his finger, and a black mist appears above the cobblestones. The scent of ash fills the air, and I wrinkle my nose. When the fog dissipates, a massive stockpile of weapons is lying on the street before us. I raise my wide eyes to the Daemon King, who simply shrugs before gesturing to the pile.

"Take what you need," he commands. "Quickly."

I nod, jumping into action. Like the beautiful juxtaposition of the city, the king has summoned both old and new weapons. I find a sword, sheathing it across my back, as Helena grabs what looks like a dozen daggers and starts hiding them all over her body. My gaze runs over her appreciatively before she elbows me in the side.

She smirks at me, her eyes twinkling. *Really?*

I shrug. "Sorry, Princess. I can't help it."

She shakes her head, bending back down to pick up more weapons. I join her, my eyes widening as I spot several pieces of elusive Summer Fae tech tucked away amongst the weapons.

There are guns here that will vaporize beings with little more than the twitch of a finger, spears to paralyze, and axes to cut through the densest bone. I recognize a grenade capable of neutralizing magic lying on the ground haphazardly next to a taser that is the size of my hand.

A ripple of excitement washes through me as I pick out my weapons. *This* is something I know.

I'm busy turning into a walking armory when the Daemon King clears his throat. I lift my gaze and freeze, my arm extended towards another weapon. His pure green eyes are staring at me, his horns reaching the sky as his wings snap out behind him.

"Captain," he says. The one word is laced with an order, and my blood chills in my veins. The Daemon's voice is garbled and sends shivers down my spine. Everything about him tells a tale of violence, death, and pain. Shadows leak all around him. The smoky air fills with swirls of inky darkness.

This is the King of the Gates of Hell.

The uncle of the woman I love. The woman I almost... Shaking my head, I clear my throat. This is definitely not the time for that.

"Yes, sir?" I manage to speak without my voice cracking, which I consider a massive feat. If I survive this day, I will remember this moment fondly.

"My niece had better make it out of this alive," he says. His voice rumbles through me, and a crack of thunder roars through the sky as though emphasizing his words. "If she doesn't, I'll make you wish my brother's so-called 'Elite' warriors had killed you."

I swallow, taking a step back. "Understood, sir."

Helena, who has been arming herself, looks up at this statement. Her eyes flash. I can hear her voice echoing through my mind. *I can take care of myself, Erik.*

"I know you can, Princess," I whisper. Reaching out, I squeeze her hand. "Believe me, I know that better than anyone."

A glimmer sparkles in her eyes, and she softens slightly. *Good.*

The king's voice is laced with violence as it echoes through the empty square. "Ready?"

I nod.

"Okay." He presses a hand against his ear, listening to someone spout an update. His mouth hardens in a firm line as his wings flap behind him. "Reports are coming in that two groups are attacking the city." Aidoneus steps forward, placing a hand on Helena's shoulder and drawing her gaze. "The two of you will go to the docks. Phaedra and I will head to the interior of the city."

Helena nods, squeezing my hand.

"Yes, sir," I reply for both of us.

"Good. Stay safe," he says, his eyes darkening.

"I swear to you, I will do everything I can to keep Helena safe. I love her," I say firmly.

A ghost of a smile flickers on the King's face. He nods before gesturing to us. "Hold on tight to each other," he says, gathering Phaedra into his arms before waving his hand.

Before I can do little more than wrap my arm around Helena's waist, the cobblestone streets disappear from view.

"Dammit!" I yell as my feet land on the rickety wood of the docks. I grab onto a wooden railing, steadying my wobbly legs as I take in our surroundings. The King has sent us to the port. Thick, gray fog swirls all around us. I can't even tell where the dock ends and the water begins.

The square, which is usually full of people, is completely deserted. Paper blows across the cobblestones like a tumbleweed in the desert. A thought crosses my mind that the people must have gone somewhere. Maybe the King had Transposed them away like he brought us here? Exactly how powerful is Helena's uncle?

Wiping my hand across my forehead, I blow out a deep breath. "He did it again. Gods, I have never met anyone who can do that. It's a sickening way to get around."

Suddenly, I'm aware that Helena is moving. I tilt my head, pursing my lips as I realize her shoulders are shaking with silent laughter. She meets my gaze, squeezing my hand as her eyes twinkle. *How else did you think we'd get here?*

"I don't know, Princess," I snarl through clenched teeth as I work to get my stomach under control. "But Transposing is officially at the bottom of my 'favorite ways to travel' list."

Six dark gray shapes materialize from the fog as the last word leaves my lips. The members of the Elite are moving towards us, their expressions grim as they take us in. The six warriors speak themselves with sign language, their hands waving as they split into two groups.

"Helena," I say urgently, drawing the sword from my back and grabbing the largest gun with my free hand. The weapons are heavy, a reminder of their lethality. "No matter what happens, I need you to know I love you. I will always love you. And if I die today, I will leave this world a better man for having known you."

The only answer is the sound of sliding metal as Helena arms herself. I can't help the awe that floods me as I study her one last time.

If her uncle is the personification of death, Helena embodies fierceness. She draws herself up, her legs spread apart as she cracks her neck. I feel a stirring deep within myself as I watch her take a step forward, then two.

This incredible female is *mine*.

I love her. And I will fight for her every second that breath remains in my lungs.

She glances over her shoulder at me before tilting her head towards the Elite. *Let's show these bastards who they're dealing with.*

"You don't need to tell me twice, Princess."

As if we have done this hundreds of times before, we move as one. The Elite surround us in a circle, and we instinctively stand with our backs to each other.

The mermen stare at us, their eyes narrowed as they take in our weapons. They, too, are armed, although we clearly have the advantage regarding weaponry. They are wearing black armor plates, leaving very little of their gray skin visible to the eye.

Not only that, but they have us outnumbered three to one.

A second passes, then two, where nothing happens. Then, my fierce warrior lunges forward.

Helena swings her sword through the air just as the members of the Elite surge towards us. They draw their own weapons, meeting us in the middle. Sweat begins pouring down my body as I move, losing myself in the fray.

The clashing of metal is the only sound I hear as I become nothing more than a soldier fighting in battle. My mind fires off commands as the Elite and I dance to a very familiar tune. They might have outnumbered a mere mortal, but though I am young, I have two decades of experience under my belt. I am calling on every drop of training I ever had now.

Thrust. Lunge. Duck. Fire. Repeat.

Seconds become minutes, as I am nothing more than a fighter. Someone slashes my cheek, and I stab them in the side.

Another Elite manages to get close enough to cut the fabric of my pants. Cursing him, I turn on the balls of my feet and slam the butt of my gun in their head.

My blood roars in my ears. As Helena and I push forward, the smell of gunpowder mixes with the acrid scent of blood. From my peripherals, I jump as one of the Elite lunges towards me. He rams into my arm, knocking the gun from my grip.

It clatters to the ground, and the Elite pulls out a dagger. He snarls, the sound silent and deadly, as he thrusts his weapon. I jump out of the way, kicking as I move. My foot comes in contact with his chest as I swing my sword.

The Elite's eyes fly wide open as my blade descends in a smooth arc toward him. The merman ducks out of the way, but he isn't fast enough.

My arm reverberates as the weapon meets bone, and I yank my sword back. A sickening crunch comes from the Elite. I watch as blood pours out of his chest, blanketing the slick cobblestones of the port in a red river. The male's mouth opens in a soundless cry of pain before he drops, lifeless, to the ground.

I don't have time to process what happened before heavy footsteps come from behind me. Reaching down, I grab the taser from its sheath on my thigh. Narrowing my eyes, I aim it towards one of the other Elite.

Pressing down on the button, my eyes widen as a flash of silver light comes from the small rectangle. Instantly, the smell of burning flesh assaults my nose as the soldier stumbles backward.

Bile rises in my throat as I realize I can see *through* his body to the cobblestones below. He isn't even bleeding as black smoke rises from the hole in his chest.

Well. That's definitely going to give me nightmares for years.

Before I can more than blink at the corpse in front of me, the sound of a body hitting the ground comes from behind me. Wide-eyed, I turn just in time to see Helena pulling a knife out of the neck of another one of the mermen.

Now, there are three.

The air in the courtyard seems even thicker than before as Helena and I return to our original positions. My heart is pounding in my chest, my lungs tight as I relish the feel of her back against mine. I brush my hand against the back of hers, squeezing her fingers lightly as we breathe heavily.

"Remember, Princess," I whisper. "I love you."

In response, she presses her ass against me. Stifling a moan, I tighten my grip on my sword.

Less than five seconds after my back lines up with Helena's, one of the mermen charges towards us. His face is contorted as his lips pull back from his sharp teeth. His eyes glimmer with threats of violence as a silent snarl escapes him. The Elite raises his sword, clearly aiming for me as he runs at full speed.

I lift my sword and meet the merman's blow with one of my own. My blade slices across his stomach, shoving him backward when another Elite appears out of nowhere. His eyes are wild as he rushes towards me, a dagger held aloft.

I duck just as the Elite's eyes bulge out of his head. He falls face-down on the ground, the hilt of a dagger protruding from his neck.

Raising my eyes to Helena's, my lips tilt up into a smile. For a split second, she meets my gaze, grinning, but then her face falls. Her eyes widen, and her mouth opens in terror as she reaches for another dagger sheathed on her forearm.

I inhale sharply when something heavy hits the back of my head. Pain, sharp and devastating, rushes through me. Black spots fill my vision as I careen forward toward the bloody cobblestones. Throwing out a hand, my sword falls away with a clatter as I slam into the ground.

Every single piece of me hurts as I fight to remain conscious. Gasping for air, my hand scrambles for my sword when a gray blur streaks past me.

Lifting my head, my mouth falls open as Helena vaults over my body. Her mouth is open in a silent scream of fury, the daggers in her hands glimmering. She moves as fast as a water wraith, her limbs barely visible as she slams her weapons into the Elite behind me. The male stumbles backward, and Helena yanks her blades out of his chest. Blood pours from the wounds as she repeats her assault once, then again.

Blood spatter from the fallen Elite is covering Helena's entire body. Others might be scared at the sight of this warrior princess, but I am filled with intense pride.

She is *mine*.

Not finished with her attack, Helena turns on her feet, engaging the other Elite in battle. They seem to be evenly matched as they dance around the docks.

Groaning, I push myself to my knees. Two Helenas appear before me as my vision blurs. Cursing, I rub my hands over my eyes.

Just as I get to my feet, a bloody Elite careens towards me. Crimson coats his body, leaking from his wounds, but he doesn't seem to care. His face is contorted into a silent scream of rage as he raises a dagger.

"Damn it," I curse as I clench my fist, turning on unsteady feet before punching the injured Elite in the side. It holds him back for a moment, but that's all. I don't even have time to consider where he came from as his mouth opens in a silent roar.

Bending down, my fingers wrap around the hilt of the small

knife in my boot. I know I'll only have one shot with this tiny blade. It was my backup. Now, it's my only hope.

The Elite realizes I'm running out of weapons because a wolfish grin spreads across his face. He snarls, his sharp canines glistening as he approaches me. Despite the blood pouring from his chest, he is still dangerous.

But I have something he doesn't. I have something to live for.

"Come and get me, fish-boy," I hiss, brandishing my blade with my prosthetic hand. My heart hammers in my chest as I stare at my opponent.

The Mer's shoulders shake in silent laughter as he charges towards me. It is ominous and sends chills down my spine. The Elite bends down, pulling a long, thin blade from a sheath on his thigh.

Twisting on my feet, I duck and swing behind him. A feral yell escapes my lips as I raise my blade and slam it into the base of his skull—the knife slides in, a perfect hit. Satisfaction roils through me as the Elite drops to the ground. His sword clatters as my knife protrudes from his neck. My heart is pounding, and I am gasping for air.

Looking up, I watch as Helena delivers the killing blow to the leader of the Elite. The male crumples to the ground as Helena's eyes lift to mine.

"Princess," my voice is barely more than a whisper on the wind as I take one step towards her, then two.

She drops her dagger, which falls with a clang as she races towards me. When Helena gets close enough to touch, I wrap my arms around her and squeeze tightly. I don't care about the gore coating her skin. I just want to be with her. To hold her. To keep her safe.

I want to show her what it means to be *mine*.

"Thank the gods you're alive," I murmur. Pressing my lips to her forehead, nose, and cheeks, I keep running my fingers down her arms. A minor laceration runs down her cheek, but other than that, she appears to be unharmed.

"I love you," I whisper.

Helena's eyes are fiery as she grabs me by the back of my neck and tugs my hair before slamming her lips against mine. For a single second, I am surprised by her boldness. Then, I take full advantage of the moment.

There is nothing gentle about this kiss. It is rough and raw and made all the more sweet by our survival against all odds.

"Isn't this sweet? And here I thought you were all about the rules, *Captain*."

That voice. My face pales as I turn around on unsteady feet. "You-you're dead."

Conrad tilts his head, his eyes gleaming as he stares at me. "Correction. You threw me overboard. But clearly, I am alive and well."

"But... what... how?" I croak. Apparently, in my shock, I'm reduced to monosyllabic words.

"Some people don't take kindly to people who break their words, Erik. It just so happens that King Phelix's men picked me up after you threw me overboard. We had a delightful conversation, and I was happy to tell him anything he needed to know about you."

"You traitor," I seethe.

This man I once stupidly called a friend laughs. He *laughs* as he approaches me. The sound is terrible and grates on my every nerve. I take a step back, shoving Helena behind me. She's so tense, she doesn't even fight me. Her skin is cold, so cold—like ice.

And *that* makes me even angrier than ever before. "Leave now," I order.

Conrad shakes his head. "Isn't this sweet?" he chuckles as he draws a sword. "You got mad at me for touching her, and here you are, ready to lay down your life for this fish-whore."

Red clouds my vision as I bend down, grabbing a sword from a dead Elite to wield against him. I never remove my eyes from his. A cold sweat coats my body as I prepare myself to fight again. "Why are you here, Conrad?"

"I'm delivering a message. King Phelix is *very* disappointed in his family. Especially his eldest daughter. He is rescinding his life debt, Erik, because he has something else in store for you. Something worse. This," Conrad gestures to the smoke-filled city behind us, "is his *gift* to you both."

Helena grips my arm with an ice-cold hand. I can feel her shivering behind me. "Asshole," I seethe. "You are working for him, now?"

Conrad ignores me, continuing. "If the rest of the Elite don't kill you, King Phelix never wants to see you again. If either of you step foot in Ice Mer waters again, your lives are forfeit. You'll wish you had died today."

Rage simmers under my skin. "You son of a bitch. People are dying here. Innocent people. Because of him. He is a *monster*. Does that not matter to you?"

Shaking his head, Conrad takes one step back, then two. He looks back at us with his feet at the edge of the dock. "This is not a joke. King Phelix is deadly serious. Helena is dead to him, and you... you are worse than dead. I have it on good authority that if the King ever sees your face again, he will personally rip you limb from limb. He *hates* traitors."

Before I can say anything, Conrad steps back. He jumps into the water with a splash. I run forward, but he has disappeared by the time I get there. Helena is close behind me, her icy hand on my arm. Slowly, I turn around and look at her. Her eyes are filled with unshed tears as she touches my cheek.

It'll be okay, her eyes say.

I don't say anything except gather her into my arms.

Seconds become minutes, and yet still, we remain together. I run my hands down her back. Slowly, she warms, and her skin loses its pallid color. I can't help but notice how her soft body feels against my harder one. She fits me perfectly. *We* fit together perfectly.

Eventually, I remember where we're standing and pull myself away.

"I love you," I say, pressing my lips to her forehead. I can't stop saying the words, afraid each time will be the last. "But maybe we should head back into the city?"

She nods, understanding glimmering in her eyes. Lacing my fingers through hers, I tug her away from the dead Elite.

32
"SIXTEEN"
HELENA

There's no way in the nine circles of hell that we are going back to the tower. Not when there are more Elites destroying things around the city. Killing people. Because of me.

Once we finish the threat, we will find my father and repeat the process. If he thinks he can send Conrad to deliver a message and expect me to take it lying down, he has another thing coming.

This war could last years, but I will take my place. I will be queen. I will take all of the power designated for me by my birthright.

And I will do this with Erik by my side. Watching him fight those Elite, battling for his life, was one of the most exhilarating things I've ever done. And I would not trade him for anyone else.

We're running through the deserted streets, the only sounds are the combination of our panting breaths and pounding footfalls. The high rises stretch upwards, creating a labyrinth of concrete and stone.

Where the hell are the rest of the Elite?

They have come for me. Conrad's message was unambiguous. This is happening because of me because of Erik and I.

But the streets are empty. They are playing a game, but I don't know what it is.

When the midnight blue uniform of one of my father's warriors flashes in my peripherals, I whip around. Before I can take a step forward, the merman is gone.

Why aren't the Elite attacking?

Erik stops and squints. He is trying to see what I did. He holds his gun with both hands now, aiming very carefully. There are innocent people inside of the buildings around us.

I signal to Erik, and we carefully walk around the corner where the Elite had disappeared. I suck in a breath when I see the soldier scaling one of the fire escapes.

So, instead of attacking us... the male would rather escape?

Erik raises his gun and fires.

The male drops like a rock, momentarily paralyzed. Another Mer warrior bursts from the nearest apartment building. Outside of their swift, graceful movements and long lives, Merfolk are no stronger than anyone else. But long lives provide ample opportunity to perfect skill, making them as dangerous as any immortal Daemon.

I'm running down the long stretch, leaving my heart behind with Erik so that he can deal with the female Mer warrior attempting to shove a knife into his throat.

Another DaePolice car rolls through the street next to us, continuing to blare a dire message. This one is different from before and, somehow, even more ominous. Cold beads of sweat appear on my neck as I listen.

"This is a complete lockdown. Stay in your homes, close your windows, keep—"

I tune the depressing message out as I sprint to the fallen Mer. Wet eyes look up at me as he twitches on the ground. I raise the knife, angling it towards the space between his ribs that will pierce his heart.

A scream erupts behind me. Like a shark rushing through a school of fish, it splinters my soul. I know that voice because it belongs to the other half of my heart.

My heart falters in my chest as I turn to watch Erik. He's engaged in battle with a member of my father's forces. They are circling each other, their swords clanging in the silent streets. The Mer is more skilled, and I watch in horror as she is working to weaken Erik.

No, no, no.

I open my mouth to shout, to distract them, but no sound comes out. My entire body is tense as I watch this man fight for his life.

Suddenly, something hard bashes into my knees. The pain is horrible, and my knife tumbles to the ground nearby just as I hit the road. Bits of asphalt tear my clothes and embed themselves into the palms of my hands. My skin is burning as blood seeps from my hands.

The Elite is on top of me in seconds, his hands wrapping around my neck. My lungs tighten, and black spots appear in my vision. My heart is pounding in my chest as I realize today might be the day my life ends.

I'm surprised when the first thought in my mind is not that I am dying but that I will miss out on being with Erik. My heart breaks as I realize I will lose the opportunity to know more about him by perishing soon after we found each other. To show him how I feel. He will never know.

My lungs continue to fight for air as a cold sweat appears on my neck. My heart is pounding as my all-too-fragile body begins to lose its battle to live.

No.

No.

No.

I will not die like this. I refuse to die like this. With the last vestiges of strength, I gather power in my legs. With a swift jerk of my knee, I aim for the sensitive area between his mortal legs. The blow lands and my assailant lurches off me, rolling to his back. His lips hold a silent growl.

Gaining the upper hand once again, I pin him with my weight and shift to grab the small dagger hidden in his forearm. My fingers find purchase with the delicate blade. There is no time to hesitate. I know about cruelty. I know about killing, even. The needle-like blade slips between his ribs with a deft movement.

I fight down a gag when the warrior grabs my hand and forces the blade up higher. I feel the moment the knife makes contact with his heart. He smiles at me as he dies.

For just a moment, I see my father's face. His smirk lurks behind the arrogance in the dying Mer's face. These Elite, they belong to him. They are his faithful soldiers. It unsettles me so deeply I can't tear my eyes away as the spark of life fades from his eyes.

Those dull, wet eyes stare at the heavens. My heart is pounding in my chest as I look up and realize...

Erik is gone.

I don't see him anywhere. Coldness floods through me as I spin on my heels, my eyes darting around wildly, but I don't see him. He isn't here. The female Mer he was fighting is nowhere to be seen either.

I refuse to let this be the end of us. I leave the dead Mer, rushing around the corner. A DaePolice tank rolls by, but Erik is gone.

By now, I feel like ice. My entire body is fighting against the fear that is filling me. As I am looking for him, I hear something. Reaching out, I grab onto a lamppost as another explosion rattles the whole damn city. The cacophony of terror fills every street.

Not again. I take off sprinting.

People scream. Some bolt from their homes while others slam doors. I watch, my eyes wide open, as bits of old architecture crumble around us.

A silent scream is caught in my mouth as one male, paralyzed by fear, stands near the entrance of his apartment building. My heart seizes in my chest as I look up and see something large careening towards him. I rush forward, but the falling gargoyle is faster than I am.

Heat stirs in my stomach, boiling through my veins and causing my vision to go red. Death is so... wasteful. Useless. Shit if I know why the male's life ended before my very eyes.

The only thing I can do now is stop more deaths. I need to stop more deaths. I need to find Erik.

Even the Daemons can't maintain peace as people choke the streets and scream over each other. My eyes fly around the destruction, seeking my captain's familiar head of hair.

"Helena!" A voice filled with power and light accompanied by the flapping of wings cut from marble silences all the other noise. Phaedra hovers above me. I look up at her, aware of how feral my features must appear.

I stare at her, trying to mime my distress. I point beside me, raising my hand to Erik's approximate height. She stares at me for a long moment before nodding. "Yes, I got him in the nick of time. He's safe."

Safe.

Relief floods through me, unlike anything I've ever felt. I sag against a nearby building as my legs wobble.

He's okay.

"Helena," Phaedra begins again. "I'll take you to him."

Nodding, I extend both hands upwards. The Angel hoists me

up easily, and we fly through the humid air. Late afternoon is preparing to give way to twilight, and I can see the future devastation of destruction for the first time from this height.

My heart stops in my chest.

Thick smoke rises to the sky, mixing with the gray clouds and turning the sun red with ash. One of the tallest highrises has been split in half, the top part laying precariously across three other buildings.

Nearly a third of all visible has been laid to absolute waste. I've never seen destruction like this.

My brain has no problem supplying the gory scenes scattered around that square. There is no point in trying to do anything other than sob.

This is because of me. Me. My fault. This is my father's personalized message.

Even if he hadn't sent that horrible man Conrad, I would have known what he was trying to say. My father's cruelty needs no words, neither written nor spoken. His words echo through every trace of disaster he has inflicted upon this city.

If you do not die easily, I will ensure others do.

And die they do, for someone they have never even seen. They will never know me. The heat of the last few days is changing rapidly. A cold front sweeps in from the south, and I shiver as my mood disintegrates.

"Helena, now is not the time to hit rock bottom," Phaedra says gruffly. "Don't you dare blame yourself for the senseless brutality of a fickle demigod."

But her words don't stop the metaphysical knife from twisting deeper into my heart or the tears from falling. Not even when she uses her magic to comfort me.

"Think of Erik," Phaedra says softly. "Center your mind on all that is good. This destruction is not your fault, but you can do good things here. I'm taking you to your uncle. He and Erik are safe in the Gods' Square."

I nod, my mind still centered on all the death. Phaedra's grip on me is firm, but it doesn't hurt.

Soon, the statue of the gods comes into view, my two uncles posing proudly on top. We swoop down to the ground, where the real thing, Uncle Aidoneus, is standing next to Erik. My captain has a dried trail of blood across his shoulder where his shirt is torn, but he doesn't have any visible wounds.

Thank the gods for that.

The king's power snakes around him, promising pain and death.

"How many?" Aidoneus asks. He directs his question at Phaedra and me, so I hold up three fingers to signify those dead at my blade.

"Seven," Erik says.

"Sixteen," the Angel replies. As if in emphasis, her glorious wings give a little flutter. She is fast, lethal, and deadly.

My jaw falls open as I look up at Phaedra. *This innocent-looking woman killed sixteen Elite by herself?*

A ghost of a smile haunts my uncle's lips as he exchanges a look with his assistant. "Nine."

Even my uncle hadn't had enough time to kill as many as her. *Shit.* Erik also swears viciously, and I nod.

Phaedra pulls a map from the watch on her wrist without so much as bragging. A file floats in the air, projected from the small device.

"Intelligence says that thirty-eight, perhaps thirty-nine, Elite came in from the sea. So far, thirty-seven have been eliminated. I would say that the threat is now contained," she says.

One of the DaePolice walks up, overhearing the last part of the conversation. He clears his throat. "Your Highness, with all due respect," he starts, his eyes flickering to Phaedra. "It only took thirty-seven of them to destroy a third of our city. If even one is left, we should remain on high alert."

King Hades considers the male. His voice is cool as he says, "Commander, thank you. Perhaps it would be best to focus on population management instead of interrupting my advisor."

The male's features turn to stone as he whirls around and shouts orders to his men.

"Ha—Your Highness," Erik says sloppily. "How did so few men do so much damage to a city like this?"

Uncle Aidoneus flicks his gaze back to Phaedra. She clears her throat. "It seems that the Ice Mer have not been so averse to technology as they had led us all to believe. I've never seen anything like those explosives before..." the Angel shakes her head as she stops the projections from her watch. "More investigation is necessary."

"Where would they even get devices like that?" Erik asks.

The King's shoulders tighten as he waves an enormous hand. "There is only one place advanced enough to rival the Summer Fae; the Northern Vampires. We will speak of this later... now we need to do one final sweep of the city and set up cleaning crews."

Everyone nods in agreement, and we start moving back to the tower. As we reach the red carpet, a rumble tears through the sky. Heavy thunder brings a cloud from the south of pure white.

King Hades looks up. "For the love of Fortuna," he breathes.

I raise my hand to my ear. The thunder has left a strange, high-pitched sound ringing in my skull. It intensifies, becoming unbearable. I press my hands to my ears, trying to stop the sound.

"Helena?" a muffled voice asks. Their voice is alarmed.

The sound is so loud I can't think. Tears are burning in my eyes. My hands tremble as they press against my skull.

"Helena, what's wrong?" my uncle says.

I open my eyes and, through the blurriness, see the last Elite running towards us. How in the hell had no one noticed him?

I point a wobbly finger, and they follow my gaze just as he plunges the blade through Phaedra's stomach. A blood-curdling scream comes from the Angel as Erik's hands snake around my waist and pull me backward. I press my body into him, into his warmth.

An unholy, guttural roar rips from my uncle's throat. Only then do I see every Daemon around us frozen, as if encased in ice.

Green power of colossal proportions jets from my uncle's body. Energy ripples from him, and in one swift motion, he grabs the Ice Mer and splits him in two. The halves of the Elite's body fly through the air, only to be caught by an electric green lightning bolt, which flashes down in the same instant.

The charred remains of the traitor scatter on the ground as Aidoneus drops to his knees where Phaedra is currently bleeding out. Her pearlescent, white blood gushes over the dark stones, and Hades holds her in his arms.

His wails fill the entire square, simultaneously drawing the attention of every being and shaking the ground.

The green magic comes from him with concentrated force as he presses his hand to Phaedra's middle. With his free hand, he draws out the sword. Phaedra cries out as the blade leaves her body.

The mysterious cloud of white is nearly overhead, and I squint up at it.

Wings.

Those are Angels clad in golden armor. King Zeus's army.

Phaedra moans, the blood continuing to pour from her chest.

"Sh-sh," Aidoneus calms her even as he appears to be a frayed electric wire sending dangerous sparks into the water.

At that moment, another flash of green electricity strikes the ground next to us, leaving nothing more than charred stone and an Angel so blindingly handsome it hurts to look at him. His wings are of the purest white, his skin like burnished gold.

Still holding Phaedra, Uncle Aidoneus vaults the blade at the newcomer.

Another flash, and the blade is gone.

King Hades looks at me pleadingly. I understand the look and slide from Erik's grasp to the ground.

The sheer amount of power thrumming through the square is incredible. Goosebumps cover every inch of my body.

"Brother," Uncle Aidoneus says warily. "Late as always, I see."

"Fashionably late," Raphael Zeus counters. He impatiently scans the surrounding scene. "Why don't you destroy the neuro emitter so your men can move again?"

"What?" the King of the Daemons asks.

His demigod brother just smiles. Then he turns his attention down at me while I am still gawking. His green eyes narrow. "Who is this, Aidoneus?"

"Raphael, allow me to introduce you to our niece."

The King of the Angels lets out a long, wine-scented breath. "For Fortuna's sake."

33
LACK ROS
ERIK

My eyes fly back and forth between the two males. Brothers. Helena's uncles. The two men are the dictionary definition of alpha males. Unadulterated power ripples off of them in waves. Though they are brothers, they look vastly different.

The Daemon King is the embodiment of death itself. His eyes flash a dangerous green as shadows swirl around him, removing Helena from view. His black crown seems more prominent as his wings snap behind him. He is so rigid, like a statue.

"What are you doing here, Raphael?" the Daemon King asks. Aidoneus looks like a snake ready to strike. He draws Phaedra nearer to him, almost sliding her body under his. Soon, his shadows cover both women.

Interesting.

The Angel's slanted eyes take on an innocent look as he presses a shimmering, golden hand to his chest. "Who, me? Can't I help my dear older brother out in his time of need?"

"Cut to the chase, Raphael. No one has the time or energy for your crap right now."

The King of the Angels sighs. "You used to be so much fun. Fine," he snaps his fingers, brushing back a lock of silver-white hair as he gestures to a fierce-looking Angel standing behind him. "Gabriel. Turn off the damned neuro emitter and get a healer here, asap. I need to have a discussion with my brother."

Gabriel nods once, his pale blue wings snapping as he vaults into the air. "Yes, sir."

No one speaks until the Angel is out of sight. The second his pale blue wings disappear from view, the Daemon King turns his gaze back to his brother. Black shadows leak from his pores as his voice deepens.

"Raphael? Why are you here?" Aidoneus growls. The words are brimming with barely contained violence.

Tension radiates through the air as the King of Angels snaps his head towards his brother. A lazy grin spreads on his face as he straightens his impeccable clothing. How the man looks that good after flying, I'll never know.

"Relax, Aidy," the Angel snickers. "I'm not here to hurt anyone," he laughs. "I just heard you had a special guest, and I wanted to see her for myself."

The Daemon King's shoulders tense at his brother's words, but he doesn't move. The air stands still as the two kings stare at each other. Aidoneus' arms are still wrapped around Phaedra as he raises a brow. He has pulled his shadows back enough that the females are visible once more. He snarls, "Don't call me 'Aidy.'"

Raphael laughs. "Still bothered by the nickname? Why is that? Do you have some repressed issues about our childhood?"

Shadows ripple through the air as the black-winged Daemon lays Phaedra on the ground before pushing himself to his feet. Helena begins to inch closer to me, but we keep our eyes on the Daemon King. His nostrils flare. "We aren't talking about me right now, Raphael. I want to know why you're here. In *my* city.

In *my* domain," his voice thunders. "You want me to believe you just happened to hear about our niece's arrival and decided to show up after disappearing to your Angelic lair for an entire century?"

Raphael shrugs. "Believe what you want. I have a question for you, though. Why would Phelix hide our niece from us? Is she hiding something special beneath that long hair of hers?"

He narrows his slanted eyes as he raises a hand as though to touch Helena. Instinctively, I shove her behind me.

"You don't touch her," I say. My voice is so low I don't recognize myself.

Raphael laughs. The sound is golden and melodic and tinged with deep echoes of violence and pain. "Oh, look. Isn't this sweet?" Raphael gestures towards me with a golden finger, and I fight the urge to recoil. "Our niece has found herself a *human* protector."

The Daemon King snarls as shadows flicker *through* his eyes. "This human just took down some of our brother's so-called Elite, so you should show him some respect. Not only that, but he is our niece's chosen partner."

Chosen partner.

The words echo as I tilt my head towards the Dameon King, who has unexpectedly defended me.

"Thank you," I dip my head. Helena is pushing against my arms, but I move with her whenever she tries to come out from behind me. Something about the King of the Angels is off, and I don't want her anywhere near him.

"Don't thank me," Aidoneus says as he shoves past me. His black, leathery wings brush against my chest, and I tense. "Just keep her safe."

"Yes, sir. I—"

Just then, sirens begin to wail around us once more.

At that exact moment, the DaePolice suddenly start moving

once again. Their cries of alarm rise through the air as a massive bang rattles through the square. I stumble backward, my body slamming into Helena's. Both of us go tumbling to the ground.

All around us, the buildings shake once more as large pieces of mortar fall. A ringing sound fills my ears as suddenly, the middle of the street seems like a perilous place to be.

I curse, rolling off Helena before wrapping my arms around her to protect her from the falling missiles. Somewhere in the back of my mind, it registers that my very mortal body will likely do little to protect her, but I can't help myself. The primal need to protect her is coursing through my body like a raging river.

She is my heart.

The tremors continue for a moment longer before everything falls eerily silent. A shadow falls over us, and I look up just as Gabriel slams into the cobblestones a few feet away. Another Angel, one with gray wings, is at his side.

Gabriel bows deeply at the waist towards his king as the new Angel hurries towards Phaedra. The Daemon King begins to pace as the healer works on Phaedra's stomach.

"My King," Gabriel says in a low voice. "It appears there were two bombs set on remote timers to go off simultaneously. One was in the square, and the other was on the water. The target was a sizable ship."

My heart seizes at the words as I push myself to my feet. "Wait. What? A ship? What did it look like?" I ask. Worry is creeping into my voice, and Helena squeezes my hand as she stands beside me.

"I didn't see much," the Angel says, glancing at his king before returning to us. "Fire was devouring what was left of the ship mere seconds after the bomb went off. It didn't look like anyone could have survived the explosion."

Helena steps forward, the expression on her face grim. She is pointing at the Angel, gesturing wildly. The Angel's brow furrows as he watches the movement of her hands, and I decide to take pity on him.

I ask, "Does anyone have a phone here Helena can use?"

Gabriel nods, pulling his FaePhone out of his pocket and handing it to Helena. She types for a moment before showing me the screen.

We have to see for ourselves. What if it's The Black Rose?

My stomach twists in knots at her words, but I know she's right. I can't leave it alone. Not now. Not knowing for sure what may or may not have happened. If it is the ship... Nodding, I pull her to my side before looking at Gabriel. "We need to get to the water."

The black-winged Daemon is glowering, his eyes flashing deep green as he looks up at us from his position beside the fallen Angel. "I can't Transpose you there right now," he says. "I won't go. I can't..." his voice trails off as his jaw tightens. The silent words echo through the square. *In case Phaedra needs me.*

A beat passes before Raphael steps forward. "I'll take you in my chopper," he says, gesturing behind him.

Sure enough, a large, black chopper is sitting in the middle of what was a busy highway yesterday. It wasn't there a few minutes ago and must have landed while we were all distracted by the bombing.

Helena's brows raise, and I can feel her surprise. She looks at me, and I can read the question in her eyes. *Do you think we can trust him?*

I shrug, brushing a piece of dust and gods-know-what off her cheek before whispering in her ear. "Honestly, I don't know, but we must get to the water. Do you think there's a better option?"

She bites her lip, studying her uncle. The King of the Angels is smirking as he watches us talk. His foot is tapping on the cobblestones as he looks at his watch. "We don't have all day, young ones. What is your choice?"

Helena brushes her lips over my cheek before squeezing my hand. The look on her face is clear. *Okay.*

"Thank you for your offer," I say. The formal words taste like sand in my mouth. "We would be grateful if you would bring us to the wreckage, Your Majesty."

A slow smile appears on Raphael's face. "Wonderful," he croons, "let's go."

He begins to stride towards the helicopter. I look at Helena, and she shrugs. Turning towards the Daemon King, I flinch when I see how pale he is. His mouth is contorted as he holds Phaedra's hand. The Healer is pressing her hands against the Angel's stomach as a soft, blue glow surrounds her.

The Healer catches my eye and looks up. "She's fading fast," she says softly. "I'm doing the best I can."

More shadows begin to retract from around the Daemon as his shoulders loosen. He looks up at me.

"Go," Aidoneus says gruffly. "When you're done, have my brother bring you back to my tower. We have much to discuss."

THE CHOPPER IS SO loud that even with the headphones, I can barely hear the pilot as he talks in my ears. I am directly behind him, but this chopper is unlike anything I've ever been in before. It's massive, and each seat is made to accommodate a set of wings.

Helena is a rigid rock next to me. Her knuckles are the palest gray as she clutches the armrest so tightly that her fingers are leaving an imprint in the metal.

I reach over, prying her digits off one by one. Pressing a kiss to her skin, I wrap her hand up in mine. "Princess," I lean over and whisper in her ear. "It's okay. I've got you."

Even though she probably can't hear me over the sound of the blades, she relaxes. Twisting in her chair, she leans her head against my shoulder. Her touch sends electricity through me, reminding me that there is a lot we have left unsaid. Feelings we have yet to explore.

There is so much to say. So much to do. In many ways, today feels like a beginning.

I told her I loved her, and she didn't reject me. I have no idea how anything will ever work for us. If we will even work. If anything, the last few days in the Gates of Hell have shown me how out of my league I am with this incredible female.

But I'll remain by her side as long as she'll have me. I'll wait as long as she needs until she is ready for me to show her just how beautiful she is. How fierce she is. I'll wait until she's ready for me to show her how she makes me feel. The irony of the entire situation is that while I thought I was giving up my life to save her, she was saving me.

She saves me with every breath she takes, every smirk that dances on those luscious lips, and every silent laugh.

When we are alone, I will show her. I will brush my lips down every inch of her incredible skin until she shu—

"I have eyes on the wreckage, Your Majesty," the pilot's voice crackles over the headset. The Were's voice is garbled as it reaches my ears.

The words break me out of my trance. I lean forward, trying to see out of the blackened windows of the chopper.

What I see takes my breath away. My heart seizes in my chest as everything seems to slow.

The once-blue waters are full of churning grays and greens. Wood and other debris burns above the water as crates bob along the waves. Broken wood and metal are strewn about as bodies litter the water between them.

Bile rises in my throat, and my stomach turns as I spot something familiar in the water. "Can you bring us closer?" I whisper. My voice is weak, but the pilot hears me.

He nods, and the chopper lowers. My eyes catch on the painted words floating in the water.

LACK ROS

A numbness spreads through me as I stare at those white letters for so long that they merge in my mind. It's not possible. I signed the ship over. I sent them away for their safety. The Consortium promised to deliver the paperwork the second I walked out of the building. We paid our dues to the League.

I did *everything* I could.

My eyes scan through the waters, seeking any sign of life. I run my eyes over one lifeless body, then another, and another. My chest tightens as the faces of my crew run before my eyes. My vision blurs, and I run my hand over my face. Dampness coats my prosthetic as hopelessness, deep and sorrowful, begins to take root.

Everyone in the chopper is silent. It is a heavy weight to bear, the realization that amidst so much death, we have survived.

All I feel is guilt. Heavy, weighty, soul-crushing guilt.

Five, then ten minutes pass as we continue to circle the wreckage. Just as we are about to leave, I see something in the churning waters. "Wait," I gasp, pressing my face against the glass. "Look. We need to get down there."

The King of the Angels glances back at me. His large wings are folded behind him, and I just know that touching them would likely set the Angel off.

Which is *not* something I want to do. Not when I need his help.

"Everyone down there is as good as dead," he says. "We can better apply our resources elsewhere."

"Bullshit," I spit out. "You can't offer to take us this far, then make us turn around. I won't stand for it. I *need* you to land."

The King of the Angels holds my stare for a minute, but I don't back down. I won't. Not now. Not for my crew. Eventually, he sighs. "Fine. Ten minutes. Then we turn around."

"Thank you."

THANK THE GODS, the chopper lands on the water a few minutes later. When the pilot gives me the okay, I unbuckle my seat belt. I draw in a long breath before flinging the door open. Helena glances at me, her eyes wide as she squeezes my hand. *I'm right here.*

Nodding, I take in my surroundings. The chopper has brought us as close as possible, but thirty feet are still between me and the body I saw from above.

Without thinking, I pull off my shirt before leaving my pants and shoes in a pile. Wearing nothing but my boxers, I take one last look at Helena and dive into the water.

Cold.

It's so cold.

It seeps into my skin. Did I once know heat? Was it possible that warmth once coursed through my veins?

Saltwater and numbness become my new reality. I'm grateful my prosthetic hand is waterproof.

It takes a full minute before my brain remembers to move.

Another three to reach the body. When I reach the makeshift raft we saw from above, my eyes widen.

Jean Luc is gripping a jagged piece of wood, his eyes glassy as streams of blood stain the choppy water behind him. It takes a moment before I see the cause. A laceration runs from his shoulder across his chest.

Gods. It's a miracle he's still alive.

"Hold on, man," I say through clenched teeth. Grabbing his arm, I start to tug him back to the chopper. He is silent, quiet moans of pain escaping his lips as I pull him to the chopper.

As if on cue, Raphael pops out of the open door. "Give me his arms."

Exchanging a grateful look with the male, I push Jean Luc forward. The King of the Angels is ridiculously strong, and Jean Luc is in the chopper a few moments later.

The moment Jean Luc's head lands on the chopper floor, he turns his pain-filled eyes to me. A thin sheen of sweat covers his forehead as he looks at me.

I clamber aboard the chopper after Jean Luc. Helena is right there, handing me a towel. I wrap it around myself before sliding down onto the ground. Reaching behind me, I grab another towel and press it to Jean Luc's chest.

"Erik," the injured man rasps, "Conrad... he's not dead..."

I take his hand in mine, squeezing tightly. "I know. We saw him. He's sided with the Ice Mer King."

Deep coughs rattle in Jean Luc's chest as blood seeps around him. "King Phelix is dangerous."

"It's a good thing I'm dangerous, too," I whisper. My heart seizes as I stare at this man who has spent the past twenty years with me. "Keep breathing, Jean Luc."

"Is that an order?" he rasps.

I smile softly. "It is."

Just then, the pilot pops his head up. He hands me a headset, which I put on. The pilot's voice crackles in my ears, "Look, we have to go. There's a storm coming in, and we need to get off the water."

"Fine," I say gruffly. "I'll stay here with him. Keep holding pressure."

Helena looks at me, raising a brow in silent question.

"Go sit," I urge her.

She shakes her head. Sitting down, she picks up my hand with one and Jean Luc's with the other. A silent sigh escapes her as she settles in.

Moments later, the chopper takes off, and I wonder if the Ice Mer King will ever leave us alone.

34
FORTUNA, THE ROMANTIC
HELENA

The second the chopper lands, Jean Luc is immediately taken to the hospital.

Erik and I are escorted back to the Tower after being thoroughly reassured that there is no further threat to the place. All the Elite are accounted for, and my uncle's men have thoroughly swept the city.

There are so many noises around me, so many people talking, shielding me, but I am struggling to feel or think anything. In the back of my mind, I realize I am in shock. I am moving, but I am not present.

Current time does not exist in linear form—it is just an endless underwater eddy that I am trapped in.

My father... is a tyrant. He killed my mother. He killed innocent people around the city just to haunt me... he tried to kill me. Again.

What does it mean that I am his progeny? Am I destined to make the same mistakes as him? Is it possible for a shark to be anything but the deadly creature they were born to be?

The problem is, this isn't even the tip of the iceberg. My

father has existed on this planet for thousands of years. His reign has been filled with terror. I thought Elva's mother had been bad, but I had been ignorant of the horrible man in my own backyard. My father deserves to spend the rest of eternity in an ocean filled to the brim with the blood of those who are no longer alive because of him.

Erik's arm is wrapped around me. His heat is like a glowing, sunlight-yellow that invades the midnight blue waters of my mind. He pushes back the ice creeping under my skin ever since that horrible man Conrad showed his face.

"Helena," Erik whispers in my ear.

I blink. We are back in that golden, or brass, colored elevator. I meet Erik's beautiful eyes and just stare. When did we make it this far?

He says, "I think we should stop at your uncle's office first."

Slowly, I nod. There is much to say to him... Erik can help me with that. I squeeze my vigilante's hand, suddenly feeling waves of emotion that are too much for my body to contain. I am so grateful for him—that we are together.

Floors pass before my eyes, but the rooms are empty this time. Not even a ghost inhabits the spaces that were once bustling with eager workers. I shake my head; the most urgent task now is fixing the shit that directly results from my presence here.

They're not working because *I* brought this horror to their city. I know that the thing that my father has started won't be solved quickly. I know that he has begun what is likely to be a war because of me.

And I hate that.

The elevator stops and dings loudly. It makes me wince. The doors slide open to reveal a room covered in shadows. As we step forward, I take in enormous white wings, white hair, and skin made of pure, reflective gold.

Uncle Raphael.

Something about him feels wrong, and I don't like getting too close. Somehow, I know he is slimy.

The King of the Angels whispers intensively, making the hair stand on the back of my neck. I can't even distinguish a word he says when Uncle Aidoneus clears his throat loudly.

"Raphael, we are no longer alone," the Daemon King says. I can just barely make out the Daemon around the enormous frame of King Zeus.

With an elegant twirl that sends his wings rustling, Raphael turns to face us. His voice is filled with forced cheer, "Helena!"

It takes an honest effort to smile and tip my head, but Erik sketches out a swift bow.

Raphael lifts one white eyebrow, looking down at us with his eyes of electric green. The weight of his gaze is heavy and makes me want to slink away, but I stand firm. He narrows his gaze, addressing me, "You still cannot speak?"

Erik opens his mouth to respond, but Uncle Aidoneus answers first. "I have a few sources I would like to consult, but from my knowledge, not even our power can reverse this. There is a cost to magic, brother. You know this. There is a give and take required for our powers to work."

Raphael shakes his head in mild disgust. "I think what you mean is *you* can't do it." he sneers. "You are too weak, brother. You've always been weak."

My mouth falls open at how the Angel dares speak to the other demigod. Even though I know Raphael is powerful, it reminds me of a worm regarding a python. I shake my head. Beside me, Erik squeezes my hand.

The King of the Angels continues, "When you explain the Divine Power like that, you make us seem weaker than common species, like Fae, or Were." Raphael's eyes take on an electric glow, similar to what I have seen from Aidoneus... and Phaedra.

"I am the highest of the Trimurti. I shall give our niece what she truly desires. And then you shall admit, once and for all, who is the best."

Before I can signal my lack of consent, his power shoots towards me like a lightning bolt. Erik gasps and steps away as the green power cocoons me in chains of pure electricity.

At first, there is no pain. There is nothing at all. I cannot move or breathe. A blinding green light fills my vision, and I am paralyzed.

And then, it is as though a thousand lightning bolts have been thrown at me all at once. My entire body is at war with itself. My heart is hammering in my chest, my lungs unable to draw breath as I double over. Silent screams escape me as I tremble.

Erik moves to touch me, but Raphael holds his large hand up.

"Halt. Touch her, and you will die," he says with an ethereal voice. It echoes through the throne room as his terrible power rips through me.

Yells erupt from around me as Erik and Aidoneus fight against Raphael's power, but I can no longer hear them. Everything sounds as though I am underwater. Nothing is easy or clear anymore. Like a fish, I open and close my mouth as breath evades me.

A silent scream escapes me. Horrific agony takes over my body. I am vaguely aware that one of the bones in my leg has snapped clean in half. I see the jut of the horrendous angle sticking out of my gray skin.

Beyond the cocoon of horrid green power, I am vaguely aware that Erik is barrelling towards Raphael.

I want to help, I do. To tell them to stop. I want to fight. To move. But I am dying. My skin has become allergic to the open air. Air no longer feeds my lungs. Because of Raphael, I am neither Mer nor human.

I have become nothing at all.

Every part of me burns and stretches in unnatural ways. My lungs feel like they will pop due to the toxic atmosphere.

Every cell begs for relief, for this pain to stop.

When it finally does, I feel my very life ebbing from my fingertips. The last thing I see is Aidoneus' power overtaking his brother before death comes to claim me.

IN DEATH, there is a song. There is peace.

My body has been laid gently on a bed of powder-soft sand, and I hear the waves crashing nearby. The stars twinkle in the heavens like pearls glinting off spell light in the deep, black layers of the sea. I'd not spent enough time gazing at the stars in my mortal form.

A female being hums, wearing nothing but robes of pure starlight.

Sensations prick at my skin, and I recognize the bitter cold. It is not welcome. At one point in my life, I loved it. But that was before my heart thawed in the warmth of daylight, of love. I push the cold away, gazing back at the stars. Instead of being afraid, I am filled with the promise of life in the darkness. The glinting lights and the majestic female bring me a sense of warmth springing from the chill.

The tune is... it's exactly what I imagine the sirens of old used to sing. Songs that could only be heard below the water, for the land robbed us of our voice.

I sit up to look at the woman. She is weaving threads of golden light at an impossibly tall, gilded loom. Her deep black skin melts into the night, and I have difficulty making out her features. A plush golden stool supports her ample arse, and her soft, curvy figure stretches high enough to touch the sky. As she works, her silken black hair shifts, revealing the low back of her dress. Her shoulder and arm muscles flex, causing the rolls around her waist to move and ripple.

She is beautiful. She is a *goddess*.

My body tenses when I take a step, but all of the damage the idiotic Raphael did is gone. Emboldened, I walk to her. She could squash me like a bug with one of her large, black toes.

Kiara? I want to ask.

When I open my mouth, still no sound comes out. A manic laugh bubbles up inside of me. Even in death, the curse persists. I have been ripped from my life, and still, I cannot speak.

The weaving stops, and my heart follows suit. A whirlwind whips at my hair, and the waves crash with more ferocity as the goddess twists around from her gilded perch. When the colossal female looks down at me, I stumble backward. She is not Kiara.

Fortuna's impossibly beautiful eyes contain galaxies that are both young and old. She smiles, and I can see stars glittering in her veins, plaiting their beauty into a fabric that makes up the robes she dons.

There is something about the air around her. It is ancient. Eons exist in the span of her body.

The goddess tilts her head and watches me.

The weight of judgment pressed down on me like the weight of holding up the world. She gazes at my heart and flicks through my thoughts. Every action and reaction from my life blooms like the purple gas from a small galaxy.

With great difficulty, I swallow. I cannot defend myself, for I cannot speak. The intensity of Fortuna's gaze is like being pelted by the icy water with no end in sight.

I am standing here before her because of my uncle's rash

actions. He is her son. Surely she would understand. My tongue is like sandpaper in my mouth as she studies me.

Her thick arms bring the fabric she's created over her soft thighs. It cascades down like a waterfall, and I see the fabric of life glimmering before me. I see it all, beings as numerous as the grains of sand on the beach. All the threads come together, and it is too much for me to understand. The one thought that floats up from the depths of my thoughts is this: We are all inseparably connected, for better or worse.

And then I see Erik's thread. It appears black, but my eyes adjust and begin to make out the complex depth of color that he is. He is... beautiful. At first, he is woven into a solid block of cloth. And then, beautiful designs start to make up his life as it twines with my own to create a delicate, blue lace. Gauzy, and yet, forever inseparable.

Fortuna opens her mouth after an eternity, or maybe just a few seconds. But she doesn't speak... she just sings.

The sound leaks from her lips, wrapping me in a warm blanket, and like the comfort of a hot shower, I feel the cold seeping out of my skin. Questions fill my mind, but blackness intercedes my sight before I can ask them.

And then I am looking up at Uncle Aidoneus.

I know that Raphael is gone from the lack of his slimy presence in the room. My under-lids flutter open, sliding across my painfully dry eyes. But that is the only hurt that persists. Everything else is... normal. I mentally run over my body, and I feel... fine. I can wiggle my toes—I have toes! My lungs can breathe. My heart can beat.

I have returned. Fortuna has blessed me with another chance —a chance to be with Erik.

"All is well," Aidoneus says. "The damage was recent enough to reverse... especially since I understand Rapheal's Birthright power well."

"Then give her back to me," Erik's gruff voice says.

"She is awake. She can go to you if she wishes."

Cradled like a child over my uncle's knee, I immediately take his suggestion and shift towards Erik. There is no hesitation between us. Time is too precious to waste, especially with a life as short as my captain's.

When he holds me, I feel just how fine my body is. A pleasant warmth fills my lower belly as every point of contact feels like sparks between us. Regardless of the tragedy that has surrounded us over the past day, my soul longs for intimacy, for comfort. Erik has always been that for me.

He is my safe place.

I catch my uncle staring at my knee, and I look down to follow his gaze. A shimmering blood that is not mine coats my leg. It's Phaedra's blood from when I held her.

Out of kindness for my uncle, I stretch a palm down and cover my knee.

As if shocked, my uncle flinches. "I apologize to both of you," he says as his eyes flutter closed. "Raphael is... a pompous ass. But I am sure he didn't intend to hurt you."

"Bullshit," Erik says. "He almost killed her!"

Aidoneus shakes his head. "He's well-meaning but doesn't understand Divine Birthright as much as he pretends to."

When silence meets my uncle's confession, he seems eager to continue. "Divine Birthright is different. If you are given the power of a god, even a demigod, you must be held in checks and balances. To give one the power to do whatever they wished without consequence would have resulted in the destruction of this world long ago..."

It feels like the King is speaking for his benefit rather than ours. The atmosphere becomes awkward and tense in the room, and I am itching to be free of the confines of the space.

Aidoneus stands and drags himself over to the enormous

window. He stares out over his city, his domain, and remains silent. His shadows wrap in dark ribbons around him as his wings snap behind him.

What is one to do with a king? How does one comfort a being so powerful? Where is decorum in moments like this?

As though sensing our discomfort, my uncle lets out a hefty laugh. He gestures towards us. "Come and look, young ones," he beckons.

Erik and I gather ourselves off the polished floor and draw near. In front of us is the statue. I hadn't gotten a good look before, but now I see how broken and smashed it is.

Except for Fortuna, Terran, and Aidoneus. Not to mention a pair of gloriously large Angel wings.

"Well, shit," Erik breathes.

"Indeed." Aidoneus nods to the rest of the city. "They will say it is a prophecy, and my brother will take offense. I had better get it fixed soon."

My eyes return to the wings. The way the Aidoneus statue looks like he is holding the disembodied wings almost appears romantic. Something about the image fills me with some sort of light. Hope blossoms within me. I meet my uncle's eyes. Despite his previous words, I see the same emotion blossoming there.

"King Hades, sections eighteen and twenty-six have reported the heaviest damages. Is there something more we can send in than the standard troops?" A voice invades the room through a speaker on my uncle's desk.

He sighs and leaves us at the window. He returns to his chair and presses a button. The space before him flashes to life with screens, plans, documents, and graphs I don't understand.

"Yes. Please send an extra auxiliary unit to every block. Tomorrow, I will come with the civil assessors to check on the damage costs. Anyone who needs a place to stay will be put in the Hotel Atheneum."

One of my uncle's dark gray palms scrubs against his face as a deep, shuddering sigh escapes him.

"As you wish, Your Highness."

"Thank you," he says. Aidoneus presses a button, and everything is gone just as quickly as it had emerged.

It feels like it is time for us to leave... but I don't know exactly where to go. I expect Hades to erupt his wrath all over us. This is our fault. *My fault.* Conrad made that perfectly clear.

But the King just sits in his chair quietly for several minutes. At last, he sits forward, bracing his elbows on the desk, and says, "Sit, please."

We obey immediately.

After we sink into the leather seats, Aidoneus takes a deep breath.

"First, Helena, I have something to say to you. You need to know that this isn't your fault. Your father and I have been at odds with each other for longer than you have been alive. This feud... he was just looking for an excuse, and he found it in you. I fear I have relaxed far too much in the past hundred years. We cannot retaliate just yet."

Erik remains silent but squeezes my hand.

The King of the Daemons leans back and addresses us both. "I see that the two of you are... together. We have had little time to speak, but I want that to change. I would like both of you to stay here until further notice. It is safe... and I believe you could provide me with useful information to... to..."

He hesitates in a way that I don't understand.

Aidoneus sighs. The sound is long-suffering and speaks to depths of pain. "I know what it is to turn against parents, to want to overthrow them. I hate it. You will hate yourself for doing it. But I'm afraid I must ask you to help me fight against your father. It will be hard, but in doing so, we will make a better future for every court in Aranthium."

I stare at him and nod. *I understand.*

"It won't be easy, overthrowing Phelix. Nor will it be without costs. Are you prepared for this?"

A long moment passes, as I think. Am I prepared to deal with the lives that might be lost because of me? More lives? More death?

The short answer is yes.

The long answer is I wish that no one else would have to die, but my father is a horrible male and needs to be stopped.

I nod once more.

"Very well," Aidoneus says. He turns his attention to Erik. "Gods have granted mortals boons for as long as mortals have walked the earth."

Erik's face is unreadable as he says, "They say that you are the father of humans."

"I am no one's father. But I have championed many a human in my day. It's been a while, and I would like to start that again."

Erik's face is pure stone, and my heart is racing. "What exactly are you talking about?" Erik asks. "You weren't at the docks, but Phelix's message was clear. This attack was because of Helena and I. He needs to be stopped. Are you going to do that?"

My uncle stares at Erik. "If it is the last thing I do, I swear I will work to restore the balance in Aranthium. Phelix has gone too far. With Helena's help, we will gather our forces and fight back against my brother."

"And Raphael?"

"He is misguided. I will get him under my wing. He will work with us, I am certain of it. Now, human, let's talk about you."

Aidoneus shuffles around several towers of precariously stacked papers to find a brown folder. He opens it, and I note the thick stack of papers inside.

"You are trouble, Captain." Aidoneus flips through the papers. "Arrested in Port City on one account of the assassination. Detained twice for public nudity. A standing warrant in the Summer Court... oh yes, this is my favorite. Three months community service for having demolished an entire factory while drunk."

My head snaps to Erik, whose face is still a blank wall.

"You have quite a high body count. But then things start to get interesting... it appears you have spent quite a lot of time smuggling overpriced medication into the Spring Mer lands—and giving it out for free."

"Hmmm," Erik says noncommittally.

My uncle smiles. "You steal from the rich and give to the poor... how wonderfully interesting."

Erik's throat bobs.

"I can take care of all of this." Aidoneus snaps the folder shut. "But you must promise to be more careful. Vigilante justice is not the future of this world... I will put you in touch with some very important people, and you will work together. But you put one toe out of line, and I will risk the wrath of my niece to banish you from my sight forever."

Erik opens his mouth and then closes it. And then he says, "I don't know if I can accept that. It has been a principle for me not to allow other species to rule over me for any reason."

Aidoneus continues smiling. "Yes, I see that. In a previous life... you were Henry Erikson? Is that right? It says you were an activist for around five years. Before you vanished."

I blink. Henry... Henry. The book. *My* Henry.

All that time I'd spent fantasizing about the Henry who wrote those words in the margins... and he has been my Erik all along. Tears burn my eyes.

"Captain Henry, Erik, whichever you prefer—"

"Erik is fine," my captain interjects.

"—Will you be a part of the change this world needs? I will help you."

Erik is silent. And then says, "How?"

"Ah," my uncle chuckles. "This is where things get interesting. I will grant you a boon."

"A boon?" Erik is just repeating my uncle's words at this point, and honestly, I would be doing the same thing if I could speak. We are both sitting in shock as my uncle continues to speak.

"Yes, a boon. A boon for my niece's companion. I will grant you a long life. You may live as long as she does."

More stunned silence. A beat passes, then two, before Erik speaks.

"Yes. *Yes*," he says eagerly.

I take his hand and squeeze. He looks at me. *I love you.*

He has said the words to me... and I didn't have time to reciprocate. But I will. I will in actions, notes, and, one day, words. When I decide I want my fins again.

"So, are we going to do this now?" Erik excitedly asks.

Aidoneus laughs, the sound deep and full of life. "Soon. Perhaps at your wedding."

"I think we are getting ahead of ourselves?"

I shoot daggers at Erik with my eyes. The hope that has taken over my body wants him to stop resisting. I want to lace our lives together, to bind us as one in every possible way.

My uncle chuckles. His amusement is written all over his face as he says, "Royal weddings have been known to happen with much less notice. It will be excellent for the city to witness another ceremony. Besides, these are my mother's rules. Fortuna is quite the romantic. That is my final condition—marry, and I will tie your lives together."

The words sit on the tip of my tongue. I grab a blank sheet of paper and write.

Because living together for thousands of years is less of a commitment than marriage...

I hand the note to Erik. And he laughs. "So, is that a yes, Helena? Are you accepting your uncle's old, antiquated offer for us?"

Aidoneus raises an eyebrow but doesn't speak.

I nod enthusiastically.

"Well, damn," Erik says. "I guess it's settled. I accept, sir."

I grin, the moment's happiness making me throw my arms around Erik's neck. If I could have laughed, I would've. I kiss his face, and Erik laughs at my exuberance.

When I finally settle into my own chair, I look at my uncle and see a pair of misty eyes.

"Very well. Leave me be," Aidoneus says as he banishes us with mock anger.

Erik is up in a moment, and I wave for him to go ahead. There's something I need to talk to my uncle about.

35

THE PISSPOOR KING

ERIK

H elena has gestured for me to leave, and logic wins out despite my every desire to remain by her side for every single second of the rest of our lives. She needs a moment with her uncle, and I need a moment to... understand. Think. Process everything that just happened. Helena's near-death experience, the bombing, Phelix, Conrad...

"I'll be right outside, Helena," I whisper.

My incredible female smiles at me, her pink eyes lighting up as she nods. The way her smile makes me feel... I can't wait to get her alone.

Show her exactly how much I love her. Teach her that words aren't the only way to show someone you love them. But I know she might need some time, which is okay with me. Especially now that her uncle has given us the greatest gift of all.

A boon.

I walk to the door in a daze. I fling it open, barely flinching as it bangs against the wall. A whoosh of cool air greets me as I leave the King's chamber, and I can't help the breath that escapes out of me as I lean against the obsidian wall.

Rubbing my hands against my eyes, I take deep breaths while I fight to process everything that has happened.

A few days ago, I was a dead man walking. The Ice Mer King was coming after me, and I would have let him have me. Anything for Helena. To keep her safe.

I had already decided to give it all up for her. I don't know when exactly it happened, but somewhere along the way, Helena taught me that a short life filled with love and laughter is better than a long, drawn-out one absent of all feelings. She taught me to feel and care, and I am so grateful.

And now... now, the Daemon King has decided to grant me a boon. When he first began speaking, I had no idea where he was going. But as soon as I realized what he was offering me, it was as though a bright ray of sunshine had filled the room.

A life with the woman I love. I would have given Aidoneus anything he asked for at that moment. Anything. And all he asks is that I take care of her? Marry her?

After watching Helena's idiot uncle nearly kill her, I knew I would do anything for her. I *will* do anything for her. Being with Helena, living with her, is inevitable. Right. Like we were always meant to be.

Marriage is nothing when you are already two halves of the same whole. I was already willing to give my life for Helena's. Marriage seems like nothing more than a formality at this point.

I'm no fool. I don't believe that things will be easy for us. For Fortuna's sake, look at this city. Anyone with half a sense can see that things will take time to rebuild. But somehow, with Helena by my side, it all seems feasible.

A few minutes pass before an awareness washes over me. My skin prickles, and I know I'm no longer alone. Lowering my hands from my eyes, they don't make it past my shoulders as I take in the large male standing in front of me.

"You," I snarl. Clenching my fists, I am lunging forward

before realizing what is happening. My prosthetic collides with a golden face that is so beautiful it's hard to look at. Drawing back my fist, I shake it as the pain radiates through my hand. "How dare you show your face here after what you tried to do?"

Helena's idiot uncle looks at me with a dangerous glint in his eye. His wings snap behind him in clear warning as he tilts his head. "Careful, mortal. I will allow you to speak your piece for one minute, but remember who you are addressing."

Right. The wings. The golden skin. King Raphael Zeus. Also known as the male who nearly killed Helena. Nodding once, I take a single step back. "You nearly killed her," I say through clenched teeth.

"But I didn't, did I?" Raphael's voice is melodic.

"The only reason you didn't was because your brother was there to save her."

The King of the Angels sighs. "Ah, yes. Aidoneus. He's always been the perfect brother. There to save everyone, it seems."

My eyes narrow. "What exactly do you have against him?"

"It's none of your concern."

I huff. "Seeing as how you almost killed my fiancée, I would say that it is, in fact, my concern."

"Fiancée?" he chuckles. "You sure work quickly, human." Glancing at his bare arm where a watch would have been, Raphael's face hardens as he suddenly slams my body against the wall. "Time's up. It's my turn to speak. You might be here under Aidy's protection, but let me make something clear to you. I am a god. The next time you touch me, I will tear you apart limb from limb. It doesn't matter to me who you are."

"*Get away from the human.*"

Black wings snap from somewhere down the corridor, and I look up as a Daemon flies down from a door up high. I hadn't even noticed it before.

Raphael jerks away from me, crossing his arms as he glowers.

I take in a deep breath as the Daemon appears in my peripherals. His black wings are spread behind him, and he is wearing a thick suit of armor.

"Well hello, Toth'toros," Raphael purrs. "Fancy seeing you here."

The Daemon doesn't appear to be impressed. He levels a flat look at the King of the Angels before grabbing my arm. "This male is under the protection of King Aidoneus. You will not threaten him again, or it will be dealt with as a threat against the king himself."

Raphael's face falls as he turns to me beseechingly. "Come on. We were just having some fun, weren't we, Captain?"

I stare at him. "No. This was not fun at all."

The King of the Angels takes another step towards me before the Daemon snaps out his arm. "I think you should leave," Toth'-toros says, crossing his arms in front of his chest.

Raphael growls, his gaze darting from me to the Daemon before huffing. "This isn't over, human."

Then, before I can reply, Helena's uncle turns on his heels. I watch as his wings disappear down the hallway before letting out a sigh of relief. "Great, now I have two demigods out for my blood," I rub my hand over my face as Toth'toros studies me.

"Ignore the asshat demigod," the Daemon says conversationally. He leans against the other wall, his wings flat. "He's always been blinded by power. Even as a young godling, he didn't understand that everything has limits. He was a piss-poor party-goer, if you get my drift."

I raise my brows. "You've known him for that long?"

The Daemon chortles, "I am far older than you could ever imagine, human."

"I see." We stare at each other for a few minutes before an idea pops into my head. I quickly relay it to the Daemon, who taps his chin briefly before nodding.

"Yes," Toth'toros says. "I can arrange that. In the meantime, the King sent me a message to escort you to your apartment. Helena will meet you there."

"Lead the way," I say.

"Speaking of Helena, I was kind of a dick to her. So, if you can put in a good word for me, I'd appreciate it. Let her know that I didn't mean any harm?"

I look at him from the corner of my eye. "What exactly did you do?"

He shrugs. "I threw her in prison."

I whip around.

"Woah, it was before we knew who she was." He holds up his hands in supplication.

I walk ahead of him, "Yeah, I think your best bet is groveling."

"Damn."

I laugh.

As we walk, I cannot help but contemplate everything that has happened. The weight of what I have agreed to settles on my shoulders. It doesn't feel heavy. Instead, it feels like life.

Long life.

With the female I love.

With Helena, I know I can do anything. Even deal with her family. As long as she is by my side.

36
A FULL HEART
HELENA

Once the door bangs shut behind Erik, I turn back towards my uncle. Aidoneus has swiveled his chair around and is now writing on scratchy paper.

I cross into his personal space and throw my arms around his neck. He freezes, but then his wings relax, and he wraps an arm around my shoulders.

"You're welcome, Helena," he says.

Extending a large hand, he hands me an elegant ballpoint pen, and I write.

Why are you like this?

He purses his lips. "I care deeply about the members of my family, Helena. You seem to be the best one I've been fated to meet yet."

I blink away tears, and I squeeze his forearm. Many words flit through my mind, and I translate them into lines on paper.

You have taught me so much. You are the first person I have seen successfully lead your people while still remaining kind. You healed something that I thought could never be repaired.

His eyes mist, and I look away. More scratching fills the silence, and I pass him the next note:

Phaedra?

He lets out a long, shaky breath. "She's at the hospital. The healers are hopeful, but only time will tell," he says through gritted teeth.

I nod and then write again.

Can you help me with a few other things?

He looks at the words and nods.

I write down everything... about the stolen clothes, the chimera, my father. The things my father said. The way he threatened Erik and me. My heart squeezes in my chest when I write about Elva. My best friend.

My uncle watches me patiently as I write. At this moment, he doesn't look frightening at all. He looks... kind.

When I'm finished, tears still slide down my cheeks, and I'm torn up for all to see. He reaches into a drawer and withdraws a disposable tissue. When he hands it to me, he holds my hand gently.

"Todd, please tell the captain that Helena will be up soon." Aidoneus makes a quick call on his FaePhone before looking back at me. "Helena, I know that life has given you and me a terrible lot. My mother is not a gentle woman... Fate can be both sweet and cruel."

I nod, dabbing my eyes with the tissue.

My uncle scratches his chin. "All my life... I've been straining to hear the ancient refrain coded into this world. The songs that are sung for families. I cannot have... offspring of my own. But I believe that we never have to be alone. There is no end to us, even when we go on."

Both of us are crying now. The formidable Daemon before me dabs at his own eyes as silver tears run down his cheek. I have never seen a male cry, and it makes me respect my uncle all the more.

Crying is not weak. It is a part of life. Aidoneus is all the more powerful to allow his emotions to run freely. He says, "There is a hand that guides the threads of light in our lives. Will you weave your old uncle into your life? Will you let me into your family?"

There are no words to express how safe I feel. For the first time, I am confronted with just how fragile I am. I have spent so long being nothing but strong. Ever since I met Erik, I realized I am capable of breaking. Not only that, but I have learned so much about myself. I need others. I need shelter. Love. People who care about me enough to put me back together again when I break.

And I have found it.

I nod, and Aidoneus stands. This male, this uncle of mine, is no ordinary man. He is a being from the most powerful family in all of Aranthium's history. A family full of trauma and dysfunction. And he is looking to change the future.

I would love to be a part of that.

When he hugs me, I feel small. Like a child. As if I can reach back through time and space and see myself as a Merling. The ice that encases my heart cracks and then boils away, billowing steam into my chest and warming the room.

Now is not the time to fight my father. That will come very soon. But first...

I am ready to embrace the flames in my life.

I am ready to be a member of a family. I want to start my own, and I already know where I will begin.

With a full heart, I take leave of my uncle.

ERIK HAS ALREADY FOUND his way to our shared apartment. Toth'toros is standing outside the door and nods towards me as I enter. I glare back at him.

The TV is on, and Erik is sitting in nothing more than his boxers. He is clean, which is more than I can say for myself. As soon as he sees me, he grins, unashamed by his state of undress.

Suddenly, there is a massive lack of oxygen in my lungs. I stand as still as a piece of coral as I lock eyes with this pirate who has stolen my heart and holds it in his hands.

We are engaged. We are alive. And the future is long. I am tired of waiting, tired of hurting. The time has come for us to be together.

"You're back," he says. His voice is deep, gravelly. "I ran a bath for you."

My skin bursts into flame, becoming ultra-sensitive. Memories of the last bath flicker through my thoughts as blood rushes to my cheeks.

When I don't move, hesitation flashes in his face. "Ummm, did you... want a bath?"

I take one step forward and slowly peel off my soiled clothes. With each article of clothing, I feel a weightless release, as if I am shedding skin that has been far too tight for many years.

Erik watches me, his eyes dancing with pleasure as they take in my exposed skin. His gaze is electric like he can't believe what he's seeing. I feel a hot flush spread across my cheeks.

When I am finished, I kneel before him, feeling exposed and vulnerable in a way that both scares and thrills me. His eyes are dark with desire as he looks at me and leans forward to cup my cheek. Then his hand slides down my neck and around the gentle slope of my breast.

"Bath?" His voice is like velvet—deep and soft—sending vibrations through my body that make me shiver with anticipation. His words give me the courage to look him in the eye - and when I do, I feel his love radiating from within him like a bonfire waiting to be lit.

I smile up at him and nod. Without further words, he sweeps me up in his arms. He holds me close to his chest like I am precious cargo. He walks swiftly to that enormous bathroom and pauses in the doorway.

He kisses me once and then again. His lips move over mine, gentle at first but then more insistent.

"Is this okay?" he asks as he trails his lips over my jaw.

I nod.

His lips go down my neck. His voice is gruff as he says, "Is this okay?"

I squeeze his hand as if to say *yes*.

The kisses deepen as he sets me into the carefully controlled temperature of the water. Just like he had done before, he washes my hair.

Then he picks up a sea sponge and scrubs away all that is left of grime and blood, leaving a trail of goosebumps across my arms, legs, and stomach. Each movement is peppered with kisses.

Then, like the wicked man he is, the sponge slides between

my legs. I gasp when it brushes over the most sensitive parts of me, which causes me to arch, but his eyes are dark.

"Do you like it?" he asks, his voice hoarse and husky.

Yes, I nod.

His grin grows wider. "Good."

The sponge moves in circles, up and down, and I let out a moan of pleasure. His eyes twinkle as he watches me, enjoying the sight of my arousal. Somewhere along the way, his boxers end up on the floor in a pile, and I behold his beautiful, scarred body.

I bite my lip.

He lifts me out of the bath, pulls me into his embrace, and carries me to the bed. The room smells of fresh linen and sandalwood. He lays me down, and I melt into the covers.

He wraps me in his embrace and whispers sweet nothings into my ear. His fingertips stroke my skin, teasing, electrifying.

Finally, when I'm panting and weak, he folds my legs around his waist.

"Do you still want this?"

My eyes flutter as I nod, already feeling the evidence of his affection teasing me. I wiggle, trying to get him to move.

"Open your eyes."

I obey and see endless pools of amber brown. He watches me with great care and slides himself inside. The feeling is exquisite. I silently cry out, gripping onto him and arching my back. He moves slowly and carefully in and out of me, caressing my body with each thrust. Somehow, I start crying. Not because I am in pain, but because I feel whole.

The air is thick with pleasure and salty with tears of joy.

Once I come down from the heavens. He joins me at my side and whispers sweet words on my gleaming skin.

"I love you," he whispers.

I place a finger on his chest and trace the words against his damp skin. *I love you, too.* He laughs and kisses me once more.

"I have so much more to teach you," he murmurs as he kisses the base of my throat. "Is that all right?"

I nod, my movements a bit stunted. I feel warmer than I ever have before. Despite what we just did, my stomach twists as I grab him to smash his lips against mine. *Yes, yes, yes,* I want to shout. Instead, I settle for pressing my hands against the tattoos lining his lower stomach.

A small growl escapes his throat as he places my hand right where he wants it. The moment is short, and he lowers himself across my body, gently parting my legs. "Excellent. There's no time to learn like the present."

WHEN I AWAKE to the knocking on our door, I bolt upright. I pull on a nearby sweater dress, untangling my legs from Erik's before stumbling towards the door.

I open the door and find a new pair of wings. I miss Phaedra's stunning color.

"My lady," the Daemon female says quickly, her eyes flicking to the ground. "King Hades has sent me with a note for you. He said it was urgent."

I take the paper and look down at the words written there.

Dear niece,

Since when has it been hard to find the personal phone numbers of world leaders?

They've been looking for you.
-Uncle A

Below his name is a thing more precious than gold and diamonds.

Elva's number.

"He's also sent you these," the Daemon says as she hands me a pair of new phones and a laptop.

I accept the gifts, bowing my head. I wish I had words to thank her.

"Will there be anything else?"

I shake my head, tears already forming in my eyes.

The female bows and I quietly close the door before returning to bed. I leap on top of Erik, instantly waking him up.

"What the hell, Helena?" he growls, his hair askew. "Don't you know humans haven't evolved past the biological need to sleep after sex?"

I punch him in the arm, and he fakes being hurt. Then I shove the note in his hand before showing him the gifts.

His eyes scan the note, and his eyebrows raise. "Damn," he says. "Are you going to call her now?"

I bite my lip.

"I think you should," he murmurs. He twists around and reaches for one of the FaePhones. He presents it to me... and I stare at it as though it is a foreign object I'd never seen before.

"Go on, my love." Erik's voice is gentle.

I unlock the phone and type out the message. It takes me a few moments to hit send.

> Me: Hey Nathaniel, it's me, Helena. I'm in the Gates of Hell. Can you ask Elva to call me when she has a minute?

I hold my breath as the little green checks go from one to two before they highlight, showing that the message was read.

Then...

incoming video call

EPILOGUE: ERIK
7 YEARS LATER,

Groaning, I roll over as my eyes draw open.

The early morning light seeps in through the large windows, and I am greeted by the most beautiful bare shoulder I've ever seen. Helena's long hair is plastered across the pillows behind her, and I raise myself on my elbow so I can stare at her.

My wife. I've never gotten used to saying those words.

Helena is lying on her stomach, her chest rising slowly while she sleeps beside me. Her chimera is resting at our feet, taking up far more space than any animal should. I know I should let Helena keep sleeping. After all, I kept her up last night until the early hours of the morning.

I should have known Helena would be such a good student. She is amazing in every other facet of life, so of course, she would be incredible in the bedroom.

A stupid grin creeps onto my face as I watch her resting. There is something so intimate about being next to someone as they sleep. The trust Helena has given me is so deep that it takes my breath away when I remember the magnitude of what it means. Her trust is a gift I cherish every day, as I do her.

I still can't believe this is my life. For those first few years, while the city was being rebuilt and the war began, it felt like things were going to be taken away from us at any minute.

But they weren't. Eventually, I came to accept that this really was our reality. Helena and I are a united front. No matter what happens, we are here together.

I will cherish this female for the rest of our lives.

Seconds tick by into minutes, and I lose track of time as I stare at my wife. Eventually, she starts to move. I watch as her eyes flutter open before they meet mine. Her brilliant pink eyes now have a ring of green around them. The same electric green that her uncle has. A signal of her god-like power.

A slow smile creeps onto her face as she pushes herself up.

The sheet slides down her body, and I can't help the way my eyes track the movement. Helena's shoulders move in silent laughter, and I force myself to drag my gaze back to hers.

"Good morning, beautiful," I say. My hands move as I speak, and she smiles.

Morning, my love, she signs back.

At first, when I asked Toth'toros to help us find someone who could give us lessons in sign language, I was nervous. I wasn't sure how Helena would feel about them, but it had turned out all my fears had been for naught. Helena had loved the idea.

The Daemon had found us private tutors, and within weeks, we were communicating by sign language.

Helena slides out of bed, taking the sheet with her, and I unabashedly watch her as she makes her way to the bathing room. Her body is so beautiful, so fluid. Even though we are on land, she still moves like she is in the water.

Leaning back against the headrest, I patiently wait for her to come back.

She doesn't keep me waiting for long. A few minutes later, she returns. I jolt upright, my eyes running down her as fire runs through my veins.

The sheet is gone.

"Gods, Helena," I groan as I run my hand down my face. "We have a meeting with your uncle this morning. Did you forget?"

She shakes her shoulders in silent laughter as she leans over the bed and crawls on all fours. She sits on my legs, pinning me to the bed. I let her.

You silly man. I didn't forget. I suppose you'll just have to be fast, she signs before pressing her lips against my stomach.

Laughter escapes me as her chimera, Cebe, gets the hint and scurries into the kitchen to find something to eat. I say, "Fast is never something I want to be with you, my love."

In response, she licks me. I close my eyes, relishing the sensation of her lips on my skin. I run my fingers through her hair and tug it gently, urging her to move up my body. She complies, trailing kisses up my chest until she reaches my neck. I moan softly as she bites down, leaving marks I know will take days to fade.

She is mine.

And I am hers.

We are late.

When we walk into the boardroom twenty minutes after we were supposed to be there, the Daemon King's eyes narrow.

"Did you two forget about our meeting?" he asks in a low voice. He looks the exact same as he did the day I first met him, although he is sporting some new crows-feet around his eyes.

The price of the war, I suppose.

The lights flicker, and Helena's eyes glow. She blinks, recognizing what she did, and the lights return. It's still a challenge for her to control her power.

Helena takes a step forward, signing rapidly in the air. *Thank you, Uncle. I'm sorry we were late. It was my fault.*

"Somehow, I don't doubt that," he mumbles.

He steps forward, wrapping his arms around Helena and squeezing her tightly. My wife returns the gesture, and I know by the way her shoulders relax that she is happy to see him.

Aidoneus continues, "Either way, I'm glad you both could join me. It's been far too long. Ever since we dealt with your father, Helena, it seems like things in Aranthium have required even more attention than normal."

She smiles as she draws back. *I agree, Uncle. Why don't you come with us next time? Get away for a bit?*

The King glares at Helena. "Not everyone has replaced their monarchy with a council, sweetheart. Even though the Ice Mer Court has changed, I am still a king."

A glint enters my wife's pink eyes, and I stifle a groan. I know that look. She's plotting something. I just hope I'm not on the receiving end of whatever she has planned.

The Daemon King either doesn't notice or doesn't care because he continues to speak. "Why don't you fill me in on your recent trip?"

Helena smiles. I pull out a chair for her, and once we are both settled, she begins to sign quickly. I sit back, happy to watch her in her element. I was pleased when Aidoneus volunteered to learn sign language as well, so he could communicate with Helena.

Over the next hour, Helena shares about our trip to the Northern Court. We have just returned from what has become our annual Solstice trip visiting Elva, Nathaniel, and their growing brood of fae younglings.

If there is one thing that being around the children has taught me, it is that I am happy to remain in the position of uncle for a while longer. Luckily for me, Helena agrees wholeheartedly. After two weeks spent with the rambunctious younglings, we were both more than happy to come back to our very quiet, very child-free apartment.

Maybe one day, we will have young ones of our own, but thanks to Aidoneus, that time doesn't need to come anytime soon.

Eventually, talk in the boardroom shifts away from visits and towards the war effort. This is where I'm in my element.

The Daemon King's voice rings through the room, power laced in every word as he asks, "How is the navy doing, Admiral?"

I lean forward, pressing a small button as a screen appears on the table. On it, a detailed map of the sea appears. The locations of all fifty ships under my command are glowing red dots. Helena squeezes my thigh; her silent encouragement all I need to begin.

"Since I took over three years ago, we have made some significant improvements to the fleet..."

I'm so glad to be home, Helena signs as she plops down onto the large couch in our living room. Her cerulean blue maxi dress rises, showing off her long gray legs as she stretches out on the piece of furniture.

The TV is on in the background as reruns of *The Real Life of Pixies* play on repeat. I drop down beside her, placing the cartons of takeout on the table. The aroma of the spiced noodles reaches my nose, and my stomach grumbles in anticipation. One of the best things about living in the Gates of Hell is the smorgasbord of food available to us.

I take the seat on the other end of the couch, handing out the cartons. We both eat in silence, enjoying each other's company and the antics of the Pixies. Once I'm done, I draw Helena's feet onto my lap. She sighs soundlessly, not protesting at all, as I begin to rub gentle circles on the bottom of her bare feet.

"I'm glad to be home too," I say as I press a knot out of her foot. "I love Elva and Nathaniel, but I could not wait to get home and be with you. Alone."

Agreed, she signs.

We pass a few minutes in silence before Helena sits up suddenly. She flicks off the TV with her magic and floats her FaePhone over to me.

My brows furrow as I take in the picture of the wooden cabin. It appears to be tucked away in the woods, with a large wrap-around deck going around the entire structure.

Helena leans over and swipes to the right. The screen is filled with another image of the property, taken further away. Water laps at the shore in the picture, as a long dock extends from the base of the deck into the blue-green water.

I raise my eyes to my wife, who is vibrating with excitement. Her pink eyes are practically purple as she bounces up and down on the couch.

"What is this, Helena?"

She tilts her head as she signs nervously. *Do you like it?*

"Do I like it? It's a cottage on the water. You'd have to be stupid not to like it. But why are you showing it to me?"

She swipes the screen again, and my eyes narrow as a document fills the screen. Pinching my fingers, I zoom in and read the words.

My mouth falls open, and I have to read the words repeatedly.

"This is... you bought this?"

I look up, my mouth wide open, as I stare at my beautiful, amazing, incredible wife.

She grins and signs, *Yes. For us. I figured that after everything with my father... It was time.*

Throwing the phone to the wayside, I gather her in my arms before my lips meet hers. Her legs wrap around me as I walk both of us backward. There is nothing gentle about this kiss. It is frenzied and passionate and hot.

I pause long enough to rip off her dress. There are too many clothes, too many barriers. The buttons clatter across the floor. Her hands work just as hard to tear off my clothes.

As the fabric pools around her waist, I have to take her in. My Helena, is fierce and beautiful, her curves only growing more luscious with time. I kiss my way down her neck, tasting the salt of her skin.

She moans, arching into me, and I know I need her now. Every part of me is tight as I lay her back on the couch. I kiss her favorite spots, those silent gasps urging me forward. I am hungry to be inside her, and yet, I want to make every moment last a lifetime. She watches me with a small smile as I crawl up her body, our lips meeting again in a fierce, devouring kiss.

Raw, electric green sparks skitter over my body.

I take my time with her, exploring every inch of her body with my mouth and hands. She writhes beneath me, her moans music to my ears.

When I finally enter her, we both cry out, the pleasure almost too much to bear. We are meant for each other, her and I.

This joining is not calm, nor is it quiet. We move together, our sweat-slick bodies filled with need, until we both explode in ecstasy.

Helena has a thing or two to teach me, and I am her more-than-willing student.

THANK YOU FOR READING!

Want to know what happened to Phaedra and Hades? Check out A Court of Wind and Wings! If you enjoyed the story, please leave us a review!

Also by Elayna and Daniela

We also write our own series! Check them out below:

The Binding Chronicles

Elayna R. Gallea—Upper YA/NA High Fantasy Romance

The Blood Tournaments

Daniela A. Mera—Young Adult Dystopian Fantasy Romance

The Ithenmyr Chronicles

Elayna R. Gallea—Upper YA/NA High Fantasy Romance

Entangled with the Enduar

Daniela A. Mera—New Adult Fantasy Romance

The Divinity Chronicles

Daniela A. Mera—Upper YA/NA High-Fantasy Romance

The Sequencing Chronicles

Elayna R. Gallea—Young Adult Dystopian Fantasy Romance

ACKNOWLEDGMENTS

We want to thank the readers that made this book a reality. To our ARC and Beta Readers, know that your comments and encouragement really propelled us onto finishing and publishing our novel.

To our writing group partner, author Sydney Hunt. She is our cheerleader and close friend. We also want to thank R.L. Davennor, Nisha J. Tuli, and Cassie Alexander for bouncing ideas off of.

Of course, we would be no where without the support, inspiration, and love from our incredible families. They were very cool with our joint-custody book baby.

Thank you to Elayna's family: Aaron, Britanny, and Jack.

Thank you to Daniela's Family: Josué, Jacqulyn, Grant, Érica, and Victoria.

About the Author

Daniela A. Mera and Elayna R. Gallea became friends through teaching languages. Daniela lives between Nevada, USA and Hidalgo, Mexico, living out her own fantastical dreams one day at a time. Sign up for her newsletter to get updates and free novellas or extra book chapters!

For print version, visit:
www.danielaamera.com

facebook.com/AuthorDaniela.A.Mera
instagram.com/authordaniela.a.mera
amazon.com/~/e/B09JDDZQX7
goodreads.com/authordanieaamera

About the Author

Elayna R. Gallea lives in beautiful New Brunswick, Canada with her husband and two children. They live in the land of snow and forests, near the lovely Saint John River. When Elayna isn't reading or writing, she can be found teaching French online to her amazing students. Tap the image or click here to see more of her work!

Made in United States
Troutdale, OR
07/14/2025